From renowned author Catherine Palmer comes a stirring new tale of unconventional love between an Osage man driven to reclaim his people's land and a Yankee woman determined to save her family from ruin . . .

Oh, if Sophie could see her sister. . . . Sophie Brownlow would swoon straight to the ground. Hannah riding bareback through the Missouri forest in the middle of the night. Hannah clutching the solid thigh of an Indian whose arm pressed her so close she could hardly breathe. Hannah savoring the feel of that very Indian's fingers, so warm and firm, so close to. . . . This was vile and sinful . . . and utterly delicious.

FALCON MOON

The glorious new novel
from the bestselling author of
Outlaw Heart, Gunman's Lady, *and* **Renegade Flame**

Falcon Moon

CATHERINE PALMER

DIAMOND BOOKS, NEW YORK

This book is a Diamond original edition,
and has never been previously published.

FALCON MOON

A Diamond Book / published by arrangement with
the author

PRINTING HISTORY
Diamond edition / October 1994

ISBN: 0-7865-0045-X

Diamond Books are published by The Berkley Publishing Group,
200 Madison Avenue, New York, NY 10016.
DIAMOND and the "D" design
are trademarks belonging to Charter Communications, Inc.

PRINTED IN THE UNITED STATES OF AMERICA

10 9 8 7 6 5 4 3 2 1

For my friend

SHARON BUCHANAN McCLURE

who has taught me to treasure my Missouri roots.

Author's Note

As I observe people and study history in preparation to write my novels, one concern continues to tug at my heart. Across the centuries, human beings have faced an overwhelming obstacle to peace: the inability to accept one another's differences. We group ourselves by race, religion, gender, culture—and we defy anyone who tries to bridge the hostility between us.

In preparing to write *Falcon Moon,* I pondered the barriers to harmony and love. Could a white woman have a best friend whose heritage was African? Could someone from an upper-class Boston family accept the labors of a Missouri pioneer? Could a proud Indian warrior learn to appreciate and respect a white woman? Could he ever truly love her?

North and South, white and Indian, male and female, rich and poor . . .

Falcon Moon

"The red rose whispers of passion
    And the white rose breathes of love;
O, the red rose is a falcon,
    And the white rose is a dove."

—JOHN BOYLE O'REILLY (1844–1890)
   "A WHITE ROSE"

"Here lived and loved another race of beings. Beneath the same sun that rolls over your heads the Indian hunter pursued the panting deer . . . The Indian of falcon glance and lion bearing . . . the hero . . . is gone."

—CHARLES SPRAGUE (1825)

Chapter
One

A gray rabbit bounded from the woods just off the narrow rutted road. A heartbeat later, a falcon swept into the sky above the line of towering oak trees. Hannah Brownlow straightened on the wagon seat and watched the bird.

Wings outstretched, the raptor hovered on a current of warm summer air. When the rabbit paused at the edge of the road to sniff a dandelion shoot, the falcon dived. Wind sizzled through its feathers as it plummeted. Startled by the hawk's shadow, the rabbit tried to bolt, but the force of impact and the falcon's curved talons stopped it cold. The only sound was Hannah's strangled cry.

"Oh, no!"

"Got 'im!" Willie Jefferson swung a clenched fist through the air. "I never seen such a grand sight."

Eyes squeezed shut, Hannah clung to the seat of the lurching wooden wagon as it rolled along. "The poor helpless thing!"

"Amen to that," Willie's wife concurred. "Ain't that the way of it? Little critter didn't stand a chance against that big ol' feller.''

Hooded brown eyes locked on the approaching rig, the falcon perched atop its kill. Satisfied that the strangers posed no threat, the raptor broke into its meal.

"Lands, I reckon he's gonna eat it, too, and right in front of us." Seated between her husband and Hannah, Ruth Jefferson shook her head. "Let's get on by. Set the mule to goin' faster, Willie."

"What are you worried about, woman? I think I'll take that rabbit for our own supper."

As Willie started to pull up on the reins, a lone figure stepped from the shadowy forest. The falcon lifted its head. A tall man stood silhouetted by late afternoon sunlight, his broad shoulders gilded in a coppery sheen.

"Lawsy, now what?" Ruth whispered.

"It's an Indian," Willie said, reaching for his shotgun. "Damn."

Hannah's mouth went dry. "A savage."

The man paused in a patch of grass between the sheltering oak trees and the open road. His dark eyes darted first to the falcon, then to the rattling wagon. He scanned the three people riding side by side. A glance absorbed the older two, a middle-aged couple, their skin as dark as polished walnut. Then his focus settled on the younger passenger.

Hannah held her breath, staring back. As the stranger's scrutiny burned into her, an unexpected heat suffused her cheeks. Her palms went damp inside her white silk gloves. She swallowed at the knot in her throat and tried to accept that she was looking at a real live Indian warrior. And he was looking at her.

She shouldn't be so surprised to run across an Indian, she reminded herself. This was Missouri, after all, the uncivilized frontier. But the warrior wasn't at all what Hannah had expected.

Fascinated by the untamed West, she had borrowed books from the library in Boston. In newspapers she had read true-life memoirs written by famous travelers and explorers. Most of these accounts had described the native American Indian as a shabbily clad savage, inferior of stature, and filthy in bodily habits.

This man was magnificent. Standing well over six feet, he was a giant not only in height but in build. His bare shoulders swelled with muscle. His massive chest might have been plated in smooth copper armor. Tendons corded his great arms, snaking downward to his powerful hands. One hand was gloved in thick leather. The other held a bow. Buckskin leggings clung to his solid, well-formed thighs.

"Scalp locks!" Ruth's gasp broke the silence. "Willie, that Indian's got scalp locks! Turn this wagon around!"

Hannah frantically studied the stranger's head of glossy black hair. "What's a scalp lock?"

"Them fringes hangin' off the sides of his britches. Those are made of human hair. White folks' hair."

"Now, you two just calm down," Willie put in. "He ain't gonna want to scalp a couple of old folk who been slaves all their life. What threat are we? And I won't let him get near Miss Hannah and her pretty red hair."

Instinctively Hannah reached up to her ribboned bonnet. How would her deep cinnamon-hued curls look fringing this savage's buckskin leggings? No doubt the man would consider her hair a worthy prize. A bead of perspiration formed under her corset and trickled down between her breasts.

The Indian took a step toward the road. Hannah could see on his back a quiver of feathered arrows, twenty or more. A leather knife sheath hung from his colorful beaded belt. He gave a short, piercing whistle.

"Saints preserve us—it's a signal to his cohorts," Hannah cried, fully expecting an ambush. "Give me the shotgun!"

Before Willie could respond, the falcon lifted from its prey and glided across open ground to settle with a rustle of wings on the Indian's gloved fist. The stranger raised his head, his dark brown eyes focusing on Hannah once again. A shiver of dread tingled down her spine.

"Hand that over, Mr. Jefferson." She grabbed the shotgun and set its stock against her shoulder.

As silently as he had emerged, the Indian turned and melted into the forest. Only the whisper of leaves echoed his presence as the trees and scrub oak closed completely around him.

"I'll protect us," Hannah announced. "Drive, Mr. Jefferson." Aiming into the woods in the direction of the vanished Indian, she hooked one finger around the trigger.

"What the hell you doin'?" Willie shouted, lunging for the weapon.

The gun went off with a thunderous roar, plowing buckshot into the ground at the edge of the road. The stock of the weapon slammed backward, knocking Hannah's shoulder half out of its socket. She tumbled over the back of the seat, her steel hoops telescoping one inside the other beneath her skirt, and landed in the wood plank wagon bed with a thud.

"Lawsy!" Ruth swung around and stretched out a hand. "Oh, Miss Hannah, are you all right, honey?"

"Crazy white woman's gonna get herself killed one of these days. And us, too," Willie muttered as he retrieved the shotgun. "Ruth, didn't I tell you we shoulda left her standing on that street corner in Jefferson City and let her find her own way down south? Didn't I say, 'Ain't no good never come of trying to help out white folk'? Didn't I reckon we was gonna have trouble? But no—you had to tug on my shirtsleeve and start that dadblame motherin' talk of yours. 'Look at that poor child on the corner there, Willie,' you says. 'Sure as I live, she's all alone here in the big city without no one. Come on, let's see what she needs. Let's help her, Willie.' Next thing I know, Miss Highfalutin Boston Lady is climbin' aboard my wagon and expectin' me to drive her to Bolivar. I'll swan."

"Now, Willie Jefferson," Ruth said as she leaned over the wagon seat. "Miss Hannah ain't been no trouble a-tall."

"Humph," he snorted. "First we got us a fancy dancy Northerner who ain't got sense enough to spit downwind. Then we got a bird-totin' Indian with a butt full of lead. What's next? Huh, you tell me that, Ruth?"

"Hush up, Willie."

"Say, Miss Hannah Brownlow, don't you know better'n to fire off a shotgun like that?"

"I didn't pull the trigger on purpose," Hannah protested. "You knocked my hand. I only wanted to keep him covered until you could drive the wagon to safety."

"This ain't no fine-tuned machine, missy. You put your finger on the trigger, chances are it's gonna go off. You might have killed that Indian. And then where'd we be, Ruth and me? Folk round here'll take any excuse they can to string up an old black feller like me used to be a slave. Missouri ain't the free North, Miss Hannah. No matter what the laws say. I get accused of murder, I'll be swingin' from a rope.''

"Shet your mouth, Willie, and stop the mule so I can look after Miss Hannah," Ruth said. "She's fair knocked herself silly with that tumble. You'll have a head-busted white woman on your hands, and right now that's a good sight worse than a buckshot Indian.''

"Aw, she's still kickin','' Willie snorted under his breath. "You tend her, Ruth. I'm gonna fetch me that rabbit. Might as well get somethin' for our trouble.''

Hannah struggled to her elbows as Willie descended from the wagon. Ruth clambered over the seat and slid her warm brown arms under Hannah's shoulders. "You got a knot the size of a walnut on the back of your head, child. You settle down now. Rest yourself.''

Hannah let her head relax into the soft folds of faded cotton skirt covering Ruth's lap. The older woman loosened the ribbons beneath Hannah's chin and set the bonnet to one side. Dark fingers stroked across a pale, damp forehead.

"Sweet Jesus," Ruth murmured in prayer, "put your healin' hand upon this child. Unswell this knot on her head and take away the hurtin'. Make her fit for the day when we all cross the Jordan to find sweet peace on the other side. Amen and hallelujah.''

Hannah smiled as the caress of Ruth's hand continued to smooth over her hair. In the course of their journey she had grown accustomed to the older woman's determination to make every occurrence a matter of prayer. Brought up to view religion as a social ritual more to be endured than cherished, Hannah had never experienced such spiritual unity with God. In the past days, she had come to respect Ruth's deep, unpretentious, and constant communion with her creator. In fact, Hannah had caught herself humming along as Ruth sang her favorite hymns again and again. She admired her companion's inner assurance that the world turned in God's hands, which were stronger and much more capable than her own.

"You'll be fine now, Miss Hannah," Ruth said softly. "That bump's goin' down already. Ain't no trouble too big, see?"

"What if that Indian comes back for us?" Hannah asked. "He might bring his whole tribe."

"He ain't comin' back. You scared the fire out of him with that shotgun, sure enough. I don't know what he's doin' round these parts. I ain't seen more than one or two true-blooded Indians in thirty years. Government ran 'em all off to Kansas."

Hannah let out a sigh. "Everything's so different out here, Miss Ruth."

"Different from what, child?"

"From what I expected. I thought I had this journey all planned out. After my mother read the telegram that told of my father's death . . ." She swallowed. "And we finally were able to have his funeral. . . ."

"Now, don't fret yourself. What's done is done. Your daddy's gone to a better place, sure enough, Miss Hannah. No weeping and wailing, no troubles nevermore."

Hannah gazed at the patch of evening sky overhead as she tried to make the image of her father in heaven seem more comforting than the thought of him at home in Boston. "After we learned about my father," she explained, "I knew I had to come to Missouri and find Ethan. My mother was frantic. She's convinced my brother is the only hope for our family, Miss Ruth. You see, my father founded the Brownlow Print Shop in downtown Boston before I was born, but its doors have been closed for almost three years now."

"It's that fightin' betwixt the North and the South that's done it. Lawsy me. Turned rich folk into poor folk, sure enough."

"During the war, my mother did her best to see that my four sisters and I lived as well as we ever had. I helped her, of course."

"Sure you did. You're a good woman. I knew that right off, the minute I laid eyes on you."

"With my father sending us his soldier wages, and my own labors earning a steady income, we never knew true suffering. But now that the war's over . . . and Father's gone . . . and Ethan is somewhere in Missouri . . ."

"You need someone to run your family business. A man. Of course, you do."

"I told my mother I would open the print shop myself. I could, too, Miss Ruth. I know how to operate every one of those machines from watching Father at it. But do you think our old customers would trust their printing business to a lady?"

"I reckon not. Machines is man's work."

"Besides, Mother wouldn't hear of it. Her daughters are all to be married off to fine Boston gentlemen."

"You don't sound too happy about that now, Miss Hannah."

"Pasty-faced dandies," she muttered. "It's the worst possible fate."

Ruth frowned. "A husband? A fine home? Children of your own? What's wrong with them things, child?"

Hannah studied a drifting cloud, rose-hued with the setting sun. She half expected to see the falcon hovering overhead, its piercing eyes trained on another helpless victim. Instead a gentle breeze stirred the treetops, bringing with it the scent of rich, loamy earth and thick green grasses.

"I have other dreams," she whispered. Then she looked into Ruth's brown eyes. "Have you ever read a really wonderful book, Miss Ruth? A novel, I mean. One that made you laugh and cry and vow you'd change your life?"

Ruth chuckled. "Land, I never read nothing at all, let alone a whole book."

"Do you mean to tell me you can't read?" Hannah sat up and studied Ruth's smooth face, wrinkled only at the corners of her chocolate eyes. "Haven't you ever been to school?"

"Who you think you're talkin' to, honey? Ain't you paid no heed to this ol' wrinkled black hide of mine? Lawsy, I been a slave for nigh onto fifty-three years. I was born a slave, and I always figured I'd die a slave. Why, I'd be a slave yet if it wasn't for Mr. Abraham Lincoln."

"God rest his soul," Hannah added solemnly, remembering the great man who had so recently been assassinated.

"I weren't no bigger than a tadpole when I was put to haulin' wood for Miss Janie's cookstove," Ruth went on. "I spent every wakin' hour totin' water from the creek. Scrubbin' floors. Shellin' peas. Hoo, them were long days! Then when I got big enough, Master John sent me out to the fields to plant and hoe and weed. Now, that was hard work, I tell you. I didn't have time for school, Miss Hannah. Weren't no school for us slaves anyhow round these parts of Missouri."

Absorbing Ruth's memories, Hannah studied the thick tangle of oak, dogwood, and walnut trees threaded together by long, leafy vines. For days now, up and down countless hills, this was all she had seen. Forest . . . dense, humid, and impenetrable.

"Slavery and wild Indians and trees as far as the eye can see," she said finally. "Miss Ruth, this is the most backward, primitive, godforsaken wilderness I have ever known."

"Now, you watch what you say about Missouri. Let me tell you a story about me and Willie, honey. See, when things was hot down here in the southward part of the state during the fightin', we headed north like there was ants up our pants."

"You were runaways?"

Ruth nodded. "Willie had been seen talkin' to some of them Kansas jayhawkers. The bushwhackers got wind of it. We figured we better run before we got our throats slit."

Hannah frowned in confusion. Jayhawkers? Bushwhackers?

"But back in April," Ruth continued, "when Willie heard that the South had give up the ghost, why, we set our minds to come back. We'd heard Master John and Miss Janie had hightailed it to Alabama where they had kinfolk, and we knew we done seen the last of them."

"But without your master, where will you live?"

"Willie's got a nephew in Bolivar by the name of Jim Strickland. Jim and his wife, Martha, got set free just before the war busted out. Fine folks as you ever saw. They'll take us in. Willie's got plans to hire out and earn us some money. Then we're aimin' to buy a piece of land and put up a house all our own. There ain't no place we'd rather be than good ol' Missouri. This is home, child. Home."

Hannah cast a skeptical eye at the forest. She couldn't imagine that the dripping maze of thorns, spiderwebs, and leaf rot could ever foster such fondness in her own heart.

"I suppose people always love the place where they're born," she acknowledged. "But it's not what I expected. When my mother agreed to let me search for Ethan, my sisters and I all sat around the table and talked about what we thought I could expect from my travels. It was supposed to be fragrant and peaceful out here. We envisioned babbling brooks, cooing doves, blossoming apple trees. There were supposed to be quaint farms with picket fences, meadows dotted with cows, barns painted bright red. You know what they write in books—"

Hannah caught herself.

Ruth's soft brown face broke into a smile. "Seems books ain't all they're cracked up to be, Miss Hannah."

"Oh, but books are wonderful! As a matter of fact . . ." She glanced at Willie, who was doing something unpleasant to the rabbit. Then she lowered her voice. "As a matter of fact, Miss Ruth, I write books."

"No, ma'am!"

"Yes, I do. I am a literary domestic, and a very successful one."

Ruth eyed her. "Do tell?"

"It all began when my father went off to war, and we women were faced with the prospect of destitution. Like many ladies of high breeding in Boston and the eastern states who have endured the loss of masculine financial support—"

"What you talkin' about, honey? Speak plain."

"I wrote books to earn money. I've penned four novels and a host of short stories in the past three years. My publishers are clamoring for more. My books have sold thousands of copies. Of course, I haven't sold as many as Wilkie Collins did with *Woman in White,* which was serialized in *All the Year Round.* That's a magazine you might have seen at the mercantile. Mary Elizabeth Bradon had wonderful success with *Lady Audley's Secret.* But Mrs. Henry Wood has outdone us all, I'm afraid. *East Lynne* was wildly popular when it was published four years ago, and it still is to this very . . ."

Hannah stopped, aware that Ruth had fallen into silence. The older woman's gaze lowered to her folded hands.

"I don't catch your meanin', Miss Hannah," she said in almost a whisper. "Novels and publishers and women in white, and all that. You might as well be talkin' German like them folk in Jefferson City."

"Well, it doesn't matter. The fact is, you would love the characters in *East Lynne,* Miss Ruth." Hannah settled her bonnet over her hair and began to retie the blue satin ribbons.

"You see, Isabel Vane left her husband for an utter scoundrel named Francis Levinson. And that dear Barbara—''

"Gutted him, skinned him, and he's all ready for the stew pot.'' Willie tossed the rabbit carcass beside Hannah in the wagon bed.

"Great ghosts!'' Hannah gathered up her skirts and edged her hoops to a safe distance. "That poor creature.''

"That's our supper, Miss Hannah,'' Willie returned. "And if we don't make it to Bolivar before dark, it'll be yours, too. Now, let's go. We've fooled around these parts long enough.''

Giving the rabbit a last leery glance, Hannah took her place beside Ruth on the wagon. After riding with the couple for almost five days, she had learned how to maneuver her hoops to cause everyone the least amount of discomfort. All the same, Willie had made it his purpose in life to point out his traveling companion's every shortcoming.

"Sure hope we don't meet nobody comin' thisaway,'' he would announce. "Miss Hannah's skirt is stickin' out halfway across the road.''

"Ain't you never skinned a squirrel, Miss Hannah?'' he would ask. "Why, where'd you grow up—in a swamp?''

"Don't ask Miss Hannah to pull up no onions,'' he would instruct Ruth. "Might stink up them purty white gloves of hers.''

It was all true, too, Hannah had quickly realized. She knew almost nothing about how to survive in this wretched wilderness. After sleeping under a thin, homespun blanket in the wagon bed for four nights, all she could think about was the safety and comfort of her family's red brick home in Boston.

Even now, her sisters were probably gathering in their bedroom to dress for dinner. They would brush and pin their hair, adjust their crinolines and hoops, strap polished shoes on their feet, and pull clean white gloves over their fingers.

In the dining room below, the housekeeper, Molly, would place starched white napkins on the lace cloth, set out silver forks and knives, and arrange a vase of fresh flowers from the garden. In the parlor, Mother would alternately gaze at the portrait of her husband, then dip her head to the beads in her lap and murmur her rosary.

During dinner everyone would tell riddles, bouncing them

back and forth like a shuttlecock at a game of badminton. Certainly there would be talk of the war and the nation's attempts at recovery after the devastation. Not that Boston itself had been affected much by the conflict. Pearl would probably discuss some new fashion illustration she had seen in her favorite ladies' magazine. Sophie would weigh the merits and liabilities of the latest soldier who had come to court her. Hiding behind her napkin, Brigitte would imitate Pearl, and little Elizabeth would chuckle merrily.

After the meal, everyone would settle in the parlor to hear Brigitte play the piano. Pearl and Elizabeth would sing. Mother might weep softly into her handkerchief. Sophie would likely demonstrate a new dance step she had learned from one of her beaux.

By the time the moon had risen, everyone would have begun the evening process of turning down lamps, setting out the cat, kissing Mother's soft cheek, and climbing the long stairway to bed. Brigitte would slip into bed with Elizabeth. Pearl, who had always slept with the two youngest sisters, now took Hannah's spot beside Sophie.

After a rustle of cool sheets and a whisper of last-minute intimacies, the bedroom would grow quiet. The four sisters would drift off to sleep, secure in the certainty that their dear Hannah—oldest and bravest of them all—would soon be bringing Ethan home again to restore the Brownlow fortunes.

With a sigh Hannah glanced behind her at the empty road. The tall oak trees seemed to close in on every side. Shadows slanted across the grass. An owl hooted, and night approached.

Jean Luc Mabille watched the retreating wagon until the robes of evening folded around it. The strangers had stolen his dinner.

Now it would be too late to fly his falcon at another rabbit or a quail. The strips of dried venison hanging in his small lodge deep in the forest would have to do. He could dig some wild potatoes from the parfleche where he stored his supplies, and then he could bake them in the coals of his fire. It would make a meal. All the same, he had been looking forward to that rabbit.

"And what do you think, Gthe-don?" he asked the prairie

falcon perched on his fist. "Should I have challenged that old *Nika-sabe* whose skin was like the night and whose eyes spoke of suffering?"

The bird ruffled his wings, and the long, pointed feathers clicked and rustled. Dipping his head beneath one extended wing, the falcon began to preen.

"No, I don't think so, either." The Indian stroked a finger over his hawk's sleek head. "My father would not have approved. He would have said, 'Gthe-don-wa-kon, my son, never use force against the old ones. They're close to the ancestor spirits, and they wield great power and wisdom.' And Father Schoenmakers at the mission school would have told me the same thing. 'Return good for evil, Luke, my boy. Always do good to those who spitefully use you. Always turn the other cheek.'"

The falcon lifted his head and gave its master what seemed a scornful look. Luke laughed. "I know, Gthe-don. The old man *did* steal our supper. But when my two fathers' teachings agree, I guess I'd better listen."

Luke studied the road for a long time. A lot of wagons had passed down it in the past few weeks. They brought families who were returning to their farms after the war. Riders on horses traveled the trail, too. Soldiers searched for missing wives and children. Weary and gaunt, they journeyed toward homes that had been burned, and fields stripped bare.

Luke often came to this place after his work in the nearby town of Bolivar. It was the only time of the day he knew true peace. Strolling through the forests, he could be alone with his thoughts. He could intimately touch the land he had grown to love with such passion. Just the scent of rich soil or the sight of mist curling upward from the surface of a pond lifted his spirit and restored his strength.

The well-traveled road also drew Luke. His prairie falcon needed open space to hunt, and southwestern Missouri with its dense woods, rolling hills, and narrow valleys offered little of that. Near the trail, Luke could sometimes flush out a small rabbit or a quail. Doves and pigeons were easier to spot against the background of the dark, leafy forest. Squirrels liked to search for fallen nuts on the cleared ground, and they, too, became the hawk's prey.

During these twilight hours, Luke had seen many of the Heavy Eyebrows with their horses and wagons. But this was the first time he had spotted one of the *Nika-sabe*. The recent long war had focused on black men who had been slaves to the Heavy Eyebrows, but Luke realized he knew almost nothing about the ways of the *Nika-sabe*. Now he had learned they weren't so different from their former masters. They, too, drove wagons and carried shotguns. And they would think little of stealing a man's supper.

"Did you see that other one, Gthe-don?" Luke asked his falcon. "The one in the green dress? She had skin like milk. And when the *Nika-sabe* woman took off the other's bonnet, did you notice?"

The hawk fluffed his breast feathers.

"Her hair was like a fire." Luke pondered the memorable sight. "A fire in the darkest midnight when a man is cold and hungry after a long hunt. That's what her hair was."

When the old woman had stroked a hand over the other's pale skin and onto that flame of hair, Luke had half expected her to cry out in pain from the heat of it. In his village in Kansas, all the Osage women had beautiful black hair. As straight and true as an arrow, a woman's hair fell to her waist.

Luke had seen a lot of Heavy Eyebrows women, too. Their hair was brown like a beaver's pelt. Or as yellow as the sand on a riverbank. It might be black, too, if they were lucky. Or some strange mixture of colors like the bottom of a muddy stream. But never in all his years at the mission school, or in his months in the small town, had Luke seen hair that glowed like a torch.

"Did you see her try to shoot me?" he asked the falcon. "Instead she gravely wounded the road."

Smiling at the image, Luke turned into the woods to follow a path that only he knew. The bird rode on his clenched fist, keeping his balance with a flutter of wings as Luke picked his way beneath towering oaks, over fallen logs, across narrow streams.

"She fell off the seat, too," Luke added, "right into the wagon like a sack of wheat. I don't think I'll have to worry about *her* shooting me. Unless she happens to be aiming at a road when she pulls the trigger."

Smelling the woodsmoke from his fire before he saw it, Luke felt his heart lift. The night would be warm and the stars bright. He could make a decent enough meal of venison and potatoes. Gthe-don would settle on his perch for the evening, and Luke could stretch out beneath a tree to watch the Moon Woman rise.

He could think about the events of that afternoon, when the team of county surveyors he worked with had begun to move across a piece of land near the Pomme de Terre River.

"Here's a cave," Thomas Cunnyngham had called out as the men carried their chain down the steep slope of a bluff. "Looks like Indians mighta lived in it."

Even now in the darkness, Luke could see that cave with the ancient gnarled oak tree growing to the left of its mouth. And he could hear his grandfather's words.

"Once the Little People lived in a land of flowing streams, a country rich with deer, beaver, and bear. There our women grew pumpkins, corn, beans, and squash. They gathered nuts, wild potatoes, persimmons, berries, the fruit of the prickly pear cactus, and milkweed sprouts."

"Where?" Luke had asked his grandfather many times as they sat beside their lodge on the dry, flat prairie of the Kansas reservation. "Where is this wonderful place?"

"It is called Missouri. Our clan built a village on the rise above a winding river. *Wah'kon-tah* had formed a cave for his people there, and he had placed beside it an oak tree that had dug its roots around the cave's mouth. Near that cave the deer made their beds. A slope of mossy rocks led down to the river. And on the highest point stood a dead tree, like a finger pointing toward the sky, as if to ask *Wah'kon-tah* why the lightning had been sent to kill it."

As Luke stepped into the clearing around his solitary lodge, he paused and shut his eyes. That very afternoon he had seen such a cave. He had seen an oak tree growing around its mouth. He had walked down a slope of mossy rocks. And on the highest point of the bluff above, he had touched a tree struck dead by lightning.

Tonight, after his dinner, he would think about that place. He would turn his thoughts to his people, the Osage, who had been driven from their homes by the Heavy Eyebrows. He would retrace his plan to take back the beautiful land of his fathers and make it his own.

And then, when the crickets had begun to chirp and the Moon Woman hung overhead like a silver coin, he might also think about a woman. The one whose hair burned in his thoughts like fire.

Chapter
Two

Willie Jefferson drove his wagon the last mile of the journey to Bolivar in the dark. As they rolled through the small town with its collection of rough cabins and clapboard houses, its doors barred and its unlit windows shuttered, Hannah reached for Ruth's hand. The older woman's fingers felt small and fragile against the smooth white silk of Hannah's own gloved palm.

Training told her she should give no heed to an elderly, uneducated, backwoods creature. Society had taught Hannah she was superior, with her ladylike arts and her genteel upbringing to see her through a life of culture and elegance. She should disdain even the touch of such a commonplace creature as Ruth Jefferson.

But Hannah's heart told her a different story. From the moment they first spoke together in Jefferson City, she had felt an affinity for the older woman. Though she told Hannah she had no children of her own, Ruth immediately took the role of comforting mother. Hannah discovered that she felt like more than a daughter to Ruth. While she respected Ruth's wisdom and maternal protectiveness, she also realized she could open her heart to Ruth as she never had to her own mother in Boston. They had talked of this and that—"women's nonsense," Willie had snorted—and Hannah had truly enjoyed the long hours on the bumpy road. Differences in skin color, age, and background faded away beneath the sounds of lighthearted laughter and comfortable chatter.

"Sherman House," Willie announced as the mule pulled the wagon up to a two-story hotel on the west side of the Bolivar town square. "You stay here, Miss Hannah. It's a fine place."

Hannah lifted her eyes to the hotel's facade, and a chill crept around her stomach. As on every other night of this long journey—except the past five—she would once again be alone. There would be no one to talk to, no dreams to share, no news to discuss. She would sleep in a cold bed, awaken to an empty room, eat alone at the breakfast table, and continue the weary search for a brother who might not even be alive. In Boston, the travel to Missouri had seemed a wonderful adventure. She had not counted on loneliness.

"Will you go to your nephew's house at this late hour?" she asked Willie. "Perhaps you and Ruth could . . ."

But even as she spoke the words, she knew two former slaves would never be permitted to sleep in a hotel like Sherman House. Not that they could afford such a luxury anyway.

"Jim and Martha be happy to see us anytime, day or night," Willie stated as he began to unload Hannah's trunk and hatboxes from the wagon bed. "They'd take in a dog off the street, them two would."

"Would they have room for me? I could sleep anywhere they might find a place to lay a blanket."

"You?" Willie shook his head and gave a laugh of disbelief. "You're the most backward woman I ever laid eyes on, Miss Hannah. Jim and Martha wouldn't let you set foot in their house. What kind of dadblamed idea is that? They spent too many years bein' slaves to want to get friendly with white people. Besides, there's a good many in Bolivar who wouldn't look kindly on a white woman staying with us black folk. It plumb ain't natural. Come on and get down now."

Natural or not, Hannah knew she would deeply miss Ruth's

company. She took Willie's callused hand as she descended from the wagon for the last time. "The truth is," she told him, "I don't care what anyone thinks."

"You better start carin'. Everybody in this world has got a place. There's black and white, North and South, menfolk and women, rich and poor, smart and backward. You, Miss Hannah, is a rich, white, Northerner woman. If you don't want trouble, you better stay in your place, and don't go tryin' to cross over into ours, hear?"

"Here, now, Willie," Ruth said softly, "Miss Hannah don't need your preachin'. Listen, child, you get on inside the hotel and take you a nice room. Get yourself a good night's sleep, and I reckon you'll be bright-eyed and bushy-tailed in the mornin'. That brother of yours can't be too far away now." She touched her husband's arm as he climbed onto the seat beside her. "Set the mule to goin', Willie. It's time we be about our own business."

As the wagon rolled away, Hannah lifted a hand in farewell. Despondency settled around her shoulders like a heavy cape. Ruth was gone, the prospects of finding Ethan were dim, and her purse had grown disturbingly light during her journey. The train ticket from Boston to St. Louis had eaten a large chunk of her savings. The stagecoach fare to Jefferson City had taken another sizable amount. She had paid Willie more than she thought prudent for transporting her in his wagon. And now she would have to pay for a hotel room.

Weary to the bone, she walked across the deep porch and pushed open the front door. The scent of burning oil lamps, old carpet, and worn leather upholstery drifted around her as she pulled the bellrope. A tall clock in the foyer ticked away the minutes. Hannah ran her fingertip down the edge of the hotel ledger, and suddenly the image of the Indian she had seen that evening filtered into her mind.

A real Indian, she thought. *A savage.* Oh, the way those brown eyes of his had drilled into her. She had felt almost paralyzed. And those scalp locks on his leggings! The very idea . . . It was a wonder such a man was allowed to live in this area. With his arrows, his falcon, and a pair of hands that could probably snap a man's neck, he was more than a menace—he was a danger.

Thinking of it now, she almost wished she had shot him. Perhaps Willie was right in reminding her that each man had his place. That Indian's place was his reservation in Kansas, and such a feral brute should be sent back there at once—or at least locked up to keep decent people safe. She had a mind to tell the authorities at the courthouse tomorrow that a murdering savage was on the loose.

A sleepy man with matted hair and a wrinkled coat emerged through a door behind the front desk. "Room?" he muttered and jabbed a finger at the price list on the wall beside him. Hannah selected the cheapest room, though it still cost far too much.

But when the clerk had carried her luggage up the stairs and opened the door onto a room with an oil lamp, a fine brass bed, and velvet drapes on the windows, Hannah decided it was worth the exorbitant cost. She would sleep well tonight, and perhaps in the morning she would understand what it meant to be bright-eyed and bushy-tailed.

Hannah woke to find that the gray sky outside her hotel window hung heavy with the threat of rain. She dressed carefully before going down to breakfast. A basin of water provided a much-needed wash for her hands and face, and she brushed the dust from her hair until it gleamed like a new penny.

Wanting to appear as fine as possible for her visit to the courthouse, Hannah tied the laces of the corset to the bedpost and pulled until her face turned red, her lungs felt as if they might collapse, and her waist shrank to the slender circumference of eighteen inches.

Letting out a breath with some difficulty, she stared at herself in the full-length pier glass that stood in one corner of her little room. She was hardly the belle she had been in Boston, that was for certain. What with precious few hours of sleep each night, a brown fringe of dust edging her small-clothes and stockings, and enough humidity in the air to wilt the best-dressed curls in the state of Massachusetts, Hannah knew she looked more like a rag doll than a well-bred Bostonian on a noble mission.

Her spirits flagged as she thought of the day to come. Once

again, she would face the prospect of trying to track down her missing older brother. And if military and civil authorities in Jefferson City, Missouri's capital, had been unable to unearth any record of Ethan Brownlow, why might a small courthouse hidden deep in the Ozarks have information of significance?

All the same, Hannah had been advised to search the southern half of the state. Ethan had written letters from Polk County three years ago—the Brownlow family's last contact from him. So Hannah would check the records in Bolivar, and then she would try the next town the authorities recommended. If need be, she would travel through this entire dismal state until her money ran out. Then, whether she had found her brother or not, she would hurry home to Boston, where she belonged.

"Oh, Ethan," she said with a sigh. "Where are you?"

As she slipped on her hoop and turned the cumbersome bell-shaped undergarment until the steels were in their correct position, Hannah tried to piece together memories of her brother. Ethan was much older—almost a full-grown man by the time she had been born. Actually he was her half brother, though no one ever brought up the fact in conversation. Her father's first wife had passed away during Ethan's birth. The little boy had been reared by a nanny for several years, until his father married again. Then, in quick succession, Hannah, Sophie, Pearl, Brigitte, and Elizabeth had appeared to provide young Ethan with a bevy of admiring sisters.

Oh, they had all adored their brother in the beginning, Hannah recalled as she fastened a stiff crinoline over her hoop. Before the tragedy that altered his demeanor, Ethan had loved to tease and play silly games with his sisters. Once he had taken them all to the circus. That had been a fine afternoon!

Lost in memory, Hannah opened her trunk and selected a blue percale day dress trimmed in navy velvet. It sported a round waist and a short, bolero-shaped jacket that would display her waist to advantage. She slipped it on and began fastening the small covered buttons that ran up the front of the bodice. That particular shade of ice blue, Sophie had informed her sister, gave Hannah's eyes an almost sapphire glow and provided an alluring foil for her cinnamon hair.

As she studied her reflection, Hannah recalled that Ethan

had not inherited any of his sisters' Irish characteristics. The four female Brownlows boasted hair in various reddish hues from carrot to auburn, and eyes in all shades of green and blue. But of course the girls' Irish blood had come from their mother, a proud O'Rourke from Tipperary.

Ethan was short and stocky like their father. His olive complexion and thin brown hair gave him a dark look. With the heritage of his deceased mother's pale blue eyes in startling contrast, he could sometimes look almost menacing—especially in the years after the woman he loved had spurned him for another man. Of course, that was only a product of Hannah's overactive imagination, Sophie had hastened to remind her. Ethan had never been anything but civil. Perhaps rejection had blunted his carefree spirit, perhaps he had grown quiet and distant, perhaps he had withdrawn into himself, but never could Ethan be called alarming.

As Hannah tied on her spoon-shaped bonnet and adjusted the high arched brim, she had to admit that Ethan had not actually played a very important role in her life in recent years. In fact, after he had been cast off as a suitor, he had gone away someplace. But where?

She frowned at herself in the mirror. Georgia, was it? Ohio, perhaps? Or had he gone farther west? She couldn't recall. And then, quite suddenly, Ethan had returned to Boston. That part Hannah remembered clearly.

"Father," he had said, while seated in the parlor with the family at tea, "I have determined to make something of myself. Perhaps I shall never know the true meaning of love and family, but I cannot roam forever. I mean to learn the printing business."

Everyone had been delighted, of course, although Hannah had turned Ethan's words over and over in her mind. *Perhaps I shall never know the true meaning of love and family,* her brother had said. Somehow she couldn't believe he was referring only to his failure as a suitor. Had she and her sisters been unable to give him a true sense of family? Had their mother, his stepmother, lacked the ability to truly love Ethan, to make him a part of her heart?

At the Brownlow Print Shop in town, Ethan had taken a job cleaning the presses and making deliveries. Though he lived at home, he spent most of his free time alone in his room in the garret. He seldom emerged for meals, and he never made social calls. The girls, busy with lessons and friends, hardly gave their brother a thought. Their mother stayed so busy with her engagements she had little time to spend with a reclusive stepson.

One evening while Ethan was away on a delivery, their father had informed everyone at the dinner table that his son was not making a go of the printing business. Ethan was, in fact, a dismal failure. Disinterested, hostile, restless, the young man was not living up to his father's dreams.

"He knows the business," Mr. Brownlow had stated, "he is twice as intelligent as any man, and he certainly has the social training to cater to our customers. But he will not try. Something eats at him, and I'm not certain how much longer I can tolerate it."

Not many days later, actually, Ethan informed the family he was leaving Boston once again. He intended to become a merchant in the West. He wanted to go to Missouri, where he had heard opportunities for business were expanding and a fortune could be made in the mercantile trade.

Nothing anyone could say would dissuade him, and he had left within the week. Hannah's father had speculated that this adventure could only be good for the young man. Ethan would develop self-reliance and ambition. When the time came to call him back to Boston to take his rightful place at the helm of the Brownlow Print Shop, he would be prepared and eager to accept the challenge.

But Ethan's father was never to see his son's success. A week later, war broke out. Ethan had written several times that year, describing his adventures in Missouri and his attempts to start a trade. And then they heard no more from him.

Hannah pulled on her gloves, gave her cheeks a pinch, and collected her parasol. How could someone vanish so completely? And why would he? Ethan had a family. A home. A business in Boston he was destined to inherit. Had he disappeared on purpose? Did he want to remain hidden?

Or had Ethan been killed?

Hannah took a breath and set her shoulders in preparation to venture out from the haven of her room. Searching the lists of war dead had not been a pleasant part of her plan for this journey. But she had done it—often enough to sense the devastating loss of human life Missouri had suffered.

Now she would eat a small breakfast and then make her way across the unpaved street to the courthouse. She would speak to the sheriff, the county clerk, the recorder, the military personnel—anyone in authority. She would search lists and give descriptions. And maybe, if she were lucky, someone would have heard of a man named Ethan Brownlow who had vanished in Missouri three years before.

"Luke, what do you make of this map?" Thomas Cunnyngham called across the room. "None of us can puzzle it out."

Straightening from the open ledger in which he was recording the past day's surveys, Luke observed the group of men huddled around a long table in the Polk County Courthouse. Tom, the county surveyor, was the only one among them who could read, and he was not particularly good with maps. The government had been selling land in this area since 1837, and the Homestead Act of 1863 had brought a huge demand for surveyed property. But few men were qualified for the complicated, arduous task.

"What do you have there, Tom?" Luke asked as he rose from his own table. "Something Ezekiel Campbell drew up?"

Tom laughed. "I reckon. Him or his deputy. Anyhow, we can't make heads or tails of it."

Campbell had held the position of surveyor in the thirties, followed by Thomas Jarnagin and James Boone. By the time war broke out, six different men had made the attempt to record and plot the land around Bolivar. Their entries in the logbook were difficult to read and not always accurate. Their maps were worse.

Luke took a position at the table beside Tom and studied the tattered diagram. "Looks like Campbell had been tipping back a jug of whiskey when he drew this thing."

"Reckon he even used a ruler?"

"More likely a strip of siding off his old barn." As the men around him chuckled, Luke traced a finger down the ragged blue lines. Here was a stream, there a large pin oak, at the bottom of the map a hill. "Looks like that spot north of Granny

Ledbetter's place to me. Here's where her old man put up the windmill, and here's where they built the house. See how it slopes south-southeast? She got that patch of a garden right there. And here by the pin oak is where that troop of Federals spent the night on their way to Jefferson City."

"Sure enough, it is!" Tom clapped Luke on the back. "I don't know what I'da done if you hadn't walked into the courthouse this spring, Luke. You got an eye for this land like nobody I ever seen, don't he, boys?"

The deputy surveyor nodded. "But we thought you was fixin' to have a heart attack, Tom, when you first laid eyes on the Indian."

Chuckling at the memory, Tom scratched his chin. "Sure enough, I did. There you was, Luke, tall as a pine tree and broad as a barn across the chest, your skin red, and them brown eyes lookin' straight through me like a pair of dadblamed arrows—why, I half expected you to tomahawk me right then and there."

"Only time I wanted to tomahawk you was when you sent me up that bluff the other morning."

"Hoo! Can't blame you for that one!" Tom grinned, and his face lit up from ear to ear.

It was that smile, Luke supposed, that had finally broken the barrier between the two men. How could he remain distant from a man who was as genuine, honest, and friendly as Tom Cunnyngham? Though their conversation had never delved any deeper than the subject of surveying, Luke felt comfortable with his employer. They laughed together, worked side by side, and shared meals.

"Fact is," Tom told the other men, "I'd trust Luke Maples with my life. I have, too, climbing around on them steep bluffs and slippery riverbanks. Yessir, when I hired Luke Maples to be my chainman, I done the right thing. If you wasn't an Indian, Luke, why, I'd be tempted to make you my deputy."

"Now then!" the current deputy surveyor cut in. "And run me off my job?"

"Seth, you can't read a damn word, you got no notion about maps, and you can't add two and two."

The deputy feigned irritation. "Well, Luke spent all them

years at that mission school learnin' his lessons from the priest. Me, I was out hoein' taters for my pappy."

"What you think, Jim?" Tom called to the county clerk who was seated at a desk near the door. "You think I ought to hire Luke as deputy surveyor?"

"Can't do it," James Jones returned. "He ain't a citizen. Ain't registered to vote. Ain't even livin' here legal. Ought to be on the reservation in Kansas, and everybody in town knows it, Tom. Only reason Luke ain't been run off is he don't cause no trouble, and you ain't got nobody else to be a chainman for your crew."

"Hell, who'd run him off?" Tom glanced at Luke. "You got any reason to go back to Kansas? You got a wife?"

Luke stiffened. For three months he had managed to avoid divulging personal information to these men. He had worked hard to earn their trust and their respect, but he didn't want them to know too much about his life. He had come to Missouri to reclaim his tribal lands for himself and to track down and kill his father's murderer. The less the townsfolk of Bolivar knew about him the better.

"My family knows where I am," he said in answer to Tom's question. "I'll go back to them when the time is right."

"Well, I hope that time don't come too soon. I need you to read these damned maps for me."

Luke nodded, then lifted his head with the other men as a whiff of fresh, early-morning air announced a young woman. Tall and slender, she wore an ice-blue dress that rustled when she walked, a frilled bonnet to cover her hair, and a pair of the whitest, silkiest gloves Luke had ever seen.

Raising her chin, she stepped up to the front desk. When Luke caught sight of her blue eyes and the tendril of copper hair against her cheek, his heart slowed to the pace of a turtle climbing a sandy bank. He had seen the woman before.

"My name is Hannah Brownlow," she stated in a crisp voice. "I'm searching for a missing person."

The clerk's shoulders sagged. "Well, you're the fifth person today, and we only just got started on the morning. I'm James Jones, Polk County Clerk. So, who you lost? Man, woman, or child?"

"A man. My brother."

"Name." Mr. Jones dipped a pen in his inkwell. "Last name first and first name last."

"Brownlow. Ethan."

At a sharp sound from the back of the room, Hannah lifted her head. It was so dark in the close quarters she could hardly see. Behind the clerk's desk, a group of men huddled around a table as they searched through a collection of large books and maps. But one of their number had straightened and was staring at her.

A shiver slipped down Hannah's spine. She had seen the man before.

"Age?"

Disturbed by a memory she couldn't place, she glanced at the clerk again. "Ethan was thirty-seven last December."

"Height and weight?"

"Five feet eight inches. One hundred seventy pounds."

"Last seen?"

"Boston." Hannah looked up again. The man had stepped into the corner away from the others. Arms folded across his chest, he was openly listening to every word of her exchange.

"Not where, ma'am," Mr. Jones said. "When? When did you last see your brother?"

"Oh, 1860. Shortly before the war started." She couldn't place the man. He was tall—too tall for this room. His head nearly touched the ceiling. And his eyes seemed to burn into her. But she couldn't recall ever seeing—

"And last time you heard from him?" the clerk cut in. "Your brother."

"In 1862. May was the last time he wrote."

"Long time back. Well, I'll look through my records of deaths, marriages, and such. But things got sorta mixed up during the war, you know. We just got the surveyors back in action," he said, jabbing a thumb in the direction of the men behind him. "And we been goin' through the files. Nobody kept records too good, I'm afraid."

Hannah nodded. It was the same story she had heard before. At worst, county and city records had been burned, water-damaged, vandalized, or stolen. At best, they were a collection of disjointed lists. Often they had great gaps that reflected times when the war brushed too close to a town and all thought of record-keeping was abandoned.

While the clerk flipped through his books, Hannah tried to covertly study the man in the corner. He hadn't taken his eyes off her for a second, and she felt absolutely certain she had seen him. Searching her mind, she reviewed the images of every tall, black-haired man she had met in her recent travels.

This one was not so distinctive that he would stand out in a crowd. Only his height and physique set him apart. He was dressed exactly as his companions in a pair of faded indigo jeans, a yellow-gray homespun shirt slightly frayed at collar and cuffs, and dusty leather boots. He carried no gun, wore no belt, had not even a watch chain to indicate the smallest measure of wealth.

His face, largely hidden in shadow, revealed the shaven masculine angles of a strong jaw and high cheekbones. His nose had a slightly Roman quality that was also reflected in his smooth mouth. As well as Hannah could discern in the poor light, the man's skin seemed darker than most, as though he had spent hours in the sun. And why not? He was a surveyor, after all.

But she didn't know any surveyors, did she? And this was her first time ever to set foot in Bolivar, Missouri.

So, who *was* he?

"Your brother ever join the army, ma'am?" the clerk asked.

Hannah returned her attention to the task at hand. "Not that we know of. If he did, he'd have been a Union man."

"Union. You checked with authorities in Washington?"

"Of course."

"Jefferson City?"

"I just arrived from there last night. They had no information about my brother."

"Well, I reckon you might oughta head down Springfield way and talk to the military folk there. I can't find a thing here in my records about no Brownlows. And the only Ethan I come up with been dead and buried now five year."

"Dead?"

"Ethan Addison. You know him? Says here he was sixty-two and died of a broken leg."

Hannah shook her head in relief. "No, that's not my brother."

The congregation at the back table broke up, and the surveyors gathered flags and chains as they started toward the door. Hannah caught the clerk's attention again.

"How would one get to Springfield, Mr. Jones?" she asked. "Is there a coach?"

One of the surveyors paused. "Lady, we ain't had a stage through Bolivar since the war broke out." He slapped the clerk on the back. "Ask Jim here to tell you about that."

Hannah turned to the clerk. The other men gathered behind him, obviously eager to hear what he would say. The tallest of their number remained separate, observing the event from the corner.

"In March of 1861," the clerk began, "I was riding the Butterfield Stage near Warsaw. We was going down a steep hill when all sudden-like the driver lost control. We made it to the bottom of the hill, but the horses took it into their heads to veer off to one side. When they done that, the stagecoach pitched over directly into the Osage River."

"Oh, my!" As much as she disliked delaying her mission for any reason, Hannah loved to hear tales like this. She had discovered that Missourians seemed to have a passion for storytelling that almost equaled her own. An encounter with a runaway stagecoach would make a wonderful scene for her newest novel.

"We thought Jimmy was a goner," the surveyor was saying. "They toted him into town in a wagon, and he was so bad off you'da buried him on the spot."

"But I didn't aim to meet my Maker just then," Mr. Jones continued. "So I commenced healing up. Course, I'll never walk right again. Hip got all busted to pieces. Leg broke in near a dozen places. Neck twisted up like a corkscrew."

"He filed a claim against Butterfield for ten thousand dollars."

Hannah's eyes widened at the sum. "Did they pay?"

"Hell, no, they didn't pay," the clerk said, his voice tinged with disgust. "War busted out, and Butterfield decided the southern route was too dangerous. They abandoned it and charted a new route across the northwards part of the country."

"But that ain't the end of the story," the surveyor added. "Tell her, Jimmy."

The clerk smiled like a cat at a pitcher of spilled milk. "Well, round about May, along came a Butterfield caravan up through Polk County on its way north to join the new route. The sheriff, bearing my situation in mind, met up with the caravan and seized the equipment. See, he wanted to ensure that a settlement would be paid to me."

"And was it?"

"Shoot, no. But things ain't so bad now, is they, boys?" The clerk gave the others a wink. "Sheriff took in a hundred and ten horses that day. We got us nine coaches, eight hacks, and two wagons."

"Goodness!"

"When Butterfield wants 'em back, they'll have to see to my claim. In the meantime, we been using our assets to good advantage. County business and suchlike."

"Matter of fact," the surveyor put in, "Luke Maples is taking a wagon to Springfield here directly. Gonna fetch us some supplies."

"Springfield?" Hannah turned to the clerk. This delay might actually work to her advantage. "If there's no coach, might I be permitted to accompany your employee on his journey?"

"Well . . . I reckon so."

"Which of you gentlemen is Mr. Maples?" she asked.

The men looked at one another. James Jones cleared his throat and ran a finger around his collar. Craning his neck toward the back of the room, he studied the tall man in the corner who had remained silent throughout the proceedings.

"Luke's a good man," the clerk said, turning back to Hannah. He dropped his voice. "But he is an Indian."

Hannah's blood drained to her knees. *That's* where she knew him. The forest. The falcon. The scalp locks. "Oh, then I don't think—"

"I'll take her," the man said, stepping out into the dim light. He looked at Hannah. "You have a trunk and a bag at the hotel, ma'am. I'll pull the wagon around."

Without waiting for her to respond, he walked through a side door and disappeared as completely as he had the previous evening. Hannah's fingers tightened around her parasol as she stared at the empty corner the man had filled moments before.

The room fell silent.

Finally the clerk gave a sniff. "Wouldn't blame you for feeling a little out of sorts over the notion of riding with an Indian. It ain't the best notion a body ever hit on."

"He won't do nothing to her, Jim," Tom Cunnyngham said. "He's harmless, Miss Brownlow, I'd swear to it. Spent half his life in a mission school over in Kansas, and he talks just like white folk. You'd never hardly know he was Indian if it weren't for his looks. See, he come here searching for work a few months back, and I hired him right off. We don't have too many able-bodied men around these parts. Those who've come back to town are too busy putting their farms in order to take a job on a survey crew. But Luke's done fine work for me. Never missed a day. Comes in on time every morning. He's smart, too. He can read most anything you put in front of him, newspapers and all. He can calculate figures in his head that take me a half hour on paper. He's polite as he can be. I took him with me to supper one night, figurin' there'd be hell to pay for it with my wife, Lavinia. See, she don't cotton to foreigners much. But let me tell you, Luke Maples won her over so fast she was fairly purrin' over him—serving him tea and playing on her piano, even reading her poems to him. You don't have a thing to fear from him, Miss Brownlow. Matter of fact, Luke's real regular."

"Well, if another of you men is going along with Mr. Maples on the trip to Springfield . . . ," Hannah said. But she could see by the looks on their faces that none of them were.

"Takes a good long day's driving to get to Springfield, ma'am," the surveyor told her. "Takes yet another day to fetch all the supplies we need. And a third day to roll on back. We all got families and farms and kinfolk need looking after, see. What with the bushwhackers still stirring up trouble—"

"Bushwhackers?" That word again.

"Southern troublemakers. Vigilantes."

"Guerrillas," someone else put in, "that's what they is."

"Maybe the Union won the war back east in April when General Lee surrendered to General Grant over Appomatox way, ma'am, but out here the Rebels ain't quite got the message. General Kirby Smith didn't surrender the Trans-Mississippi Confederacy until the end of May. And General

Stand Watie's *still* got his troops fighting. Missourians hold out
to the bitter end, see. We're stubborn folk. And there's men in
the woods who probably ain't gonna surrender for a long time
yet.''

The others in the room nodded solemnly.

Hannah tried to adjust to this new information. "You mean
the war isn't really over here?''

"It's over. Legally." The surveyor let out a breath. "But in
Missouri the law don't hold a lot of sway.''

Hannah wished she could sit down. Her stomach had begun
to churn, and her knees felt like butter. She had expected to
encounter returning soldiers. She had prepared herself for the
sight of bullet-riddled buildings and burned barns. But if her
mother and sisters knew she was supposed to ride in a wagon
in the sole company of an Indian warrior and make a day-long
journey through a state that was still fighting the Civil
War . . .

"Anyhow, don't worry your pretty head none about bushwhackers," the clerk said in a light tone. "They got great
respect for women. They won't touch you.''

"They're real polite," the surveyor added. "They consider
themselves protectors of home and family.''

Hannah nodded and tried to make this reassurance cheer her.
"Well, thank you all very much.''

"You just go on down to Springfield with Luke Maples.
He'll look out for you. He don't say too much, and he wouldn't
hurt a fly.''

Obviously, you haven't seen the scalp-lock fringes on his
leggings, Hannah thought. Riding with Luke Maples was the
last thing she would ever consider. She tipped her head to the
clerk. "I appreciate your advice, sir. Thank you so much.''

"Good luck finding your brother.''

Bidding the other men good morning, Hannah lifted her
skirts and hurried out of the courthouse. Her first thought was
to find Miss Ruth and throw her arms around the woman. At
this moment she needed to talk to someone with a gentle and
sympathetic spirit.

Her second thought was to track down a ride going east. If
she took the first wagon out of this hellhole and the first train
back to Boston, no one would blame her. She had been a fool

ever to think of searching for Ethan. These Missourians were the stubbornest, most ignorant people she had ever met in her—

Hannah stopped and stared at the hotel across the street. That savage was setting her trunk in his wagon!

"Just a minute," she called. Waving her folded parasol, she picked her way around the mud puddles that dotted the road. "You there, sir!"

Luke lifted his head to watch the fire-haired woman tiptoeing toward him in her flimsy shoes. Her enormous bell of a skirt swung this way and that, its silky blue hem dipping into the mud with every step. He would never understand white women.

All the same, he needed this one's company for a little while. The mention of her brother's name—Ethan—had triggered a memory that cut him to the core.

The night his father had been murdered, there was a man among the killers. A Missouri man . . . hooded . . . armed with a whip and a gun . . . mounted on a black horse . . . The man Luke could never forget was the one who had whipped his father until the great warrior's back lay open to the bone. The man Luke had vowed to search for, find, and kill was the one who had hanged his father from a tree. The man Luke sought was named Ethan.

The woman's brother was probably a different person, Luke had to acknowledge. In the past few months, he had followed the trail of two other Ethans, and neither had been the one he was looking for. All the same, he wanted to hear more about this missing Boston man who had vanished in Missouri three years before.

"Sir!" the woman called as she approached the wagon. The toe of one shoe caught the edge of a wagon rut, and she plunged her parasol into a puddle to keep herself upright. "Sir, I'm so sorry to have caused you trouble, but I've decided not to—"

"Get in the wagon, ma'am," he cut in. "I'll take you to Springfield."

"No, I don't think—"

"Really, it's no problem." Before she could slip around him, he caught the woman around the waist and lifted her toward the wagon. In his hands, she felt the way his falcon had as a fledgling—skinny, fragile, almost boneless. Her waist vanished somewhere in his palms. Having deposited her on the seat, he took up the reins and climbed in beside her.

"Now, wait just a minute!" she said, turning on him. "I have already made up my mind to stay another day or two here in Bolivar."

"Might as well go to Springfield when you've got the chance," Luke countered. He gave the reins a shake and set the wagon rolling.

"But I haven't settled on a plan of action. I need time to work through my schedule, and I don't intend to allow a perfect stranger to . . ."

Luke turned a deaf ear to the stream of admonishments and gave Miss Hannah Brownlow a brief glance. She might look like a fledgling bird, but the spirit inside her belonged to a falcon in the fullness of regal self-confidence. The woman did not want to ride with him, and the longer she jabbered at him the more certain Luke became that he didn't want her along either. She was a pest, certain to destroy the peace and serenity of the morning drive. He considered pulling on the reins and setting her in the mud, fanny first.

While Luke mulled over his options, the horse, oblivious to the angry monologue coming from behind it, eased into a gentle pace that took the wagon past the hotel and the courthouse square. To give himself strength to endure the scolding woman, Luke conjured the memory of his father's murderer. Ethan. He needed to learn more about this woman's brother.

"Stop the wagon this instant, sir," Hannah demanded. "I will not ride another foot in this wagon with you!" She reached for the reins.

Luke clamped a hand around her wrists, locking them together in a grip that threatened to crush her bones. He looked at her for a moment, attempting to silence her with an icy glance, and then set her hands on her lap.

"I could have you arrested for kidnapping," she burst out. "If I choose to press charges, you will spend the rest of your life in a jail cell. Do you realize that?"

The Indian studied the road in silence, as if he hadn't heard

a word she'd said. Hannah tried to make her heart slow down
before it pounded a hole straight through her chest. She had to
get off this wagon! No matter what the ignorant surveyors
thought of this Indian, she knew better. She had seen those
scalp-locks. She had seen that quiver full of arrows. The man
might fool everyone in Bolivar by dressing like a white
gentleman, but in his heart he was a savage.

"You are an intolerable, rude, self-absorbed—"

"You tried to shoot me yesterday," he cut in.

Hannah prickled. "I did not."

"Your friend stole my rabbit."

"Well, of all the—!" She crossed her arms. Was he actually
daring to accuse her of attempted murder? Did he mean to
imply that she had abetted a thief? As if what she had done
were worse than kidnapping an innocent woman . . .

The wagon was rolling past the last house in town. "Now see
here, Mr. . . . Mr. *Indian*—"

"Maples. Name's Luke Maples." He held out a hand.

She stared at the outstretched palm. Torn between years of
training in the social graces and an enormous reluctance to
make physical contact with this insufferable boor, Hannah
gripped the handle of her parasol.

"Hannah Brownlow," she said, taking his hand and giving it
a perfunctory shake. Before she could pull away, his fingers
tightened around hers.

Luke lifted his head and looked into the woman's face.
"Pleased to meet you, Miss Brownlow," he said.

The lashes framing her eyes were long and dark brown, and
when she glanced up in surprise at the tone in his voice, their
tips nearly touched the arch of her red-brown brows. He had
never known eyes could be such a color. Rimmed in dark
indigo, they were as blue as cornflowers on a Kansas prairie.

He repeated a line he'd read in a book at the mission school
library—one that had made all the Osage boys snicker. "I'm
delighted to have the company of such a charming companion," he said and finally released her hand.

She crossed her arms again, tucking the hand safely away.
"Likewise, I'm sure." Then she lifted her chin. "And you may
have titled yourself Luke Maples, but I know the truth about
you. You're an Indian."

"You're smarter than I thought."

"I'll have you know I am extremely intelligent and literate, and I don't intend to be made sport of by—"

"Are you planning to jabber all the way to Springfield, Miss Brownlow?"

"I am not going to ride to Springfield with—"

"An *Indian*."

Hannah flushed. She hadn't realized how unfair her words sounded until he threw them back at her. "It would be highly improper for a woman to travel alone with a man, Indian or not."

"If you want to get to Springfield, you'll stay on this wagon."

"How can I be certain I'll ever make it to Springfield?"

"Afraid I might scalp you or something?"

Hannah gulped down a bubble of air. He was actually grinning. As if this were a matter of great amusement! Of course, she couldn't just come right out and admit that she was indeed concerned about the safety of her hair. That would be playing straight into his hands.

"You think all Indians live for is to run around scalping people," he said. "You Heavy Eyebrows know nothing about our ways."

"Heavy eyebrows?"

"*I'n-Shta-Heh.*" He glanced at her again, and the corner of his mouth tilted up. "It's the name we gave you Americans. We Osage have always shaved our heads and brows. But you have these . . ." He reached up and ran one finger over the smooth curve of Hannah's eyebrow.

She held her breath as the spark of his touch ignited on her skin. He was staring at her, his brown eyes suddenly deep and unreadable. Now he touched her other eyebrow, stroking the tip of his finger across her forehead toward her temple. His hand wavered at the edge of her bonnet where a strand of her hair had escaped. Then he dropped his arm and turned away.

"*I'n-Shta-Heh,*" he said. "The enemy of my people."

"And *that's* why you must stop the wagon," Hannah blurted. "I won't ride with someone who wants to kill me!"

"I don't want to kill you. What purpose would the death of a white woman serve me?"

Hannah pondered that for a moment. Killing her wouldn't do him much good—unless he wanted to add a new scalp to the fringes of those buckskin leggings.

"In battle we prove our bravery by counting coup," he explained, ignoring the fact that she hadn't answered. "Scalping a man slain in battle is done, but counting coup on a living man is better."

"Counting coup?"

"That means we touch the enemy." He laid a hand on Hannah's arm. "Like this."

She gave a startled jump.

He smirked. "Don't worry. A woman isn't a worthy foe for an Osage warrior."

"I wouldn't be so certain of that, sir," Hannah replied archly. "One should never underestimate one's enemy."

Luke observed the fragile creature beside him for a moment. Her fine, high cheeks had flushed a bright pink, and her eyes sparkled like a lake in the summertime. There was a flare to her small nostrils and a tilt to her head that reminded him of a proud mare ready to face down anything in her way. Maybe this fire-haired woman was right. Maybe she would prove herself a noble foe.

"Why should I trust anything you say?" she asked. "You're nothing but a sham. I saw you and your bird in the forest yesterday. You were dressed as an Indian. On the one hand, you walk about half-naked like a savage, and you purport to know all about counting coup and taking scalps. On the other hand, I notice you certainly have a full head of hair yourself. You speak with almost no accent. You wear civilized clothing. And this morning in the courthouse, you might have been a Heavy Eyebrows yourself, Mr. *Luke Maples*."

"Or Jean-Luc Mabille. The French name I was given by my father."

"French? Oh, please."

"Or Gthe-don-wa-kon. Mystery-hawk. My Osage name." He shrugged. "I'm whoever you want me to be, Miss Hannah Brownlow. If you want an Indian to thrill and frighten you, I'll put on my leggings and shoot a deer with my bow and arrow. If you want a white man to mince and bow around you, I'll tip my hat and recite a passage from William Shakespeare."

"You couldn't."

" 'To be, or not to be: that is the question: whether 'tis nobler in the mind to suffer the slings and arrows of outrageous fortune, or to take arms against a sea of troubles, and by opposing end them? To die: to sleep—' "

"All right." Hannah held up a hand. "Please . . ." She studied the gray sky and the heavy slate of clouds. The road was empty of travelers. The countryside grew thick with vines, shrubbery, and trees. No houses. No people. Again Hannah had the odd sensation that she had stepped into a world skewed by time. Men still fought the Civil War. Indians quoted Shakespeare. This was a place where the rules she had been taught didn't apply, and where reason held no sway.

No, she wouldn't let herself think this way. She had to set this tipsy feeling to rights.

"The men at the courthouse told me you went to a mission school," she said. "That's how you know Shakespeare. And I suppose that's also why you don't shave your head and eyebrows."

"Maybe."

Hannah twisted the handle of her parasol. She still wasn't certain she could trust this man to take her all the way to Springfield—Shakespeare or not. But she had let the town slip behind, and she couldn't deny that she was fascinated to learn more about a people she had only read of in books. She had planned a scene in her novel in which a horde of Indians attacked a settler's cabin. Could she learn something from this Osage Mystery-hawk that would enrich her story?

Glancing at the man beside her, she tried to imagine him riding down an enemy and counting coup. Or shooting an arrow through a man's heart and then slicing off his scalp. Obviously he had done those things.

So why on earth was she riding with him? Her sisters would be aghast at the thought. Her mother would swoon.

Hannah squared her shoulders. She had never been the swooning sort. She would sit right beside this savage all the way to Springfield, and she would pick his brain about the customs of his people. They would have a fine, interesting chat, and she would only be the richer for their chance encounter.

"All right, I'll ride with you," she announced.

"Why? Because I can recite words written by a man you were taught to admire?" He threaded the reins through his fingers before turning to her. "Or is it because you understand that, like Hamlet, I have questioned the purpose of my own existence? Because you realize that I, too, have wondered whether a man should sit back and accept his fate by allowing his enemies to steal his land and kill his family and defeat him—or whether that same man should arm himself with the weapons he has been given, and fight against the sea of trouble that threatens him? Will you ride with me because of what you hear and see, or because of what you understand?"

Taken aback, Hannah studied the brown eyes deeply set beneath the Indian's brow. He not only knew the words of an English bard, he felt them with his soul. He wasn't supposed to speak this way . . . or act this way . . . or look at her this way.

And she wasn't supposed to notice that his black hair curled slightly at his collar. Or that his leg was touching the hem of her dress. Or that his eyes were tracing the shape of her lips.

"I've decided to ride with you," she said softly, "because . . . because you interest me, Mr. Luke Maples Mystery-hawk. Because you seem . . . genteel . . . respectable . . . civilized. And because I have decided to trust you."

He raised his focus from her mouth to her eyes. "One should never underestimate one's enemy, Miss Brownlow."

Chapter
Three

~~~~≈≈≈≈~~~~

It had been a mistake to ride with him, Hannah decided. Not because he had tried to scalp her or anything. Far from it. She might as well have been a splinter on the wagon seat for all the notice he paid her. In contrast to his initial wordiness, Luke Maples lapsed into utter silence once she had agreed to accompany him.

She had tried her best to bring him out. She'd asked everything she could think of about his tribe, the Osage. What did they eat? What were their homes like? What did they wear? Did they believe in God?

He gave nothing but one-word answers. They ate buffalo. They lived in lodges. They wore clothes. Yes, they believed in God.

Irritated, Hannah had finally given up. Then it began to rain, a light off-and-on-again drizzle that made the road steam and obscured the forest with mist. She raised her parasol, which barely covered her and did nothing for Luke. Let him soak, she decided. If he couldn't talk, he could just sit there and drip.

The road turned to mud as the wagon bed collected a puddle of water that began to slosh. Snorting with impatience, the horse jerked at the reins. The sun had completely vanished behind a thick layer of gray cloud when Luke finally pulled the wagon under the branches of a walnut tree.

"What are you doing?" Hannah demanded as he set the brake. "You can't stop now. If we're ever to make it to Springfield by nightfall, we must keep traveling."

He regarded her evenly. "It's time to eat."

"I certainly don't see an inn anywhere about. And I didn't bring a lunch, did you?"

"As a matter of fact, I did." He reached behind him in the wagon and lifted a damp canvas bag. After digging around inside it for a moment, he pulled out a couple of long brown sticks. "Here."

Thankful for gloves, Hannah took the offering between her thumb and index finger. The thing resembled a knobby ribbon and looked as stiff and unpalatable as a piece of old kindling. "You don't mean to actually—"

"Eat it." He chomped down and tugged off a hunk of the stick. "Yep, I do."

Hannah watched him chew. "But what is it?"

"Jerky." He raked a hand through his wet hair and let out a breath. "Deer meat. Venison."

"Has it been cooked?"

"Dried."

"You're eating *raw* meat?" She pondered the barbarity of it. All the same . . . her stomach had been rumbling for hours. She sniffed, shut her eyes, and bit down. Nearly a minute passed before she was able to tear off a bite. Holding her breath, she chewed and chewed. And chewed.

"Good, huh?" Luke asked.

Hannah swallowed. "Is this your main source of nourishment? You Osage people?"

"Sometimes."

Another empty answer. Her novel would go nowhere with this sort of information. Hannah ripped off another bite of jerky. "Well, for heaven's sake, what do you eat the rest of the time?"

Luke observed her for a moment. Hannah Brownlow was the

nosiest Heavy Eyebrows he'd ever met. Other than Tom Cunnyngham, no one in Bolivar cared a thing about him or his life. Which was fine. But this young Boston miss seemed to be able to do nothing but ask questions.

He didn't trust her curiosity. She probably thought she could entertain future guests with stories of the wild Indian savage she had met in Missouri. On the other hand, it had been a long time since Luke had spoken more than a couple of short sentences to anyone. Though he worked closely with the survey crew and enjoyed discussing business with Tom, he had never in his life felt so alone.

Among his clan, a person was never alone. The tribe and its unity provided constant companionship. For the Osage, group living was the only acceptable way of life. To be cast out for a crime was the worst punishment a man could face. To send a child to the mission school was the greatest sacrifice a family could make. To leave the village and move away—as Luke had done—was all but unthinkable.

Until he had come to Missouri to search for his family's lost lands and his father's killer, Luke had lived in the close presence of his mother, brothers, sisters, aunts, uncles, grandparents, and more friends than he could count. But for many months now, his world had been one of silence, solitude, loneliness.

"Or is the content of your pantry yet another great Osage secret?" Hannah cut into his thoughts. "All I asked was a simple, straightforward—"

"Pumpkins," Luke said. "Squash, corn, beans. We grow those crops in the fields. At least we do when we find fertile ground. When we move into a forest, our women gather hickory nuts, walnuts, acorns. We eat persimmons, hackberries, lotus, haws, pawpaws, grapes, milkweed sprouts. Turkeys show us where to gather *ho'n-bthi'n-cu,* the wild bean. And our main vegetable is *do,* the wild potato."

Hannah focused on the dripping woods. "You mean you can find all those things out in that impossible tangle?"

"And more. For meat, we eat white-tail deer, rabbit, squirrel, wild turkey, fish, skunk—"

"Skunk!"

"On the plains, we hunt buffalo and prairie chickens."

"My goodness. In Boston it's mostly beef for us. Beef comes from cows, you know."

Luke had to smile. "Yes, I know."

"Corned beef and cabbage is my mother's favorite. She's Irish. She's why I have this red hair." Hannah motioned to her bonnet. "We like potatoes, too. Not wild ones, just normal everyday ones that you can cut up into a stew or boil with parsley. Of course, I wouldn't know how to do that. We have a cook who prepares our meals. But she's Irish, too. So there's the corned beef and cabbage all over again. Have you ever tasted corned beef and cabbage, Mr. Maples?"

Luke dragged his gaze up from her mouth to her eyes. He'd never seen such lips on a woman—pink and full and moving with words as fast as water over a cliff. Her mouth lured him, but her eyes beckoned with even greater persuasion. Blue and as deep as pools above that waterfall of a mouth . . .

"No," he said finally. "I've never eaten corned beef and cabbage."

"It's quite nice, but not if you have it every day. Since the war began, we've had to face some hardships. My father went off to fight, you see, and the shop was closed down. He's a printer. Or was." She sobered. "My father was killed."

The shadow of pain that crossed her eyes pulled at something inside Luke. "I'm sorry," he said. "My father was killed, too."

"In the war? I heard there were Indian regiments."

"No. Before that. I was a child."

Hannah shook her head. "It's a terrible thing to lose a father. We were shocked because the war had hardly touched us in Boston. True, we didn't have much money coming in, and we had to let the gardener go. I was forced by circumstances to take a form of genteel employment. My sisters and I did spend a great deal of time after the second Battle of Bull Run preparing emergency medical supplies. When I wasn't writing, I was in the Tremont Temple tearing old garments and sheets into strips or sewing the strips into bandages. We worked for hours preparing liniment, and sometimes I spent a whole day just rolling dressings. But all the same, the war seemed distant. Life was actually quite peaceful. You see, we were certain Father would be home soon, and all would be as it had been . . . And then . . . then . . . the telegram arrived . . . and . . ."

She fumbled in her sleeve for her handkerchief. How could she be weeping in front of this utter stranger? Hannah sniffled as she searched for the wayward lace scrap.

"Miss Brownlow? I don't have a handkerchief on me, but . . ." He offered his arm and shirtsleeve. "You can use this, if you . . ."

"Oh, thank you. How kind." She let out a breath and gathered a clump of the damp homespun. The fabric was warm and clean-smelling as she brushed it across her cheek. The feel of his arm beneath, so hard and strong, somehow reassured her. Had circumstances been different, she might have given in to her need to be comforted and laid her head on his shoulder. But of course it would never do to become familiar.

"I'm terribly sorry," she said, lifting her eyes to his face. "I don't mean to be a bother."

Luke said the opposite of what he'd been thinking all morning. "You're no bother, Miss Brownlow."

Her smile could have melted ice. "I try not to think about . . . the past. I look ahead. After I find my brother, Ethan, I can go back to Boston, and everything will be all right again."

Luke felt his spine prickle at the sound of that name. It was time to be done with weeping and chatter. He'd agreed to take this woman with him for one reason only.

"So you've lost your brother," he said, releasing the wagon's brake and giving the reins a shake. "Tell me about Ethan."

It took about an hour of her lengthy descriptions and wanderings down uncharted paths of memory for Luke to figure out that Ethan Brownlow was not the man he sought.

Hannah's brother had spent most of his life in Boston rather than roaming the Kansas and Missouri countryside. He was a Union man, not a Confederate sympathizer. He was charming, lighthearted, debonair—a man who enjoyed taking his sisters to the circus and the park. He definitely was not a man who would don a hood and ride into an Osage village in the middle of the night with a group of Missouri slave-owning guerrillas bent on massacre. Ethan Brownlow played with children—he didn't carry a whip and take perverse pleasure in hanging an enemy with a noose.

There was no connection, and Luke had to admit he was up against yet another dead end. It wasn't the first one he had ever faced. And he knew it wouldn't be the last.

Now that he had found what must have been his clan's tribal home atop the bluff above the Pomme de Terre River, he knew he would do anything to make it his own. But could an Indian take possession of federal land? Would he be permitted to buy the property? Or could he live on it, farm it, and eventually own it according to the Homestead Act created three years earlier?

Luke had no idea what obstacles lay ahead, but he intended to find out during this trip to Springfield. He had made up his mind he would stop at nothing to reclaim his stolen legacy. After leaving the security of his home and village, he had taken greater risks than a warrior at battle. No Heavy Eyebrows law could hold him back.

Besides, he reflected, he had nothing to lose and everything to gain. The Osage, who had survived for centuries as hunters and gatherers, had been forced onto the prairie where forests were skimpy and buffalo had become the people's major source of food. Then the reservation had been overrun by Easterners rushing westward to search for gold. Following that, settlers refused to honor the established boundaries of Indian land. Every few years, the federal government sliced off another huge section of the reservation, and it stood to reason they would not stop until the Osage people had nothing left but their names.

What did Luke and his young companions have to live for? Their hunting grounds were limited. Their future as warriors was threatened. They could offer their children no home but a bleak, flat, barren plain. And what would their grandchildren inherit?

Luke grunted. No, he had nothing to lose in coming to Missouri to find and take the old Osage lands. Whatever it took, he would own those wooded acres over the bluff where the cave with the old oak tree grew. He would build a lodge and live through the winter.

When spring came, he would return to his village in Kansas

and marry a woman of his tribe. Perhaps one day he could bring his mother and his brothers back to their traditional homeland. He and his wife would have children—Osage children. And they would inherit a rich legacy, one with promise and hope.

"Of course, Elizabeth hardly remembers Ethan," Hannah was saying as the rain pattered on her parasol. Luke realized he hadn't been listening to her for quite a long time. Oblivious, she chattered on, her blue eyes locked on the sky and her long neck curving upward like a swan's.

"Elizabeth was far too young to know our brother." She gave a deep sigh. "Ethan was much older than all of us, as I told you, and he left home that first time when Elizabeth was barely . . ."

Luke watched her bosom rise and fall. Amazing. He'd never paid particular attention to the women in Bolivar. But the longer he spent with this one, the more disturbed he felt. Her dress was the color of a frozen pond—ice-blue and shiny. She wore a small jacket that fit around her bosom like a second skin. A line of tiny, fabric-covered buttons ran up the curve between her breasts.

Luke found himself wondering what lay beneath all those layers of cloth. Her breasts must be the size of ripe melons. And her waist. Where was it? He didn't see how there was room inside her narrow torso for her heart and lungs. She certainly had difficulty breathing at times . . . especially when she looked at him.

No, he was imagining that. A woman with large breasts, a small waist, and hair like a flame would surely have attracted the attention of some young white man's family. No doubt she had been sought as a bride already. She certainly would have no interest in an *Indian,* as she had disdainfully called Luke. He ought to keep his eyes on the road and his mind on his own mission. No good could come of thinking about Hannah Brownlow's high, round breasts.

"And that's when the wagon turned the corner in Jefferson City," she was saying. "Miss Ruth spotted me, and I looked at her. We smiled at each other. And the next thing I knew, Willie was loading my trunk and hatboxes on his wagon."

Luke studied the road ahead. "Willie is the *Nika-sabe*? The black man?"

"I told you that. Haven't you been paying attention?" Hannah let out a breath. "Oh, what does it matter? I'm just blathering. I'll never see Miss Ruth again, even though she was kinder to me than anyone else on this ill-advised journey. We looked out for one another as though we were sisters, and we could talk about almost anything. You know, she was a slave all her life, and I've never known a moment of tedious labor— other than winding bandages for the soldiers—but there was something between Miss Ruth and me. A connection. I'm sure you couldn't understand what I'm talking about. You've probably never known such a thing."

"I know it with my falcon. Gthe-don reads my thoughts. We hunt as one."

Hannah pondered the odd notion. "How did you catch him?"

"I climbed a tall tree to the nest and took him as an eyas, a nestling. At the mission school I'd read a book about falconry. I was intrigued by the subject. You see, the falcon is a sacred symbol to the Osage."

"Why?"

"Haven't you ever watched a falcon fly?" He reflected on the light-colored hawk that had become his trusted partner. "He's swift and ruthless. His courage is savage. He lives a long life—some think forever. The prairie falcon can take a passenger pigeon on the wing, and he has no fear of attacking birds much stronger and larger than he. He's not a slave to the earth, but he roams the skies freely. It's thought that the falcon was born of heaven, a child of Grandfather the Sun and the Moon Woman. He's stainless and pure. When I read the book on falconry, I couldn't imagine how man could subjugate such a creature for his own uses. I made up my mind to unlock the mystery."

Regarding him covertly, Hannah turned over his words in her mind. Falcons were sacred, yet Luke Maples had possessed the temerity not only to capture one but to force it into submission. He had disregarded centuries-old tradition to achieve his own purposes. What sort of a man would break every rule—would even challenge the spiritual realm—in order to unlock a mystery?

"Gthe-don wasn't easy to train," Luke continued, "but I had little else to do in the afternoons after my classes. He soon learned to perch on my gloved fist, to fly freely without escaping, and to jump from a branch to my fist. Then I taught him to fly to a lure and then to my fist, to respond to my whistle, and finally to hunt for me. In Kansas, Gthe-don provided most of my small game—ground squirrels, doves, pigeons, grouse, quail. But he's a prairie falcon, suited to wide open spaces and treeless plains."

"So he finds it harder to hunt in the forest?"

Luke nodded. The rain had tapered off, and he found it surprisingly good to talk with this woman about his hawk. "I try to find cleared fields or roads. The falcon is more efficient."

"So that's why you were on the road to Bolivar yesterday?"

"When your *Nika-sabe* stole my rabbit."

"Willie didn't think of it as yours," Hannah returned. "Besides, you vanished into the forest without it. Why shouldn't Willie and Ruth have it for their supper?"

"Because my bird—" Luke paused and peered ahead at the edge of the forest. He thought he detected a movement. A slight shadow. A rustling sound.

Hannah straightened. "What?"

"Because my falcon killed the rabbit," Luke continued, drawing her attention away from the road. "And that means it was mine."

"Well, if you'd wanted it so badly, you should have told us so instead of slinking around like . . . What on earth are you staring at?"

"Nothing."

Hannah frowned. This man was annoying. Other than those scalp-locks, his irritating silences were the worst thing about him. He wasn't the least bit like the Indians she had dreamed up for her novel. They were going to be bloodthirsty savages, the sort of barbarians who populated the articles she had read. They would wear war paint and carry tomahawks.

Hannah reflected on the manuscript she had begun writing as the train carried her west to Missouri. She hoped it would be a breakthrough for her—the novel that would raise her to the ranks of Mrs. Henry Wood and her titillating *East Lynne*. Aware that she had to avoid anything smacking of scandal lest she offend her mother's delicate sensibilities, Hannah had decided to make her mark on readers by using a unique setting—the wild Western frontier.

She had plotted the whole book before she even left Boston. The heroine, a courageous young woman, would travel to the West with her loving husband and two small children. The family would settle into a quaint and cozy log cabin and begin to farm. But their peace would be shattered by an Indian attack.

When her beloved husband was killed by the raiders, the heroine would rally her children to keep the home fires burning. Only the help of a handsome blond man who farmed the neighboring acreage would enable the widow to survive. This wonderful man would fall in love with the young widow, and eventually he would offer to marry her. When the Indians attacked a second time, the farmer would kill the chief to ensure that his young family would live in security forever.

Lost in the beauty of her story, Hannah was startled to see two mounted men ride out of the dripping forest. Luke stiffened and placed a protective arm in front of her.

"Who are they?" she whispered.

Luke shook his head. "Don't speak."

Drawing guns, the two men rode toward the wagon. Luke mentally took stock of the knife hidden in his boot and the rifle on the wagon floor behind his feet. Both were all but useless against an ambush. If he reached for a weapon, the strangers would shoot.

"Howdy, folks," one of the men addressed them. He wore a shaggy brown beard and mustache. "We hear tell that you, sir, are Luke Maples from up Bolivar way."

Luke said nothing. If they threatened his life, he would have no choice but to defend himself. He also knew that, as an Indian, he would be held responsible if any harm came to Hannah or to either of his attackers. Even if he won, he was bound to lose by engaging in a battle with these men.

"I said, I reckon you must be Luke Maples from yonder north," the man repeated.

"What do you want, sir?" Hannah spoke up, ignoring Luke's restraining grip on her arm. "Why are you pointing your weapons at my traveling associate?"

"Well, ma'am, we wouldn't want to worry you none, but you oughta know you're in the company of a redskin."

"I'm well aware of Mr. Maples's heritage. He is driving me to Springfield on a mission to find my brother, and he has been thoroughly civil—unlike you, who seem to have no compunction against pointing your weapon at unarmed travelers."

The man glanced at his companion. The two wore muddy boots, sweat-stained clothes, and shapeless hats. "Now, we don't aim to do nothing but enforce the law," the bearded man told Hannah. "And the law says that redskins belong in Indian Territory. That's over Kansas way, a far piece from here."

"Enforce the law? Are you the sheriff?"

The man laughed, revealing a set of badly decayed teeth beneath his mustache. Hannah grimaced. These men were filthy and discourteous. Surely they couldn't claim any measure of respectability.

"Naw, I ain't the sheriff, ma'am." He swept the battered felt hat from his greasy hair. "I'm Captain Joshua Billings of the third Missouri regiment of the Confederate Army. At your service."

"Confederates? I'll have you know the war is over, Captain Billings. The Confederacy surrendered two months ago. You have no jurisdiction here."

"I wouldn't be so sure about that. What I say round these parts goes. And I say that Indian you're with better get his red hide back to Kansas where it belongs."

Indignant, Hannah twisted the handle of her parasol. "Captain Billings, are you what is commonly known as a bushwhacker?"

"That I am, and damn proud of it. Now, I suggest you get your Union fanny off this wagon and let us tend to the Indian."

"My Union *what*?"

"C'mon, Travis," the man spat. "You hold her while I take care of the redskin. And get her purse while you're at it."

"Sure thing, Captain." Digging his heels into his horse, the second man rode at Hannah.

"Stay down!" Luke warned. He grabbed Hannah's arm and thrust her onto the wagon floor as Joshua Billings lunged at him. Travis pulled up alongside the wagon and reached for her.

"Oh!" Struggling amid the tangle of her hoops, Hannah jabbed her parasol at her attacker. "Stand back!"

He swiped at her again, but she batted his hand away. With a growl of frustration, he slid from his horse onto the wagon and locked an arm around Hannah's waist. She fought, kicking and elbowing, as he dragged her off the rig and onto the muddy road.

"Now, give me that purse of yours. Ow!" he grunted as she plunged her elbow into his stomach. "Damn it, I ain't gonna hurt you. Josh and me just wanna teach that Indian a lesson!"

"I'll teach you to sully a lady!" She slapped him across the face. He staggered backward.

"Travis, help!" the other man cried out. "The Indian's got a knife!"

Shoving Hannah down into the mud, Travis abandoned her and slogged across the road. She struggled to her knees and peered between the spokes of the wagon's wheels to the other side of the road. Knife in one hand, Luke was circling the fallen Billings. Approaching, Travis leveled his gun at Luke's back.

"Luke!" Hannah screamed. "Behind you!"

Swinging around, Luke threw himself at Travis. A bullet exploded from the barrel as the men went down. Billings scrambled through the mud and fell on the wrestling pair. A knife flashed. Someone cried out. Mud flew.

"Dear God!" Using the wagon wheel as leverage, Hannah pulled herself to her feet. She picked up her sodden skirts and sloshed across the road. This couldn't be happening, she thought with every step. These men actually meant to kill Luke. They intended to rob her and leave her stranded out in this dripping wilderness. Such a thing would never happen in Boston! Decent people simply didn't behave this way. These men were animals.

Covered in mud, the three combatants had become almost indistinguishable from one another. Hannah picked up a heavy limb from the side of the road and watched for an opportunity to come to Luke's aid. When the bearded man rolled on top of the flailing figures, she swung at his head. The crack echoed like a gunshot. The limb shattered, and Josh Billings tumbled to the ground.

Instantly Travis reared up and hammered Luke's jaw. In

return, Luke flicked his knife across his attacker's arm. They fell on each other again, blood mingling with the mud.

Picking himself up from the road, Billings lunged at Hannah. She tried to back away, but he threw himself onto her. Crushing the breath from her chest, the weight of the man's body pinned her arms and legs to the ground. The world swam. She tasted blood as she struggled helplessly beneath him.

"Demon!" she croaked, barely able to make the word audible. "Get off!"

"I'll teach you to knock a man's head half off, Union bitch. You ain't seen trouble till I—"

"Josh, I'm cut bad," Travis cried out suddenly. "Let's get the hell out of here!"

"I'll be damned if I'm gonna let—" His words were cut short as Luke smashed his fist into the man's temple. Billings slumped into the mud, senseless.

"Hannah?" Luke grabbed the heavy man by his shirt and trousers and threw him off her body. Kneeling in the mud, he scooped the limp woman up in his arms. She moaned, and her ashen face sent a stab of fear into his heart. She was brave and strong—and she'd been injured trying to protect him.

"Can you breathe, Hannah?" he asked.

She nodded, blinking back tears. "But my ribs hurt."

"I'll take you to the wagon." He carried her across the muddy road and laid her in the wooden bed. "Lie still until I can get us away from this place. When I'm sure we're safe, I'll check you over."

After scanning the road to see that Billings was still out cold and Travis was nowhere in sight, Luke swung himself up onto the wagon. He flicked the reins, and the horse tugged. For a moment he feared they weren't going anywhere. The wheels creaked against the thick, sucking mud. Luke shook the reins again.

"Let's go," he told the horse. "Come on, boy."

The horse strained at the harness. The wheels turned. The wagon rolled forward, and Luke let out a breath. As the rig moved down the road, he glanced behind him again. Billings still lay unmoving in the mud. Travis and the two horses had vanished.

Luke dropped the gun he had taken and rubbed a hand across

his eyes. He blinked through the grime on his eyelashes and spat out a mouthful of blood mingled with mud. His teeth were full of grit, his jaw throbbed, and his knuckles bled.

Heavy Eyebrows. What a disgusting breed, Luke thought. Just the kind of men who had killed his father. It had taken all his control to keep from slitting the throats of those two pigs once he had incapacitated them. A quick swipe with his knife would have added a pair of scalps to his leggings.

He spat again. But those ways were behind him. The presence of two murdered and scalped white men on the road to Springfield would identify him immediately as the killer. He would lose any chance of regaining his land. He'd probably lose his life.

As much as he disliked it, Luke knew he had no choice but to continue to behave and dress as white men did. He had to suppress his Osage instincts and training in order to follow the ways he had been taught by Father Schoenmakers at the Osage Mission School. The priest, at least, had been a good example of a Heavy Eyebrows man. But those two on the road back there—

"Oh, my side hurts," Hannah murmured from the back of the wagon.

Luke swung around, instantly focused on her again. "Hannah?"

"It feels like a knife is sliding up and down between my ribs."

"Don't move. I'm coming back." He let the reins go slack and hoped the horse would continue to follow the open road. Concern flooding through him in an unexpected tide, Luke climbed over the seat and knelt beside the woman.

In spite of the dark mud splattered across her face, he could see that she was as pale as flour. Her bonnet had fallen to one side, and her hair was matted and almost black. One sleeve hung tattered, exposing her shoulder. Her blue eyes were bright with pain.

"He threw himself on me," she said in a low voice. "The Rebel captain."

"That man wasn't an officer. There's no such thing as the third Missouri regiment of the Confederate Army. Bushwhackers invent their own regiments to make themselves sound legitimate."

"It's so barbaric and primitive out here. Bushwhackers and muddy roads and trees all around. I don't know how you can bear to live here." She studied Luke's face. He looked terrible—his skin coated in thick mud, his hair tangled, blood trickling from his jaw. "You've been cut!"

He touched his chin. "It's nothing. Now, what about you? Do you think your ribs are broken?" He reached out to touch her, but stopped just before his fingers met hers. More times than he could count, he had treated wounded and battered companions after a raid. But a woman? A Heavy Eyebrows?

He searched her face, trying to read the message hidden behind the pain in her blue eyes. Did she want him to examine her? Would she let him remove her clothing? Could he trust himself to look at her without seeing? To touch without feeling?

"I wouldn't know whether my ribs are broken or not," she said softly. "I'm so filthy and wet, I probably can't even peel off this dress to find my corset. Look, it's starting to rain again."

Luke lifted his head. This time the clouds had rolled across the sky like heavy gray pillows. "It's going to pour."

"At least the rain will wash off some of this muck."

He couldn't believe she was smiling. Her face softened, and the pain seemed to melt away. Hannah Brownlow was beautiful, he reflected. The most beautiful, intriguing, and confusing woman he'd ever known. On the one hand, she stood stiffly on her prim Heavy Eyebrows principles of white superiority and female propriety. She chattered like a blue jay. She had little idea of the harsh realities of life. She was as pampered and naive and pristine as a person could be.

On the other hand, she was intelligent and courageous. In spite of her sheltered upbringing, she had ventured miles from her home to find her missing brother. Though she clearly had been taught to disdain Indians, she didn't seem to notice any differences between herself and the two old *Nika-sabe* she had traveled to Bolivar with. She hadn't hesitated to come to Luke's defense either, and she'd clobbered that outlaw over the head with every ounce of her strength. She'd been shoved into

the mud and tackled by a man twice her size, and she had come
out of it all with a smile on her face.

"I don't suppose you could find an inn," she said. "I'm so
hungry and tired. If only I could rest a little, we could make our
way to Springfield by nightfall."

Luke reached out and brushed a clot of mud from her cheek.
"I'll look for an inn," he told her as he pulled a blanket from
the stack of goods he was taking to Springfield. When he slid
it under her head, he realized it was damp, but she settled onto
the pillow with a sigh.

"Rest in the wagon," he said. "I'll take care of you."

"Thank you." Her eyes drifted shut. "You are truly the
kindest gentleman I have ever met."

Luke studied Hannah in silence for a moment before
climbing back onto the wagon seat. As he took up the reins, he
felt the first droplets begin to splatter across his shoulders.

The horse struggled through the mud, and Luke watched the
road melt into a river. It was strange, he thought as he rode in
silence. A few hours ago, he would have sworn Hannah
Brownlow thought of him as a barbaric savage. But now she
called him a gentleman. The kindest she had ever met.

Strange, too, that a few hours ago he had classed her with the
other Heavy Eyebrows he knew. He had considered her hardly
different from Travis and Josh—savages themselves.

But now, as the rain streamed into his hair, he realized he felt
an unfamiliar urge to watch over Hannah. Somehow she had
become beautiful. Intriguing. Desirable.

Chapter
Four

Rain veiled the road in a chilly gray curtain. The horse pulled the wagon less than a mile before the wheels mired in the muck, and Luke had no choice but to postpone the journey to Springfield. Deciding the best thing to do was find shelter and wait out the storm, he slackened the reins and set the brake.

He turned to study the condition of his sodden passenger. Hannah had said almost nothing since the ambush, but the pale, drawn cast to her face told him she was miserable.

"Can you ride?" he asked over the din of the rain.

She nodded.

While she huddled under the useless canopy of her parasol, he unhitched the horse and led it around to the back of the wagon. "We'll have to leave your trunk and hatboxes out here," he told her. "I doubt anyone will be on the road again until morning."

"I'd hoped to get to Springfield tonight." She looked at him through the waterfall that poured over the brim of her bonnet.

"But I suppose it's useless to think of going on. Will there be an inn ahead?"

He shook his head. "If we're lucky, we might find a farmhouse."

She gathered her sopping skirts. "There's a packet in my trunk. I must take it with me."

He waited in the downpour while she unlocked the lid and lifted out a leather pouch. Tucking it under one arm, she straightened. "You may assist me now, Mr. Maples," she said softly.

Something in Hannah's futile attempt at gentility tugged at Luke's heart as he took her gloved hand. Here they were— rain-soaked, splattered with mud, battered, and bruised—but she was determined to address him as a lady would a gentleman. After arranging her bedraggled bonnet to cover the muck in her hair, she carefully maneuvered her sodden dress with its creaky hoops and tattered sleeve. Her gloves were caked with mud as she patted down her skirt. All the same, she was as conscious of decorum as if she were in a parlor in Boston.

"Hang on, now," he said as he placed his hands around her waist. She cried out in pain and sank her fingers into his shoulders when he lifted her onto the horse's back. "I want you to straddle the horse like a man. Considering the shape you're in, it's the only way you'll stay on."

Blanching, she edged one leg over the horse's wide back and at the same time telescoped her hoops one inside the other. Luke debated helping her, but he knew she'd be mortified if he placed so much as a finger on her slender ankle.

"You all right?" he asked, looking up at her. Her eyes were squeezed shut, and she had clamped her lower lip between her teeth. After nodding, she fell silent, so he decided he would have to trust her word.

In some odd way, Luke thought as he led the horse down the road, she reminded him of himself. As he did, she insisted on clinging to a tradition that was foreign to this environment. Her Eastern manners were not only unnecessary, they were almost absurd in the wilds of the Missouri Ozarks. Was he, too, operating under a set of conventions and traditions that offered him little hope of making his way? Were his dreams of restoring his Osage culture to these hills and woods as absurd as Hannah Brownlow trying to behave like a Boston lady in a place where survival depended on strength and cunning?

Uncomfortable with the thought, Luke concentrated on the road. Before long, he spotted a trail cut into the forest. "We'll take this path," he called. "It might lead to shelter."

Hannah nodded, unable to think beyond the ache in her ribs. She clung to the horse, one hand tangled in a clump of wet mane, the other clutching her manuscript, her thighs rubbing back and forth on the damp hide. Riding with her legs astride the horse was humiliating, almost unbearable, she thought.

"There's a cabin up ahead," Luke said. "No one's living in it."

Squinting through the downpour, Hannah could barely see the faint shapes of a small tumbledown log shack with a rickety shed beside it. She had no idea how Luke knew no one lived there. But as the horse approached, she realized he was probably right.

The door hung ajar on leather hinges. There was no sign of people, dogs, or livestock. The kitchen garden beside the house hadn't been planted. No smoke drifted from the chimney.

"You go on inside, and I'll put the horse in the shed," Luke told her, lifting his hands to help her down.

"Just walk right in? It wouldn't be polite." Even as she spoke the words, she realized how silly they sounded. This was no city dwelling where visitors placed calling cards on a silver tray. This was an abandoned hovel, a shelter from the rain. "I suppose if no one's here," she amended, "it wouldn't hurt to wait out the storm."

"I don't suppose it would." He smiled as she leaned toward him and let him place his hands around her waist.

But her face crumpled with pain when he slid her off the horse to the ground. It was all he could do to keep from pulling her against his chest and holding her for a moment. Instead he lightly squeezed her arms. "I'll light a fire when I come in."

She left him and made her way around the deep puddles to the house. Pushing open the door, she peered inside. The single room was gloomy and smelled of rain. But there was only one leak, and the sight of a low rope bed drew her through the door.

Once inside, however, she stopped in amazement. Was this

really how people lived? She could hardly believe the stark poverty the abandoned dwelling represented. Perhaps a sturdy table had been carted away by the home's owners, but the two benches left behind had been hand hewn of rough bare wood with no evidence of artistic craftsmanship or finishing varnish. Apparently also left behind in haste, a moth-eaten homespun blanket in shades of gray and brown lay on the floor. A few dried onions hung from the ceiling. A pot of rancid lard sat on the hearth, and a cracked, dirt-embedded cake of soap lay on the mantel.

There was nothing to suggest comfort or civility. No crisp white tablecloth. No shiny silver knives and spoons. No sparkling crystal goblets. No carpets underfoot. No tufted settees. No bright curtains drifting at the windows. There weren't even any windows, she realized belatedly.

"Anything to eat?" Luke asked as he stepped in.

Drenched from head to toe, he stood dripping just inside the doorway. His shirt clung to his skin, outlining the muscles of his chest. He ran one hand around the back of his neck. The mud had been washed away, and his hair shone like ink.

"I don't know," she said, unable to take her eyes from him. "I haven't checked the pantry. Or . . . whatever sort of storage they have."

"This room is all there is to the house." He strode across the uneven floor, his boots making wet footprints on the bare dirt. "There's some dry kindling and a few old logs. Good. I saw a plump chicken out in the shed."

"You don't mean to kill it, do you?"

Luke gave her a long look. He had meant to do exactly that. "I'll see if I can find some eggs."

"That would be lovely. I'm famished." Hannah lifted her heavy skirts and crossed the room to the bed. "Where do you suppose the owners have gone? Are they permanently away? Should we expect them back tonight?"

"I doubt it." He knelt to stack the wood in the fireplace. "They probably ran off during the war. A lot of Heavy Eyebrows fled this part of Missouri. Union or Confederate— neither allegiance was very safe, they tell me. If a man sympathized with the South, the jayhawkers went after him."

"Jayhawkers. I've heard that name."

"They're raiders from Kansas. Abolitionists."

"And I suppose if one's loyalty lay with the Northern states, the bushwhackers attacked."

"That's what they tell me."

Hannah peeled off her jacket and examined the torn sleeve in dismay. "I intend to report that awful Captain Joshua Billings and his friend Travis to the authorities in Springfield," she said. "They had no right to treat us so despicably."

Luke studied the small flame crackling amid the kindling. He couldn't afford to have word of the incident spread around. The less people heard his name, the better.

"You'd do best to leave it alone," he told Hannah. "Bushwhackers are well hidden in these woods, and their friends protect them. Don't stir up trouble."

She swung around. "*They're* the ones who stirred up the trouble, not us."

"And I'm asking you to ignore it." He stood and faced her. "I don't want you to tell anyone about what happened."

"Why not? They committed a crime. They should be brought to justice."

"Around here, attacking an Indian is no crime."

"But you're not really an Indian the way they think you are. You're a regular . . . Well, you're a man."

"I *am* an Indian," he countered. "Just the way they think I am. Joshua Billings was right when he said I belong on the reservation in Kansas. Legally that's where I should be. But I'm not going back and I don't want to call attention to myself."

With a sigh she sank onto the bed. "All right, I won't say anything. But they meant to kill you, you know. What's to stop them from trying again?"

"I'll stop them." He ran his gaze down the bedraggled woman. "And if I'm fortunate enough to have you around, I know you'll do your part to stop them, too."

Hannah looked up in surprise. He was leaning against the stone fireplace, his hands in his pockets, and his brown eyes filled with a warm light. She flushed at the flood of response his remark evoked inside her.

"They had planned to steal my purse," she said quickly. "It's all I have to see me back to Boston."

"I know that. But you spoke up in my defense before you had heard what they wanted. And after Travis abandoned you, I saw you go after him and Billings with a tree limb." His mouth softened into a smile. "Thank you, Miss Brownlow."

The heat in her cheeks flared. "You may call me Hannah."

"So, how are your ribs . . . Hannah?"

Uncomfortable with the familiarity of his address even though she had permitted it, she knotted her fingers. "They hurt."

"Why don't you take a look while I step outside to fetch the eggs?" He pulled a tattered flour sack from between two logs, where it had been stuffed for insulation, and started for the door. "You could put on that old dress while yours dries out."

As he left, Hannah turned and studied the row of wooden pegs hammered into the wall behind her. The rag hanging there was a dress? She reached out and touched the limp fabric. It was hard to imagine a more plain, forlorn-looking garment than the one she lifted from its peg. The color of rancid butter, the shapeless dress looked as though it had been sewn for someone half her size.

She worked open the buttons on her own ravaged bodice and stripped it off. Glancing to the door to make sure Luke was gone, she unfastened her skirt, crinoline, and hoop. They sank to the floor as if weighted with lead. Oh, she was soaked all the way to her skin! She took off her muddy shoes and damp stockings. Her smallclothes stuck to her chafed thighs as she tugged them down her legs. Around her waist she wrapped the homespun blanket—dusty though it was—and began to un-hook her corset.

Just as the stiff cinch tumbled onto the bed, she heard Luke knock on the door. "Wait!" she called out. "Not yet!"

The crazy thought of him seeing her naked body sent a flicker of heat skittering down her thighs. A respectable woman never revealed herself, her mother had instructed. A decent woman not only wore floor-length dresses, but she used gloves, bonnets, and stockings to protect every available inch of bare skin. Other than the face, a woman's body was intended for privacy. Even in bed, one wore a long gown and a cap to cover the hair. Men were hardly different. Jackets, vests, trousers, hats, gloves, shoes—all served to make them look uniform and dignified.

But Luke Maples seemed to ignore such customs. He wore his collar unbuttoned and his sleeves rolled to the elbows. His denim trousers fit like a second skin. How could any woman ignore the tight curve of his buttocks? How could she help but notice the turn of his muscles and the expanse of his broad back?

All the same, Hannah knew she must keep her eyes to herself. It would never do to ogle her traveling companion—as fascinating as he might be. In the close proximity of the cabin, she should do all she could to keep covered. She gave herself a quick perusal before tugging the dry dress over her head. Her ribs were bruised and sore, but she doubted any were broken. The waist of the dress was as tight as a bandage, and she realized it would help with the pain.

She fastened the row of mismatched buttons that ran up her back, then attempted to puff out the hopelessly limp skirt. Without a hoop or crinoline, it hung like an old sack. If only her sisters could see her now, she thought as she padded barefoot across the floor to the door. How humiliating.

"Five fresh eggs," Luke announced as he walked into the house. One look at Hannah, and he stopped in his tracks. This couldn't be the same prim miss who had set out from town with him that morning. Though her hair was still splattered with dried mud, it seemed to glow with an inner light. One lock had fallen from its pins to lie like a cinnamon river against the butter-colored dress.

Her long neck was bare all the way down to the deep front curve of the bodice that revealed the swell of her breasts. She crossed her arms beneath them and around her little waist. The action that was meant to be modest and protective only served to lift her bosom and draw his attention to the curve of her hips.

With some effort, he raised his focus to her eyes. "You look . . . very . . . very natural."

"Naturally appalling." She touched the rumpled yellow skirt. "My sisters would swoon if they saw me in this."

"Naturally beautiful," he countered. "I like it . . . the dress, I mean." He turned quickly before he said something else he might regret and unhooked a rusty iron skillet from the rafter overhead. The coin-sized hole in the pan's center had obviously rendered it worth abandonment by its owners. "So, how are your ribs?"

"Sore. But I don't think anything's broken." She smiled. "Probably my corset was a great protection."

"I guess so." He couldn't imagine what a corset was. He set the skillet on a bench. A chipped crock in one corner of the fireplace produced some solid lard—ancient but, he trusted, edible. It wouldn't be much of a meal for a hungry man, he admitted, but it would be better than jerky.

"I like mine scrambled," he told Hannah as he placed the sack of eggs beside the skillet. "And if you can find some coffee in the house, I could sure use a cup."

He walked to the window and began to unbutton his shirt. It was late, but the heavy clouds couldn't hide what little was left of the evening light. All the same, the wagon was stuck good, and there'd be no chance of making it to Springfield even if the rain did let up. That meant he and Miss Hannah Brownlow would be spending this night together.

He didn't like it. Glancing at her, he saw that she was studying the skillet's sizable hole. He wished she'd get on with the cooking. He wanted to heat some water in the old kettle he'd found outside so she could wash her hair and he could scrub the mud out of his socks.

It had been a mistake to bring her along. Her brother obviously wasn't the Ethan who had murdered his father. And no good had ever come of an Osage associating too closely with a white person. It wouldn't be any different with this Boston lady.

If she chose, Hannah could cause him a lot of trouble. Despite her promise, she might complain to the authorities about the bushwhacker attack and accuse him of failing to protect her. She could publicly lament this night alone with him in the cabin. If he didn't behave to her liking, she could claim he had taken advantage of her in one way or another. It wouldn't matter what he said in his own defense. She held the power.

Unfamiliar with the feeling of helplessness, he regretted the situation he'd gotten himself into. Not that she seemed inclined to cause him such trouble. He covertly observed her again.

Sleeves rolled to her elbows, she had taken a large spoonful of lard and dropped it into the skillet. The truth was, Hannah seemed to have a good heart.

Luke grunted and turned back to the window. Of course, that very illusion about the Heavy Eyebrows was what had gotten his people into trouble in the first place. They had trusted the "good-hearted" white men and had traded away their rich hunting and gathering grounds.

No, nothing good ever came of trusting. Luke hadn't trusted anyone—not even his own Osage companions—for many years now. Not since his father's death. He certainly didn't intend to start with this fire-haired white woman.

At least she'd begun the dinner, he noted as he walked across the room to dry his shirt by the fire. She bent over to set the skillet on the grate, and he noticed the way the borrowed dress draped down over her hips. Tempting. So tempting. Her cornflower eyes and heavy breasts had been haunting his thoughts all day. He would have to put a stop to that.

"And then I suppose one would place the spoon just so," she was saying to herself as he hung his shirt over a bench. "If one stirred the tiniest bit . . ."

Luke looked around her shoulder at the skillet. "Wait—you don't . . . What are you doing?"

"What?" She raised her head and banged it against the mantel. "Ouch!" The skillet slid off the grate and into the fire, nearly spilling the eggs over the side.

"Heat up the fat before you put eggs into it," he told her as he wrapped his shirt around the handle of the hot skillet. "And you had the pan on the hottest part of the flame. The eggs were burning before they'd even started to cook. Now we've got ashes in here, and half our supper went through the hole in the middle of the skillet."

He looked around his shoulder at her. She was standing in the corner by the fire, her lower lip tucked between her teeth and her blue eyes luminous.

"I'm sorry," she said, lifting her chin. "I was doing my best. I've never actually . . . cooked before."

He straightened, the smoking skillet in one hand. "You don't know how to cook eggs?"

"I can certainly learn."

Luke frowned. It hadn't occurred to him that she would know nothing about preparing their dinner. But she had told him her family employed a cook, hadn't she? He wished he'd listened better on their trip.

"I'll cook, and you watch," he said. "Next time—if you ever need to make eggs again—you'll know how."

"All right." Hannah took her place beside him. It was a relief to have him take over, but she felt uncomfortable in his presence. He had taken off his shirt, and his bare shoulder was so close to hers she could smell fresh rainwater on his skin. In the firelight, his chest took on a coppery hue that made him seem more primitive to her—as raw as a wild stallion.

Studying him secretly, she noted the way the muscles in his arm bunched and rippled as he adjusted the skillet on the grate. How would a man ever develop such sinews? Had Luke been born with a naturally strong physique? Did all Indians look like him? She let her eyes roam across his chest to the flat round coins of his nipples. Before she could stop it, her mind formed on image of herself leaning across him, her lips touching the tip of one brown nipple.

"Good heavens!" she said out loud.

When he gave her a questioning glance, she amended, "I mean . . . good heavens, we never ate our eggs like this. We had ours soft-boiled or poached . . . Have I ruined them beyond hope?"

"They'll have a little extra flavoring is all." He dipped out more than half the lard she had put in the skillet and gave the eggs a stir. In moments, a comforting, evocative aroma filled the small room. "Did you find any coffee?"

"No. I think the owners of the house took everything edible when they left. But never mind. These eggs look wonderful."

Luke glanced at her. She was leaning over the skillet, eyes shut and nose tilted to drink in the aroma. He let his focus trail down her neck to the curve of her bodice. The dress had gapped a little, and he could see down into the rounded shadows of her bosom. At the thought of her bare breasts beneath the tight dress, a spark flared to flame inside him. It flickered up and down his thighs and settled in his loins.

No, he had to concentrate on the meal. He gave the eggs another stir. She was white and Eastern and genteel and definitely beyond his reach. He couldn't touch her, or he'd pay for it the rest of his life.

"It smells exactly like breakfast at home," she said wistfully. "May I?"

She took the spoon from his hand and pushed it through the fluffy eggs. Firelight bronzed her slender arm. As she stirred, the dress slid slowly from her shoulder. Luke couldn't keep his eyes from her soft, pale skin and delicate bones.

"My sisters won't believe it when I tell them about this," she said. "Fried eggs for supper."

"We're scrambling them."

"Oh." She flushed, and a smile softened her pink lips. "I can do a great many things, you know, and not one of them is useful out here."

"What can you do, Hannah?" Luke watched as her long eyelashes drifted to her cheeks. He had never seen such a woman—all softness and sighs, and a mysterious dreaminess that almost made her seem an illusion, a mirage.

"My crewel work is the envy of everyone," she told him. "I'm very good at parlor games. I can play croquet better than any of my friends. And you should just see me waltz."

"All right, show me." He said the words before he'd thought through the consequences.

Oblivious to his discomfort, she rose and drifted around the small room, her bare feet almost noiseless on the dirt floor. At her ankles the yellow skirt billowed, its hem dotted with charred holes made by cooking-fire cinders. Her hair tumbled around her shoulders like a sheet of molten copper. As she turned and swirled, she hummed a song Luke didn't recognize.

Imagining himself stepping between her outstretched arms and catching her around that tiny waist, he swallowed, and his heart began to thud like a drum. He could go to her now, draw her tightly against his chest, and carry her to the bed in the corner. With a single tug, the old yellow dress would fall away and she'd be naked to him. He could stroke his hands down her body and teach her how to please him. At the thought of lying beside the woman, tangling his fingers in her fire-hair, knowing the taste of her breasts, his breath grew shallow and labored.

"Oh, my aching ribs!" she said with a sudden laugh. Spreading her arms, she gave him a final deep curtsy that enticingly displayed the curves of her breasts. "Do you see what I mean? The waltz is a delight, but what good would it ever do me in the wilderness of Missouri?"

Unaware of the effect she was having on him, Hannah rejoined Luke by the fire. Her skin was damp in the close, hot room, and her breath came in short gasps. He forced himself to give the scorched eggs a turn and take the skillet off the grate.

"Your waltzing might make a man take interest." His voice sounded harder then he'd intended. "Then you could marry and bear lots of children to do your cooking and cleaning."

Hannah stared at his back as he went to the bench. Now, what had he meant by that? He was laying out two wooden spoons, his bare skin outlined in the fire's red glow. She didn't want any man paying undue attention to her. And she certainly hadn't meant to make Luke Maples interested. Had she?

He set the skillet in the center of a bench and sat down at one end. "Planning to eat?"

She rose and joined him at the other end of the same bench. As she instinctively made the sign of the cross, she noticed that he had bowed his head and was moving his lips in a silent prayer. In a moment, he, too, crossed himself and then dipped his spoon into the eggs.

"You're Catholic?" she asked.

He shrugged. "I'm a believer. My grandmother and grandfather taught me to worship *Wah'kon-tah.* That's the Osage name for the Creator you call God. At the mission school, Father Schoenmakers taught me to believe that Jesus Christ is the son of God, and I was baptized into the Catholic church. Somewhere in the two sets of rituals I've found a faith that goes beyond rites or ceremonies. I've made peace with God."

"Well . . . how interesting," Hannah said. Never once had it occurred to her that Indians might have a god of their own. She'd always thought of them as heathens. Godless savages needed missionaries, of course. And priests like Father Schoenmakers were doing God's will in teaching such pagans about Christ.

What had it done to Luke to be brought up with one religion and then suddenly introduced to another? She couldn't imagine. As he ate, she watched him in silence. The man was fascinating. His black hair, still wet on the ends, touched the back of his neck. His bare arms were ridged with sinew that she decided must have been honed by hard labor. In all her life, Hannah had never met a man as physical. At times it had seemed to her that he was nothing but brawn. Yet Luke Maples was proving himself far more complicated than she had first thought.

As the hours had passed on their journey, he had become more than just a tall, massively built man with deep brown eyes and a mouth that could show warmth one moment and disdain the next. He was intelligent—extremely so. His mind traveled paths hers had never taken. He possessed a spiritual depth she could only guess at. What other mysteries lay beneath the sculpted physique?

"Do Osages pray regularly?" she asked.

He looked up, as if surprised she was still interested. "Daily."

Another one-word answer. "When do you pray? Please, won't you tell me about it?"

He considered for a moment. If he spoke of his people, he would make himself vulnerable to her ridicule or to the disgust he had read in white men's eyes. But he didn't think this Hannah Brownlow intended to mock him. Her curiosity seemed as honest and innocent as everything she did. But to trust her with secrets of the Osage? Instinct told him it would be a mistake.

"Our religion is private," he said.

"You're like a book, Luke. A secret journal," she said softly. "You're shut tight and locked with a key that was lost a very long time ago . . . lost when your father was killed, I suppose. Inside the hard, sealed covers of that book are wonderful tales and thrilling adventures. There's knowledge that I shall never possess as long as I live. There's understanding of things I've never seen. There are pictures of places and people I'll never know." She let out a breath. "I would so like to read that book, Luke Maples Mystery-hawk."

He looked into her blue eyes. She was simple and complicated. She was naive and wise. She was as much a mystery to him as he was to her. But to tell her the things in his heart? To step out to her in trust?

No matter what passed between them, he told himself,

tonight would be the last time he would see her. Swallowing, he set his uncertainty aside.

"The Osage people rise and speak the Dawn Chant to our grandfather, the sun," he began slowly. "We offer one prayer as Grandfather's first rays emerge, another when we see him fully, another when the plume-like shafts of light appear, and again when Grandfather is fully risen."

"So, you worship the sun?"

"No, Grandfather is the manifestation of *Wah'kon-tah*'s power. Without him, there would be no light, no warmth, and therefore no life." He leaned back and slipped his hand into his pocket. Then he drew out a necklace and laid it on the table. Its leather thong supported a round white pendant. "This is my gorget. The disk was carved from the shell of the freshwater mussel. It represents Grandfather the Sun."

"It's beautiful." She touched the large pendant. "Why don't you wear it?"

"For the same reason I don't shave my head or wear my leggings in public."

"You're trying to be a Heavy Eyebrows."

"No." He swept the gorget from the table. "Hear this, Hannah Brownlow: I will never be a white man. I am Osage. I might believe in Jesus Christ, and I might be able to see the good in a man like Father Schoenmakers. I might understand your history and read your books. I might grow my hair and wear your clothes and eat your food. But my blood is Osage. My heart is Osage. And the Heavy Eyebrows will always be the enemy of an Osage warrior."

Hannah set her spoon on the bench and leaned toward him. "If white people are your enemies, then why are you so much like us?"

"Never!" He stood suddenly, almost knocking the skillet from the bench. "I can't be someone I'm not. What you see of me is only the outside—the shell. Inside, I'm Osage."

"That's ridiculous. You can't separate the two. You're a mixture, and you might as well accept it."

"You're wrong. There are some Osage whose fathers are of the Heavy Eyebrows. French fur trappers took our women as wives. English traders did the same thing. Those mixed-bloods are the children we send to Father Schoenmakers's mission school. But I'm not a mixed-blood. I went to school because my father had been murdered when I was a boy, and there were many children in my family—too many for my mother to provide for. At the school I learned the white man's ways, but I am not white. I'm Osage."

"All right." She swept up the skillet and the two spoons and started toward the fire. "But don't make the Heavy Eyebrows sound so despicable."

He leaned against the mantel, one arm propped on the heavy wood beam. "And don't make Indians sound so savage."

"I'm not responsible for your reputation." She set the skillet on the hearth and straightened to face him. "If you want to be thought of in a positive light, you shouldn't go about scalping my people."

"And you shouldn't go about stealing my land."

"I never stole anything from you!"

"I know your history, but do you know mine? More than sixty years ago, this state you call Missouri was Osage territory. My people lived and hunted in these valleys and on these streams. Our chief was named Pawhuska, or White Hair to your government. When your president, Thomas Jefferson, bought the Louisiana Territory from Napoleon, he immediately began sending the defeated eastern tribes onto our land to make room for white settlers. The Cherokee, Choctaw, Creek, and Chickasaw joined our traditional enemies the Potawatomi, Sac, and Fox."

"I should think there was plenty of room," Hannah retorted. "These forests seem to go on and on."

Luke grunted. "Your government threatened to cut off all trade with my people. We were forced to sell two hundred square miles of southern Missouri and northern Arkansas for seven thousand, five hundred dollars in cash and goods."

"That's all?"

"That happened in 1808. In 1815, the eastern emigrant tribes massacred our women and children while our warriors were away on a buffalo hunt. With our strength so drastically reduced, your government again forced us to sell our territory—this time everything north of the Arkansas River."

"But why?"

"So Heavy Eyebrows could settle the land. In 1825, the few

Osage still living in Missouri agreed to give up their claims to all the remaining land. A reservation was drawn up for us in southeastern Kansas."

"And what's wrong with that?"

"It's fifty miles wide and a hundred twenty-five miles long. It has few forests, only one major stream, and little game. Once we ate a wide variety of foods, but now we live only on buffalo. Your government promised to maintain neutral lands east of the reservation. Gradually these neutral lands were violated by the Heavy Eyebrows settlers, and now they're officially open for settlement. When gold was discovered in California in 1849, your people overran our land with no thought of the boundaries. When the Civil War was brewing, your people rushed to Kansas to settle, in order to declare it an abolitionist state. Hundreds of Heavy Eyebrows families have ignored the reservation borders and set up farms on Osage land. Now do you know what these Heavy Eyebrows have done?"

Hannah shook her head. She couldn't imagine.

"They want to do away with the reservation."

For a moment she couldn't speak. "You mean . . . the Osage will have no home? No lands or houses or anything? But what will you do?"

Luke regarded her in silence. "What would you do?"

"I suppose I would . . . I'd do exactly what I'm doing now. I would take whatever measures were necessary to keep my family alive and well. Perhaps I would fight to keep my old home from those who were trying to take it. Or I'd find someone who could help me keep it legally. Or . . . I suppose . . . I suppose I would search for a new home. Yes, I know I would. I'd search high and low until I found a perfect place where no one could disturb my family for the rest of our lives."

A slow grin tilted the corners of Luke's mouth. "You understand better than I thought, Hannah Brownlow," he said. "You would make a fine Osage."

"But I can't be someone I'm not—can I, Luke Maples? Your blood is Osage, mine isn't. Your heart is Osage, mine isn't. And as you said, the Heavy Eyebrows will always be the enemy of an Osage warrior."

Chapter
Five

Hannah turned away from Luke and bent to inspect her dress as it lay across the bench near the fire. She didn't want to talk to him anymore. She was so tired she felt as if she might fall over, and her ribs hurt with every breath. Besides, the man bothered her. He said things she didn't want to hear. He challenged her thoughts, and he countered what she had always been taught was true. It would be such a relief to step down from the wagon in Springfield and walk away from him forever.

Her dress was drying quickly, but the crinoline could take days. No doubt the steels in her hoop would rust and would be forever ruined. Oh, for a clean dress, a new pair of shoes, and a stroll down a Boston street!

"Do you want to bathe?" Luke asked behind her.

Hannah glanced over her shoulder. He had hung a black iron kettle over the fire. Steam curled upward into the chimney.

"Oh, I don't know," she said.

"Here's some soap." He took the small, withered cake from

the mantel and set it on the bench. "It's strong, but I doubt it'll burn you."

Hannah lifted a hand to her hair. "I realize I'm still muddy, and I'd like to wash my face but . . . well, my mother taught me it's unhealthy to bathe too often. One simply can't trust water. My mother always said, 'If the exposure to chill doesn't give you pneumonia, Hannah, the invisible creatures in the water will surely make you ill.' There's cholera, yellow fever, typhus. The list is endless."

Luke shook his head in bemusement. This woman and her views were so alien. Whoever heard of fearing water—the source of life, strength, and health? No wonder so many Heavy Eyebrows men smelled worse than caged animals.

"My mother taught *me* that water, like breath, is essential to life," he countered. "Water purifies. The Wah-Sha-She are the group of Osage who've taken the name Water People. One of their *wi-gi-es* is the song of the water, 'Behold the hollow bed of the river; I have not made it without a purpose. When the Little Ones make of it the hollow of their bodies, they shall free the hollow of their bodies from all causes of death.'"

Hannah tried to absorb the startling idea. "Who are the Little Ones? Your children?"

"No, the Little Ones are all the Osage people in every age group. We call ourselves Children of the Middle Waters, and our leaders are known as the Little Old Men."

"And *all* of you like to bathe?"

"Every day, winter and summer. We swim in the river near our village no matter what the weather or temperature. We insist on purity and cleanliness. Our women wear a perfume made from the sweet flag plant, horsemint, and crushed columbine seeds. We wear loose garments—leggings, breechcloths, moccasins." He picked up his drying shirt and tossed it over one shoulder. "Body odors can't escape these Heavy Eyebrows clothes. My family and friends would ridicule me if they could see the way I dress now."

Hannah stared at his broad back as he walked to the door. How odd to think that every book she had read called Indians filthy and foul-smelling. And all the while the Indians considered their white acquaintants as foolish and malodorous.

Did Luke perceive *her* as putrid? What an appalling thought!

Hannah looked at her expensive blue gown as if seeing it for the first time. She couldn't deny that it was tight and hot—and with all the layers of undergarments beneath, the costume really was stifling. But to actually bathe every day? Heavens, she would catch her death.

"I'll be outside for a while," Luke said from the door. "I want to see if there's anything around here we can eat for breakfast. You sleep in the bed. I'll take the floor."

He was gone before Hannah had a chance to respond. She stared after him, lost in bewilderment. An Indian who quoted Shakespeare, calculated figures in his head, read maps, trained falcons, and bathed every day. Imagine!

Lifting her skirts, Hannah went to the fire and peered into the simmering pot. Should she really bathe? What if she took a chill out here in the wilds of Missouri? Who would tend her? How would her mother find out where she was? What if she died?

But the thought of Luke regarding her as a smelly Heavy Eyebrows impelled her to take the kettle hook and lift the heated pot from the fire. She hung the ragged quilt over an abandoned drying rack. It made an inadequate curtain, but better than nothing. Kneeling behind the screen, she slowly stripped away the old yellow dress.

Anyway, what did it matter how Luke Maples thought of her? She would bathe—but not because of him. She had to be fresh for her interviews in Springfield tomorrow, she told herself as she dipped the cake of soap in the hot water. The military and government authorities would have little respect for her if she stood before them with mud-splattered hair and dirty hands.

She ran the soap down one arm and then the other. The water felt deliciously relaxing as it dripped from her elbows. What did crushed columbine seeds smell like, anyway? And horse-mint? She wouldn't mind wearing a sweet perfume—not for Luke's benefit, of course, but simply for her own. How uplifting it would be to waft through life on a cloud of fragrance. Was that how it was for the Osage women?

Hannah studied the soap in her hand and thought of the man who had brought her this far. Was an Osage woman waiting back in Kansas for Luke to return? Did he have a lover? A wife?

She shut her eyes and smoothed the warm soap around her breasts. Free of the encumbrance of her corset, her chest felt light and her skin silken. She stroked the soap up and down her cleavage and then slid her fingers beneath the heavy globes. With the caress of the smooth soap, her nipples beaded into tight peaks. For a moment she let her eyes play across her own body. The crests of her bosom stood out against her white skin like rosebuds in the snow. She drew the soap over one nipple and then the other, enjoying the tingle. Washing felt good, she decided. Very good. Maybe there was something to this business of bathing after all.

As she sponged her legs and feet, the tuft of dark curls between her thighs caught her attention. That secret place had always been forbidden territory. On an impulse, she slipped the soap over the sensitive curls. Goodness . . . Oh, heavens . . .

If the stroke of soap and the trickle of warm water felt this alluring, what would it be like to know the touch of a human body? She bent over the kettle and dipped her head into the water. As she scrubbed, she recalled her mother's terse explanation of the production of babies.

"You must allow your husband to do as he likes with you," she had told Hannah and her sisters as they sat wide-eyed in the parlor one afternoon. "You are to be an obedient and humble servant to his needs. Your husband is the only person allowed permission with your privy parts. He may touch you there, and you must not flinch away. In due course, you will find yourself with child—a blessed reprieve from your bedroom duties."

As Hannah rinsed the soap from her hair, she pondered what exactly a husband would want to do with his wife's privy parts. Why would it make her flinch? And why would childbearing be a reprieve? The experience must be awful, whatever it was. She was certainly thankful she never intended to marry.

All the same, the brush of the rough cotton towel over her body suddenly felt so titillating that she couldn't help imagining the feel of a man's hands stroking her skin. Had Luke Maples ever touched a woman's privy parts? Hannah had studied his fingers at great length as he held the reins that day.

Large and strong, those hands would surely know how to make a woman shiver. Well, it was lucky he was an Indian and certainly not of any interest to her—nor was she to him.

Sighing, she slipped the yellow dress over her head again and fastened the buttons. As she padded across the room to the fire, she couldn't deny that she felt fresher and more relaxed than she had during this entire journey. She knelt near the dying embers and used her fingers to comb through her thick, straight hair.

There was little hope of transforming herself into a woman of any social stature by tomorrow morning. Her curling iron lay at the bottom of her trunk on the wagon. There weren't any oil lamps in the cabin with which to heat the device anyway. Her gloves were soiled and her bonnet nearly ruined. She had so little money left in her purse, she couldn't consider replacing the items. She simply would have to make do.

When she turned her head to finger-comb the other half of her hair, she realized the door was standing ajar. Startled, she sucked in a breath of warm air. Then Luke's familiar form moved into a shaft of moonlight, and her shoulders unknotted.

"I didn't hear you come in," she said. "I thought those awful bushwhackers might have returned."

She saw him swallow and turn to the pegs by the door. Outlined in silver moonlight, he scrutinized her. "When I'm with you," he said, "you have no need to be afraid."

As he approached the fire, she realized his brown eyes were transfixed on her face. "You washed your hair," he said in a low voice.

She held up the long, damp hank and regarded it for a moment. "You were right about the soap. It felt lovely."

He crouched near her, one arm resting on his knee. "I've never seen such hair."

"All the Brownlow girls have red hair. Little Elizabeth's a carrot-top. Sophie is a strawberry blonde, and Brigitte's hair is almost brown, but not quite. It's the Irish in my mother that did it. She's a redhead herself. What color would you call mine? Copper?"

"Fire," he said. "A blaze on a cold winter night."

At the tone in his voice, Hannah glanced up. Their eyes met. His expression was intense, riveting. Her heart began to thud, and she knew she should look away. She should ask him if he'd found anything for breakfast. She should busy herself washing the dinner dishes.

But she couldn't move, couldn't speak as his falcon gaze peered through her—reading, analyzing, scrutinizing. Unable to catch her breath, she watched his focus lower to absorb her lips. She dropped her own attention to his mouth. His lips were strong, male, compelling. In a rush of shattering sparks, it came to her that at any moment Luke Maples might kiss her. And that she wanted him to.

The thought sent a shower of flames to the tips of her breasts. They swelled slightly inside her tight bodice, and their tips tightened with anticipation. She felt herself tilt toward him . . . drawn as if she were bound to him by an invisible cord. Something damp and alive curled through the pit of her stomach and nestled between her thighs. Pulsing, it demanded attention.

If he didn't kiss her, she would melt from the need of it. And if he did, she would die of mortification. Her first kiss . . . from the lips of a savage. But somehow she knew it would be the best kiss . . . the most magical . . . she would ever have.

"Luke," she whispered, "I—"

"Pork," he cut in, standing suddenly and turning away. "They left a loin hanging in the smokehouse. We'll eat it for breakfast."

The spell shattered, and Hannah felt herself unravel like the threads of a lace shawl. "Wonderful," she managed.

He let out a ragged breath. "Are you finished with the water?"

"Yes, of course. Certainly." Flushing, she gathered her skirt and hurried to the bed. What had she been thinking? What had she been wanting? She had actually pondered kissing Luke Maples—a stranger, an Indian! Perhaps that bath had touched her brain already. Maybe she was coming down with something.

She took the bedraggled quilt from the drying rack. No sheets tonight. No bright oil lamps. No velvet curtains. Not even much of a mattress. She spread the quilt on the rustling corn-husk pallet and hoped there were no bedbugs lying in wait to feast on her tender skin.

"Good night," she called softly as she lay down and tucked her bare feet under the quilt. "God bless."

Luke bent and stirred the fire as he spoke. "Good night, Hannah Brownlow. Don't be afraid of the bushwhackers."

She drew the corner of the quilt over her arm and studied the silhouette of his broad shoulders. It was no longer the bushwhackers she feared.

Luke hung his wet socks over the bench. The room felt close and hot, and the fire didn't help. With no windows in the little cabin, the only fresh air seeped through chinks in the logs. He wished he could sleep outside, but the rain had turned the ground into a wet, steaming bog.

Taking an old scrap of canvas he had found in the shed, he spread it before the door and hunkered down. The woman had finally fallen asleep. Her breaths came deeply now, punctuated by great sighs that spoke of her exhaustion. He wondered how her ribs were healing. The night of rest would help to fade her bruises.

Lifting his head, he peered through the darkness at the curves of her body on the bed. Hannah Brownlow was a wonder. A mystery. How could a woman know nothing of cooking? Dancing was her greatest skill! What good would that do her in life? He himself would marry a fine, strapping Osage woman who could dig wild potatoes and sew moccasins and butcher a buffalo.

Luke stretched out on the quilt and placed his hands behind his head. He wove his fingers together and stared up into the blackness. Osage women knew how to dress, too. They would never dream of wearing a garment made of steel—one that hung as heavy as a stone and would rust in the slightest damp.

What would Hannah Brownlow look like in an Osage deerskin dress? A belt made of woven buffalo-calf's hair would cinch her small waist. Earrings and bracelets would adorn her body. Might she consider tattooing her skin as Osage women did? No, it was obvious she took pride in her pure, spotless complexion. But she might wear her hair loose. It would hang down her back like a sheet of flame. Hot . . . fiery . . . lit with sparks.

He rolled onto his haunches again and studied her. She had turned onto her back. Her hair draped over the side of the bed, almost touching the floor.

Coming to his feet, he crept across the floor to the bed. He crouched at her side to study the fine web of copper hair. He was driven to touch it. Just once. Tonight he had come so close! As they sat beside the fire, he had almost caught her in his arms. He had nearly lifted that sheet of flame in his hands and buried his face in its mystery. He had almost pressed his mouth against her full lips and known the taste of the woman whose image played through his mind, even though he fought to fill his thoughts with his future and his dreams.

Lifting a hand, he reached toward her hair. His breath shortened. If he touched even one strand, it would burn on his hand until he could make the woman his. She would never leave his thoughts until he laid her upon his buffalo robes.

Curling and uncurling his fingers, he lifted his eyes and observed the rise of her breasts. They jutted into the air, two rounded hills. The thought of her peaked nipples sent a bolt of lightning through his loins, and he swelled with hunger for her. Had she known the pleasures of a man? He doubted it.

Most likely, she had been as carefully sequestered as the young girls of his tribe, who were protected and guarded until marriage. Boys, too, kept themselves pure until the wedding. Of course, Luke had joined his companions in secretive, detailed discussions of the mechanics and mysteries of mating. They had watched the elk in rut and had known a similar relentless drive for satisfaction. But unlike the animals, Luke and his friends had learned to hold back from women, to wait until the marriage ceremony gave them the right to explore the magic of union.

At the thought of satisfying his hungers with Hannah Brownlow, who lay so trustingly beside him, Luke sensed a mixture of emotions. How easy it would be to overpower her. At this moment, his aroused body demanded the satisfaction that only a woman could provide. The image of suckling her breasts and easing himself into her moist depths sent him almost to the brink of need. One touch would sever the slender thread of control that restrained him.

And yet, how could he plunder her? She lay sleeping in utter confidence that he would honor her. Protect her. Guard her. She *trusted* him.

How long had it been since anyone had trusted him? How long since he had trusted? Luke shut his eyes and took a deep breath. He didn't want her faith. He didn't want those blue eyes looking to him as defender and champion.

Rising to his feet in a surge of frustration, he clenched his fists. No, she was nothing to him. He was nothing to her. He began to pace the room, his footsteps as silent as a panther's. She probably dreamed of marrying some Union soldier or Boston businessman. No doubt, if he approached her for her favors, she would scorn him. Her shunning would pierce more deeply than any arrow.

Though his body burned for her, he would never take her by force. The honor of his people would not permit such depredation on a woman who had placed herself in his care. Missouri authorities, too, would call the act a crime and hang him high.

More to the point, Luke had to admit, was the knowledge that he could never touch Hannah against her will. She was too pure, too kind, too loving. She had helped to save his life. The least he could do was drive her safely into Springfield and walk away.

He raked a hand through his hair as he returned to his place by the door. He would keep her safe, and she would have no one to fear. Not even him.

A delicious aroma tickled Hannah's nostrils. She rolled to her side in bed and drank deeply of the thick scent. Eyes shut, she traveled through a land of lace tablecloths and steaming platters of eggs and bacon. Something rustled . . . corn husks.

Now white mist drifted around her. It covered her arms and legs as she lay high on a pile of freshly husked corn. Something was soaring overhead, up and up in wide, lazy circles. A falcon. It gazed down at her, searching, hungering. Fear mingled with desire inside her, stirring and compelling, and she tried to reach for the falcon. But she was in the clouds—and the bird was such a far, aching distance above her.

The white mist bathed her skin, silky and warm. Watching the falcon ride the winds, she stroked her fingers over her chest. Her breasts glowed. She waited breathless, almost eager for the falcon to begin its dive. Like a warm river, her thighs pulsed. She shifted, and her hips floated on a soft pillow. Oh, how her breasts ached! If only he would come to her . . .

Again she drew her hand over her bosom. The liquid inside her throbbed. What if the clouds enveloped her and the falcon lost sight of her? She had to go to him! She stirred, moaned, but she couldn't move.

Now something was climbing up through the clouds toward her. Something dark. Shaggy. Greasy hair. A bear! Enormous and threatening. Would he seize her before the falcon could?

She opened her mouth to call for help. Please! Aching ribbons trickled down her thighs. Her nipples sparkled like twin stars. Which would reach her, falcon or bear? Why couldn't she move? She stretched out her arm to the falcon. His wing brushed her fingertips.

"Luke!" she cried out, seizing the wing and discovering, instead of feathers, the shock of solid, warm flesh.

"*Tha'-gthin-xtsi* . . ."

"What?" Her eyes drifted open, but she felt disoriented. Where was she, and why was her cheek pressed against Luke Maples's shoulder?

"Are you all right?" he whispered.

"It was horrible . . . I think I was . . ." Comforted by his voice, she slid into the dream again. "There was a greasy bear and . . . and that bushwhacker kept climbing . . ."

Luke's brow furrowed with concern as he debated whether or not to place his arms around her and draw her closer. She had melted against him, but he held himself stiffly distant, his hands knotted into fists at his side.

"I was on a bed of corn husks . . . ," she murmured, her lips moving against the bare skin of his neck. "Or perhaps it was a cloud, and you were . . . No, it was a falcon . . ." She rubbed her cheek against his shoulder. "I'm not sure. I only know I've never felt so . . . so strange."

As she nuzzled him, her hair spilled across her back.

Clenching his jaw to maintain self-control, Luke watched the strands sift and slide into place. He had been watching, too, as she slept. He had seen her hand cup her breast, her fingertips glide over the tightened tip, her pink lips part in desire. She had been dreaming of the vigilante . . . and also of him.

Now he could take her. She was aroused, in need of appeasement, and very confused. He could capture her in his arms, kiss her mouth, stroke her breasts. He could lead her so far in sensual pleasure she would believe she was still dreaming. He could caress her until it was too late to turn back.

He lifted a hand toward her hair. He spread his fingers.

She sighed, a deep, endless release, and he suddenly understood it would be too late for him, too.

Gently laying her back on the bed, he stood and strode to the fire. He couldn't look at her. He was losing the battle for control. His loins burned as he crouched on the hearth to turn the slab of sizzling pork. In his chest, his heart beat like a pronghorn-skin war drum. Would he have to spend the rest of this day avoiding her blue eyes? The rest of his life running from her memory?

"The breakfast smells wonderful," she said softly. He could hear her moving across the floor behind him as she approached the fire. "Is it the pork from the smokehouse?"

He grunted in acknowledgment.

"The rain stopped," she went on. "I'll step outside to the privy. Do you suppose it's safe?"

"As long as you don't fall in."

Glancing over her shoulder, Hannah gathered her skirt and walked to the door. My, the Indian was terse in the morning! She couldn't imagine why. She herself had awakened to find him cooking breakfast by the fire, and though she thought she might have had a bad dream or two, she was in a decent humor.

But then some people were naturally sullen in the morning—like Sophie, who always stayed up so late with her beaux that she could barely open her eyes for breakfast. Hannah had always enjoyed the start of every new day, and now, as she walked barefoot through the tall grass, she drew in deep breaths of the fresh, rain-washed air.

Thank goodness she would return to civilization in a few hours. No more savage Indians. No more barbaric bushwhackers. In spite of her dwindling finances, she would engage a hotel room and eat a full dinner. She might even take the time to curl her hair and remove a clean bonnet from one of her hatboxes before setting out in search of Ethan.

The privy was small, dark, and thick with flies. A putrid odor clung to the old damp wood. In and out again as quickly as possible, she hurried back to the cabin.

"What a dreadful life these people must have had," she said as she entered the room. "It's all so backward and primitive."

Luke thunked the skillet on the bare bench. "At least they owned their own land." Avoiding her eyes, he went back to the fire.

"Is that what you want?" she asked. "Land of your own?"

He stabbed a slab of pork with his knife. "Yes."

They were back to one-word conversation. Lovely. She could hardly wait to start the long journey. "But you own miles of reservation land," she tried. "Won't you build a house there?"

"No." He sat down on his stool, crossed himself, and tore off a hunk of the meat with his teeth.

"Why not? It's your land. You could farm. You could set down roots for your wife and children . . . Do you have a wife?"

He chewed for almost a minute. "No."

Hannah bit into her pork steak. At least something about this morning was good. She watched Luke as she ate. In contrast to his behavior the night before, he was all but ignoring her. He wore his shirt buttoned to the top, his hair combed back from his face, his knife hidden away. Gone was the bare-chested warrior. Gone the falcon-eyed predator. Luke had sealed himself away, as though his thoughts and vision were trained on something in the far distance.

"I'm not married either," she said, deciding it was better to talk to herself than eat breakfast in the unbearable silence. "I've had any number of gentlemen callers. If you've ever read *Harper's,* you'll have heard their notorious analysis of fashionable men—stunted, pale, pasty-faced things with matchstick legs. I couldn't agree more. With most of the ambitious young men away at war, there's been no one to interest me. Sophie enjoys the soldiers flitting in and out, but I don't give

them a moment's heed. I have more important things to do, you
see—"

"Waltzing."

She looked up. "What?"

"Waltzing—that's what you do."

Bristling, she lifted her chin. "I may not know how to cook
eggs or do anything terribly useful in this wilderness, but that
doesn't mean I'm idle at home."

"Mm-hm."

"I'm a literary domestic," she announced. "I write books."

"Mm-hm." Luke took another bite of pork and focused his
attention on the grain of wood in the bench. In spite of himself,
he was curious. What would this naive, inexperienced woman
possibly know enough about to write a book?

"I write novels," she told him, heedless of his studious
avoidance of her. "I'll admit, I'm not nearly as popular as Mrs.
Henry Wood. She, of course, writes pure scandal. Adultery,
divorce, betrayal. Wonderful stuff! But I could never write a
book like *East Lynne*. My mother would have a fit of apoplexy.
So I've decided to make my own mark by penning novels
about the wild Western frontier."

Luke couldn't help but look up. What on earth did she know
about the wild Western frontier? There she sat, blue eyes
shining, bosom rising and falling with excitement, cinnamon
hair streaming over her shoulders. She gave him a smile that
burned the edges of his heart.

"I've already written several chapters," she said. "Would
you like to hear them while we ride?"

What could he tell her—that he didn't want to hear her voice
because it had echoed through his dreams all night?

"Sure," he said.

"All right!" Beaming, she popped the last bite of pork into
her mouth. "You will be totally riveted! Entranced!"

Luke picked up his skillet and walked to the fire. He was
afraid he already was.

After riding on the knobby horse from the cabin to the main
road and then all the way back to the wagon that morning,
Hannah thought she would do almost anything to take her mind
off the realities of the day. Luke's trousers were coated

knee-deep with mud, and he had spent more than an hour freeing the mired wheels from muck. All the while, they both had been pestered by mosquitoes and biting flies, while the sun grew so hot not even a parasol could keep Hannah from sweating.

When they were finally on their way again, she decided to strike up a conversation and inquire further about Luke's Osage customs. "Now, about this business of eating raw meat," she began. "I should like to know how one would go about building a place on which to smoke the venison. If the smoking rack were constructed of wood, wouldn't it burn?"

She could have sworn Luke rolled his eyes. Instead of answering, he tossed the packet that contained her manuscript into her lap. "Read," he commanded.

Deciding not to take offense at his tone, Hannah unbuckled the leather packet on her lap and slipped out the stack of papers. She felt a swell of satisfaction as she read the words she had written in neat blue ink: *Bittersweet Heart.* It was the name of her new novel.

She cleared her throat and began to read.

A sunlit valley lush with trees, rivers, and open fields stretched below the hillside on which stood Elizabeth Heartshorn, her husband, and their gentle son. Between his father and mother, the boy trustingly lifted his round blue eyes to the reassuring smiles on their faces. Elizabeth cradled her newborn daughter tightly against her throbbing heart as if she might protect the infant from the grave harms and willful curses of the harsh life that waited ahead.

Harsh indeed, though the innocent young family knew only what lay behind them, for they had journeyed hundreds of miles from their snug home in Connecticut, leading their wagon and team of oxen across forlorn prairies and windswept plains, through raging torrents, and over towering mountains. They had endured the ravages of a harsh winter that had parched their skin and frozen one of their oxen in its tracks. Summer had quickened their spirits with hope, only to dash them on the dunes of wilting, arid deserts.

But now, bright with promise, the vista of bright roses and thick green grasses spread before them in the Missouri valley where they would build their cozy log cabin. The endless sea of

*wildflowers and hardy trees offered no hint of terrors to come,
many though they would be, nor of perils left behind. It was a
paradise. A haven. Or so Elizabeth perceived it, having the
sober yet cheerful temperament of a woman whose strength lay
in the kindness of her heart and the heavenly cast to her eyes.*

*A peaceful woman was Elizabeth Heartshorn. Not that she
had escaped the perplexing trials of growing up in a poor
family of four sisters who, when they were not at odds over
some whimsy of thought, were industriously engaged in the
pursuit of survival. They labored as sellers of vegetables in
the town market, some tending the garden and others minding
the pitiful stall from which they sold their wares. Fortunate in
fact was Elizabeth's upbringing, for it prepared her to endure
what she could not know lay ahead.*

*With eyes of emerald green that sparkled when she laughed,
and tresses as bright as poppies—*

"I named Elizabeth after my littlest sister," Hannah broke
into her story. "Lizzy has hair like that, and she was always
after me to put her in a book."

Luke nodded, but it seemed to him that Elizabeth Heartshorn
sounded more like Hannah Brownlow than anyone else. The
woman's unfinished book lay on her lap, the pages rustling in
the slight breeze. Her hair hung loose down her back, and her
fingers played across the paper.

Having been brought up on stories told around the fire at
night, Luke had always been fascinated by the Heavy Eyebrows' love of writing down their tales. And—other than the
Bible—these tales usually were pure invention, he had learned
at the mission school. Unlike Osage legends, they didn't
explain the creation of the world or the arrival of people from
the heavens. They didn't teach a man how to live within his
tribe. They didn't laud the majestic buffalo or admire the crafty
coyote.

Instead, they merely described the experiences of one man
or one woman. The main actor in these Heavy Eyebrows books
usually struggled alone against insurmountable odds, and
finally overcame all obstacles to achieve some self-prescribed
goal. There was little sense of loyalty to community, of
oneness with nature, of devotion to God. It was a man—or, as
in Hannah Brownlow's story, a woman—against the world.

Luke had decided he didn't much care for the stories of the Heavy Eyebrows.

"What do you think of Elizabeth?" Hannah was asking. "Can you see how strong she is to have made it all the way across the deserts and mountains?"

"There are deserts between here and Connecticut?"

Hannah let out a breath of exasperation. "One has to allow for some sense of imagination. I'm trying to show how courageous Elizabeth is."

"Courageous, yes. But she might look more intelligent if she hadn't tried to go from Connecticut to Missouri by way of New Mexico."

"Oh, all right! I'll cross that part out. You needn't be so particular."

Luke fought the smile that tickled the corners of his mouth. "And roses were brought here by the Heavy Eyebrows. Your Mrs. Heartshorn wouldn't have found them in her uninhabited valley."

"Really?" Hannah stared at her manuscript. How odd to realize that her book reflected the inaccuracies of her own limited knowledge. "Do you suppose I should actually try to make it true to life in Missouri?"

"Why not?"

"Because it's so awful here. The trees are choking, and the roads are pathetic. I certainly couldn't think of putting Elizabeth and her dear children in a hovel like the one where we stayed last night."

"You're going to build her a mansion?"

"No! But at least her log cabin will be solid and clean. Not full of chinks that let the air and rain right in. Not wide open to snakes and spiders. She'll have brightly flowered curtains fluttering in the windows and a nice nickel-plated stove to cook on."

"Did she carry the glass windowpanes all the way from Connecticut?"

Hannah glanced at Luke and gave him a scowl. "All right, how would you write it, then?"

He shrugged. "It's your novel."

"Then will you please listen and stop interrupting?"

"As you wish."

Forgetting it was she who had stopped the story in the first place, Hannah cleared her throat and tried to find her place. Luke Maples was the most irritating man alive. She had written lots of books. She knew how to make them sound good.

With eyes of emerald green that sparkled when she laughed, and tresses as bright as poppies, Hannah read, *our young Elizabeth might have been mistaken for an angel had not the trials of her journey worn gentle lines about the corners of her eyes. Indeed, despite her humble state, she had often been the envy of much wealthier young women in her eastern town, for she was delicate of cheek and fair of brow, with a neck and shoulders smoother than a fawn's. Her beauty might have led to vanity had not the dear child an equal measure of sweet innocence and untarnished virtue.*

It was this very virtue that had led the youthful lady to accept the courtship of a hardworking farmer, Jonathan Heartshorn, a man she might easily have shunned in favor of some gallant roué who would have used her shamefully for her beauty and then cast her aside for her lower class.

Oh, but do not pity Elizabeth, gentle reader, for her humble choice. Love and admire her; for while the storms of fate gather on the horizon, it is her simple generosity, her benevolence, and her timid sensitivity that well may see her through the terrible trials that lie ahead. Were the destiny that was to overtake this gentle woman foreseen by her husband, he would have set her in his wagon and turned the oxen immediately toward the east again, rather than suffer her to endure it.

Hannah turned a page. "Now, you can't find any fault with that," she said. "There's not one thing wrong with it."

"As a matter of fact, I can't wait to find out what this terrible fate is that's lying in store for our young, gentle Elizabeth."

Hannah glanced at him, trying to read his expression. Was he teasing again, or did he really want to know? "Too bad for you," she said, deciding that he thought her story was silly. "I haven't finished writing the book, and you won't ever get to find out what happens to Elizabeth."

Luke mused on her words for a moment. "I hope . . . I hope she stays safely in her snug log cabin with her two children and her handsome Heavy Eyebrows husband," he said. For the first time that morning, he turned and looked into Hannah's blue eyes. "And I hope she lives happily ever after."

Captured, unable to breathe, Hannah met the eyes of the falcon. "I hope so, too," she whispered.

Chapter
Six

Springfield, Missouri, was hardly better off than Bolivar, Hannah decided as Luke drove the wagon into the small city. She had heard Springfield was considered strategic from both a commercial and a military standpoint. During the war it had been fought over bitterly.

From the look of things, the city had been used as a base of operations and supply for one army or the other until the end of the war. In spite of the devastating Union defeat at the battle at nearby Wilson's Creek in September 1861, Federal garrisons had held the city since early the following year. It had been a military depot for the army of the frontier and the army of the southwest.

Hannah guessed that Springfield had once been a successful little town. Its founders had laid out their city in neat lots with streets, alleys, and a central public square. Through the charred facades of burned-out buildings and the tangle of trampled gardens, she could make out what once had been a thriving community of mercantiles—saddle and harness shops, shoe shops, a gunsmith, wagon shops, a hatter, meat markets, tailor shops, jewelry stores, and tin shops. She found evidence of printing offices, churches, schools, a foundry, a bank, a livery stable, even a dentist's office. There must have been sign painters and house painters, she reasoned, and on the outskirts of town the wagon had passed the ruins of two tobacco factories and a planing mill.

But Springfield's former glory had been erased during its military occupation. Houses and outbuildings were torn down to provide firewood. Churches had been converted into hospitals or arsenals. Private homes had served as barracks for soldiers. Tents dotted former parks and gardens.

The shattered city still reeled. Soldiers roamed the streets. Cannons sat on corners, ominous reminders of the constant threat citizens of the town had lived with. Rubble lay in piles. Fences had been knocked to the ground or burned. There was an isolated, stricken look in people's eyes, an expression of despair that crept into Hannah's bones and made her shiver.

"Oh, my," she murmured at the sight of a cluster of ragged tents. Nearby a tattered man sat under a denuded oak tree and smoked a corncob pipe. He regarded the passing wagon as a wreath of smoke curled around his ears.

"What's wrong?" Luke asked.

"This place. I feel as if I've come to the very end of the earth."

He grunted. If only she knew—the end of the earth was the Osage reservation in Kansas.

"Springfield's not so bad," he told her.

"I can't imagine people actually live here. I'd have left long ago. No . . . I'd never have come here in the first place."

"Unless my eyes are playing a trick on me, you *are* here."

"But I'm not staying. The moment I find Ethan, I'm taking the first train back to civilization."

Luke had to acknowledge that Hannah meant what she said. The Ozark hills might be a paradise to him, a place where he could find peace and solitude, where he could touch the source of his own soul. But they were hell to her. It wouldn't be long before she would leave for good.

Deciding he could trust himself to look at her now that they were safely back in populated territory, he allowed his eyes to wander over her familiar face. Pale, fragile, she hardly looked strong enough to climb down from the wagon, let alone find her brother and make it all the way home to Boston.

"How are your ribs?" he asked.

She chewed her bottom lip for a moment. "Fine. And don't worry—I won't tell anyone about the bushwhackers."

It wasn't that, he wanted to say. If she chose to tell the sheriff about the attack, Luke would find some way to handle the consequences. What he wasn't comfortable about was leaving her alone in this city. Human scavengers roamed the streets. Women who had followed the military from camp to camp lolled on the sagging porches of abandoned houses and called to passersby. Soldiers whose minds and bodies had been ravaged by war wandered amid the disorder. Drunkards, gamblers, ruffians of all kinds ruled the town.

On the other hand, Hannah had made it this far on her own. She was a survivor. If she could fight off a bushwhacker, she could last a day or two in Springfield. Besides, Luke reminded himself, he wasn't responsible for her. He'd agreed to bring her to Springfield, and here she was. Safe and sound.

"There's a nice-looking hotel," she said, pointing to a two-story building down the street. "If you would be so kind as to drive me there, I'll engage a room."

Luke cleared his throat. "That's not a hotel. It's a saloon. A . . . a bordello."

Flushing, Hannah gave a quick laugh. "Of course it is. I suppose it was the gilt trim that threw me off."

Inwardly Luke groaned. If she couldn't tell a whorehouse from a hotel, she probably thought those wolves leering at her from the street corners were just nice, polite gentlemen. Hannah was like a young doe—innocent, unwary, delicate. Luke knew how easily she could be cheated or robbed . . . or worse. The thought of abandoning her didn't sit well.

"How about that establishment just ahead?" she asked. "Lyon House. It's not too far from the courthouse. I could walk the distance easily." She picked up her purse and set it on her lap, wishing she could count her money again without being too obvious about it. How much would a room cost? And how many days would she need to stay in this godforsaken place? "I wonder if they'll take me in, dressed as I am."

As he headed the horse toward the hotel, Luke gave Hannah a lingering gaze, aware that this was the last time he would be allowed the luxury. In her yellow dress, with her coppery hair, she was more beautiful than any woman he'd ever known.

"I really should have pinned up my hair this morning," she said softly, "and this skirt is so wrinkled."

"You look fine, Hannah. Just fine."

Her heart lifted at his words, and she smoothed her long hair over her shoulders like a cape. But as the wagon jolted down the rutted road, it occurred to her that she had no reason to feel at ease about this latest step in her journey. She had so few coins left she was in danger of destitution. In fact, she surmised that the return train fare to Boston would eliminate the rest of her purse. Worse, she had no transportation, and she was miles from any railroad. A telegraph line was all that linked her to Boston, and she still had not a single clue as to Ethan's whereabouts.

She scanned the narrow boardwalk and long glass windows as the wagon approached the hotel. She would go on searching for her brother, she knew, until she had spent her last penny. But for the first time since beginning her journey, she felt reluctant to be on her own.

"You'll be all right?" Luke asked as he pulled the reins to bring the horse to a halt.

"I'm fine," she said, squaring her shoulders. "I'm sure the authorities here will know where Ethan is. If not, I'll continue on my way until I do find him."

"Where will you go?"

"Wherever I'm told would be the best place to search. Rolla, perhaps. Or Joplin."

Again Luke felt a protective urge well up inside his chest. Joplin, with its violent history, was the *last* place Hannah needed to go. Reminding himself that he couldn't fall into the trap of becoming concerned with the affairs of a white woman, he jumped down from the wagon and walked around to help her down.

"Sounds like you'll be keeping busy," he said, forcing indifference into his voice. "Best of luck to you, then."

"And the same to you, I'm sure."

She gathered her purse and manuscript, adjusted her bonnet,

and extended her bare hand. But as her fingers touched his, Hannah felt a shower of sparks scatter through her. Her eyes flew to his face, and for the first time since she had met Luke, she clearly read the message in his expression. It was desire. Need. Hunger.

Swallowing hard, she placed her palm on his shoulder as his hands slipped around her waist. The feel of hard muscle beneath his shirt stirred the coil of yearning deep inside her. She felt it slide through the pit of her stomach and begin to throb.

As he lifted her down from the wagon, his brown eyes burned through her, consuming in their intensity. Inches away, his body was so close she could feel the heat emanating from his chest. Her feet touched the ground, but she couldn't move.

"Luke, I . . . I want to . . ." Her voice sounded breathless, husky. What did she want? She wanted this moment to go on forever. She wanted him to hold her closer, to bend his head, to brush his lips across hers. *Please, please, kiss me,* she heard her heart beating in a faltering rhythm. *Please, please.*

"Take care of yourself, Hannah Brownlow," he said. But he didn't hear his own words. His attention was focused on her mouth, her soft damask lips tilted toward him, parted slightly, damp from her shallow breath. Mesmerized, he fought the need to cover her mouth with his, to taste her sweet lips and touch her silken tongue.

His hands tightened around her waist, and he pulled her closer, so close he could feel the tips of her breasts graze his chest. Her eyelids drifted shut, and she blossomed toward him like a spring wildflower—open, willing, ready. She wanted him. She trusted him.

He swallowed, fighting . . . fighting. One kiss. One touch of her hair. He would be lost to her.

"Hannah." He gritted his jaw as her eyelids fluttered open. *"Tha'-gthin-xtsi."*

"Luke?"

"You are beautiful," he whispered. Then he set her away from him and turned his back so that she couldn't see his face as he walked to the wagon.

Hannah pressed her manuscript against her chest as she watched him unload her damp trunk and hatboxes onto the hotel porch. Silently he situated the last soggy box and then jammed his hands into his pockets.

Hannah cleared her throat. "May I pay you for—"

"No." He didn't look at her. "I was coming anyway."

His face was a mask as he climbed onto the wagon. When he took the reins, his dark eyes focused on the road ahead.

So, he was leaving. Just like that. He gave the reins a shake, and the horse pulled at the harness. The wagon began to roll. It passed the end of the hotel porch, then the courthouse.

"Luke!" Hannah dropped her book on the porch and dashed down the muddy road. "Luke, wait!"

"Hannah?" He reined the horse with one hand, and with the other he reached toward her. As she caught up to him, he took her outstretched fingers. "Hannah, what is it?"

She stood on tiptoe and looked up at him, her blue eyes shining. "I want to thank you," she said. "For bringing me safely here. For everything."

For one brief moment, she laid her cheek against his arm. Her loose hair slipped over their clasped hands. Silky as thistledown, warm as sunshine, the fiery strands burned against his skin. He stared, transfixed, as he watched his own fingers slide into her hair . . . thread through the flame . . . gather it in his palm . . . crush and sift and stroke it.

And then she was backing away. "I shall never forget you, Mystery-hawk," she said.

She turned away, her fire-hair swinging like a copper sheet. Lifting her ragged yellow skirt in her hands, she ran back down the road. A lumber wagon crossed between them, blocking Luke's view. When it finally rumbled past, Hannah had vanished into the hotel.

For a moment he could do nothing but stare at his hand. His palm burned as though he had lifted a pot from the cooking fire unprotected. But it wasn't her hair, after all, that engraved Hannah Brownlow in his mind.

It was her heart.

"We don't take no butternuts here."

Hannah blinked in confusion at the elderly clerk behind the hotel desk. Though the top of his head was as bald and shiny white as a crockery bowl, wisps of thin gray hair stuck out around his ears in disarray. Like an old, wild alley cat, he regarded her with a mixture of disdain and indifference as his snaggletoothed jaws worked a plug of chewing tobacco.

"Butternuts?" she asked.

His wrinkled brown tongue repositioned the wad before he spat a long arc of juice into the brass spittoon near her feet. It hit the bottom with a loud *ptang*. Wrinkling her nose, Hannah gathered her skirt and stepped a pace away.

"That's what I said," the clerk told her finally. "We don't take no butternuts at Lyon House."

"I have no idea what you're talking about, sir. I've just arrived from Bolivar after two difficult days of travel, and I'd like to engage a room."

"And we don't take no butternuts."

"*What* is a butternut?"

"*Yew* is a butternut."

"I am not!" Hannah lifted her chin. "And if you would be so good as to tell me what a butternut is, I'll tell you why I'm not one."

The clerk eyed her before shooting another brown arc into the brass spittoon. *Ptang.* "Butternuts is poor country folk. They wear yellow clothes just like that'n yew got on, 'cuz butternuts is all they got for dye. They slop hogs and make whiskey and go barefoot 'cuz they ain't got shoes. And they sure ain't got enough money to stay in a fancy hotel like Lyon House." *Ptang.*

Hannah looked down at her dress. She'd had no idea she was wearing a butternut's cast-off clothing. But that morning her hoop had been creaky, her crinoline still wet, and her ice-blue gown torn at the sleeve. What choice had she had?

She returned the old man's disdainful stare. "I should think," she told him, "that a person of your venerable age would have learned to avoid judging a person solely by appearance."

"What the hell you talkin' 'bout?"

"I am not a butternut! But even if I were, you shouldn't assume I can't pay for a room here, because I most certainly can." She slapped her purse on the desk. "How much for one night?"

"Two bucks."

"Two dollars? That's robbery!"

"Like I told yew, honey, we don't take no—"

"Butternut or not, I shall meet your outrageous price, sir, and you will refrain from addressing a lady in such a callous and disrespectful manner."

Fingers trembling with anger, she dug two coins from her purse and plunked them on the table. The very idea that she would be turned away by a lowly hotel clerk because of the color of her dress! Who were these poor butternuts that they had earned such disrepute? And who did this clerk think he was—the King of England?

"Fetch your trunk on upstairs to room three," he told her. "Seems to me I put fresh sheets on that bed a week or so back."

"A week—"

"Now, don't get yourself all riled up, honey." *Ptang.* "Your cheeks are redder'n a turkey's ass in pokeberry time."

"I've a good mind to go and find Luke Maples. He could teach you a lesson on gentlemanly behavior."

"That Indian who drove yew up? He set one foot inside Lyon House, and I'd have the sheriff string his hide from the nearest tree. We don't tolerate no redskins 'round this hotel. This here's a decent place, now. Ain't no vermin allowed."

Hannah could hardly breathe. *Vermin!* She studied the two coins in the clerk's hand. She'd have dearly loved to snatch them away and find somewhere else to stay. But she doubted she could overpower him, and she wasn't sure she could even find another hotel that hadn't been burned to the ground.

"I'm to carry my own trunk upstairs?" she asked tartly.

"'Less you want to leave it out on the porch all day."

"Very well." Gathering her purse, Hannah marched across the lobby and out the front door. Luke Maples was not vermin. And she was no butternut. How utterly unfair to be regarded as such.

She pushed her sleeves up her arms and grabbed one of the handles of her trunk. Certainly she could carry her own trunk. She could sleep in a bed with dirty sheets. She could eat jerky and wear a butternut's dress and fight off a bushwhacker with her bare hands if that's what it took to find Ethan. She could and she would.

Bracing herself, she lifted one end of the trunk and began to drag it backward into the hotel. The marble threshold provided a slick surface on which to ease the trunk into the lobby, but the carpet on the floor inside might as well have been glue. As she tugged against the heavy weight, her ribs ached, but she tried not to think about the pain—or the stairs.

"Pardon me, ma'am—may I be of assistance?"

The voice behind her was richly toned. Hannah turned her head. A medium-sized man with dark hair and a full mustache gave her a broad smile as he swept his hat from his head.

"J. B. Hickok at your service," he said. "Friends call me Bill."

Hannah assessed him for a moment. The man smelled rather strongly of liquor, but he was wearing a large gold ring, a fine tie stuck with a diamond pin, and a flashy gold hunting-cased Waltham watch. A gentleman at last.

"Hannah Brownlow," she said, tipping her head in greeting. "Lately of Boston."

"An Easterner? Well, you've come a far piece. You staying here at Lyon House?"

"Only for one night. I'm in search of my brother and I plan to speak to the military authorities here."

"A Union man, your brother?" When Hannah nodded, Bill Hickok grinned. "I'm a Federal myself. Served in northern Arkansas and right here in southwest Missouri. I was a scout for the army of the frontier."

"My goodness, you must have become well acquainted with danger during the past few years."

"Danger means nothing to a man like me, Miss Brownlow. I have no fear of man or beast. I would fight to the death for the honor of my country."

"Hoo-hee!" the clerk cackled from behind the desk. "You tell her, Hickok. She's sucker enough to believe every word." *Ptang.* "Paid me two whole dollars for a room!"

"Don't give him no nevermind," Bill confided to Hannah. "He's a mite tetched in the head."

He tapped his temple knowingly, then bent and swung her trunk into his arms. Giving the clerk an angry glare, she followed Bill Hickok up the stairs. Her room could hardly have been more of a shock. A rusty iron bed stood in one corner, its stained and filthy sheets in a tangle on the floor. Tattered curtains hung from one window; the other was bare. The glass in almost every pane had been smashed out. The washstand near the door held an empty pitcher and a washbowl plastered with dry black whiskers from a previous tenant's shave.

"Heavens!" she exclaimed.

"Listen, that old feller down there'll cheat you blind if he can, Miss Brownlow," Bill Hickok said as he set the trunk on the floor. "He's as worthless as tits on a boar. But don't you worry, now. Go do your talkin' to the authorities, and then come on back to the hotel. I'll buy you a drink, how's that? Make you forget all your worries."

Hannah tried to smile. "Thank you, but I don't drink."

"Shoot. Well, how about supper, then? They got right tasty food here. Beans. Stew. Cornbread. You name it."

"Perhaps."

"Hey, Hickok, you ol' bastard!" a man called as he leaned into Hannah's room. "You comin'? . . . Oh, excuse me, ma'am, I didn't know you was here. I'm David Tutt."

"Hannah Brownlow." She hesitantly shook the stranger's hand.

"Miss Brownlow here's from Boston," Bill said. "You ought to know, Tutt's a Rebel. Fought for the Confederates in Arkansas."

"So what?" Tutt snapped. "Damn, I wish you'd quit bringing that up, Hickok. You're making me mad enough to chew splinters."

Both men straightened and faced each other. "What you gonna do about it, Tutt?" Bill returned.

Hannah's blood dropped to her knees. "Thank you so much for your assistance, Mr. Hickok," she said quickly, giving his shoulder a slight push. "Now, if you gentlemen would excuse me, I have business to attend to."

Eyes fastened on Tutt, Hickok gave a curt nod. "Sure thing. Hope to see you this evening, Miss Brownlow."

With a sigh of relief, Hannah followed the two men to the door and shut it behind them. Sinking onto her trunk, she buried her face in her hands. Confederate and Union soldiers in the same hotel . . . a thieving old clerk . . . a filthy bedroom . . . What was she doing here?

She had to think on better things. Boston, perhaps? But it was so far away and her life there so out of touch with the realities of the rest of the world. Ethan? No, thinking of her brother only made her feel more hopeless.

Taking a deep breath, Hannah let her mind drift until it settled on something peaceful. A cracking fire . . . the scent of scrambled eggs . . . the drip of warm water on tired skin . . . the whisper of a deep voice . . .

Tha'-gthin-xtsi . . . you are beautiful.

Luke! Oh, Luke . . .

Hannah had just dipped a spoon into her bowl of beans—all she had been able to afford for her supper—when the thunder of a horse's hooves on the hotel's front porch broke the quiet in the saloon. What now? she wondered.

All evening she had been struggling to accept the fact that while Springfield's court records had shown several Brownlows, none of them was an Ethan. The lists of Union soldiers had not included her brother's name either. Her last hope was to check with Confederate regiments in the morning—but, of course, she knew Ethan would never have joined the Rebel troops.

As shouts and shrieks filled the lobby, Hannah grabbed her purse and clutched it against her stomach.

"It's Hickok again!" the proprietor hollered. "Everybody move the tables and take cover!"

The saloon erupted as men began shoving tables against the walls, and silk-clad ladies dragged chairs to safety. Hannah reached for her beans, but someone jerked away the table and sent her bowl to the floor with a crash.

"Oh, no!" She knelt to the floor where her precious food had splattered. At that moment a huge brown horse clattered into the saloon, its rider waving a hat in one hand and a half-empty whiskey bottle in the other.

"Howdy, howdy! Bill Hickok's the name!" Spotting Hannah crouched alone at the center of the room, the rider made a gallant dismount. He swaggered toward her. "Why, Miss Brownlow! So glad you could join me this evening. You certainly do look lovely."

Abandoning her dinner, Hannah rose to face him. "Mr. Hickok," she addressed him evenly, "you have brought your horse into the dining room."

"I have?" He gave an incredulous look at his horse, then

broke into loud guffaws. "Well, what do you know? I sure have!"

"I shouldn't think that is appropriate."

"Why, I don't know. These folk have been waiting all evening for me to bring some life into the place, ain't you?"

"Now, Bill," the saloon keeper said. "We all seen this act of yours plenty times before. So, if you wouldn't mind takin' your horse back outside—"

"And make Miss Brownlow miss the show?" He gave Hannah a wink before taking a long swallow of whiskey. "Look here what this fine steed can do."

He tapped his horse on the nose and made three exaggerated bows. Then he began to shout at the poor animal to sit. Wild-eyed, the horse tried to back up, but stepped on a fallen chair. It trotted forward a few paces, and Bill gave it another slap.

"Sit, you mangy ol' cuss!" he hollered.

The horse finally managed to lower its back legs before collapsing onto the floor with a whoosh of sawdust. Bill swung around and flourished his arms. "What d'you think, Miss Brownlow? Ain't he a sight?"

Hannah eyed the door. She had to find Luke. He would rescue the poor horse from this devil.

"Roll over!" Bill commanded. "I said, roll over, you flea-bit cayuse!"

The horse snorted and shook its head, bridle jangling. Approaching, Bill flicked the animal with the tip of a small whip.

Hannah's spine prickled. "You can't expect the creature to roll over," she said. "It's wearing a saddle!"

"You don't know what a genius I am, see? Now watch this." He whipped the horse again. "Roll over!"

Kicking wildly, the animal rolled onto its side. More sawdust flew. The whip cracked. Hickok's laughter mingled with the horse's loud whinnying. Hannah watched in horror as the creature finally worked itself over onto its back, then dropped onto its other side. Sides heaving, it lay limp for a moment, before Hickok began to use the whip again.

"Up, now," he called. "Come on, let's show Miss Brownlow

how you can dance. Then maybe she'll dance with me, huh? You like to dance, Miss Brownlow?"

Hannah lifted her skirt. "I dance with gentlemen," she said. "Never with you."

His laughter ringing in her ears, she hurried out into the lobby, aware that she had lost both her supper and her appetite. If only she could find Luke before that ruffian killed his poor horse! Adjusting her bonnet, she strode out onto the porch.

Night had closed in around the city, draping it in such utter blackness that nothing but the saloon across the street was visible. Where was Luke? Did she have any chance of finding him? Or had he already made his purchases for the survey team and started back to Bolivar that afternoon?

Realizing she had no hope of finding him without traipsing from one saloon to another and placing herself in danger from vagabonds and reprobates like Bill Hickok, Hannah went back into the hotel and climbed the stairs to her room. She probably couldn't find Luke if she searched all night. Even if she did find him, she doubted he would accompany her into the hotel.

He was an Indian, she reminded herself as she locked her door. He was unwelcome in such high-class establishments as Lyon House. To "civilized" Missourians, he was *vermin*. As she reflected on Luke's fine nose, his deep-set brown eyes, his compelling mouth, she wondered if he had been forced to sleep in a barn somewhere. Or worse.

She sighed and settled into a rickety chair by the window. Her hoops creaked. Her corset cut into her breasts. The skirt she had taken from her trunk that afternoon felt hot and clammy compared to the lightweight butternut dress she had worn on the journey.

Picking up her manuscript, she ruffled the edges of the pages. It had been fun to read her book to Luke. Even though he had questioned and even teased her, she knew he understood. He cared about the story she was trying to tell.

She opened her purse and took out her pen and a small bottle of ink. Maybe if she wrote a few pages, she could escape this stifling room and her hopeless quest for an hour or two.

From the saloon below she could hear the sound of the whip, the cries of the watching crowd, the shouts, and the skittering hooves. The horse whinnied in desperation, and Hannah gritted her teeth. *Barbarians,* that's what they were! *Savages.*

As the word registered in her mind, Hannah suddenly pictured herself only two days before. A savage, she had called Luke on the road into Bolivar. An Indian. Barbaric. She had judged him by his clothes, his skin. She had unfairly labeled him, just as the clerk had unfairly labeled her a butternut because of her dress.

But she had been *taught* that Indians were savages. She had read how filthy they were. She had heard tales of their barbarity, ignorance, paganism. Was Luke an exception? Or had all the accounts been wrong? Whom could one trust? What could one believe?

Staring at the tattered calico curtains, Hannah felt a wash of cool air from the broken window stir across her skin. If only she could see Luke. If only she could hear his voice. But he was as lost to her as Ethan.

She opened the bottle, dipped her pen into the ink, and scanned the last page she had written on the train to Missouri.

"So, you're the farmer who lives over the hill," said John, his tone light and agreeable. He opened wider the front door of the cabin and admitted the visitor who had just stepped down from his carriage. "We've been hearing reports of you since we moved to this valley two months ago. My wife, Mr. Williams, Elizabeth Heartshorn."

"A pleasure, madam," returned the handsome gentleman, his hand warmly grasping Elizabeth's. "And, to be sure, you must call me Caleb."

"Welcome, Caleb, to our humble home."

"Humble, indeed?" he expressed with genuine surprise. "Why, you have made this common dwelling an enviable abode."

Two roses flew to Elizabeth's pale cheeks as she regarded her visitor's kind smile. She had indeed taken great care with her choice of paints and wallpapers—

Hannah stopped reading and frowned at her story. Wallpapers? In a log cabin? What had she been thinking? She recalled the rough-hewn structure where she had spent the night with Luke. Wallpaper wouldn't have a hope of clinging to those smoke-stained, splintery walls. She scratched through the sentence and added several new words in the margin.

She had indeed taken great care to keep her cabin clean, the ashes in her fireplace swept, her quilts mended. But to think that Caleb Williams could appreciate feminine touches. They would seem of such inconsequence to a man whose thoughts must be consumed with the rigors of survival on this rugged frontier. Even John, whose eyes now shone with pride at the praise rendered so gallantly on his wife's behalf, had hardly noticed the results of her labors.

As Caleb turned away to discuss matters of farming with her husband, Elizabeth found her attention drawn to the fine cut of their visitor's suit. Caleb was known in the valley as a wealthy man, one who lived in a fine brick house—

Again Hannah frowned. She had hardly seen a single brick since coming to Missouri. And Caleb wouldn't be wearing a suit, would he? Not a working farmer. She drew a line through the words and changed "brick" to "stone" and "suit" to "linen shirt."

Caleb was known in the valley as a wealthy man, one who lived in a fine stone house with a large barn and vast fields. It was rumored he had been married once, but his dear wife had been laid to rest not many days following the birth of a son. The child, too, had passed to the bosom of heavenly peace, leaving a father to grieve so deeply he had never considered the possibility of finding another to fill the emptiness left by his lost loved ones.

Understandable, such grief was, Elizabeth knew, yet she also wondered at the man's decision to refrain from the solace of hearth, home, and family. Certainly she had heard of the many desirous glances cast his way, for Caleb Williams was considered by far the most sought-after bachelor in the valley.

If not for his wealth, his appearance would have drawn him plentiful attention. Hale, he was, and strong of limb, though not a tall man or so very strapped with muscle. While the hand of time had treated him with kindness, he was no longer young, and Elizabeth felt her heart ache with the years of his solitude. His golden hair and pale skin—

Hannah stopped reading. She chewed on her lower lip for a moment as she stared blankly out the window. Then her heart began to thud, and her eyes misted. Dipping her pen in the inkwell, she crossed out the final paragraph. With bold black strokes, she penned in new words.

Hale, he was, and strong of limb, a towering man well endowed with muscle that broadened his shoulders and hardened the plane of his back. He was a young man still, and Elizabeth felt her heart ache with the years of solitude he had suffered already. His raven hair and deeply tanned skin might have given him the look of a savage had not his warm touch and kind words been so evident of the true spirit within him. He was a gentleman, she realized, of the noblest ilk.

He was a man any woman might desire.

Hannah laid down her pen and lifted her eyes to the window once again.

Chapter Seven

~~~~~~~~~

Luke fingered the hilt of his knife as he crouched in the shadows across the street from Lyon House. He could hear the desperate whinnying of a horse inside the saloon. A life spent riding bareback on the plains of Kansas had taught him every nuance of meaning in the sounds creatures made—horses, birds, squirrels, even frogs and crickets. The animal in the hotel was frightened, bewildered, and in pain.

Once again, Luke fought his instincts. He had no doubt that in one swift motion he could silence the devil who handled his horse with such cruelty. The swaggering drunkard who had ridden into the hotel a few minutes before had a fine crop of hair. Luke could almost feel his own fingers gathering a hank of thick curls and slicing his blade through warm flesh. One quick jerk and he would hear the familiar pop of scalp tearing from bone. Then he could calm the frightened horse with a word or two, mount it, and ride out into the night. In a few days, he would be in Kansas.

Kansas was exactly where Luke knew he would have to go

if he did a fool-headed thing like scalping a man in a crowded saloon in Springfield, Missouri. But why shouldn't he exact a final revenge on the Heavy Eyebrows and then return to the reservation? Nothing stood in his way but the threat of a hanging—or a bullet. At this moment, he almost felt he had nothing to lose.

The events of the afternoon had confirmed Luke's suspicions. In the process of buying supplies and conferring with the survey team in Springfield, he had casually inquired about the prospects of purchasing land in Missouri. And he had been told time and time again what he already suspected—Indians were not free to buy property in the United States.

As Luke listened to the distant sound of laughter and the clatter of the horse's hooves on the saloon's wooden floorboards, he reflected on his conversation with an official at the Springfield Land Office. The office controlled land sales in most of the southwestern part of the state, including the acreage in Polk County where Luke had found the withered oak tree.

"Look, fellow," the official had said, "ain't you an Indian?"

"Osage," Luke had confirmed.

"What're you doing over here anyways? You folk gladly sold your land to the federal government back in 1825. You'uns got your own property in Kansas now. Go on home to Indian Territory, why don't you?"

"Just out of curiosity, what rights *do* I have around here?"

"You got no rights, red man. Now, head on out of here, huh? I got work to do."

Luke had paused only a moment. "What about the Homestead Act? Could an Indian homestead land in Missouri?"

The official glanced at an associate and gave a snicker. "Fellow, the Homestead Act of May 20, 1862, granted the right to homestead one hundred sixty acres of surveyed land to every qualified *citizen* of the United States of America. Now, tell me this—when was the last time you recall voting in an election?"

The men had chuckled as Luke turned to leave.

"You never voted, because you ain't a citizen," the official had called out. "You ain't a citizen because you're an Indian. And that means you can't buy our land, nor homestead our land, nor no other way get your red hands on our land. So, ride

on back to your teepee and stop poking your nose where it
don't belong."

As he tested the blade on his knife, Luke felt his blood rise
at the injustice of the land official's words. So many things the
man had said were wrong. The Osage had never willingly sold
their Missouri land. They had been coerced, backed into a
corner, their rights stripped away by lying Heavy Eyebrows
agents.

Like those people the Heavy Eyebrows men considered
inferior—the black *Nika-sabe,* and all women—Indians had
been denied privileges of citizenship such as voting and government representation. His people were in the worst position. Not
only couldn't they vote, but they could never own land outside the
reservation. The Heavy Eyebrows men even permitted their
women to possess property.

Luke gritted his jaw and was starting to rise when the front
door to the hotel swung open and Hannah Brownlow stormed
out onto the porch. She planted her feet in an angry stance,
crossed her arms, and glared into the darkness. The sound of
her short, rapid breathing drifted across the street.

At the sight of the woman, Luke felt his stomach take an
unexpected dip. *Hannah.* This was why he had crept through
the night and waited in the shadows for more than an hour. One
last look at Hannah. And there she was, the one who had
bewitched him.

Once again, she was the woman he had seen riding in the
wagon on the way to Bolivar. Her shiny dress swung around
her ankles like an enormous bell; her spoon-shaped bonnet
framed her fiery hair; her bright eyes fairly outshone the stars.
With skin as white as the moon and a dress of billowing green
silk, she might have stepped from the hand-painted color plate
of a storybook.

As beautiful as Hannah looked in her swishy skirts, Luke
couldn't help thinking of her in the old yellow dress she had
found in the cabin. He had enjoyed the fine view it provided of
her full, round breasts, her narrow waist, and her curved hips.
That dress had been soft enough for a man to touch and thin
enough for a woman to feel the warmth of his hands through
the fabric.

So, Hannah, how are your ribs? he wanted to call out to her.

Are you still sore? Did you find your brother, Ethan? Have you eaten a good meal yet? What has made you look so angry?

But the woman on the porch was no longer a part of his life. He had little doubt that he would soon be a faded memory among the many that filled her mind during this long journey from Boston. Perhaps she had forgotten him already.

Striding to the edge of the porch, she looked from side to side. Whom was she searching for? She placed one foot on the step that led down to the street. Luke's eyes narrowed. Would she walk away from the hotel and out into the darkness? *Don't do it, Hannah. You won't be safe.*

She took another step. He straightened, his knife loose and ready in his palm. He would follow her . . . trail her silently through the darkness to guard her from any ruffian who might be lurking on a street corner.

Again, a battle raged inside him. Why should he concern himself with this Heavy Eyebrows woman? Let her go. Let her stumble into her own fate.

No, he couldn't do that. There was no doubt in his mind that he would protect her with his life. Why? Because she had tempting breasts and magic hair and because he desired her as he'd never desired a woman of his own people?

It wasn't that . . . not at all. Not her body. Not her hair. It was her spirit. It was the way she had gone after that bushwhacker on the muddy road. It was the expression on her face when she had first tasted the jerky. It was the way she loved the old *Nika-sabe* woman who had been kind to her. It was that book she was writing—silly, preposterous, riddled with errors . . . and yet somehow deeply moving. Luke had found himself wondering all afternoon what would happen to the young Elizabeth Heartshorn and her Heavy Eyebrows husband.

In the distance Hannah again peered from side to side. Whom was she looking for? Luke frowned. Had she met a man in the city that afternoon? Someone she hoped would come to the hotel to warm her bed? A lover?

The thought sent a flame of jealousy roaring through his chest. No man deserved to part Hannah Brownlow's thighs. No man but himself. *A ridiculous idea.*

Now she was climbing up the steps again, turning her back

on him, walking across the porch to the door. Forget her, Luke instructed himself. Let her return to her world of silk dresses and dinners of Irish corned beef and cabbage. Release the memory of her fire-hair. Ride to Bolivar in the morning with a free mind. Leave the supplies with the surveyor and head for Kansas.

Kansas. Home. The fire would burn brightly in his mother's lodge. The chants of his people would rise to Grandfather the Sun with the first light of dawn. Luke's brothers would welcome him in the summer buffalo hunt.

And, if he chose, he could join the resistance movement of the warrior Pa-I'n-No-Pa-She, Not-Afraid-of-Longhairs. Like Luke, Not-Afraid-of-Longhairs had attended Father Schoenmakers's mission school on the reservation, and he was deeply opposed to selling more Osage land to the Heavy Eyebrows. Not-Afraid-of-Longhairs had chosen not to leave the protection of the tribe, as Luke had, but to work from within it to defeat the enemy.

As much as Luke respected Not-Afraid-of-Longhairs, he felt sure the Osage warrior's dream was futile. The two had argued. Luke urged for Osage assimilation into the white man's way of life while maintaining tribal customs and beliefs. Not-Afraid-of-Longhairs insisted that the tribe must draw more closely together rather than spread itself thin within the Heavy Eyebrows' world. He wanted to fight for Osage rights within a treaty system that Luke saw as a lost cause.

Watching Hannah disappear into the lobby of the hotel, Luke felt his own spirit sink. He didn't want to go back to Kansas. He didn't want to join Not-Afraid-of-Longhairs in his doomed battle. What he wanted was the rich land where the gnarled oak tree stood and the stream rushed over smooth, round stones. What he wanted was deep soil, thick trees, deer, squirrels, raccoons, hills, valleys, water. What he wanted was the peace of home.

An oil lamp lighted the window of an upstairs room. Luke studied the panes of broken glass until he saw Hannah's silhouette appear in the frame. Holding the manuscript of her book, she drew a chair to the window and sat down. Her hands turned pages one by one. She dipped a pen into a bottle of ink and began to write.

And Luke knew what he really wanted more than anything else.

Stepping out onto the boardwalk in front of Lyon House, Hannah drank in a deep breath of fresh morning air. At last the rain had stopped falling, the gray clouds had rolled back, and the sun glinted off puddles in the street. Springfield looked almost new, almost pretty.

Lifting her chin, she set her shoulders toward the square. Though she didn't relish the idea of speaking with officers of the Confederacy—defeated though they were—she knew they provided her last hope of finding Ethan before she must leave Springfield for some other town where her brother might have been seen.

Not that she would be too sorry to leave this wild city.

Talk at the hotel's breakfast tables had concerned the antics of Bill Hickok. It seemed the man loved nothing better than to ride his horse down sidewalks and into hotels, saloons, stores, and other public places, and make the poor animal perform tricks. He was known for drunken sprees during which his favorite activity became bullying nervous men and showing off to women.

Hannah chastised herself for failing to recognize immediately that the man was a cad. His fine jewelry and expensive watch had fooled her into thinking him a gentleman. Once again, she had to admit, she had been swayed by appearances.

When would she learn to look patiently into the heart of a person before forming an opinion? With a sigh she shook her head. Luke Maples, of course, was the prime example of her failure to judge correctly.

The thought that the handsome Osage Indian might still be in town had buoyed her all through breakfast. But as she approached the courthouse, she reminded herself that he probably had already gone. He had lost a day of travel to the rain, and the surveyor would be impatient for his supplies.

No, Hannah knew she was mired in this city with no one better than Bill Hickok for company. Her breakfast companions had savored the details of Bill's gaming adventures the night before. Evidently the showman had played poker with David Tutt, the ex-Confederate, and had come out the loser.

First his money went, then his fancy Waltham watch, and finally his diamond pin and ring. Drunk and angry, Bill had warned the cardplayer not to show the watch around town.

"It'll give me as much pleasure wearing it on the streets as it has already given me to win it," Tutt had bragged. "I intend wearing it in the morning."

Hickok had sworn a vile oath and retorted, "If you do, I'll shoot you."

Now everyone was eager to see whether the Rebel would make good on his boast—and, if he did, whether Hickok would follow through with his threat. Hannah understood that this was a great joke to the hotel patrons, because Bill Hickok was known as a hopelessly poor shot.

Oh, to be in Boston! She clutched her purse as she climbed the courthouse steps and entered the cool building. Because of the numbers of people searching for missing relatives or applying for pensions, former Union and Confederate military garrisons had set up temporary offices there. Hannah joined the long line outside the room where a Confederate officer was searching through lists of names and regiments.

As she waited, she found her attention wandering down the long halls to the warren of offices in the building. Had Luke been inside this courthouse? Were the surveyor's offices here? Could he have found the supplies he needed at another place in the city or would he have come here? What would she do if she saw him? Could she greet him and then watch him walk away once more?

"Name?"

Startled, Hannah glanced down and realized she had arrived at the front of the line. Quickly she gave the familiar litany of information about her missing brother. The officer flipped through a book, running his finger down the lists of names.

"Brownlow, did you say?" he asked.

"Yes." Hannah's heart jumped a beat. "Ethan."

"I've got an E. Brownlow here. Enlisted March 23, 1862."

"Enlisted . . . in what?"

"In the Confederate Army, ma'am," the officer said impatiently. "Isn't that why you're standing at my desk?"

"Well, yes, but . . . a Confederate? Ethan would never—"

"It doesn't say Ethan. It's just plain E."

"What happened to him—this E. Brownlow?"

"Don't know. We lost more than twelve hundred men at the Battle of Wilson's Creek, but that was in '61. We fought at Newtonia in '62. Won that one, too, but lost a fair number of troops. To tell you the truth, there were almost a dozen battles or campaigns here in Missouri from the time this E. Brownlow joined up until the end of the war. I don't have many names of the dead, except for the Wilson's Creek troops. What I have is mostly enlistment records."

Hannah nodded, trying to think quickly. "Can you trace this E. Brownlow? Can you find out what became of him?"

"I'd have to put through a request. Could take a while. Things are in sort of a . . . well, a mess. We lost records, or they weren't kept up. Volunteers swelled the ranks without ever bothering to enlist. A lot of them saw action, and some died in battle without leaving much of a record. Others joined on the spur of the moment but fled when the going got rough. Enlisted men deserted. Some troops just vanished into the woods—"

"Bushwhackers. Yes, I know about them."

The officer regarded her. "So, what do you want? Shall I try to find this Brownlow fellow for you?"

"I know Ethan would never join the Confederacy, but . . . this is the closest I've come to finding his name . . . and yet—"

"Ma'am, there's a long line behind you. You want me to forward a request on this or not?"

"Yes. Please." She swallowed. "How long might it take?"

"No idea. A few weeks. Months. What's your address?"

"Months!" Hannah rubbed her hand across her forehead. "Oh, I'll have to think . . ."

"Ma'am, please—"

"All right. Have the information sent here—to the courthouse in Springfield. I'll give you an address when I've decided whether to return to Boston or not."

The officer scribbled out a note and handed it to her. "Here's the fee for services. Pay up now, please."

She stared at the slip of paper. "There's a fee to search for military records? They ought to be available to the public! Besides, that Confederate soldier probably isn't even my brother."

"Look, ma'am, it's all the same to me whether he's your brother or not. You want records, you pay your fee. This was a civil war, ma'am. You think the Federals are coughing up their own money for a Confederate officer to sit here and jaw with you?"

Hannah drew open her purse and took out the required money. The night before she had laid each remaining silver coin on the bed and planned exactly how she would put it to best use. Now she would have no choice but to go back to Boston. What she had left would hardly pay her fare, let alone provide her a place to stay in Missouri while she waited for news of this missing Rebel soldier who couldn't possibly be Ethan.

She set the fee on the desk and closed her purse. "Where might I find the telegraph office?"

"Down the hall, ma'am." The officer dropped her money into a metal box and shut the lid. "Next!"

Hannah stepped to one side, her mouth dry. All right, she would send a telegram to her mother stating that she simply had done the very best she could. Then she would find transportation to Rolla, purchase a train ticket there, and hope she could make it to Boston before she starved to death.

Why in heaven's name had she given that officer her money? Ethan was a Boston man—a Federal born and bred. His own father had fought for the Union and had been killed in service to his country. Of *course* E. Brownlow wasn't her brother.

Entering the telegraph office, she heard the *click-click* of the machine as it relayed messages over a network of wire from Springfield to Rolla to St. Louis and on to the East.

"I want to send a message to Boston," she told the young clerk. "My name is Hannah Brownlow."

"Brownlow?" He frowned and began to search through sheets of paper in a pigeonhole desk. "Seems to me we got in a message for you a few days back. I believe I recall that name . . . yes, ma'am. Here 'tis. Hannah Brownlow. You told someone in Boston you'd be passin' through Springfield?"

"Yes, my mother . . . but I didn't expect . . ." Taking the message, Hannah unfolded it.

"You know how to read?" the clerk asked.

She lifted her head in surprise. "Of course I do."

He shrugged. "Just askin'. I'll read a telegram for a nickel."

Hannah returned to the message. Everyone in this state, it seemed, was out to take her money.

"Find Ethan and bring him home soon," she read. "Military pension only a token. Desperate. Have let cook go. Can live two months on savings. Sophie and Brigitte may look for work."

A chill slid down Hannah's spine. She read the telegram again. How could her father's military pension have been merely a token? A family whose sole support had died in battle deserved the most financial assistance the government could provide! The cook . . . well, that part didn't seem so terrible. In the past weeks of travel, Hannah had certainly seen people facing greater hardship than adjusting to the loss of household help.

Was her mother correct in calculating that the family could live just two months on the savings from Hannah's book royalties? And would Sophie and Brigitte actually lower themselves to search for work? Perish the thought!

Hannah folded the telegram and slipped it into her purse. Almost no money and hardly a trace of Ethan. What if he had fought as a volunteer in some battle and been killed? She might never find him. But how could she return to Boston without him? Could a family of five live on the earnings from her books indefinitely? She had managed to support them through the war. But forever?

Hurrying back down the hall to the Confederate office, she caught herself chewing her lower lip. "Where else can I look for my brother?" she asked an officer standing near the door. "We last heard of him in southwest Missouri. Where should I go?"

"Been to Joplin? There was a battle near there at Carthage in '61. A lot of the trouble with Kansas was centered in that area. Officials in Joplin ought to have some records."

"Joplin, then."

"'Course, Forsyth saw a lot of action, too. Now, that town's directly south of Springfield. You'll find a Union outpost there with hundreds of refugees—mostly women and children. I don't know if I'd go if I was you, though. Lots of renegades in those woods."

"Bushwhackers?"

"Yep. They can stir up a heap of trouble and then ride for Arkansas if things get hot. Forsyth's a rough place."

"All right, Forsyth." She lifted her chin. "I'm sure I can take care of myself, sir. Thank you very much."

"Good luck to you. If you go to Forsyth, you'll need it."

In spite of her bravado, Hannah realized her hands were knotted into tight fists as she left the office. For the thousandth time, she ground out the question: *Where* was Ethan? If he were alive, why hadn't he written to the family long ago? He must be dead. But if he had been killed, what would the Brownlows do?

As she walked out of the courthouse into the sunshine, Hannah turned the question around and around. First, she decided, she *must* finish her novel—and quickly. The sooner it arrived in New York, the sooner she would be paid.

Second, she must think of a way to obtain enough money to continue her travels until she had exhausted her search through Missouri. She had already covered the northern half of the state by speaking with authorities in St. Louis and in the capital, Jefferson City.

Springfield had turned up only the Confederate E. Brownlow, but Joplin might provide information. Forsyth, too, should be explored. That would take care of the southwest.

Then she could travel to Rolla and ask there. The southeast was no good—almost uninhabitable swamps. It hadn't played much of a part in the war, so she could avoid it and still consider her mission accomplished.

Hurrying down the steps, she thought about the possessions in her trunk. Perhaps she could sell something. Her pearl earrings? Would anyone in this backward place actually want earrings? How much would they earn? She didn't want to be swindled again.

Hannah crossed to the west side of South Street. As she stepped onto the boardwalk, a hand touched her arm. The human contact brought her quickly back to reality. Luke? She caught her breath and turned her head.

"Morning, Miss Brownlow." Bill Hickok doffed his hat.

"Oh, Mr. Hickok. Good morning."

He was dressed as before—minus his fancy jewelry and

watch. The revolver strapped around his waist was an obvious addition to his dandy outfit. "Nice day, ain't it?" he asked.

"Passable."

"Say, you seen anything of David Tutt? He's that Rebel I introduced you to yesterday."

"No, I haven't seen Mr. Tutt. I haven't been looking."

"Well, I been looking, but I ain't been finding." He sniffed and fingered his revolver.

"I see you're armed this morning, Mr. Hickok."

"This here's my Colt's dragoon. Cap and ball, you know. Finest weapon in the West. So, what'd you think of my show last night? Ever seen a horse could do tricks?"

"I can't imagine that your horse enjoyed it particularly. How is he faring today?"

"Ain't checked on him yet. He's over to the livery stable on the northwest corner there." Hickok leaned forward suddenly and squinted. A scowl formed on his face. "I'll be damned. That's Tutt!"

Hannah watched as the former Confederate stepped out of the shadows of the stable and began to walk south along the square. The moment passersby became aware of the approaching encounter, they began to gather in excited clusters. Children pointed. Doors fell open, and people hurried out onto the sidewalk.

"I understand Mr. Tutt is your friend," Hannah said, hoping she could somehow defuse the confrontation. "Perhaps he's coming along to chat with you."

Hickok snorted. "Well, it's all right if he ain't got my watch on, but if he does, there'll be merry hell, you bet your life!"

"Mornin', Bill." A young man tipped his hat as he and a group of onlookers surrounded the showman. Hannah tried to step aside, but she was caught up in the crowd of men.

"Hey, Freddy," Hickok returned. "Is your big brother wearin' that watch?"

"Reckon so. Mighty pretty one, too. A Waltham, ain't it?"

"Damn right."

"Gold hunting case, I understand. Gold chain and seal, too. Why, I'd say it's the finest sort of a watch, wouldn't you, Bill?"

"I'd say it is, Freddy."

Hannah looked from one man to the other. They reminded

her of schoolboys baiting one another for a fight, and she had
the urge to give each of them a sharp rap on the knuckles.

"You'd better go and tell Dave to take off that watch,"
Hickok snapped.

"I think he has a right to wear what he pleases if it belongs
to him."

"He shan't wear that watch anyhow."

By now, David Tutt was clearly visible as he walked toward
his younger brother and Bill Hickok. Hannah saw that the
Rebel also wore a sidearm.

"There he comes now," Hickok said. He took a few steps
forward and drew his Colt.

"There's gonna be a shootin'!" someone shouted. "Lay
low!"

The crowd scattered.

Hannah picked up her skirts and ran for the courthouse. This
couldn't be happening. Men didn't really fire guns at one
another in broad daylight, did they? Shooting was for wars, not
for silly gambling debts. These two were as bad as the
bushwhackers—or worse! As she scampered the last few
paces, she saw Tutt reach the corner of the courthouse and
Campbell Street.

"Dave, don't you come across here with that watch," Hickok
warned as he placed his gun hand on his other arm to steady his
aim.

Tutt drew his pistol. Instantly Hickok fired. The bullet tore
into Tutt's chest. Blood splattered across his shirt, scarlet
against white. A look of terror and disbelief crossed his ashen
face before he collapsed to the ground in a shapeless heap.

The watching crowd erupted. Women shrieked, and men
began to shout. Cries of "Murder, murder!" mingled with calls
for help. The acrid scent of gunpowder suffused the air.
Belatedly arriving on the scene, the sheriff called for order and
calm.

Shuddering, sickened, Hannah shut her eyes and sank
backward to rest her shoulders against the wall of the courthouse. Instead of meeting with cold stone, she felt a warm arm
slide around her waist and draw her into the haven of a solid,
male chest.

"Hannah," Luke said against her ear. "I'm here."

"Oh, Luke . . ." As someone began to wail, she turned her face into his body and pressed her cheek against his shirt. His hands molded around her shoulder, his fingers massaging her skin as if he might pour his own strength into her.

"Come away from this place, Hannah," he whispered.

"But Mr. Tutt . . . Will he live?"

"No," Luke said simply. "The bullet entered near his heart. He walks in Spiritland." He began to lead her away from the milling throng, back toward the hotel. "You've seen death now, Hannah. It has an ugly face."

She could only nod. Images of the moment swirled through her mind—the confusion and disbelief, the single gunshot, the crimson bloodstain, the look of horror on Tutt's face before he fell. And then Luke's warm body engulfing and protecting her.

Where had he come from? Had he been nearby all morning? Or had the disturbance on the street drawn him from some errand? The reason hardly mattered. It was enough that his arm was around her and his clean scent surrounded her.

"Here's the hotel," he told her. "Do you want to rest?"

"No," she managed. "I want to get away. I have to leave this awful city."

They climbed the steps, but he stopped on the porch before entering the lobby. "Where will you go, Hannah?"

"Forsyth."

"Forsyth is too dangerous. Worse than Springfield."

"Joplin, then."

"Let me take you back to Bolivar. You can stay in a hotel there. That old *Nika-sabe* woman is your friend. You'll have someone to talk to."

"But my brother. I—"

"Write letters to Forsyth and Joplin."

"I wish I could go to Rolla." She swallowed at the lump in her throat. "There's a train, and I could . . . No. I have to check Joplin first. My mother needs . . . She needs me. She needs Ethan."

"Is your mother as strong a woman as you, Hannah?"

For the first time she lifted her eyes to his face. The sight of him—real, touchable—sent a physical ache deep into her core. Gold flecks shimmered in his brown eyes. A lock of ink-black hair had fallen onto his forehead, and the tip of it touched the slash of one black eyebrow. His mouth mesmerized her as his lips moved over the words he repeated.

"Is your mother like you—a woman of courage and power?"

"Sometimes she's strong," Hannah acknowledged in a low voice. "But she has relied on the support of men all her life. She won't survive without—"

"She *will* survive. If she's like you, she'll survive—with or without a man." He glanced over his shoulder at the crowd milling around the courthouse. "While they're outside, I'll fetch your trunk. We'll ride for Bolivar."

Hannah pressed her fingertips over her eyes as Luke slipped through the hotel door and took the steps two at a time. He was wrong! Her mother wasn't strong—and neither was she. She had spent or been tricked out of most of her money. She had failed to find a confirmed trace of her brother in all these weeks. She had come face-to-face with her utter ignorance of survival outside the protection of her Boston household. She had stood inches away from a man moments before he committed murder! Everything about this trip had taught her that she was weak, naive, and foolish.

"Tutt fired first!" the hotel clerk announced to the saloon keeper as they stepped onto the porch. "I seen it with my own two eyes."

"Hell, you're blind as a bat, you old coot."

"I saw the sheriff studyin' Tutt's pistol, did you? One chamber was empty. I'd swear I heard two shots."

The clerk paused and worked up a gob of tobacco spittle. Remembering her two dollars, Hannah glared at him. He sneered and spat a long brown arc into the flower bed.

"Is Mr. Tutt really dead?" she asked.

"As a doornail. Took everybody by surprise that he missed. He was a crack shot, Tutt was."

"I certainly didn't hear two shots fired."

"Aw, what do you know about anything, woman?" He ran his brown tongue around the inside of his mouth, then turned back to the saloon keeper. "I'd wager Hickok's shot was a pure accident. Seventy-five paces? That was a chance shot, sure as hell."

"Circuit court's in session, anyhow. They'll indict Hickok, arrest him on a bench warrant, and bring him to trial."

"I reckon so. You think he'll stand a chance?"

The bartender shrugged. "You keep tellin' your story about hearin' two shots, and he might."

Both men were chuckling when Luke shouldered his way out the front door with Hannah's trunk in his arms. As he started across the porch, the old clerk stiffened. "Hey, you! Indian!"

Luke paused and turned around.

"You been inside my establishment, Indian?"

"Just collecting the lady's trunk."

"The hell you say!" The old man stepped up to Luke and spat a stream of red-brown tobacco juice onto the toe of his boot. "We don't tolerate no savages at Lyon House. Get your red hide out of this town before I call the sheriff to arrest you. Won't nobody testify on *your* behalf, I guarantee."

"I would," Hannah announced. "And if there is an uncivilized worm to be found at Lyon House, he's working behind the front desk."

Tucking her hand around Luke's arm, she gave the clerk a disdainful sniff. "You may escort me to the wagon, Mr. Maples," she told Luke. "Twenty-four hours in this bestial city are enough to convince me that I should like nothing better than the company of a gentleman."

Chapter
Eight

"I'll pay you two dollars to take me to Joplin," Hannah told Luke as the wagon rolled out of Springfield. "Two silver dollars."

He gave a short laugh. "It's seventy miles from here to Joplin, Hannah. One way. The round trip would take me a week—assuming I wouldn't get stuck in the mud again. And if I don't show up in Bolivar tonight or tomorrow morning with these supplies, I'll lose my job."

She studied the thick growth of oak, walnut, and hickory trees that closed in along the sides of the narrow road. Vines tangled the higher branches, and scrubby brush filled in the spaces between the trunks. A familiar constricted, confined feeling slipped around Hannah's throat like a noose. "All right, three dollars."

"Why do you want to go to Joplin anyway?" he asked, though he already knew. Her determination to find her brother ate at her as relentlessly as his own need to find his father's killer.

"They might have some word of Ethan there," she said.

"I thought you wanted to go home to Boston."

"I do—with all my heart. But I can't leave Missouri without Ethan." She gnawed at her lip. "If you won't take me to Joplin, then how about Forsyth? I'll pay you three dollars."

"I wouldn't drive you to Forsyth for three hundred dollars."

She glanced at him in surprise. "Three hundred dollars would buy you all the land you could ever want."

"And a trip to Forsyth would probably mean the end of Hannah Brownlow." Realizing that he'd revealed more of his concern for her than he intended, Luke gave a shrug. "Besides, I couldn't buy land in Missouri even if I had three thousand dollars."

"Whyever not?"

"I'm a savage," he spat. "Or did you forget?"

Prickling, she met his steady gaze. "I might have thought you a savage once, but not anymore. You heard what I told that disgusting hotel clerk."

"I did. But your defense won't do me any good, and it might hurt your own reputation."

"I don't care what anyone thinks of me. I never have."

"Something's bothering you, Hannah," he said, the combative tone leaving his voice as swiftly as it had appeared. "You've torn the skin from your lip."

He reached toward her, and with the tip of one finger he dabbed the bead of bright blood. Her eyes followed his hand as he brought it to his own mouth and touched the scarlet droplet to his tongue. He paused a moment, then spoke in a voice so low she could hardly hear.

"I have felt your fire-hair, Hannah Brownlow," he said, "and now I understand the taste of you."

A shiver slid down her spine at the feral gesture. Disturbed yet fascinated, she struggled to grasp the meaning behind his words. He was staring at her, as if waiting for some response. What could she say? She could barely breathe.

Searching for a reply, she pressed her fingers against her lip to stanch the seeping blood. When that proved useless, she touched the spot with the tip of her tongue. He watched every movement, his falcon's eyes intent.

"What bothers me at this moment," she finally managed, "is you, Luke Maples."

"Why?"

"Where did you come from today? How did you find me at the courthouse? Why am I on your wagon riding back to Bolivar?"

"And why does my touch make your desire flow like the sap of a tree in springtime? And why do you wish that it hadn't been my finger against your lips . . . but my mouth?"

For a breathless second, she gaped at him. Then she squared her shoulders and narrowed her eyes. "Stop this wagon at once. I intend to get down."

"Calm yourself, Hannah." He couldn't keep the smile from his face. She was as jittery as a young doe—and he had to admit that around this woman he felt like a buck in rut. But he knew he had to control his urges. She was off limits.

"I was near the courthouse today for the same reason everyone else in town was there," he said, telling her something close to the truth. "I wanted to see the confrontation between Hickok and Tutt. I spotted you by the wall and thought I'd ask how your search for your brother had gone. When I started across the grass, Hickok fired."

Hannah had scooted as far to the edge of the seat as her hoop would allow. Did he actually expect her to listen to him? He had tasted her blood! He had said things that should never be voiced between decent, respectable men and women. He *was* a savage after all. She had to get off the wagon.

"So, did you find any trace of your brother?" he asked.

"I asked you to stop this wagon." She crossed her arms. "Do it now, please."

"I won't touch you again, Hannah."

"Why should I trust you?"

"Because you know you can. We spent a night alone together, and I kept my distance . . . Not that I wanted to."

At his confession she felt her cheeks flame. "This entire situation is intolerable. I don't want to go back to Bolivar. I don't want to ride in this rickety wagon. And I don't want to listen to you."

"Then read to me again. I'd like to hear more of your book

about the red-haired woman and her Heavy Eyebrows husband."

"There isn't any more," Hannah said in a bald-faced lie. She
certainly wasn't about to tell him she'd spent almost the whole
previous night adding pages and pages to her story. Her
life—and especially her book—were none of his business, and
the less he knew about her the better.

"Then tell me," he said, "what you were writing in your
room until the Moon Woman was bright in the sky."

Again Hannah could do nothing but stare at him. His face,
impassive, was turned to the road. His eyes focused straight
ahead.

"How do you know what I was doing last night?" she
demanded.

"I watched your bedroom from the street."

"What? Why in heaven's name did you do that?"

"To make sure you were safe." He propped one foot on the
front board of the wagon and regarded her evenly. "You tell me
you wrote nothing new, but I saw you writing. Maybe *I*
shouldn't trust *you*, Hannah Brownlow."

"I . . . I . . ." Flustered, she felt the heat rise in her
cheeks. "I don't think my writing is any of your affair."

"Why not? You read your whole manuscript to me on the
way to Springfield. Besides . . . I'm interested. I want to
know more about that blond-haired farmer who lives over the
hill in a fine brick house."

"Stone house. I changed it."

"Hmm." Luke pondered this for a moment. He knew he had
disconcerted Hannah, and he didn't want to drive her farther
away. But he couldn't seem to check his words. Everything
about her interested him—her thoughts, her feelings, her
reactions. And he knew those facets of her would be reflected
in the book.

"It seems to me," he said finally, "that our young Elizabeth
might have some romantic interest in the farmer."

"Of course she doesn't," Hannah snapped at him. What did
he know about her characters anyway? "Elizabeth is happily
married. That should have been obvious from the start of the
book."

"Why aren't you happily married, Hannah?"

"Because I—" she began, and then cut herself off before she said something she might regret.

She studied the tops of the trees, aware that the wagon was taking her farther and farther from Springfield. Should she insist that Luke return? Or should she ride with him to Bolivar and wait for news of Ethan there? In Bolivar, she knew she would rest. In Bolivar, she could counsel with Miss Ruth. In Bolivar, she would see Luke Maples . . . perhaps every day.

"I have never desired a husband, and I never shall," she said quickly before her train of thought got out of hand. "I wish to write books for the remainder of my life."

"A husband wouldn't let you write books?"

"Certainly not. Any husband I'd marry would have to meet my mother's requirements. Foremost, he'd have to be wealthy. A wealthy husband would not require additional income from his wife's employment. A wealthy husband would not approve of a working wife. A wealthy husband would exist in a social strata that frowns on the literary domestic."

"Why would anyone frown on what you do?"

"Have you never heard of the magazine *The Round Table*?" When Luke didn't respond, she gave a shrug. "It's highly respected. Last year a critic deigned to comment on the writing of novels for and by women. He called our books shoddy, flippant, and bombastic. He said they were trash. Literary quagmires."

"And you place value on what this man wrote?"

"He's a highly regarded critic. He said that women's novels have but one wretched thread of a plot upon which to hang the incidents. He said they're full of dreary platitudes and sickly sentiment. Do you know what he called our books? 'A strange farrago of the namby-pamby and the disgusting.' That's exactly what he said. *The Round Table*. You could go to a library and look up the articles, both of them. January and February, 1864."

Luke ventured a glance at Hannah and observed the fine flare to her nostrils, the hot pink in her cheeks, and the shimmer in her blue eyes. She was angry. Angrier than he'd ever seen her.

Her rage at the critic's attitude told him that her books were as important to her as she had said they were. She had been furious over the bushwhacker attack and livid at the hotel clerk's prejudice. But one critic's low regard of women's novel writing had utterly outraged her.

That a woman might place her work over marriage and family was a new idea to Luke. He knew he himself had ranked marriage far beneath his twin goals of regaining his tribe's lost Missouri lands and seeking out his father's killer. But a woman forgoing motherhood? He wanted to explore this passion in Hannah.

"This critic must be a very important man," he said. "He must know a lot about writing books. I suppose he's written a good many himself."

"I have no idea. They usually don't, you know, these critics. I have my doubts that some of them even read our books."

"Then he must have talked to people who read the sort of novels he criticized. But maybe not too many people read your kind of books, Hannah. Is that it?"

"Honestly!" She fixed him with a look that would have set fire to water. "Novels were the second largest number of books issued during the war, I'll have you know. Only juvenile literature ranked higher. Even though the price of paper doubled, the cost of printing and binding went up, and skilled labor was scarce, more novels were published than ever before. Popular authors sold forty thousand books in two or three months. My novels came very close to selling that number. Many books sold fifty thousand copies, and a few even one hundred thousand. Now, take *East Lynne*—"

"I'd rather take Hannah Brownlow," Luke cut in. "And I think those who read her books would, too. You've given that critic too much power. Draw power from those who enjoy what you do."

Hannah shot him a look of surprise. "You're defending me?"

"I like the book you're writing. It has depth and strength. Within its words, I can read your heart."

She gazed at the road ahead for a moment, hardly knowing what to say next. One minute this man was tasting her blood, the next he was defending her literary style. Was he a savage or a gentleman? Should she flee the wagon at the first possible moment, or should she trust him to take her safely to Bolivar?

"So your mother would have you marry a wealthy man,"

Luke said suddenly. "And then you would stop writing your books."

"I *won't* stop writing."

"What else does this mother of yours expect you to find in a good husband?"

"Education. College at the very least. She'd prefer a physician, of course, or a lawyer. If not that, then the owner of some profitable business in downtown Boston."

"And these things are important to you, too?"

"If I were to marry, which I won't, I suppose I would want a man like that." She studied his face. He was watching the road, alert for signs of travelers, wildlife, or outlaws, but she knew he was listening intently to her answers.

"Personally," she said, "I've always thought politicians were fascinating."

Luke grunted. *Politicians!* Like those scoundrels who had tricked his people into selling their land? Yes, he could just see it now—Hannah living in a big house in New York with fine carriages at the door, hundreds of *Nika-sabe* servants to wait on her, and so many swinging silk skirts they would fill her trunks to overflowing.

In spite of her passion for writing books, she would marry someday. Of that Luke felt sure. A woman like Hannah had too much fire to live alone forever. And although she had an independent streak as wide as the Missouri River, she was bound by the societal conventions her mother had instilled in her.

Hannah's husband would probably be some wealthy Heavy Eyebrows man with lots of money in the bank and a fine university education. They would have intellectual conversations over dinner and stimulating visits with others in their circle. And when the lights went out, they would sleep beneath layers of quilts and gowns, and she would bear his children.

"And what sort of woman will you marry?" Hannah asked, breaking into his thoughts.

"Osage," Luke shot back. "I want a woman with black hair and brown skin and the eyes of a swan. She'll wear dresses of deerskin scented with crushed columbine seed. Beautiful tattoos will cover her body. My wife will know the ways of the Osage. She'll understand how the Little People came down from the stars, and she'll sing *wi-gi-es* to Grandfather the Sun and the Moon Woman. She'll know how to build a strong lodge, a home warm enough to keep out winter winds."

Speaking his dream aloud, Luke felt the flame rekindle inside him. A woman like that was exactly what he desired. A fit wife would know the right things and be able to do all the necessary tasks to make life full and healthy. She would be full-blooded Osage, and within the nest of her body he would create a future for his people.

"My wife will know how to butcher a buffalo," he continued, "and use its hide to make blankets and rugs, its sinews for thongs, its horns to carve spoons, its tallow for preserving meat, and its paunch for making kettles. She'll know how to smoke its meat and dry strips of it on the rocks. The woman I marry will be skilled in planting and gathering wild vegetables. She'll make our clothing. She'll bear me many sons and daughters. And together we'll rebuild the line of the Osage."

"How absolutely perfect," Hannah said. "I wish you all the happiness."

Luke heard the chilly note in her voice and wondered what it meant. Had his picture of the Osage wife he wanted somehow reflected on Hannah—as the image of her in bed with a Heavy Eyebrows husband had reflected on him? He hadn't intended it to. But he couldn't deny that this white woman on the wagon seat beside him would make the worst sort of wife imaginable.

Of course, he would make a terrible husband for her, too. He wanted land, not money. He cared nothing for city life, mercantile trade, banks, or politics. His days were filled with fresh air, sunshine, and hunting with his falcon. At night he often slept naked beneath the silver light of the Moon Woman.

It was a good thing he recognized that the Hannah Brownlow who walked in his dreams was merely an image of sexual desire. She was a woman—intriguing, beautiful, sensual—and she had triggered the male needs he kept carefully suppressed. At least he understood these feelings for what they were, and therefore he could keep them separate from his true desire for a woman of his own people.

"I don't suppose you Osage know the first thing about love,

do you?" Hannah asked. "I have read that romantic love was a late medieval development evoked by the necessity of lords to leave their ladies at the castle alone for great lengths of time in the company of unwedded knights. Then the French troubadours got hold of the notion and began to popularize it in their songs until—"

"We know about love," Luke cut in.

"That's good. I thought you might have those horrid arranged marriages where some distant relative sets everything up."

"My uncle."

"I beg your pardon?"

"My uncle is the man who'll find a wife for me. He'll look for a girl from a different clan and then visit her parents. They'll engage the girl's uncle, and the two men will arrange everything—the feasts, the exchange of gifts, the joy-weeping, the race for prizes, and after the wedding, the instructions about married life and its duties."

"Oh." Hannah clamped her mouth shut. She had heard of formulated marriages, but she could hardly fathom how they survived.

"In time an Osage man and his wife learn to love each other," Luke explained. "They care about the same things— their home, their children, their future—and so they build a dream. Out of that dream, the love is born."

She considered this for a moment. "I suppose when you put it that way it doesn't sound so different from the way we marry in Boston. A man might fall in love with me and court me, but in the end it would be up to our parents to arrange everything. Still, I wouldn't like the idea of marrying someone I hardly knew."

"I probably won't ever have seen the woman I marry."

"Really? What if she's homely?"

Luke had to laugh. "I don't know of an ugly Osage. You, with all your reading, should have heard that Mr. Washington Irving called us the finest-looking Indians he had seen in the West. We're all tall—most of our men are well over six feet. Our people are strong, muscular, handsome."

"And modest." Hannah gave him the hint of a smile. Then she leaned her back against the seat, tilted her face upward to the rose-tinted evening sky, and took a deep breath. "Ah, well, I hope you're terribly happy, Luke Maples," she said. "I hope you build the grandest Osage lodge in all the world, marry the most beautiful woman God ever created, sire fifteen strong children, and hunt for countless rabbits with your falcon, because I have decided you are really quite a decent man and you deserve the best life has to offer."

Luke ran his eyes down her form as she stretched out, her eyes shut, her face hued with the light of the setting sun. Her hair caught fire, and beneath her bonnet, it glowed and sparked a bright orange-red. In spite of all he had just said about the woman of his dreams, he wanted to touch Hannah. He wanted to hold her body tightly against his. He knew he would never tire of hearing her laughter, her chatter, her thoughts. He wanted to know her completely, inside and out.

Under her bodice, her breasts rose and fell with each breath. Her pulse throbbed in the tiny hollow of the base of her throat. She smelled of soap, and he couldn't help turning on the seat, bending near her neck to take in the full measure of her scent. If God had ever created a most beautiful woman, it was this one . . . this Hannah Brownlow.

"I hope you're happy, too," he told her in a low voice. "I hope you write a hundred books and sell so many copies that the *Round Table* critic is forced to speak well of you. Because I have decided you are a most intriguing and beautiful woman . . . and you deserve the best life has to offer."

She smiled at his words, but then her face went solemn again.

"You know, there are times," she murmured, her eyes still closed and her breath soft against his cheek, "when I almost feel happy, Luke. And there are times when I think I shall never ease this unbearable ache inside me."

"Which time is this?"

At the sound of his voice so close, she opened her eyes. He was a breath away. "I'm aching."

"Hannah," he whispered, "you are a mystery woman."

He lifted a hand and touched a tendril of hair that had escaped her bonnet. Sifting the lock through his fingertips, he tried to steady the drumbeat of his heart. As the strands of fire-hair slipped to her breast, he ran his finger across her lip.

The moistness there told him of other places on her body . . . places he might find damp were he to touch her at this moment. She was everything he wanted, and everything he couldn't have.

"Your lip is soft again," he said.

"You must have a magic touch." She watched the effect of her words on him, and realized that she had said too much. He was so near she could feel the heat emanating from his skin. His eyes seemed to pierce and consume her. She knew if she tilted her head the barest inch, her lips would brush against his mouth. And she wanted to. *Oh, please, Luke. Kiss me.*

"You have magic hair," he told her, tugging the ribbon beneath her chin so that it came loose and her bonnet tumbled into the bed of the wagon. "Your hair burns in my dreams."

Her heart danced as he slipped his fingers through the curls she had so carefully arranged that morning. One by one, he drew out the pins and dropped them until her hair tumbled to her shoulders and then slid down her back. He took clumps of her hair, weighed it, crushed it, sifted it, his eyes never leaving her face for an instant. She could hear his breath, ragged and labored, and she knew he was turning over the consequences of desire as he stroked her hair.

She should say something . . . put a stop to the madness . . . spurn him as she had spurned so many. But the dusk covered them in a warm blanket, and she knew no one but God would see. Would He care if she succumbed for just one moment to this man whose path had crossed hers and who would soon travel on alone?

Swallowing her fear, she lifted her hand and touched the side of his face. His skin was as smooth and tight as she had dreamed it would be. She allowed her fingers to trail across his cheekbone and then down to his jaw. The rounded muscle clenched and loosened as he gritted his teeth in a struggle for control.

And then his neck . . . oh, but it was warm as her fingers slipped beneath his collar. His own hand had left her hair and formed around her shoulder. As the horse plodded on, Luke drew her closer . . . easing her shoulder against his chest . . . running his hand down her arm . . . bending toward her cheek . . .

Sparks showered through her, scattering across her breasts, shooting to their crests, filtering down to her stomach, lighting fires deep inside her body. She could feel his breath heat the soft down of her ear. The side of his finger stroked up her neck, paused beneath her chin, tilted her face toward his. *Kiss me! Oh, Luke, kiss me now* . . .

She could see him above her, silhouetted in the gathering darkness, his hair lifting in the breeze that was the blessing of night. Though she couldn't see his eyes, she could feel them . . . falcon's eyes, watching, assessing, measuring the moment. She could almost hear the questions rippling through him. *If I kiss you, Hannah, what will it mean? Will you reject me? Will you want me? What will become of us?*

She didn't care what happened. At this moment she knew only one thing—this man had awakened something inside her, and only he could satisfy it. Her hand moved down his neck and over the front of his shirt. The hard pectoral muscles tightened at her touch, and she marveled at the swell of brawn and the power of bone in his body.

What would his bare skin feel like? The image of touching his naked flesh sent a melting heat through her core. It settled between her thighs and began to purr . . . like a cat waiting to be stroked.

She let her hand fall to his thigh, her fingers spreading over the thick, taut ridges of sinew. At her touch he let out a deep groan of release and jerked her hard against his chest.

"Hannah!" he ground out.

Her breasts were crushed against his chest, and the breath was forced from her lungs. His fingers curved behind her neck, his thumb beneath her jaw. Roughly he pushed her chin up.

But his mouth, when it covered hers, was gentle.

His lips searched . . . explored . . . caressed. They dampened hers and brushed over the sensitive, delicate skin again and again. The purring inside her grew louder, more demanding, more urgent. She drank his kiss, reveling in the intimacy of his mouth moving on hers.

When his tongue moistened her lips, it was a feral sensation, wild and savage, and she blossomed inside like a new flower. As his fingers slid through her hair, she parted her lips and met his touch.

He shuddered. Opening to each other, they tasted inner secrets like explorers at a well of mystery. She caressed the inner lining of his mouth, and felt him stroke across her teeth. He entered her, hard one moment, tender the next. The purring inside her became a throb, the incessant beat of a war drum. She crossed her legs, hoping to ease the pulsing, but her action merely increased the tempo.

"Hannah," Luke murmured, drawing away for a moment. "*Tha'gthin-xtsi.* Beautiful."

Never in his life had he kissed a woman in this way. Never had he held one so close. But this Hannah kept nothing from him. Trembling with need, she responded to his every touch, every caress. He knew she was as morally bound to restraint as he was . . . but if she were free to give herself to him, would she come willingly? Would her body light him on fire and would his draw forth the sweet milk of her response? Was it possible that this woman—so far from him in culture and outlook—would meet him on equal ground if they lay together?

How many times had he heard of the magic a man might draw out of a woman if he loved her with tenderness, skill, patience? Could he take Hannah to that meeting place where the sun joined the moon and the stars fell from the sky?

Pulling her closer, he took her shoulders and turned her so that her breasts fully pressed into his chest. She wrapped her arms around him and let her lips trail down his neck. Her kisses lit a flame on his skin, a fire that burned through his heart and heated the coals that always lay lurking in his loins. Instantly he grew rigid and hot. His thoughts tangled. They swirled and twisted beneath the demanding pressure in his body.

How could a man be patient and tender? He wanted Hannah now. He had to have her! Her hands danced down his neck, stroking his singing muscles. Her breasts pushed into his chest, and he could feel her nipples like tiny cherries just waiting to be plucked and savored. Her mouth moved up and down his neck, her tongue tasting his skin.

He couldn't wait. He wouldn't. The horses had abandoned the journey and wandered to the road's edge to sample some grass. Luke didn't care. He couldn't think about tomorrow and his lost land. He couldn't think about the past and his murdered father. He only knew that now this woman was warm, alive, hungry for him.

Touch her, his body demanded. Know her. Taste her. Capturing her mouth again, he slipped his hands from her shoulders down to the rise of her breasts. Her breath caught and hung as he slowly molded his palms up, around, over the twin mounds of full, ripe flesh. At the feel of her cherried nipples, a surge ran through his loins once again, swelling, hardening, pushing for release.

Oh, she was beautiful. Perfect. He cupped her breasts and lifted, enjoying their weight. He brushed his thumbs across their tips and heard her gasp. He was pleasing her! Again he stroked her nipples, running his fingertips around them, then cresting over their tips until she was breathing like a winded doe.

He would take her. Tonight. Here, in the bed of this wagon. He would strip away her clothes and lie naked with her—a man and a woman alone beneath the eyes of the Moon Woman. He reached for the button on her bodice and began to work it loose.

"Oh, Luke," she whispered, a tremble in her voice. "Luke, please."

"Please what?" He brushed apart the edges of ruffled fabric and let his fingers drift over her bare skin.

"Please help me to think."

"I don't want to think. Not tonight."

"This can't be happening." She shut her eyes and fought the sensations he was evoking. How many times had she said those words, and yet these were amazing things happening to her . . . they had happened . . .

"I won't hurt you, Hannah," he said.

"But you will. It's not only my arms that want you tonight, it's my heart."

He lifted his head and gazed into her face. Moon Woman had risen just enough to reveal the expression of fear and longing in Hannah's eyes. Luke touched her cheek. He listened to the hoot of an owl. Ahead of the wagon, the horse tore up a clump of grass. A breeze cooled his heated skin.

"Hannah, don't give me your heart," he said.

"I won't mean to. But I'm a woman. My heart is a part of my body. What one desires, the other must have, too."

Pulling back from her, Luke raked a hand through his hair and took a deep breath. "This is a mistake."

"I know," she acknowledged, her voice barely audible. "It's my fault. I've been lonely and confused, and you're so . . . so kind and different from other men."

"I take full responsibility." He leaned forward, elbows on his knees, and rested his face in his hands. Even now—when his brain had begun to work again—his body demanded her. He was swollen and in pain from his need. His fingers shook with the desire to touch her again. So close . . . he had come so close to uncovering the mystery of her breasts. He could still feel the rounded pebbles of her nipples on his fingertips. He tasted the sweet fragrance of her mouth. Her hair burned on his hands.

Gritting his teeth, he prayed for restraint. He had to let her go. Had to give her up. Not even the knowledge that she was still beside him, still ripe, still warm and soft and ready for him, could stand in the way.

"It's this place," she whispered. "Missouri. Nothing is predictable here. I thought there would be quaint farms and apple orchards—but there's only wild forest. I thought the war was over—but here it's still alive. I thought you were a savage, a heathen—but you're . . . you're wonderful."

"I'm not wonderful," he exploded, sitting up and grabbing her shoulders so that she was forced to face him. "I'm an Osage Indian warrior, just like all your books say. I've counted coup seven times—twice on the dead bodies of my enemies. I wear a knife, Hannah. Before you take another breath, I could slit your throat and slice your scalp from your skull. I'm trained to hate you and kill you. Your people betrayed and robbed mine. I was taught to despise you for that. Don't mistake me for a Boston gentleman. Don't dream me into someone I'm not, Hannah."

"And don't underestimate my intelligence. I know who you are. I also know you won't slit my throat. I know you're honest and moral. I know I can trust you."

"Don't trust me! Don't trust anyone, Hannah." He shook her roughly. "You are my enemy!"

"I don't believe that. I won't believe you despise me. If you hated me, you couldn't have kissed me so gently. And you wouldn't have stopped when you did. You *did* stop, Luke."

"Because what I want from you is wrong."

"What do you want from me?" She waited, studying his face as he searched for the answer to her question. When he said nothing, she took his hands from her shoulders and laced her fingers through his. "Perhaps the kiss was a mistake. Perhaps we'll regret it for the rest of our lives. But not because it was a sin. Not because you and I are enemies. We may regret that kiss because it was the one moment when we forgot we're supposed to be enemies, and instead we accepted that we enjoy one another's company, we take pleasure in our conversation, we appreciate our similarities and differences, and we each find the other desirable. We may live to regret our kiss because we let it go. We did the proper thing, and we stopped. And we know we shall never capture that moment again."

She slipped her hands out of his and took up the reins. "If you will please drive me into Bolivar now," she said, handing them to him, "I shall take a room at the hotel, and from there I shall see to my future."

Chapter
Nine

❦

Grandfather the Sun lit the sky with the first hues of pink just as Luke spotted the distant courthouse on Bolivar's central square. He reached to his boot and wiped a clump of mud from the toe. Pressing it to his forehead, he shut his eyes.

"Sacred is the act by which my hands are blackened," he murmured in his native Osage language. "It is the act by which I offer my prayer. Sacred is the act by which my face is blackened. It is the act by which I offer my prayer. Sacred is the light of day that falls upon my face—the morning on which my prayers are lifted up."

For a moment he sat in silence, aware of the sun warming his skin and transforming the dew into mist. A butterfly danced around the purple petals of a coneflower. An orange-furred fox squirrel darted across the road in front of the wagon. In a hawthorn tree near the road, a crimson male cardinal whistled its distinctive cry of "pretty, pretty, pretty."

Luke turned to look at Hannah. Her head, heavy in sleep, lay on his shoulder. Sometime in the darkness she had drifted off, and he had slipped his arm around her to support her tired body. She had sighed, snuggled against him, and slept on.

Watching as the coral light slowly revealed her face, he memorized the soft curve of her cheeks, the deep red-brown tint of her lashes, the smooth damask hue of her lips. The cardinal's song insisted she was pretty . . . but Luke denied that refrain. Hannah was beautiful. Completely, perfectly, amazingly beautiful. His upbringing had taught him that a lovely woman had black hair and copper skin. Hannah had shattered that image in a breath.

As he committed her face to memory, Luke also tried to force down the thoughts and dreams that had swirled through his head all night. He couldn't have her. Couldn't need her.

"Our Father in heaven," he whispered, changing to the tongue of the priest at his mission school, "Your name is holy. May Your kingdom come and Your will be done on earth as it is in heaven. Give me today my daily bread, and forgive me for . . . for wanting Hannah . . . as I try to forgive those men who have done me wrong. Lead me away from temptation, and keep me from evil."

"Amen," Hannah said softly.

Luke swallowed and opened his eyes. Her head was still on his shoulder, but she had lifted her hand and was crossing herself. How much of his prayer had she heard? Was she aware how he had struggled through the dark hours? It didn't matter—it wouldn't be long before he would leave her forever and return to Kansas. Now the wagon was rolling past the charred remains of houses and entering the first populated streets they had seen since Springfield.

"You pray more often than I." Her voice was still soft with sleep. "I never think about God much . . . except at Mass."

"I think about Him all the time. His hands have touched everything important to me—trees, birds, rivers, stones."

"People?"

"Of course." He couldn't help moving his fingers over her shoulder, learning the exact feel of her slender muscles and bones. "God created us, Hannah. You know that."

"Both of us . . . yet you insist we're enemies." She brushed a hand across her cheek as if she could dispel the lure of sleep. "It's odd to think God touches us every day. He must be sad to see how we're taught from birth to despise each other. I don't hate you, Luke. I dreamed about you last night . . . all night."

He stiffened. "Hannah."

· "It was a silly dream, with things drifting in and out. Flowers and rivers and such. I was a falcon, soaring through the sky. Oh, the fresh, clear air . . . the sunshine. Utter ecstasy! I can still feel the wind rippling through my feathers. And you were a bold, majestic golden eagle—"

"Don't tell me this dream, Hannah," he warned. "What happened between us last night was nothing. It meant nothing. I've forgotten it already."

"So have I." She sat up and moved away from him. Of course he didn't want to hear her dream, she realized. He didn't want to be reminded of their kiss. He had told her it was a mistake—and it was. The best thing now was to put all dreams and memories of Luke Maples aside and plan for the future.

Stretching carelessly to show him how little she thought about any of it, she stifled a yawn. "All I can possibly think about is finding Ethan," she said. "I have dozens of letters to write, and I'll want to pay a visit to Miss Ruth. Then there's the matter of money. Do you know of anyone in Bolivar who might want to purchase a pair of pearl earrings?"

"Earrings?"

"Very nice ones—the drop sort. They dangle from a woman's earlobes on little gold chains. I should think they're worth at least . . . oh, ten dollars."

Luke tried to keep a straight face. He couldn't bring himself to look at Hannah now that the sun was fully up, but he had no trouble seeing the poor, bedraggled citizenry of Bolivar town. Not a woman in view wore earrings. Most, in fact, wore nothing but the same kind of faded yellow dress Hannah had found in the cabin. Many had bare feet. Their heads were bonnetless, and they wore patched aprons tied to their waists.

"I doubt you'll find a person in this town with ten dollars to spend on earrings," he said. "Don't you have enough money to stay at the hotel for a few weeks?"

He had dropped the question without thinking, but her silence told him the answer. The little purse she clung to so fiercely must be almost empty. She would be forced to find some way to go on living in Missouri until she could locate her brother.

"I have enough to stay at the hotel," she said carefully, "but I might need extra money for postage and travel and such."

Luke drew the tired horse to a stop in front of the hotel, then sat in silence as he studied the reins in his hand. He wanted to look at Hannah one last time before he left Missouri. He *had* to look at her. But it would kill him—he knew it.

"You might take a job somewhere," he said, keeping his focus on the reins.

"A job? I can't imagine that. Doing what?"

"Cooking."

"Cooking!" She laughed, a bright tinkling sound that tore through his heart. "Scrambled eggs! Oh, dear, I'm afraid that would never do. Perhaps I could teach waltzing lessons." Her laughter turned into a sigh. "No, I'll have to think of something to sell."

Luke swallowed. "Be careful, Hannah. There are men here who would want to buy something other than your pearl earrings."

Without giving her a chance to react to his warning, he stepped down into the street. As he rounded the wagon, he could feel her slipping away from him with each step. She would walk into the hotel, disappear behind the door, and he would never see her again. Never touch her. Never hear the sound of her voice.

A pain he'd never felt before twisted through his chest as he heaved her trunk from the wagon bed to the porch. A knot like a fist swelled up in his throat. Gritty, hard as stone, it settled there, and nothing he could do would dislodge it. He clenched his teeth and made himself repeat the comforting *wi-gi-e* of the hawk for whom he had been named.

"Far above the earth I spread my wings," he murmured, "as across these broad lands I soar. Far, far above the earth—"

"Luke?" Hannah's voice was soft. "Are you speaking to me?"

"No." Still unable to look at her, he kept his eyes on the wagon wheel as he approached.

"Were you praying?" When he didn't answer, she took a breath. "When we're apart, Luke, will you pray for me?"

"If I think of you . . . Summer is a busy time."

"Of course." She gathered her purse and reached for her bonnet where it had fallen behind the seat. "I suppose you'll have a lot of land to survey with all the people coming back to town and searching for land to homestead."

"I won't be with the survey crew."

"Why not?"

"I'm leaving for Kansas." He held out his hands as she finished tying her bonnet. "Back to the reservation."

Hannah couldn't keep the look of dismay from crossing her face. She had counted on seeing Luke—at least catching a glimpse or two—during her time in Bolivar. But he had told her he could never own land in Missouri, and he'd had no luck finding the man who had killed his father. What could keep him here?

She leaned toward him and felt his hands slide around her waist. The touch sent a shiver racing through her bones. Placing her palms on his shoulders, she set her foot on the edge of the wagon. As though she were made of air, he lifted her over the side and lowered her until her feet touched the porch.

"Good-bye, Hannah," he said quickly, and turned away.

"Luke!"

He swung around, and his eyes locked with hers. The shock of meeting clashed between them in reverberating waves. She sucked in a breath.

"I said good-bye, Hannah," he repeated.

"Oh, Luke." She knotted her fingers.

He stared at her a moment longer. Then he turned away again and climbed into the wagon. As she stood alone on the porch, she watched him flick the reins and stir the horse to life. The wagon rolled down the street, and in the morning sun Luke's black hair gleamed like polished ebony.

"Mercy, child! I figured you long gone by this time." Ruth Jefferson peered at Hannah through the half-open door. Remembering that the Jeffersons would be staying temporarily with Willie's nephew, Hannah had traced Ruth to the Stricklands' small log cabin on South Lillian Street. "Ain't you found that brother of yours yet?"

"Not yet, Miss Ruth. I've been to Springfield in search, but I decided to come back here to wait for news from the army."

"Back to Bolivar? How come?"

"Because . . ." Hannah shifted from one foot to the other. "Because you're here."

"Me?" The soft brown eyes narrowed. "What do I got to do with anything? You ain't in some kind of trouble now, are you?"

"Who's there, Ruth?" A younger woman's face emerged around the edge of the door. Seeing Hannah, the woman scowled. "What you want, ma'am? I don't do white folks' washin' here no more."

"No, it's not—"

"This here's that young'un I told you about, Martha," Ruth said. "From back East, you know?"

"The book writer? What you doin' at my door?"

"I . . . I wanted to speak with Miss Ruth. May I please come in?"

The two women looked at each other. Finally Ruth opened the door a little wider and slipped outside. "Miss Hannah, child, you can't be comin' over here. What if somebody saw you? What would the folk in Bolivar town say if they knew you was talkin' to us?"

"I don't care what they'd say." Hannah let out a weary breath. "Oh, Miss Ruth, I don't care what anybody thinks about anything. I'm so tired and confused. I've been back in Bolivar two days now, and things couldn't be worse. I'm almost out of money, nobody wants to buy my earrings, there hasn't been a single word from the Confederate army about Ethan, and . . . and Luke Maples has gone back to Kansas."

"Luke Maples?" Ruth regarded Hannah with a skeptical eye. "You meet a man someplace?"

"Luke took me in his wagon to Springfield. We talked and laughed and argued almost the whole way. I read my book to him—I think he liked it, too. And the night he brought me back to Bolivar, Miss Ruth, he kissed me."

"No! Lawsy, you in love. Martha!" Ruth called back over her shoulder. "Get on out here now, and help me with this. I'm too old to remember what it was like to be courtin'."

The younger woman stepped out into the sunshine, and Hannah saw that she had beautiful jet-black skin and eyes as dark and bright as a doe's. A red scarf covered her hair. Her yellow dress, though faded, was clean and carefully patched. Two children peered at Hannah from the folds of their mother's skirt, and a baby was bound to her back with a length of checkered cloth.

"What's the problem here?" Martha Strickland asked Ruth. Her voice was rough, almost hostile.

"Seems Miss Hannah loves some man done rode off to Kansas without her."

Softening, Martha clucked. "Now, ain't that just like a man? Listen here, girl, you're too pretty to worry yourself over some no-gooder like him. You get on back East and marry you a nice Union soldier."

"I don't want to marry," Hannah protested, "and I'm not in love with Luke. I just . . . I miss him. I enjoyed his company. That's why I thought I'd come here to visit with Miss Ruth."

The two women looked at each other. After a moment of silent communication, Martha let out a sigh of resignation.

"Well, sit yourself down anyhow," she told Hannah. "If we gotta have a white woman in the front yard we might as well look like we doin' you right. Want somethin' to drink? Sassafras tea?"

"Tea would be lovely." Hannah sank onto a carved wooden bench by the front door and drew apart the ribbons of her bonnet. "I am so hot. Miserably hot."

Ruth sat at the far end of the bench, and Martha's two older children—a boy and a girl—climbed into her lap. When Hannah took off her bonnet, the little girl gave a shriek and buried her face in Ruth's bosom.

"My goodness, what's the matter?" Hannah asked.

"Your hair. She ain't seen nothin' like it, I reckon." Ruth stroked the child's soft cheek. "It's okay, Hattie. This white woman ain't gonna hurt you."

One dark eye peeked out. "She gonna make Mama be a slave again?"

"No, of course not," Hannah cried. "Oh, Hattie, I would never do such a thing to your dear mother. Why, my own father fought in the war to free the states from slavery—and he was killed in battle, too. We Brownlows have been staunch abolitionists for years."

"Tea, Miss Hannah?" Martha held out a chipped white cup

filled to the brim with a fragrant, steaming liquid. "Good for what ails you."

As Martha seated herself on a stool nearby, Hannah tipped the cup and took a sip of the tea. Odd-tasting but delicious, it slid down her throat and calmed her stomach. The past two days since Luke had left her in Bolivar had been terrible— long, hot, sleepless nights, and frustrating, futile days. Relaxing, she leaned back against the bench and let out a deep breath.

"Now, honey," Miss Ruth said, "tell Martha and me what's got you in such a state."

Hannah took another sip of tea. "I'm down to the bottom of my purse, Miss Ruth. In Springfield, I spent far too much for a hotel room, and then I paid a fee to find word of my brother. I've attempted to sell my jewelry here in Bolivar, but nobody can afford it. I was warned to be careful of tricksters. I suppose I'm an easy mark."

"Well, now, you're a good woman is all." Ruth patted Hannah's knee. "Folk take advantage of gals like you whenever they can."

"I don't believe I'll ever find Ethan, and yet I can't go home to Boston without him. My mother sent a telegram saying that the family has fallen into dire straits."

"Where'd they fall?" Hattie asked.

"Hard times," Martha explained. "Miss Hannah, these days we all got hard times."

"I know, but I can't bear to think of my sisters going to work in a factory. It would be . . . abominable."

"Might do 'em good. Hard work never hurt nobody."

"You don't know Sophie." Hannah shook her head. "I've tried to find my brother, but he seems to have vanished into thin air. I thought if I could quickly write my book, then I might sell it and use the money to help my family. But every night when I sit down in my hotel room to work, nothing will come! I haven't managed to write a single page since I've been back in Bolivar. It's as though there's a gigantic cork halting the flow of my thoughts and feelings."

"It's that Luke feller," Ruth said firmly. "He's done stopped you up, Miss Hannah."

"Pull out the plug," little Hattie put in.

Hannah couldn't help but laugh. Reaching out, she brushed her hand across the child's fluffy black hair. "If I could think of a way to pull out the plug, Hattie, believe me, I would. But that plug is large and very deeply embedded. My money is running out, my brother is nowhere to be found, my family is on the verge of starvation, and I'm trapped here miles and miles away—with little chance of even being able to purchase a train ticket home."

"My, my, my," Martha said, shaking her head. "You stuck in blackstrap molasses, girl."

"Set to prayin'," Ruth instructed. "Amen and hallelujah."

For a long time, the three women sat gazing out across the clearing in front of the house, Ruth humming a hymn. Bored, Hattie and her little brother finally clambered down from Ruth's lap and scampered around to the back to play. A fat puppy wandered up and plopped down in the shade beneath the bench. In a moment, a second puppy joined the first.

Away from the bustle of downtown, Hannah felt a sense of calm slip through muscles that had been taut and cramped for weeks. The sweet perfume of honeysuckle hung in the air, and huge bumblebees murmured around the yellow-blossomed vine. Sunflowers, tall and golden, nodded their heads in the afternoon breeze. A chicken crossed a patch of bare ground and pecked at the scattered corn kernels someone had sprinkled.

"I feel at peace here," Hannah murmured. "You have a lovely home, Miss Martha."

The woman gave a soft laugh. "Why, thank you kindly."

Again the three fell silent. Hannah shut her eyes, and as always, the picture of Luke's face drifted before her. The ends of his hair curled around the collar of his shirt. Black and white—a startling contrast. But his eyes were brown and warm, and so deep she felt lost in them. His mouth seemed to move, speaking her name, calling her, beckoning.

Oh, Luke . . .

"You reckon you could write that book of yours here, Miss Hannah?" Martha asked in a low voice. "We got us a big ol' sweet gum tree out back by the stream. Ain't nobody would see you there. Wouldn't cause a lick of trouble. I could haul out a table and a stool, and you could sit yourself down there in the cool quiet."

Hannah studied the woman's face, reading acceptance in her brown eyes. "I can hardly thank you enough," she whispered. "Your offer is too kind."

"Just be sure you don't get here till after seven of a mornin' and you leave before sundown. Willie and Jim's got jobs mixin' mortar for the masons in town. But if they get wind of our little secret, we'll catch hell sure enough."

Ruth chuckled. "Think of it, Martha. You and me—who both been hid out by white folks when we was slaves and we run off—we gonna turn around and hide us a white lady ourselves."

"You reckon this is what freedom is all about?"

"Girl, if it is, it sure tastes sweet. Amen and hallelujah."

Laughing, the women rose from the bench and walked around the house to look for the children. Hannah stretched out her legs, took another sip of sassafras tea, and decided she might just find Missouri to her liking after all.

Though his impulse told him to leave for Kansas immediately, Luke spent five days after his return to Bolivar working with Thomas Cunnyngham and the survey crew. He needed the extra week to earn a full month's pay, and he knew he couldn't leave without readying his supplies for the long journey.

In the evenings, he packed his belongings. While preparing for winter, he had spent the spring and summer months gathering and drying mushrooms and herbs. In his lodge he had stored a huge supply of wild potatoes, nuts, persimmons, berries, and squash. Now he sorted out the best of these and placed them in containers made from the dried, stiffened paunches of buffalo.

He flew his prairie falcon often. Before long the raptor had killed enough squirrels, doves, pigeons, and quail for Luke to set up a smoking rack. Smoked meat and the other provisions would enable him to travel without stopping to hunt.

With the weather warm and dry, he slept outside beneath the stars each night. Slowly he dismantled the lodge he had built that spring—taking down the buffalo skin coverings and rolling them up, untying the hickory saplings that formed the frame. He wanted to leave his camp as much the way *Wah'kon-tah* had created it as he could, so he carried his fireplace stones back to the streambed and tore out the small garden he had planted in neat, artificial rows.

During the day, he joined the survey team and walked over the land he coveted, measuring out acre after acre for the Heavy Eyebrows who would one day claim it. He stayed away from the place of the oak tree and the cave, knowing he should never go back there. His thoughts were afflicted enough.

He couldn't claim the land, and though he had searched diligently, he had failed to find his father's killer. The man was almost certainly a bushwhacker, Luke realized, and unlikely to be parading around in public. It would be difficult to learn the names of all the bushwhackers, and impossible to ferret out one particular man. These guerrillas specialized in furtive solitude.

More persistent and tormenting than thoughts of his failure to attain his goals were images of Hannah Brownlow. Every waking hour she danced through his mind. He saw her glowing hair in the flame of his fire, in the blossoms of the butterfly weed, in the plumage of the woodpecker. Her blue eyes smiled at him when he knelt to drink from a gurgling creek and when he watched jays flit from branch to branch overhead. Her breath played across his skin in the warm night breeze. Her laughter bubbled in the waterfalls he crossed.

The harder he tried to hide her memory, the stronger it surged forward—Hannah stirring eggs over the fire, Hannah striking the bushwhacker over the head with a tree limb, Hannah reading her book, Hannah moving into his arms . . .

It was the last Hannah who haunted him at night. Like a figure from Spiritland, she came to him in his dreams. She walked through shimmering green mists, her blue eyes sparkling and her hair aflame. And every night she slipped out of her clothes and lay with him. Her hands stroked his fevered skin. Her lips dampened his neck. Her tongue tormented his flesh. Her breasts pressed into his chest, and her thighs parted to take him in.

And every morning, he woke exhausted and aching. Hard, hungry for release, he struggled to make himself stand and walk to the cold spring. But even dousing himself with frigid water did little to ease the mounting need he felt for the woman.

Again and again, he chastised himself for having agreed to

take her in his wagon that morning in the courthouse. Even more often, he cursed himself for the moment when he had pulled her against him and kissed her lips. What a fool he'd been! Now he would live with that memory for the rest of his life. Would she haunt him forever?

The only solution was to get away from Bolivar as quickly as he could. In Kansas, many matters would take his thoughts from Hannah. He would help his tribe contend with the loss of reservation land. He would join his brothers in the summer buffalo hunt. He would marry . . .

No! Luke slammed his fist onto the ground where he sat. Startled, his falcon fluttered up from his perch, brown wings rustling with irritation.

"What shall I do, Gthe-don?" he demanded of the bird. "Marry a woman I've never seen and be tortured by one I'll never see again?"

The raptor regarded him evenly, his brown eyes conveying a regal disdain for the problems of a common race.

"What would you do in my place?" Luke went on. "Would you fly back to Kansas and live the rest of your life on the prairie?"

The bird cocked his head. Luke had to smile.

"Of course you would. The prairie is where you belong, isn't it? Wide-open spaces where the hunting is easy and game is plentiful. You were born there, and there you'll find others of your kind." He fell silent and watched the stars come out one by one, like budding flowers.

"Tomorrow I'll go to the courthouse and pick up my pay. Then we'll go out to my people's lost land one last time. I know it's unwise, but I have to see it again. I want to carry that memory with me back to Kansas so I can pass it on to my children. And after that, Gthe-don, we'll ride for the prairie."

The falcon ruffled his wings then turned from Luke to stare into the night.

Luke took off his hat as he stepped into the courthouse and walked into the room where the recorder and clerk kept their offices. As usual, the surveyors were gathered around a back table attempting to read the maps they found so baffling. Luke had to smile. Tom and his men loved this land as much as he did, but their lack of schooling hindered their ability to translate flat diagrams into images of rolling hills and limestone bluffs.

"Luke!" Tom Cynnyngham spotted his chainman across the room. "Thank God you're here. Come on over and see if you can piece out this map. I reckon the land is right over to the west edge of the county, but Ab here thinks it might be down yonder south."

Knowing he needed to collect his pay and head out, Luke hesitated a moment. But the sight of the tall, thin surveyor who had befriended him from the moment he set foot in the courthouse softened the edges of Luke's heart. He strode across the room and glanced over the others' shoulders. At once, he knew the place.

"It's west," he said. "Just the other side of Half Way."

"Told you!" Tom's voice bore a note of triumph. "That there is where they put in the road to Buffalo, ain't it, Luke?"

"Sure is."

"Luke, could you calculate out where Tom Abernathy's place is? Jack Dean claims Abernathy's built a fence over on his property. We got to sort it out before we can do anything else today, or them two are gonna come to blows."

"I'd work it out for you, Tom," Luke began, "but I need to talk over a matter with you in priv—"

"Which one of you gentlemen is James Jones, County Clerk?" a loud voice sliced off Luke's words. The surveyors turned their attention to the front door. A short, stocky man whose long black hair draped to his shoulders in thin wisps was regarding them with a mixture of amusement and disdain. "I represent the Butterfield Stage Company. I've come to settle Mr. Jones's claim."

"Jim ain't in yet," Tom Cunnyngham said. "He don't move so good of a mornin'. He's been stiff with rheumatiz ever since his accident, you know."

"And you gentlemen are . . . ?"

"County survey team. I'm Tom Cunnyngham, Surveyor. This here's Seth Tinker, Deputy. These are Herman Borscht, Jeb Smith, and Luke Maples, my sworn chainmen and flagmen."

The man's pale blue eyes scanned the group, then locked on

Luke. He frowned. "You employ an Indian, Mr. Cunnyng-ham?"

"Sure do. What's it to you?"

"I would assume it's against the law for a county to employ a non-citizen. Especially when there are able-bodied white men in need of work."

"Listen, we Missouri folk do the right thing, legal or not. Luke's the best man I got on the job, and not a one of these fellers here would deny it. He might be an Indian out of Kansas, but in his bones he's Missouri through and through. Where you from anyway, mister?"

"Boston, originally. I live in Kansas City now." The man's eyes hadn't left Luke for a moment. As hard and cold as icicles on a winter morning, they pierced into him as if probing for answers Luke wouldn't give. "You're from Kansas," the man commented. "I've been there once. So, are you Osage?"

Though he knew he was leaving Missouri within the hour and had nothing to fear from this stranger, Luke's heart was hammering against his ribs. Every instinct rose to the alert, every sense heightened with warning. Slowly he nodded. "I'm Osage."

"Vermin," the man spat. "Every one of you lice should be exterminated."

"Now, just a minute here!" Tom exploded. "Ain't nobody talks to my man like that. Get your ass out of this courthouse, mister."

"I'll nail *your* impertinent, lawless ass to a tree, Cunnyng-ham. I'll report you and your two-bit survey crew to the federal government. You can't have an Indian working here. He and every redskin like him deserves to be whipped and strung up. Them and these niggers roaming around on the loose!"

"You bastard," Tom growled.

The man's blue eyes glittered in his pink face. "I'll return to interview Mr. Jones when he has seen fit to rouse himself from bed. In the meantime, I suggest you round up the wagons, carts, stagecoaches, and livestock your sheriff impounded from my company. Butterfield is not pleased with the authorities of Polk County, Missouri. We are considering pressing charges."

"You do and we'll whip your hide and string you up, mister—"

"Mr. Brown." The man tipped his hat to reveal a shiny bald pate above the long black strands that hung to his shoulders. "Mr. Ethan Brown, at your service."

Turning, he settled his hat on his head and strode out of the room.

"Pussyfoot dandy," Tom hissed after him. "Let him try to report me. Just let him tangle with a Cunnyngham! I swear I'll kick his fat butt all the way back to Boston. Don't you fret none over this, Luke . . . Luke?"

Trembling with barely leashed anger, Luke turned his focus on his friend. Could it be? Was it possible his enemy had just walked into his hands? Ethan. A man who had been to Kansas. A man who hated the Osage. A man who spoke of whipping and hanging.

But his name was Ethan Brown! And he was from Boston. Could he be Hannah's brother? What if the man they were looking for was one and the same? Should he find Hannah and tell her? Should he confront the man and then slit his throat if he'd killed Luke's father?

"Luke?" Tom touched his arm. "Never thought I'd see a red man turn white. You look like you just seen a ghost. C'mon, now, don't let that Mr. Ethan Brown get to you. If he's lookin' for trouble, he'll find it here in Bolivar, I guarantee."

"He's probably a bushwhacker on the sly," the deputy put in.

"I reckon so." Tom shook his head. "Troublemakers. Herman, you better go tell the sheriff what's up. He's the man who impounded the Butterfield equipment, so that Brown bastard will be lookin' for him. You others keep on piecin' out this map. Luke, you and me'll take a walk. You said you had somethin' you wanted to talk to me about in private."

Luke forced a deep breath into his lungs. He had to stay calm. Had to think. If he acted hastily, he could destroy this opportunity. "On second thought, I think I'll take a ride out of town," he told Tom, leveling his voice to an even tone. "If you can spare me for a few hours, I need to do some thinking."

"Sure, sure. You go on, Luke. We'll be back into the office around lunchtime, and you can catch up with us then. Say, how about you comin' over to the house tonight for supper? Lavinia's been after me for weeks to invite you again. What do you say?"

Luke smiled. "I'll let you know, Tom."

Stuffing his hat on his head, he gave the other men a nod and then left the room. The morning sunlight struck him almost blind as he stepped out of the courthouse. As he walked down the steps, he felt his spirits lift like dandelion seeds on a gust of wind. He would ride out to the land where the old oak tree grew. He would sit in the cool shade at the mouth of the cave. And he would ponder the miracle of this day.

Adjusting her load of manuscript pages, pens, inkwell, purse, and lunch basket, Hannah elbowed her way out the front door of the Sherman House hotel. This was going to be a glorious day!

Lifting her chin, she drew in a deep breath. The morning was hot, but she wasn't concerned about the weather. Miss Ruth had taken time away from her chores to alter two of Hannah's simplest dresses into the common style worn by women in Bolivar. She had removed ruffles and braids around necklines, cut off sleeves to the elbow, and detached heavy overskirts.

Now Hannah had only to wear a foundation of crinoline and corset to achieve the correct shape. Her hoop lay in the hotel room along with her tight jackets and woolen undergarments. In a pale green skirt, white chemisette, and light straw bonnet, she felt she could endure the Missouri heat even if she were damp with perspiration by the end of the day.

"Good morning, Mr. Gorden," she greeted the hotel owner, who was sweeping the sidewalk. The evening before, he had agreed to allow her to stay on the entire following week for one dollar and the time it took to mop the saloon every morning. That would take no more than two hours a day, she had calculated, and then she could hurry to Martha Strickland's house to work on her book.

"A lovely day, isn't it?" she added.

He grinned, his gray eyes crinkling at the corners. "Sure is, Miss Hannah. You're all gussied up. Where you off to?"

"Business, Mr. Gorden."

He leaned on his broom handle and watched her walk past. "You want me to check the mail for you over to the post office?"

"Yes, please," she called over one shoulder. "Mighty kind of you."

Chuckling to herself, Hannah stepped down from the boardwalk and started across the road. She was already starting to speak like these backwoods Missouri people. Well, they weren't so bad after all. Mr. Gorden had been nice enough, especially once she had explained her predicament. The cook at the restaurant where she ate her evening meal had been more than kind. And of course, Ruth and Martha had gone out of their way to welcome her. Already she had written more pages of her book than she had during her entire train trip from Boston.

Words for each new scene played through her thoughts while she slept at night. Even now as she walked, she heard her characters deep in conversation. *"Dear wife, how I adore you,"* whispered Elizabeth's loving husband. *"When I ponder the extent to which you have labored for our family, I cannot help but marvel. You have quilted such fine warm bedding and laid back stores that will surely see us through the coming winter."*

A smile softened the corners of Elizabeth's mouth. Though the darkness of night blanketed the snug cabin, the light of her husband's affection cast a gentle glow upon her heart. Were she to know, dear reader, that the darkness held more than just the moon and stars that night, our young Elizabeth would have little just cause to smile.

Observe her now in these final moments of peace and contentment. See the softness of the hand that lies upon her husband's sleeve. Hear the quiet hymn that slips from her lips. Know that love and happiness and hope, for but this single moment, are possessed by Elizabeth in full measure. But, alas, not for long.

"Hark!" cried her husband suddenly. *"In the distance, my sweet! What do I hear?"*

In alarm, Elizabeth glanced at the low rope bed where her children lay in innocent slumber. Then she looked at the window, its shutters rattling of their own accord. "Someone is outside!" cried she.

"You must hide the children. I shall step to the door and learn who approaches our abode."

"Take care!"

"Make haste!" As he opened the door, a cry from the bowels of hell itself assaulted their ears. Wicked arrows sped through the night and buried their evil blades in the wood. "Elizabeth!"

"My love!" screamed the terrified woman. "Indians! Indians!"

A fearsome figure leapt toward—

"Good morning, Hannah." Luke Maples stepped out from the doorway of the City Drugstore and took off his hat.

"Oh!" Hannah stopped and clutched her throat. "Luke! You're supposed to be in Kansas."

"Not yet."

"My goodness, I—I . . . It's such a surprise to see you."

"I figured you'd probably gone back to Boston by now. The last time we talked, you were about to run out of money."

Her hands had gone damp on her bundle of writing supplies. "Mr. Gorden has given me one week to . . . I'm going to sweep and mop for him and . . . that sort of thing."

She shrugged, trying to act as indifferent as she could. But at the sight of him she felt as though a heavy boulder had dropped onto her chest. She could hardly breathe. Her nostrils flared as she tried to drink in air.

How was it possible he looked as wonderful as she remembered? Didn't absence paint a rosy glow on memories? But Luke was just as tall, just as broad-shouldered, just as male as she had recalled. His brown eyes roved up and down her, absorbing and devouring her. His mouth—silent and unsmiling—hypnotized her.

"Where are you going?" he asked.

"To Miss Ruth's." Her voice was almost a whisper as reality began to sink in. Luke was here, still in Bolivar! The empty place inside her heart filled with a warm, throbbing glow. "I've been writing my book there."

Luke's expression softened. "How's our young Elizabeth?"

"In trouble." She cleared her throat. "That is . . . the cabin is under attack."

"What about the neighboring farmer? Can't he save her?"

"He's not really part of her life, you know. He's been by once for a visit. He brought some . . . jerky." She flushed. "I put that in to make the book more true to life."

"Did Elizabeth like the taste any better than our young Hannah did?"

She had to smile. "Not much."

For all his outward calm, Luke found it hard to believe he was talking to Hannah Brownlow. She was here—as real, as beautiful, as vibrant as before. More so, maybe. Her blue eyes shone brighter than morning glories after a summer rain. The moment she had seen him, her cheeks suffused with pink like the sunrise. And that dress . . .

He couldn't decide where to look—her face, her hair, her body. She was food to him. And he was a starving man.

"I'll carry your things to the *Nika-sabe*'s house," he said. Without giving her the chance to let reason intervene, he took the bundle from her arms. "Which way?"

"Lillian Street." Hannah felt as though she were drifting through water as they started down the walkway. She couldn't feel her feet. Her head was light and dizzy. She didn't think she'd taken a breath since Luke's sudden appearance.

"What will you do after next week?" he asked. "Will the hotel owner let you stay on?"

"Our agreement lasts only till Saturday. I sent word to the Confederate office in Springfield that I'm staying in Bolivar. I hope to hear something by mail within a few days."

"It might take longer."

"I know. But I have no money."

He glanced at her as he weighed the implications of her statement. They weren't pleasant. "What will you do if no word comes, Hannah?" he demanded.

She stopped, surprised by the harsh tone of his voice. "Perhaps I'll stay with Miss Ruth—"

"The *Nika-sabe*'s husband won't take you in. It would mean disaster for him at the hands of the bushwhackers. You're already risking more than you know by spending time at that house. And they've taken a great chance to allow it."

"But—"

"You remember what those men wanted to do to me? They would have killed me for the color of my skin. Would they think kindly of you for associating with the old *Nika-sabe* woman? They would hang her husband from a tree if they thought he was being too friendly with a white woman."

"I never meant to cause Miss Ruth any trouble."

"Of course not. But what will you do, Hannah?"

She gripped the handle of her lunch basket. "I don't know."

He looked into her eyes, trying to read beyond the despair he had provoked. "Do you know what happens to women who fall on hard times? Do you know how women in Missouri make money when they run out of hope, Hannah?"

A picture of the bordello she had seen in Springfield formed in her mind. "No," she whispered. "I won't do that."

He regarded her for a moment, and then his heart began to hammer. "Hannah, walk with me to the edge of the spring. I have something to ask you."

Chapter
Ten

~~~~~~~~~~~~~~~~~

Like a gossamer silver ribbon, the rippling spring wound between its grassy banks. A purple-stalked cluster of blazing star wildflowers lifted tall, fuzzy stems above a swath of rose verbena. Compass plants with yellow blossoms mingled among pink asters. Scarlet trumpet creeper climbed up the trunk of a cottonwood. Beneath the shade of the tree's triangular leaves, Hannah set her lunch basket down and then straightened to face Luke.

"Speak plainly," she told him. "I'm sure our meeting this morning was no accident. What do you have to say?"

As he placed her bundle of writing materials on the long green grass, Luke bolstered himself to lay before Hannah the idea that had been no more than a seed in his dreams—a seed that had germinated in the early hours of morning when he met the man who might have killed his father, and when he last looked on the lost Osage lands—a root that had sprung to life in the instant he had seen Hannah emerge from her hotel.

"What do I have to say?" he repeated. "That I wanted to see you again."

"Why? You walked away from me a week ago with only the barest good-bye. You made it clear I meant nothing to you. You told me you were leaving, and I gave you up as gone."

"There were two things I had to lay eyes on again before I could ride for Kansas."

"Which two things?"

"You, for one."

"Me?" She couldn't suppress the heat that flushed upward across her cheeks. "Why?"

He studied a gold-and-black butterfly as it sat on a white stone by the river, its delicate wings fanning back and forth in the sunlight. Could he tell Hannah that her memory had danced through his dreams as though he walked in Spiritland? Could he tell her he had missed the sound of her voice more than he missed his own mother's laughter?

"I wanted to see if you'd found your brother."

"No," she said. "I've heard nothing."

He bit back the urge to tell her about the stranger in the courthouse. If she knew, she would want to find the man. If Ethan Brown were really Ethan Brownlow, Luke would lose Hannah. He wasn't ready to face that again, in more ways than one.

"The other thing I had to see before I left for Kansas was the land," he said. "My people's lost home."

"You found the place where your tribe used to live?"

He nodded. "It's not far from Bolivar. I couldn't stay away. Now . . . now I feel the old desire. The old hunger. I want that land, Hannah."

"Has it been settled?"

"No. Tom Cunnyngham and I surveyed it a couple of weeks ago so it could be opened up for homesteading."

"Could you homestead it?"

"No." He let out a breath. "But you could."

She stared at him. What would she want with a piece of this miserable, mosquito-infested state? All she had desired for months was to go home to Boston, where it was safe and civilized.

"One hundred and sixty acres," he said. "A large, deep river edging the boundary. A smaller stream running through the center. Trees of every kind. Rich, loamy soil. Wild game—deer, squirrel, possum, raccoon, rabbit. It could all be yours if you filed at the land office in Springfield."

"Luke . . . you know I don't want to own land here."

"But I do." He squared his shoulders. "So marry me, Hannah."

"What?"

"Marry me. I'll provide for you until you find your brother. I'll give you a place to live. Food to eat. I'll protect you. In return, you file for the land under your name as a citizen."

Staring at him, she realized he was deadly serious. "And then?" she asked. "Suppose I do claim land for you and find my brother? What's to become of me after that?"

He shifted from one foot to the other. "You can go back to Boston."

"But we'd be married."

"Legally. But only so you can file on the land I want. In spite of what happened between us that night on the road back to Bolivar, I don't want to truly wed you, Hannah. I have plans to marry a woman of my own people and continue the line of my fathers. I want my children to be full-blooded Osage."

She crossed her arms and stared down at the stream. This was preposterous. The man was out of his mind.

And yet she knew she had only one week of grace left in Bolivar. When the hotel owner could no longer help her, what could she do? She had no place to turn.

Surely there could be some other solution. Maybe if she tried again to sell her jewelry. Or her clothes. Maybe she could look for a permanent job somewhere, though it was obvious women weren't needed or wanted as workers in Bolivar. All the women she'd met were wives and mothers. Their husbands earned a living by the sweat of their brows.

And what about Luke? Was this farfetched plan really his last hope? Was the dream of owning land in Missouri so strong that he would resort to such an extreme?

"Can't you take out a request for citizenship?" she asked him. "Immigrants do it all the time. My own grandparents came from Ireland."

"I'm an Indian, Hannah. Osage Indians can't become citizens. I can't change my race any more than you can change the fact that you're a woman."

"Well, this woman doesn't want to get married. Not even to help you get your hands on some land."

Luke clenched his jaw at the finality of her words. He had admired her stubbornness before—now it was an obstacle to his dream.

"I can't get that land any other way," he told her. "As my wife, you could file on it. You could stay there with me until you found your brother. I'd even help you look for him."

"You would?"

He glanced at her, realizing he'd found the chink in her armor. But again the question ran in circles through his mind: Should he tell Hannah about Ethan Brown? If he convinced her to marry him and then told his secret, she might never forgive him. Did he care? Could he deceive her?

No, Luke made up his mind he would find out more about the stranger before he told Hannah anything. He didn't want to raise her hopes, and he did want her to marry him. This Ethan Brown might not be her brother at all—and he might be the man who had killed Luke's father.

"If you don't get word by mail pretty soon," he said, "I'll drive you to Joplin and Forsyth. I'll give you half my surveying pay, too. You can save up for your train trip home."

"How could I go home if we were married?"

"Marriage is different out here. If you left for Boston after a while, no one would think too much about it. Especially if you had married an Indian. Running off would seem natural."

"But the marriage would be listed in the county records."

"Do you ever intend to marry anyone else, Hannah?"

"No."

Though he expected that out of obligation to her mother Hannah would one day wed a man of her own race, Luke couldn't allow her to ponder that possibility. "Then what difference would it make? No one will have to know that the old spinster who lives down the street in Boston is really married to an Indian in Missouri."

Hannah shut her eyes, suddenly picturing herself as that aging, lonely creature—a woman who had lived her life through books. Did she really want to end her days like that? She had always been so certain of her dream, and yet . . .

Why not solve her financial problems and have an adventure along the way? It might be interesting to live in a cabin in the wilderness. She could write about it when she returned to Boston—omitting her marriage, of course. She could send the story to *Godey's Ladies' Book*. "My Pioneer Enterprise: Being the Exploits of a Lady Traveler on the Missouri Frontier."

And she'd be able to prepare for her journey home to Boston at the same time. With half of Luke's earnings at her disposal, she could afford the train fare in a matter of a few weeks.

"What about you?" she asked. "Won't your Osage bride object to a husband who's already married?"

"Some men in my tribe have more than one wife. It shouldn't be a problem. Besides, I'll divorce you in the Osage way before you leave Missouri."

"Divorce me?" Hannah bristled. "I'd rather be a bigamist than a divorcée."

He shrugged. "All right, we'll stay married. It'll help me keep the title to the land clear anyway."

"The land, then. That's what this is all about."

"That's right." For some reason, Luke realized he couldn't make himself look into Hannah's blue eyes. It *was* the land that pulled him, he told himself. This arrangement had nothing to do with the woman herself. It had nothing to do with the fact that the sight of her that morning had sent a shaft of desire like a hot arrow through his loins. It had nothing to do with his nightly dreams of her. It had nothing to do with the silent emptiness of the past few days without her.

It was the land. Only the land.

"And you would swear not to touch me?" she was asking.

He swallowed against the knot of need that had formed in his throat. Now, while the moment was ripe, he would seal their separation by placing on it a fiery brand of prejudice and hatred.

"I swear, I'll never touch you," he vowed. Then he hardened his voice. "I don't want to risk the chance that you would bear a child from my seed. My children will be Osage. I would never defile them with the blood of a white woman."

She turned on him, her eyes flashing with cobalt fire. "And I despise the very thought of bearing a half-breed savage."

"Then we understand each other. Come with me to the courthouse, Hannah. We'll marry and be done with it."

"Fine." Sweeping her lunch basket into her arms, she swung away from him and marched toward the street.

"Married!" Ruth Jefferson's eyes widened until they seemed to fill her face. "What you talkin' about, girl?"

"I got married at the courthouse this morning," Hannah repeated, pushing her way into the small cabin. "I'm Luke Maples's wife."

"Him? I thought he run off to Kansas."

"He didn't." Hannah glanced around the dimly lit room. "Where can I store this, Miss Ruth?"

"What is it? And what you doin' in here anyhow? Martha'll have a conniption if she sees you inside her house."

"It's the book I've been writing. I want you to hide it for me while I'm away in Springfield."

Ruth placed her hands on her hips and glared at Hannah. "Now, you start this story from the beginning, girl. And talk plain."

Clasping her manuscript to her stomach, Hannah settled onto a bench beside the fireplace and brushed the strands of damp hair from her temples. "Luke Maples found me this morning. He's that man I told you about—the Indian."

"Indian? Glory be! You never said nothin' about that!"

"He is, but it doesn't matter. He's very nice." Hannah's own words flashed back across her mind. Not two hours ago she had called him a savage. Well, he had deserved the label after what he'd said about her heritage.

"Anyway," she continued, "we made an agreement, Luke and I. He's going to feed and house me and give me half of his income—"

"You gonna be a kept woman? Shame, shame! Lawsy, Miss Hannah, I never had you figured for the type."

"No!" Rising again, Hannah began to pace up and down the small room. "It's nothing like that. Not at all. We've agreed there will be nothing fleshly between us."

"What? Fleshly?"

"He won't . . . you know." She rolled her eyes. "We won't sleep together in the same bed. Not as husband and wife."

"You got married to a man you ain't gonna get no pleasure out of? What good is that, girl?"

"We didn't marry for pleasure, Miss Ruth. As I started to tell you, Luke is going to provide for me until I find my brother. He has even agreed to help me look for Ethan. In exchange for that, I'm going to file on a homestead for him. It's his old Indian lands he wants."

"You mean to tell me you got yourself married to this feller just so's you can get him some land?"

"And he's going to help me by—"

"Ruth, what's a-goin' on in here? Don't you know we got greens to pick?" The door swung wide, and Martha strode in. At the sight of the intruder in her cabin, she clamped her mouth shut, set her baby on the bed, and shook her finger at Hannah's nose. "What you doin' in my house? You better get on outside before somebody sees you."

"But I need to hide my novel—"

"She done got married," Ruth cut in. "Married to an Indian."

"No, sir!"

"Uh-huh. She done it. Just like a business, too." Ruth clucked. "Ain't even gonna know his pleasures."

At the sound of the two older children starting through the doorway, Martha turned and shooed them out. Then she pulled the latch string. "Now, then. You tell me you got yourself hitched and you ain't plannin' to roll down the thunder with your man?"

Hannah felt a flush spread from her neck to her cheeks. "I don't see what that has to do with anything. I need money and help finding my brother. Luke needs land. We have an arrangement. If you'll agree to hide my book, Miss Martha, I'll go. A supply wagon is leaving for Springfield in an hour, and I'm to be on it."

"He gonna be on it, too?"

"No, he's going out to the land to start building himself a house. That's part of the Homestead Act, you see. You build on the land, live there, and cultivate it for five years, and then the Land Office issues you a title."

"Wait a minute now—you gonna live with this man for five

whole years and never know his pleasures?" Martha inquired. "You crazier than I thought."

"Not for five years!" Hannah burst out. "A few weeks at the most. And what's so wonderful about a man's pleasures, anyway?"

Ruth and Martha looked at each other. Finally Ruth cleared her throat. "Miss Hannah, sit yourself down. It's time we had ourselves a little talk."

"I'll bring the sassafras tea," Martha put in. "Got a pail of it chillin' in the spring for when Jim and Willie come home."

"But I have to meet the wagon—" Hannah could see it was no use. She let out a sigh and sat on the bench again.

Ruth seated herself on the opposite bench and regarded Hannah in silence. In a moment Martha returned and handed out mugs of cool tea, each with a sprig of mint sprouting from the top. She picked up her baby, settled beside Ruth, and unbuttoned her bodice. After she lifted out one ample breast, the baby began to suckle.

Uncomfortable at such privacies, Hannah studied her own white-gloved fingers curled around the teacup. She had been taught to regard the human body as shameful, sinful, and certainly not meant for exposure—not even in bed. Every night of her life, she had worn nightgowns that fell to her toes and lace-edged caps to cover her hair. During the day, it was bonnets, gloves, dresses, jackets, stockings, and shoes from head to toe.

Being presented with a woman's bare breast was bad enough, Hannah thought. Far worse was the idea of talking to Martha and Ruth about what it meant to know a man's pleasures. She and Luke weren't even really married—not in that way. Such topics were intended to be secret and unspoken, not bandied about.

"What's your mammy told you about men, girl?" Miss Ruth spoke up after she had taken a deep drink of her sassafras tea. "She told you very much?"

"All I need to know, I'm certain. She told me it's a wife's duty to her husband to allow him his way with her. And that's how babies are created."

"She didn't tell you about the joy?"

"No. She didn't mention joy at all . . . in fact, she spoke of . . . of pain."

"Aw, that part lasts no more'n a minute right at the start. Honey, I'm here to tell you 'bout the God-given joy. Between a husband and wife the good Lord planned for fun, shiverin' pleasures, thunder and lightnin'. Now, when you and this Luke feller see your way past this addlepated notion that you ain't gonna touch each other, go ahead and set yourself free to do whatever you want. Do whatever it takes to make him feel so good he wants to worship you like you was a queen. You let him do the same thing to you. After a while, honey, you gonna be so happy you'll be fit to bust your britches."

"You ain't never felt nothin' like the joy a husband can give his wife," Martha concurred. "Makes life worth livin'. Makes up for all the chores, all the pain of birthin', all the sorrow of death. If I was you, I wouldn't hold back from that husband of yours. Not a bit."

Hannah drifted a moment, pondering what Ruth might have meant by "shiverin' pleasures" and how she and Luke might give them to each other. But enough of that nonsense.

"Thank you both very much for your advice," she told the two women. "I appreciate your concern, but you must understand that Luke and I have a perfectly rational agreement. Neither of us is interested in the sort of arrangement you're talking about. Our marriage is merely a way to achieve our goals."

"Sounds to me like you'uns made a bargain," Ruth said, "not a marriage."

"That's right." Standing, she brushed down the folds of her skirt. "I'll be back in Bolivar in three days. Martha, will you please keep my book safe until then?"

"Sure, honey," Martha said as she and Ruth stood to see Hannah to the door. "You go to Springfield and lay claim to that land. Then come on back here and start livin' with your man."

"I'll do just that." With a wave Hannah lifted her skirts and started for the street.

She could hear the two women chuckling behind her. "She ain't gonna last long," Martha said.

"I better brush up on my midwifin'," Ruth murmured. "Won't be too long before we have us a birthin'."

Hannah rode to Springfield with a group of three families who were on their way to homestead some land near the James River. With men and their grown sons to guard the wagons, she felt safe from bushwhackers. Though the journey proved uneventful, she recognized the place where Luke's wagon had stuck in the mud, and she saw the cut in the forest that marked the trail down which they had found the little cabin.

Had she really married him? Hannah turned the question over and over as she rode down the bumpy, narrow road. There was no denying the marriage license carefully folded inside her purse. There was no denying the memory of the moment when she and Luke had stood before the justice of the peace and repeated vows to love, honor, and cherish each other.

But how could she have done such an impulsive, reckless thing as to legally wed a man she hardly knew? After pondering the situation from one side and then the other, she finally concluded that since she hadn't married Luke in the church with a priest and a proper Mass, it really didn't count. Their marriage wasn't a sacrament. Therefore breaking it couldn't be a sin. Could it?

The more she tried to reassure herself that she had done the right thing, the more certain she was that—priest or no priest—God had been watching her that morning. He knew. He had heard those promises she'd made. And He wasn't going to be the least bit happy when she climbed on a train back to Boston and left her husband behind.

Worse, Hannah knew there was only one reason for a man and woman to get married—and that was to have children. After all, wasn't that what she'd been taught? Procreation— the whole purpose of marriage. But she didn't intend to let Luke Maples near enough to breathe on her, let alone procreate.

It was hard to imagine a worse sin than the one she had committed that morning. The more she thought about it, the more contrite she felt—yet there was nothing to do now but go forward with the plan. Meanwhile she would just hope God didn't decide to send down a bolt of lightning to strike her dead.

The wagons arrived in Springfield late at night. Luke had given Hannah enough money to take a room, but she stayed at another hotel rather than at Lyon House. She didn't see Bill Hickok, who had indeed been arrested and brought to trial.

She learned from breakfast diners the following morning that the killer had been vigorously prosecuted, but witnesses had testified to hearing two shots that morning on Springfield's square. Since David Tutt's revolver proved to have a single empty chamber, Hickok was acquitted on grounds of "reasonable doubt."

So this was Missouri, Hannah thought as she walked into the Land Office to file her claim. Liars. Murderers. Bushwhackers. Thieves. Mosquitoes. Ticks. Snakes. And here she was, placing a stamp of ownership on one hundred and sixty acres of the miserable state.

"You over the age of twenty-one?" the clerk asked when she stepped up to the desk. He was a beefy young man with a wispy blond beard. Dipping his pen into a bottle of ink, he stared through thick-rimmed spectacles at his ledger.

"I am twenty-one," she stated.

At the sound of her voice, he lifted his head and looked her up and down. A smile lifted the corners of his mustache. "Well now . . . we don't get many women in here. 'Specially not young, pretty ones. You a citizen of the United States, ma'am?"

"Indeed. I was born in Boston." She placed on his desk the packet of identifying papers she had brought. "That's in Massachusetts."

He glanced up again, but the appreciative gleam in his eyes had vanished. "I know where Boston is. Yankee territory."

After flipping through Hannah's papers for a moment and making several notations in his ledger, he asked for the survey of the land she wanted to claim. Hannah unfolded a map Luke had given her and carefully pointed out the acreage he had chosen.

"Here it is, just above these bluffs. There's a stream running through the middle, you see?"

"I see it." He recorded the coordinates. "That'll be eighteen dollars, ma'am. Four dollars commission for the entry, and another four for the certificate. Add to that a ten-dollar fee."

Hannah took out the coins Luke had given her. How long

had he worked to earn this money? As the clerk counted out the money, she gazed at the plot of land on the map. It was her home now—hers and Luke's. He had paid for it; she had filed for it. It belonged to them. Together.

"Here's your duplicate receipt," the clerk said. "I've logged the entry here in my ledger and I'll report it to the General Land Office. Now, you understand that you have to settle and cultivate the land for a continuous period of five years?"

"I understand. My husband is building a house, and he plans to farm the land."

"You're married? Why didn't your husband come file? He could have put his name on the claim as easy as you. If you was to pass away while bearin' a child or such, it would make things a lot simpler to have his name on record."

Hannah swallowed. "Luke is . . . My husband is busy."

The clerk shrugged. "If you say so. Anyhow, when five years is up, or within two years after that, you come on back here and show me proper proof that you been living on your claim and farming it. Then you pay your dollar-twenty-five-an-acre price. Now, ma'am, that's gonna run you two hundred dollars. You sure you got a husband can plow and plant up that land for you?"

"I'm sure." Without thinking, she added, "I have the finest husband a woman could ever want."

"All right, all right." The tips of the clerk's ears grew red as he bent to write again. "I don't have time to hear no love stories this mornin'."

"Love? Oh, no, you don't understand—"

"Now then," he cut in, "once you pay your two hundred dollars, I'll give you a final certificate. Then I'll send word to the General Land Office, and they'll issue you a complete title to the land. If you don't want to live out there five years, you can pay for your land with cash or warrants. Then you only have to stay six months before I can issue you a title."

Hannah pondered this a moment. "I feel sure it will take my husband five years to earn the two hundred dollars. He is not a wealthy man."

"I understand. Ain't too many of us these days that is. All the same, if he's a hard worker and as fine a man as you say, he'll earn you a good living. That's some of the best land in Polk

County you just laid claim to. I hear tell Indians used to live out around them woods."

"Really?" Hannah tightened the strings on her purse as she regarded the man. "What sort of Indians?"

"Osage, I reckon. This whole bottom half of the state used to be their land. But they sold it all off and moved to Kansas."

"I wonder if they're happy."

"Don't much think so. All they got over there is prairie— flat, open, and windy as hell. Here, we got hills and hollers, and all kinds of fruits and nuts and wild game. We got rivers aplenty and good dirt for farming. A man out here's got to be tough and as stubborn as a Missouri mule. He's got to have a good head on his shoulders and fire in his blood. But if he's got them things, and if he loves this land, he's gonna do just dandy."

"I'm sure my husband will, sir," Hannah said softly. "He loves this land more than you can ever imagine."

Three days after his wedding, Luke waited beside the Bolivar courthouse for Hannah to return from Springfield. He watched the fingers of Grandfather the Sun wrap around the late evening sky. Oak trees, their leaves outlined in gold, formed a solid bank across the distant ridge. Against his shoulder, the stone wall grew cold as he leaned on it, waiting. A chill crept over the moccasins on his feet and curled around his ankles.

Hannah could have stolen his money. The thought had chased itself through his mind since the moment he had placed his leather pouch—heavy with coins—into her white-gloved hands. He had given her eighteen dollars for the land fee and commission, another five for a hotel and meals, and ten more to purchase seed and a plow. Thirty-three dollars. Almost the entire sum of his savings. More than enough for one-way train fare to Boston.

Knowing it would not have taken her long to file a homestead claim on the land and to buy the supplies, he had been eagerly waiting for her return. Wagon after wagon had rolled through town that evening. None of them carried Hannah.

Could she have had trouble laying claim to the acreage? He didn't think so. She was the right age. She had proof of her citizenship. She had the survey map. What could have gone wrong? Nothing . . . unless she had mentioned her marriage to an Indian.

Luke crossed his arms over his chest and stared out at the darkening road. Shadows crept across it. A deep indigo veil hung over the sky. Grandfather the Sun had slipped beneath the oak trees, and the Moon Woman would soon show her silver face.

Oil lamps burned in the windows of homes down the street, but all the storefronts were dark. Luke was the only person outside—everyone else had taken refuge from the whine and sting of the mosquitoes. A shaggy dog strolled past, gave Luke a baleful look, then wandered off to find a bed for the night. Somewhere in the distance a great horned owl uttered its resonant six-noted hoot.

If Hannah had stolen his money, he was ruined. He would have trouble even making the journey back to Kansas. But what tore through his gut was the loss of the land. He had come so close. Close enough to taste the sweetness of victory. His own land. His own hunting grounds. His own forest, deer, stream. His future lay within his grasp. Yet as the stars began to peep out from the blackness, he felt that future slipping through his fingers like sand.

Finally he had no choice but to admit that once again a white person had made the Indian a fool. For one sliver of a moment, he had dared to trust. He had let himself reach out. He had placed his faith in Hannah. And she had stolen his money, his land, his dream.

Anger as sour as an unripe persimmon in his mouth, Luke lifted his shoulder from the courthouse wall and turned to leave. His horse would be eager to move from the post where he was hitched. His falcon would want company, though his fierce brown eyes would reveal no joy when Luke appeared. He started across the thick grass and stepped onto the road.

"Luke!" The voice sang through his veins like a waterfall. "Oh, there you are!"

He spotted her instantly, and chills scattered down his spine. She was running down the boardwalk, her skirt swinging like a bell and her gloved hand lifted high. In her fingers she clutched a roll of papers. White papers. Official papers.

"Hannah!" He took off toward her at a dead run.

"I got the land," she cried. "All of it!"

In five paces he reached her, caught her around the waist, and lifted her high in his arms. She laughed and gasped and laughed again. He felt sure his heart would pound straight out of his chest. But as he lowered her to the ground, he realized it wasn't the news about his land that had sent a flood of warm rain through his veins. It was Hannah. This beautiful woman.

"Hannah," he said, his voice so low he could barely hear it. "You came back."

"Of course," she whispered. Her blue eyes filled with a surprised light. "I promised I would."

"I waited for you," he said, unwilling to move away from her, drinking in the sweet scent of her skin. "Lots of wagons came from Springfield this evening."

"I had to go to five mercantiles to find your supplies. Only one store carried seed that could be planted this late in the growing season. Then I had to find a farmer who had room in his wagon for a woman in a hoop skirt, plus a plow and five bags of seed. Almost everybody was loaded to the brim with goods. Finally I found a man who would take me, but when I got here I couldn't find you. So the farmer left me off at the hotel down the street. The seeds and everything are there—"

"Hannah, it's all right now."

Her eyes narrowed as she studied his face. "You thought I stole your money. You thought I wouldn't come back, didn't you? You don't trust me."

He removed his hands from her waist and stuffed them deeply into his pockets. "I told you once, Hannah, I never trust anyone."

"Am I supposed to trust you, then?" she asked. "Am I to place my protection and care in your hands—when you have not the slightest faith in me?"

"You can believe what I tell you, Hannah."

She met his gaze. "And you can believe what I tell you, Luke. I promised I would come back, and I did. I brought the seed and the plow . . . and the receipt for the land."

A knot formed in Luke's throat as he watched her unroll the papers as delicately as if they had been made of butterfly wings. Though it was almost completely dark, the moonlight shining on the first white page revealed the coordinates that marked the land's boundaries. *Eighteen dollars,* the receipt read. *Paid.*

"Here, Luke," Hannah whispered. "Here's your land."

She drew his hand from his pocket and laid the receipt in his open palm. He stared down at it, unable to speak, fighting the emotion that stung his eyes. With a piece of paper this very land had been stolen from his people. With another piece of paper, it would belong to them again. Land. Hope. A future.

"Come, Hannah," he said gently. "Let's go home."

Chapter
Eleven

❦

Butterflies danced through Hannah's stomach. They flitted and flirted; they turned somersaults and flips. Their wings ruffled inside her as they teased up and down, around and around in a hundred tiny circles.

It was Luke, of course. The butterflies were all his fault.

Only moments before he had lifted her onto the bare back of his enormous gray horse. Thank goodness her hoops had telescoped correctly and prevented the hem of her dress from flying up in his face, revealing her crinolines, petticoats, and—heaven forbid—her legs!

Hannah had just adjusted to the notion of a genteel ride when Luke leapt behind her onto the horse. He wedged her bottom tightly between his thighs, wrapped one arm just beneath her breasts, and gave the horse such a jab with his heels that it bolted into the darkness as if a demon were after it.

Gasping in shock, she had grabbed the nearest handholds— the horse's long mane and Luke's rock-hard thigh. So much for gentility, she thought as she struggled to take air into her lungs. This was as wild a ride as she could ever have imagined.

"Where are you going?" she cried when Luke turned the horse off the road and headed into the woods.

"To our land." His mouth was almost against her ear. She could feel his breath, hot and damp on her chilled cheek. "We'll take this trail."

"Which trail? It's far too dark to see anything!"

"We know the way."

Prayer—it was the only hope she had. *Our Father,* she began to mouth as the branches of oak trees whipped past only inches above her bonnet. *Our Father, which art in heaven* . . .

"Are you hungry, Hannah?" Luke asked, and his breath made hot shivers run down her neck.

The butterflies swirled upward and danced at the top of her stomach. Hungry? Who could possibly think about food? This man . . . this savage . . . was pressed so close to her she could feel his heart beating against her shoulder blades.

"No," she managed.

"I am. Starving."

The butterflies sank to the pit of her stomach and fluttered between her thighs. Why was she hearing messages in every sentence he uttered? Why had the thought of marrying him and spending the next few weeks with him sounded sane and reasonable three days ago? Now it seemed the maddest thing she'd ever done.

And it was. Oh, if Hannah's sisters could see her now . . . Every one of them would swoon straight to the ground. Hannah riding bareback through the Missouri forest in the middle of the night. Hannah clutching the solid thigh of an Indian whose arm pressed her so close against him she could hardly breathe. Hannah savoring the feel of that very Indian's fingers so warm and firm, so close to the sensitive skin of her lower breast.

This was vile and sinful . . . and utterly delicious. If she turned her head just so, she knew his lips would brush against hers. Would his mouth part as it had before? Would their tongues collide in a rainbow of shimmering stars?

If she sank against him just the barest bit, she felt certain his palm would slide beneath and then over the rounded curve of her breast. At the delicious image of his bronzed fingers cupping her, the butterflies zipped out of her stomach and flew straight to the tips of her breasts. Her nipples tightened and swelled beneath her chemise. Her thighs began to tingle.

"Lower your head now," Luke murmured. His words slipped down her spine like warm maple syrup. "I haven't had time to clear this section of the trail."

Before she could react, he placed his hand over her bonnet and pressed her head firmly against his chest. He, too, crouched over, shielding her with his arms and body. In the dark haven, she took in the scent of him—clean, male, magnificent. Her nostrils dilated as she instinctively rubbed her cheek against his shirt. My, but his chest was as hard as stone.

"We're almost there," he told her. "Hold on tight."

Oh, Lord. She gripped his thigh, certain her fingers weren't making a dent in his solid flesh. His hand spread out around the curve of her waist, and his thumb nestled in the fold of her overhanging breast. One slip . . . just the tiniest slip . . . and his hand would cover her . . .

What was she thinking? She didn't want this! She'd made him promise never to touch her. He'd told her he didn't want to . . . that any intimacy would defile him.

So why was she dreaming such wicked visions? Why did she wish this ride would go on and on forever? And why, oh, why had those butterflies melted into a droplet of juicy golden butter that had slid down between her thighs and begun to throb?

"Can you hear the river below us now?" Luke drew on the reins to slow the horse. "It's called Pomme de Terre."

Hannah tried to translate the French, but her brain wouldn't work properly. His chin was just above her shoulder, and she could feel his black hair brush her cheek. His arm supported the weight of her breasts. His thigh pressed against hers. Oh, heavens! She tangled her fingers through the horse's mane.

"My people lived here long before French fur traders came to give their own name to this river," Luke was saying. The horse came to a complete stop and lowered its head to nibble at a patch of ebony grass. "Frenchmen built trading posts and forts. They brought horses, guns, whiskey. They slept with our women, who then bore their children. They gave us French names."

"You once told me your French name," Hannah said, remembering.

"Jean-Luc Mabille." He paused for a moment, as if weighing his next words. When he spoke again, his voice was low. "So, what name did you give the judge in Springfield? Are you Hannah Maples, now?"

She nodded. "Would I wear your name if I were your Osage bride?"

"You would keep the identity of your own clan, but our children would belong to mine."

"What's your clan, Luke?"

"Hunkah A-Hiu-To'n."

"Does that mean anything?"

"The clan means everything to an Osage." His voice wore a smile. "There are two main divisions among the Osage, Hannah. The Tzi-Sho, the Sky People, are men and women of peace. The Hunkah, the Earth People, are warriors. I'm a Hunkah."

"I might have guessed."

"The Hunkah are divided into two groups. The first of these groups has seven clans. The name of my clan refers to the golden eagle. We call him the stainless one."

"Why?"

"Because it honors him. Long ago, the Little Old Men chose this bird as the symbol of my clan. The golden eagle attains great heights, and he circles indolently under the eyes of Grandfather the Sun. He's brave and ruthless. More important, he carries the color of sacred charcoal on his body, talons, and beak tip." Luke paused, recalling the evenings when he had sat beside his mother's lodge and watched the firelight flicker on his grandmother's face as she related the history of his people.

"But since you have no clan," he said to Hannah, "I suppose your name has no meaning."

"Hannah means graceful one." She listened to the river for a moment. Her heart had calmed a little, and she began to relax.

"You are graceful, Hannah."

"But I'm not an Osage."

"No." He fought to keep back words he didn't want her to

hear. He couldn't tell her she was more compelling than any Osage woman he had ever known. He couldn't reveal that her hair tempted him and her body called to his. Yet he didn't want her to remember only the harsh words he had spoken on the morning of their marriage ceremony.

"You're not an Osage," he acknowledged. "But you're as brave and as beautiful as any. I'll give you an Osage name. I'll call you Gthe-non'-zhin. It means Returns-and-Stands."

She glanced up at him in surprise. Their eyes met and locked. "Why that name?"

"Because you came back to me." He could feel her breasts, full and rounded against his arm. In the light of the Moon Woman, her damp lips glistened. Her eyes searched his face as he continued to speak. "Because I believe that no matter what happens to you, Hannah, you'll always stand strong. You may face battles, struggles, but you'll return in victory, standing tall and beautiful in your triumph."

A shiver coursed upward to the tips of her breasts. "Say my name again, Luke."

"Gthe-non'-zhin."

"Returns-and-Stands. It makes me feel invincible."

He smiled. "There's power in a name. You deserve that one."

"Gthe-non'-zhin," she whispered. Her eyelids slid shut. "Gthe-non'-zhin."

"Invincible woman . . ." Irresistibly drawn, he covered those compelling lips with his mouth.

She melted against him like a warm breath of wind. Her lips molded to his, soft, damp, hungry. Ignited by the intensity, the immediacy of her response, he dropped the reins and took her fully into his arms.

Adjusting her body to the shift in position, she slipped her hand higher up his thigh. "Hannah!" he growled. At the movement of her fingers, a thousand burning arrows shot through his skin to pierce his loins. A flaming wall of desire engulfed him.

But he knew she was an innocent dove and didn't understand the power of her touch. All the same, her need for him was a woman's need. And he needed her as a man needs his wife.

As he found her lips again, he tried to quell the sparks her fingertips had lit on his thigh. It was impossible. So close, her hand was. So near the source of his urgent, boiling hunger. Did she know? As his mouth played over her, his heart beat out the message . . . *Touch me! Touch me, Hannah. Touch me!*

"Hannah . . . I want you to . . ." His mouth slanted across hers. Could he ask? Could he demand satisfaction of her?

"Oh, Luke," she murmured against his mouth. "Luke, we promised each other."

No, he couldn't ask. They had given a pledge.

But her hand was so hot. Her fingers so tight. So close.

A bolt of lightning tore into his groin as he felt her tongue wet his lower lip. "Hannah!" he ground out again. He couldn't keep the images from his thoughts—her pale fingers stroking his rigid flesh . . . her soft hands playing velvet music up and down his sensitive sheath . . . her fingertips drawing him out until he stood up like a spear, bold and hard and male. He couldn't keep away. He didn't want to. Nothing had ever felt more right than the touch of this woman.

"Hannah, your mouth . . . your hands . . ." He ran his finger over the wet curve of her lower lip before kissing her again.

"Luke, we agreed not to." But as she spoke, her body belied every word. "We said . . . We promised . . ." Her mouth parted, and she took him in.

Penetrating the silken, intimate warmth, he sensed his body rear up like a panther. Every muscle coiled. Every nerve taut.

Her breath came in tiny gasps as he stroked her lips, played a dance of intimacy with her tongue, taught her the meaning of magic. He turned her so that her breasts crested against his chest. Oh, sweet heaven! The pressure of those full, womanly curves . . . the rounded points of her nipples . . . the image of touching them . . . tasting them . . .

"Please, Hannah—"

"Gthe-non'-zhin," she whispered against his neck. Returns-and-Stands. A woman alone, powerful, mysterious, strong. Yes, she was strong! And yes, she desired this man whose kisses made her throb deep inside. She wanted his mouth, his hands, his body.

"I swore to myself," he began, but her hands had slipped

around his back, and her tongue was making a damp trail down his neck. "I made a vow . . ."

"Oh, Luke, I know. I know it's wrong. A mistake. A sin—"

"No!" He caught her shoulders. Her blue eyes went wide as he shook her lightly. "It's not a sin. Not between husband and wife. This is God's gift. This desire. This spirit that has drifted around us and pulls us together."

"But we promised each other. We said we didn't want—"

"Do you want me, Gthe-non'-zhin?"

She drew in a breath at the power of his question. Did she want him? Yes. Oh, yes! But to allow the liberties of a husband with his wife? To procreate?

"I want you to kiss me," she told him. "I want you to kiss me and hold me every day and every night as long as I'm with you."

"And nothing more?" He could almost hear the roar of the panther in his loins—aroused, pulsing, demanding satisfaction. "You would have me kiss you until the hunger between us burns like a fire. And then?"

"You said you didn't want me to bear you a child. What more can there be without that?"

He looked into her face. "Oh, sweet Hannah. Oh, my Gthe-non'-zhin. Let me show you."

Luke let his horse pick its own path up the final hill. They had come this way a dozen times or more in the last three days—clearing stones and brush, felling trees, hunting. The horse knew the way, and Luke wanted only to think—about the stranger Ethan Brown, about marriage to a white woman, about the buffalo blanket that lay waiting and whether he should spread this woman's thighs.

But finding a trail of thoughts he could follow was harder than tracking a deer down a riverbed. His brain had stopped functioning. His body had taken over. There was only instinct. Only the mating call.

He had heard about this mystery—that the right woman could make a man lose his reason. Once the body demanded satisfaction, nothing else would do. It was the madness of the wapiti bull in rut. Mating became the only aim, the only hope to ease the all-consuming desire.

But Luke knew he was not an animal, not completely subject to the whims of nature. He knew, too, the enticing secrets his friends had spoken of in the darkness of the forest. Though Osage maidens were carefully guarded at all times, and Osage men stayed pure until marriage, it didn't keep them from talking. From imagining. From wondering.

Pleasures could be had, Luke and his friends theorized, without the final act of mating. A woman could touch a man, they assured each other, and with her hands and mouth give him every pleasure he needed without the chance of creating a child. A man might be able to do the same for a woman. It could be done; they were all certain of it.

None of them, of course, had ever been given the opportunity to put such a theory to the test. All the same, they talked, they speculated, and in their beds alone at night, they dreamed of finding such a woman—a woman who could work magic with her hands . . . and with her mouth.

Would Hannah agree? Luke studied the side of her face as they rode the last paces up the moonlit hill. Would she hold him in the darkness and run her fingers over his naked body? Would she allow him to undress her, to know the mysteries that lay beneath those stiff clothes she wore?

"Are we almost there?" she asked, turning slightly. Her breasts brushed his arms.

He nodded. "On the crest of the hill."

Did her question mean she was as eager as he? Did white women speak of the same things Osage men spoke of before marriage? Did they wonder aloud about the pleasures of the body?

"I'm so hot," she whispered. "Is there a stream near the house you've built?"

"Very close."

"Oh, Luke . . ."

"Here, Hannah." He felt his heart again begin to hammer as the horse emerged into the clearing he had worked so hard to prepare. This was the place he had readied for her . . . the haven for the explorations . . . their hideaway . . . "This is your home."

In dismay she stared at the long, hulking shape in the distance. It had no roof, only rounded sides that curved upward to meet in the middle. The walls seemed to sag. They weren't made of logs or stone or brick, but of layers and layers of something—something that looked like old, rotted leaves strung together. There were no windows. No chimney. No porch.

"This is the house you've been building?" she whispered.

"It's a lodge."

"When will you finish it?"

"It is finished."

"But it . . . it looks like a . . . like a shack."

Luke stiffened. "It's a lodge," he repeated.

"You mean I'm to live inside there?"

"Of course. We both will."

"But the walls are—"

"Buffalo skins. While you were in Springfield, I cut hickory saplings and drove their bottoms into the ground in a large rectangle, see? Then I tied the tops together. It's tall enough inside that I can stand without touching my head to the roof. After I'd formed the outer framework, I interlaced smaller saplings to fill it in."

"Then it's . . . it's like a basket. You brought me here to live in a basket."

She knew her words were too harsh, but she couldn't restrain them. From the moment she'd agreed to the rash idea of marrying this man, she'd clung to his promise of a snug home, good food, and protection. For the past three days she'd been anticipating this moment. They would ride up to the front of a cozy log house with a wide front porch and a split-rail fence around the yard. The kind of house in her book. Not this. Not this . . .

"It's a twig house," she said. "I thought you were going to build a log cabin."

"In three days?" He dismounted and held up his hands to Hannah. The magic of their ride through the forest was drifting away like smoke on a windy day. "Besides, a lodge is better than a log house. Come, I'll show you. This is how we live in my village in Kansas. You'll like it."

She placed her hands on his shoulders and slid into his arms. For a moment he considered drawing her close against his body and making her forget all her hesitation. But he knew her thoughts were no longer dwelling on sweet kisses, but on that so-called basket of a house behind him.

He set her feet on the ground and took her hand. It felt small and as fragile as a bird's wing. There would be hours later for exploration. Now it was time for patience.

"We Osage live in lodges," he explained as they walked across the clearing. "Sometimes our women make the outer walls of woven cattail reeds. But I used buffalo skin, as we often do. They'll keep the lodge warm in winter and cool in summer. There are two fireplaces inside, one at each end, and I left an opening at the top for smoke to escape. I put the doorway in the eastern side so you can see Grandfather the Sun as he rises each morning."

"I never get up before sunrise," she said quickly.

Now it was Luke's turn to stare. "When do you get up?"

"When Cook rings, of course. She comes into my room with a tray of hot tea about . . . Oh, eight o'clock. After I've taken my tea, I dress and curl my hair. My sisters and I assist each other, or the process would last twice as long—corsets take forever to lace, you know. And one has to heat curling irons and tie ribbons and arrange bonnets. When cook rings a second time, breakfast is served. It's nearly nine by then. The rest of the day is frightfully busy. If we began it at dawn, we'd swoon with exhaustion by luncheon."

When he said nothing, gaping at her as though she were speaking a foreign language, she decided she'd better explain. "After breakfast," she said patiently, "it's time for morning calls or needlework or painting. Then we take our luncheon. Following that, we rest for a bit to aid digestion, then we rise to greet our afternoon callers. We might do a bit more needlework if we like, but that's when I usually write my novels. Then it's time for afternoon tea. After that, we rest again, and finally we dress for dinner. Then it's music and perhaps dancing until rather late. Sometimes we're invited out. Finally, it's off to bed. Don't you see? One couldn't think of getting up too early when one has to stay up so late with one's dinner guests."

Luke regarded the woman standing outside his lodge. She was gazing up at him with eyes like two shining blue moons. Her face was solemn, serious, honest. He didn't know whether to grab her shoulders and try to shake some reality into her, or laugh out loud.

"And as for a house made with basket walls," she was saying, "with a covering of buffalo skin . . . That wasn't at all what I had in mind when I agreed to our arrangement. I expect to be provided with the basic comforts to which I'm accustomed, Luke. Solid walls, for example. A carpeted floor. A wooden door."

She gestured at the buffalo hide that hung over the opening to his lodge. "I can hardly believe you expect me to live in there—with nothing better than a musty old hide to keep out the dangers of these woods. What about insects? What about bears?"

He stared at her, bemused, as she continued. She could be the most annoying creature. More irritating than an ankle covered with raw chigger bites.

"I don't know what we could do about a stove either," she went on. "We can't very well place a hot stovepipe through a wall made of sticks. We'd burn the whole thing down. And what if it's windy? The slightest draft can cause terrible illness—"

"Be quiet, woman." He scooped her up in his arms, kicked open the door flap, and carried her inside. "You talk too much, you know that? Talk, talk, talk. I knew you were trouble the moment I agreed to take you to Springfield that first time."

He dropped her onto a soft, springy surface and vanished.

"Luke?" Sitting up, she felt around in the darkness. Beneath her there was something warm and fluffy, like a thick-pile rug. There was a mesmerizing smell, too. Woodsy and fragrant. And then she heard a scraping sound somewhere in the distance.

"Luke? Is that you?"

When there was no answer, she reached out into the darkness. Was this a wall beside her? Or a curtain? She couldn't see a thing in the utter void. Why didn't Luke answer?

She maneuvered her hoop until she was kneeling on the soft rug. Straightening, she felt around in the blackness. If she could find the wall for balance, she could stand. Was she on a bed or on the floor? How dare Luke leave her alone like this. Where was he? What was he doing?

She groped around in the blackness until her fingers touched something warm and soft. Something alive!

As she was pulling away, a sudden sharp pain tore through her hand.

"Ouch! Oh—what was . . . ?" Wincing in pain, she jerked her palm against her breast. Her fingers went numb. "Got to get out of this . . . basket . . ." Cradling her hand, she began to scramble through the darkness in the opposite direction from her attacker.

Someone was after her. Someone with a knife. Luke? Visions of his scalp-trimmed leggings danced through her mind. She slid to the edge of the furry rug and tumbled to the ground in a heap. Reaching blindly, she groped for a handhold. Something. Anything!

Just as she found what she thought must be the wall, a pair of warm hands clamped down on her shoulders. She swung around and jammed her elbow into a wall of solid muscle.

"Uhh!" Luke's voice was unmistakable.

"Get away from me!" Tangled in her hoop, she shielded her wounded hand as she tried to fend off his grasp. "Leave me alone!"

"Hannah!" He grappled with her flying elbows. "Hannah, it's me. Luke. What's wrong?"

"You knifed me!" She bit the hand gripping her arm.

"What? Ouch!" A flood of words in his native tongue cut through the air. Then he grabbed her again. "Hannah, what's going on?"

As if he didn't know! Still struggling against him, she worked to free her foot from the two steels that somehow had gotten crossed in her attempt to crawl across the floor.

"Hannah, talk to me," he demanded.

Before she could bite him again, he pushed her shoulders to the floor and straddled her. She let out a screech that would have raised the rafters had there been any. For a moment she struggled beneath him, kicking and twisting. And then the breath went out of her. She lay still, hardly moving, barely trembling.

"Kill me first," she whispered.

"What?" he asked, incredulous.

"Before you slice off my scalp . . . kill me first. If you have any mercy in your heathen blood, do it quickly."

He said nothing. Then he began to chuckle.

"What is so amusing?" she demanded.

He laughed out loud. "You think I want your scalp?"

"You tried to kill me. You stabbed my hand." A new wave of pain washed over her as the numbness in her fingers began to fade.

He debated moving to one side, but he was afraid she'd try to bolt again. "Hannah, I didn't stab you. And I don't want your scalp."

As the burning sensation in her hand grew sharper, she tried to suck in a deep breath. But Luke's body was lying on top of hers, pressing her into the ground and crushing the air from her lungs. "Somebody stabbed me," she managed.

"There's no one in my lodge but the two of us, Hannah," he said in a low voice. "Only you and me. Now, will you stay put while I light a lamp?"

She thought it over for a moment. This savage had scooped her up and carried her into his house. Then he had dropped her as though she were a sack of flour. Then he . . . or someone . . . had knifed her. Why should she trust a word he said?

"Hannah?" he asked again. His mouth brushed across hers. Warm, reassuring. "I give you my vow. I will never hurt you."

She shut her eyes. She was a fool for the man's kisses. "All right," she whispered.

The weight of his body lifted. In a moment she saw a golden light. Luke's face emerged in the glow of the lamp he was carrying. He peered down at her, his brown eyes luminous.

"Can you sit up?" he asked.

"I'm tangled."

He helped her disengage her foot from the hoop. Then he lifted her onto the fluffy rug—a tanned buffalo skin lying on his bed. Sitting down beside her, he placed the lamp on a small table. "Let me see your hand, Hannah."

She uncovered it and confirmed that the flesh on one side was torn and bleeding. Luke frowned as he inspected the damage. Gently he touched the open wound. What had caused this? He lifted his head and scanned the inside of his lodge. Nothing was out of place. No enemy lurked in the darkness.

"Hannah, what happened?"

"I don't know," she said. "You picked me up and carried me into this wretched dark . . . cave. Then you threw me down and walked off. When I reached out to try to find a wall or a . . ." She looked up at the place where she had stretched her hand.

In the shadows a pair of sharp, bright eyes stared back at her. Brown eyes. Deeply hooded. Unblinking.

"Luke!" she gasped.

He swung around. "Gthe-don!" Realization washed through him. "My falcon attacked you."

For the first time Luke's anger burned against his hunting companion. He stormed up from the bed and stalked toward the perch where the raptor was tethered.

"Why?" he demanded. "Why did you do this to my woman?"

The falcon turned away and regarded the oil lamp. Giving Luke a clear view of his sharply curved beak, the bird seemed to relay a message of disdain and superiority. Brown feathers ruffling, he readjusted his taloned feet on the perch and then rotated his head again to study the pair of watching humans.

"You'd better get used to her," Luke snapped at the hawk. "She's my wife, and she's here to stay. If you attack her again, I'll prepare a dinner of roasted prairie falcon. Do you hear, Gthe-don?"

The raptor looked at Hannah, then at Luke. Then he turned completely around on the perch until nothing was visible but his large brown back and long, striped tail feathers.

"Pompous bird," Luke muttered.

He sat down on the bed beside Hannah again and took her hand. Spreading her fingers across his thigh, he checked to see that they still moved well. Her face was as pale as the moon, and her eyes were bright with pain, but she was silent.

"I'm sorry this happened, Hannah," Luke said as he stripped off his shirt. He tore a length from the hem and placed it across the gash in her hand to blot the blood. What a wonderful welcome, he mused. Hannah's first view of her new home— and it's an Osage lodge instead of a snug log cabin. Then a falcon tears a hole in her hand. This makes her think she's about to be scalped by the very man who swore to protect her.

"Can you bend your fingers?" he asked gently.

She winced as she tried to tighten her hand into a fist. "It hurts here, along the edge."

He carefully touched the place she had indicated. "The flesh is deeply torn. You should see a doctor."

"No," she said. "I'd go to my doctor in Boston, but not . . . not out here. Just bandage it up. I'll heal."

Again he muttered in his native tongue. "Hannah, I am sorry. The bird is . . . aggressive. What makes Gthe-don a good hunter can also make him difficult to live with."

Hannah studied Luke's long, bronzed fingers as he tied another strip of his shirt around her hand. How could she stay angry when he was so apologetic about the whole incident? Yet, as she observed his thick black hair and penetrating brown eyes, she wondered how different this man was from his falcon.

Aggressive. Irascible. Difficult to live with.

"Intelligent," Luke said, breaking into her thoughts. "Nothing escapes the falcon. He's disdainful of anything or anyone he perceives as inferior. You should see the way he harasses birds that are much bigger. Ravens, hawks, eagles—he's unmerciful. And he's so fast. He can strike swifter than lightning. He's trained to be a killer. You don't ever want to cross him. You never want to trust him too much, Hannah."

"I know," she said. "You've told me before not to trust."

"Especially not the falcon. You'll think you know him. You'll think there are no more surprises. And then—boom." He smacked his hands together. "He attacks. Never trust him."

Nodding, Hannah tucked her bandaged hand in her lap. "Never trust the falcon," she repeated. "Never trust anyone."

He glanced up, surprised at the tone of her voice. Her blue eyes were fastened to his face, assessing, almost cold. "Did you really think I would scalp you, Hannah?" he asked.

"Would you have?"

"Never."

"Why not?" She tried to read behind the veil that had slipped down over his eyes. Moments before, he had called her his woman . . . his wife. He had said she was here to stay. What had those words spoken in a rash moment meant? She had to know.

"Am I not to trust you either, Luke?" she asked.

"No," he answered quickly. "Never trust."

"What should I fear about you, then? What might you do to me?"

He was silent a moment, his predatory eyes searching hers. "I might want you, Hannah," he said finally. "I might want you too much."

Chapter Twelve

"I built two beds," Luke said, standing and moving away from Hannah. "One is at this end of the lodge. The other's down there. You can see I hung a divider between. I'll sleep here near the door. You can have the other bed."

"All right." Hannah picked up the oil lamp. His confession of desire had shaken her, but she didn't want him to know he could have such an effect on her equilibrium. "Will there be any supper this evening?"

"Not if you expect a cook to ring a bell and bring your meal on a silver tray. If you want to eat, you fix your own food." His voice was harsh, almost indifferent, as he walked to the door. "I'm going to the stream to bathe."

Hannah watched him hook his finger through a hole in the hide that covered the doorway. He swung open the flap, stepped through the opening, and vanished into the darkness. For a moment she listened for the sound of his footsteps. Nothing. The man was as silent as a panther.

She examined her bandaged hand again, then lifted her eyes to the falcon in the corner. "You," she said, "are a pest."

His back still facing her, the bird swiveled his head almost all the way around and stared at her with sharp brown eyes.

"One more trick like that," she announced as she rose, "and I shall pluck out your feathers and use them to wipe that insolent look off your saucy little beak. It's bad enough I have to live in this . . . this hovel for the next few weeks until I find my brother. It's bad enough that I'm miles from the faintest trace of civilization. It's bad enough that I have no one to talk to except a man I can't trust. But—you!" She set one hand on her hip and shook her finger at the falcon. "You are not going to make my life a torment. Do you hear me, bird?"

The raptor turned around on the perch. His long talons gripped the well-peeled branch embedded in the earthen floor. Proud, unmoved by her heated speech, the animal stared at her.

Gthe-don was magnificent, Hannah had to admit. Pure white feathers surrounded his neck, while two contrasting black streaks ran downward from each eye—almost like war paint. The pair of hooded chocolate eyes missed nothing, and the hooked gray beak looked as wicked as a curved scimitar. Dark, tear-shaped spots ran in a neat pattern down the white front of the bird's breast, as though the creature were clad in a fine morning coat. But the gentlemanly image ended at the pair of long, razor-sharp talons.

"Your master may think he's a fearsome devil with his vicious bird and his nasty scalp-lock leggings," Hannah said as she walked around the lodge to survey the place that would be her home for the time being. "And you may think you can drive me away by pecking my hand. But I think both of you are just bluster."

She pulled open the drawstrings of a long, elaborately decorated bag and ran her fingers over the beautiful needle-work on a stack of Luke's shirts. Ribbons had been embroidered down the front of each woven garment. Carefully stitched underlays created patterns that revealed layers of contrasting fabric. Blue, pink, purple, red, white, green—the colors were bright and satiny. But the ingeniously worked symbols delighted Hannah even more—geometric arrows and butterflies, even stylized handprints. Deeper in the bag lay beaded belts and vests adorned with designs created of small metal disks.

Everything smelled wonderful, with a light scent that was sweet and at the same time undeniably masculine. When she shook open a shirt, tiny black seeds tumbled to the ground, and small fragrant leaves fluttered from the folds. No wonder Luke always smelled so good, she mused. He tucked these aromatic herbs into all his stored clothing.

Holding the shirt to the light, she turned it this way and that. "How magnificent!" she whispered. "Now, Gthe-don, you mean old bird, what do you think of this? How could a man who's meant to be a savage wear such a shirt as this? This is a work of art. Did Luke's mother stitch it?"

The falcon regarded her stoically.

"All right," she went on, "be sullen if you like."

She placed the shirt back into the bag and retied the drawstrings. She had been right about the stove. There wasn't one. But Luke had made some sort of a fireplace out of smooth river stones set in a circle. She could see he'd been cooking. An iron kettle sat near the fireplace, and a few odd-looking containers full of supplies were stacked against the wall.

"Luke told me to eat," she said to the falcon, "and so I shall. But you've already had your dinner, haven't you? I hope my hand tasted lovely. You took a big enough chunk out of it."

She lifted the lid on one of the containers and found a collection of those jerky strips Luke had been so keen on. She didn't want that for supper! But her inspection of the remainder of the containers provided nothing more appetizing than a bunch of old roots, some withered greenery, a few brownish mushrooms, and several other items she couldn't identify. None looked edible.

Jerky it would be, then. She had just torn off her first bite when she heard Luke step back into the lodge. "How was the stream?" she asked as she turned toward him. "Chilly, I should th—" She nearly choked.

The man was naked.

Well, except for that little leather apron-thing tied around his waist, he was. Stark naked! She gaped at him—at his enormous copper chest sporting two flat brown nipples, long tanned legs, bare male feet—then she whirled around to face the opposite direction. Oh, heavens!

"Find something to eat?" he asked.

She swallowed at the forgotten lump of jerky in her mouth. It seemed to have swelled to twice its former size. "Uhh . . . mmm . . . yes, I did."

"Good."

He was striding down to her end of the lodge. She could hear his footsteps on the earth floor, but she couldn't look. Where were his clothes? Did he actually intend to parade around in that leather apron all evening?

"Here are some pawpaws in this basket," he said. "Ever eaten a pawpaw, Hannah?"

She shook her head quickly, then glanced at him out of the corner of her eye. He had hunkered down in front of the fireplace and was sorting through the containers. The short apron was split up his thigh to his waist. One of the leather flaps had draped back, and she could see all the way up it to his golden buttocks! Oh, Lord!

"They taste something like a banana," he was telling her. "But there are other flavors mixed in. Try one. And here are some walnuts. Do you like walnuts?"

He turned toward her. At the sight of her shocked expression, he stood quickly, concern prickling down his spine. Then he recognized the significance of the bright spots of pink on her cheeks and the flush of embarrassment spreading up her neck. Her blue eyes darted from his chest to the wall, back to his bare legs and then to the fireplace. She swallowed, and as he approached, he could see the moist sheen that had broken out on her forehead.

A smile began to play on his lips. "Hannah," he asked again, coming to stand right in front of her. "Do you like walnuts? Or are you hungry for something else?"

The spots on her cheeks flamed red. "I'm perfectly fine."

Her voice was low and throaty. He could see her breathing like a sparrow caught in a trap. Her fine, high breasts rose and fell, rose and fell. How interesting, he thought as he pulled one of her bonnet ribbons to release the bow. Hannah was as disconcerted by his bare body as he had been at the mere image of hers.

"Are you still hot, Hannah?" he asked. "You look a little . . . damp."

Her fingers tightened around the strip of jerky. "Aren't there any windows in this lodge of yours?"

"We don't feel the need for windows. But then, we Osage don't usually wear as many clothes as you Heavy Eyebrows do."

He lifted the bonnet from her head, and for a moment he stared in awe at the pile of cinnamon hair pinned up in great coils and loops. Tossing the bonnet onto the bed, he let his eyes trail down her neck to the high, tight bodice of her dress. How could there be so many buttons on one garment? And why? It was as if these Heavy Eyebrows women were afraid the slightest gust of wind might expose their precious white skin to the sun.

"You could put on something cooler," he said, running the side of his finger down her heated cheek. "What I'm wearing is very comfortable."

She glanced down at him, then bit her lower lip.

"Haven't you ever seen a breechcloth? This is a long strip of leather," he explained, taking her hand and stroking her fingers down the front of the garment. "It flaps over my woven belt in the front, then it goes between my thighs and flaps over the belt in the back."

Hannah thought she was going to melt onto the floor in a puddle as he lifted back the apron to reveal the sueded buckskin pouch that barely contained him. His smooth, taut skin stretched from his bare buttocks around and beneath the bulging thong in front.

"Very nice," she managed, then flushed as hot as a flame again at the implication of her own words. "The apron, I mean. Or rather . . . the breechcloth."

He was grinning at her, a lazy, insolent smile that sent sparks shooting through her stomach. Did he think she would swoon at his feet with the briefest glimpse of his grand, masculine body? Well, she thought, two could play at such a game.

"I would never dream of wearing so few clothes," she said, giving a stretch that she knew would draw his attention to her bosom. "I should think the mosquitoes would find you a feast."

"A feast?" he returned. "I wouldn't mind being a feast . . . for the right diner."

She caught her breath and turned away. Pulling the pins from her hair, she dropped them casually onto the low bed. "Who can think of eating now anyway? I'm exhausted from traveling."

Swirling around to face him again, she gave him a full view of her long hair tumbling over her shoulders to her waist. Transfixed, his eyes softened to deep mahogany velvet. She ran her fingers through her hair, working out the curls and checking for stray pins. Aware that she was playing with fire, she fluffed and toyed with her tresses, winding a strand around her finger, then brushing it aside as her fingertips swept across her breast.

"We Heavy Eyebrows," she said, "never run about half-naked as you Osage do. We wear decent clothing that covers us properly. We eat food that's been cooked, not hung over a rack to dry in its own blood. And we sleep until a civilized hour of the morning beneath our bedding made of fine linen and goose down. We do not rise at dawn after a night of lying on buffalo hides."

She started to turn away, but he caught her arm and swung her around. "Hannah, have you ever lain on a buffalo hide with a half-naked man who eats raw meat dried in its blood?"

"No," she whispered, suddenly afraid that her coy teasing had pushed him too far.

"Then perhaps you don't know what you've been missing."

"Perhaps not . . ."

She stared at him, struggling to remain calm as his hands slid up her arms and into her loose hair. He was right—she talked too much. Her mouth had always gotten her in trouble. She was wicked. And, oh, the look in Luke's eyes made her feel sinful . . . so sinfully delicious.

"Perhaps there are many things you don't know, Hannah," he said, his mouth a breath away from hers. "Perhaps you don't know what I meant this evening on the horse when I kissed you."

"About . . . about not procreating?"

His lips formed a half smile. "About learning how to touch."

"Luke, I—"

"I think so, Hannah. I think you're as intrigued as I am."

She shook her head, but the words wouldn't come. His fingers threaded through her hair, drifted up the side of her neck, touched the row of buttons at her throat.

"I'm not experienced in such matters," she whispered. "I wouldn't know—"

"Neither would I. But I'd like to find out. You've made me curious, Hannah. Have I made you curious?"

She couldn't say a word as his fingers began slipping open the buttons on her bodice one by one. As her breasts were released from the confining fabric, the placket gaped apart. And then his hands formed around her waist, molding the curves and sliding down her hips.

"You're very hard here," he murmured. "Not soft, like your shoulders."

"It's my . . . my corset," she explained.

"Can it come off?"

"Yes, but—"

"How?"

She watched in breathless fascination as his large hands brushed back her bodice to reveal her chemise and corset. She could see that her breasts had swollen, and she was certain their tips were tight little buds of excitement.

Something told her this game was dangerous, yet she didn't want to stop it. He had assured her it was safe. Not sinful—for they were married. But how could she be certain? It felt so wicked to stand here in the half light and allow this man to strip away her garments one by one.

Now he had tossed her bodice to the floor and was examining the row of hooks on the front of her corset. "Like this," she said suddenly, and sucked in a deep breath before flicking them apart.

But when the corset tumbled away, and she saw the look of bold hunger in his eyes, she knew she had made a mistake. He was staring at her chemise, devouring the sight of her bold nipples as they jutted against the thin white fabric. Fear mingled with the desire she felt as he lifted a hand and ran it down her bare arm.

"Will you touch me, Hannah?" he asked, meeting her gaze with his brown eyes. "I won't hurt you."

"You warned me not to trust you."

"Don't trust me. But always trust yourself, your own instincts. How do you feel?"

"Savage," she murmured.

His eyes burned. "Hungry?"

She nodded. "And frightened."

"Curious?"

"Fascinated."

"Do you want to know the feel of my bare skin?" He took her hand and laid it on his chest, covering the circle of his nipple.

Beneath her palm she could feel the heated flesh, the mound of solid muscle, the tension of his sinew. "I like it," she said.

"Taste it."

Her eyes flew open . . . but intrigue won over surprise. Nostrils flared, she leaned against him and placed her lips on his skin. He drank in a deep breath as her mouth moved over his chest, exploring, savoring.

"The skin of my belly is flat and hard," he said when she lifted her head. He moved her palm across his stomach just above the line of the woven belt that held his breechcloth. "Are you also hard there, Hannah? Or are you soft like a flower?"

Her eyelids drifted shut as his hands moved from her hips to her stomach, his fingers testing the flesh beneath her full skirt. Then he was unhooking her garments one by one—skirt, crinoline, hoop, petticoats—and letting them puff to the ground in a heap of billowing fabric.

"Oh, Luke," she murmured. She was standing before this man . . . this stranger . . . in nothing but her smallclothes. But his hands pulled her slowly closer until their bodies pressed together . . . and she liked it. Very much.

She liked it even more when she felt his fingers creep up the front of her chemise. Her breasts began to tingle. How did he know? How was he so certain of the exact things to do to draw out such magic inside her? She knew nothing about him. Nothing but the hard pressure against her stomach, the sure sense of urgency about his body as he stroked and manipulated hers.

"I feel your fear," he murmured against her cheek. "Fear is

good, Hannah. It heightens your senses. It makes you alert, aware of everything in this game we play."

"Is this a game, Luke?"

"Nothing more." He trailed his fingers up and over the hill of her breast, enjoying the silken fire of full, rounded female flesh. Flames curled down his thighs as he cupped her breast in his palm. His hands were large, but one palm could barely contain her as he lifted and weighed the heavy globe.

"This is our mystery game," he whispered. "A hunt for secret pleasures. Always, in the midst of the hunt, a man feels fear. His heart beats like a war drum. His breath hangs in his chest. His muscles swell and tense. He feels and knows everything around him. Like the falcon, he hovers, ready to plunge, ready to penetrate."

She could hear his voice through the swirls of fog in her mind, but she couldn't find words to respond. While one of his hands caressed her breast, the other tugged at the pink ribbon holding her chemise. She could feel the thin fabric sliding away, baring her skin to his touch. And, oh, the wonder!

His hands were huge and warm and work-callused as they covered her. His breath came hot and ragged across her skin as his fingertips circled around and around her bare flesh. Yes, she liked this game. She savored the danger, the uncertainty.

Opening her eyes to thin slits, she watched through the veil of her lashes as his thumbs stroked her milky skin. Never had she seen her own breasts so full, so swollen. Her nipples had cherried into sweet, aching rose-hued crests that seemed to beg for his touch. He was so close, so very close.

"Luke, touch me," she pleaded.

"Touch me, Hannah," he returned.

With a deep breath that quelled the flickering uncertainty in her stomach, she allowed her hands to slide down his chest. Yes, she understood what he meant. She could feel the source of his own desire pushing against her pelvis, hard, demanding.

"Are you certain this is just a game?" she queried again as she covered the pouch of his breechcloth with her hand.

He stiffened at her touch. His biceps tightened, expanded. His eyes fell shut, and his face went slack. Slowly, tentatively, she moved her hand down him.

"Only a game," he confirmed. "But a dangerous game. Hannah . . . you make me weak."

Thrilled by her own sense of power, she stroked her hand over his hardened length. She could feel his body, pushing, thrusting against her palm, wanting more and more. He was marvelous, majestic, an animal in the essence of its element. As her massage increased in tempo, he returned his attention to her breasts.

But when his thumbs stroked over her nipples for the first time, she gasped. "Luke!"

His eyes opened. "Hannah?"

"Luke . . . it's not a game."

"I want to taste you," he whispered.

She couldn't speak aloud, but she knew her eyes said yes. Yes, yes, yes. "Oh, Luke . . . I'm melting."

He smiled as he bent his head and ran his tongue over her pebbled nipple. She sucked in a breath. Her knees went hot. A damp, throbbing heat curled into itself and nestled between her thighs.

"Luke, I don't think this is a game," she repeated, more certain than ever that this was a mistake—and equally certain that she wanted to ride it to its culmination.

"It's a game with high stakes," he countered. "A gamble. I wager we'll both be winners, Hannah."

"But I'm losing," she said as she sank onto the bed because her knees would no longer support her. "I'm losing control."

He looked into her eyes, his own deep and searching. Moving to lie beside her, he ran his open hand down her body. He reveled in the feel of womanly curves and hollows. He wanted her to lose control. He wanted her to writhe against him, as women were said to do when a man touched them the right way. He wanted her to gasp and scream out loud with pleasure. He wanted to give her that, this fire-haired spirit-woman in his arms.

Bending over her, he ran his tongue around and around her nipples until they were wet and glistening in the lamplight. She gripped his shoulders, her head thrown back on the buffalo robe that cushioned their bodies. She was beautiful, hungry, a woman in need of his touch. He had awakened her—and the knowledge stirred him.

"You like this, Hannah," he told her. "You enjoy my mouth on your skin. I think you feel happier now than you have since you came to Missouri."

She nodded, lost in a haze of lights that drifted around her head. "It seems as if I'm on top of a mountain," she whispered, "and I want to jump off."

He knew he could take her even higher. He felt that power, that innate certainty within himself. But he had promised her there would be no risk. No danger.

"Are you on the mountain, too, Luke?" she asked him through glazed eyes.

He swallowed. "I'm still climbing."

"Mmm." The thought that she could lead him to feel what she felt gave her a sense of incredible desire. She slipped her hands over the mound of his breechcloth, then she felt for the tie that bound the leather thong to his waist.

"I'll take you with me," she whispered, and she pulled the woven belt. It came apart, and the leather apron fell away with the forward thrust of his shaft.

She bit her lip in wonder as he emerged fully into her hands, a flaming rod of male flesh. At her touch on his bare skin, he groaned aloud. It was an animal sound, rich and resonant, deep with need. Shivers rippled through her as she began to stroke him, her palms and fingers drawing out his need.

"Hannah!" he cried when she pushed her breasts against his chest. Driven, he stared into her blue eyes and saw the fatal effect of their game. She wanted him as much as he wanted her. And his need was strong, a raging flood that pushed against the dam. He had to find release. He had to ease himself—but the only source of comfort lay within the velvet of Hannah's body.

"Hannah, this is enough for tonight," he ground out.

"No," she whispered, shaking her head. "I don't want to stop. I like the game too much."

Rolling onto her knees, she began to kiss his stomach. The scent of his clean skin drifted around her as she trailed her tongue down his body.

"Hannah!" he cried out again. He grabbed her shoulders, but she refused to be drawn away.

"I'm aching inside, Luke," she mouthed against him. "Touch me, Luke. Play the game with me."

"Hannah, this is far enough." But he knew his words carried no conviction. Her sweet lips had covered him, her tongue making wet strokes over his sensitive arousal. This was what he had dreamed of. This was exactly the moment he and his friends had whispered about in the still, silent darkness of the night. A woman's hands. A woman's mouth.

But this was stronger. Much more powerful than he'd ever imagined. This was more than a game. More than a brief interlude from which he could walk away.

"Luke, please caress me," she begged.

If he obeyed . . . if he discovered a molten pool between her thighs—that magic pool of which he had heard so many rumors—he would want to drown himself in it. He would be driven over the brink of restraint. He would have to take her completely.

"I'm so hot," she murmured. "I feel so strange. I'm trembling right down to the tips of my toes. Please do something, Luke. Please . . . help me."

"Hannah." He cupped her head and lifted her away from him. Her breasts grazed his chest as she shifted to lie at his side. "Hannah, what have we done?"

"We're playing the game. It's safe . . . you promised."

"I was wrong." He gritted his teeth as he felt the pressure of her hardened nipples pressing into him. "It's not safe. I want you too much, Hannah. I want to make you my mate."

She closed her eyes, unable to think past the miracle of his fingertips as they played across her stomach. *Lower,* she felt herself urging silently. *Lower, Luke. Touch me. Ease me. Satisfy me.*

"All right," she whispered heedlessly. "Make me your mate."

He clenched his fist, fighting. Wanting her. Awash in the demand she had stirred. "No," he muttered.

Rolling away from her, he stood. Dear God, how he needed release! His body jutted out, so ready to penetrate. So ready to thrust away the last barrier between them.

"I gave you my word, Hannah," he managed. "I swore a vow."

She stared at his broad back, at the hard outlines of his shoulders, the rounded muscles that defined his naked buttocks, the fine sinews of his legs. His skin glowed with a light sheen. His fists knotted, released, knotted again.

He turned on his heel and strode out of the lodge.

"Luke!" she called.

"Go to sleep, Hannah."

His voice cut through the night as he disappeared. She lay for a moment, breathing hard, blinking in the mists that swirled around her head. Blood pounded in her temples. Her breasts throbbed. The small of her back ached with a delicate, curling pain. The nest between her legs pulsed.

She slipped her hands around her bare breasts. Oh, Luke! Why had he led her down this path? Now she knew! He had wanted to torment and dominate her. He had wanted her to taste the pleasure he knew he could give her—but wouldn't. He would never satisfy her. Never complete her.

To Luke she was a foolish Heavy Eyebrows woman. She was white. He wouldn't want her to bear his son. He wouldn't desire her the way he desired an Osage woman. Hannah was inferior.

Gingerly she placed her fingers over the throbbing place between her thighs. Sweet heaven, but she needed release! For a moment she lay in silent agony, uncertain where to turn. She shut her eyes, clenched her teeth, and shoved her hands into the dark fur of the heavy buffalo robe.

She rolled onto her stomach and breathed into the musky hide. *Help,* she prayed. *Help me! Make it go away. Make the pain of his rejection go away. Make the power of my need go away.*

For a long time she lay fighting. Unable to calm herself, she rose in the dim light and slipped into her smallclothes before stretching out on the bed again. The oil lamp sputtered out, and the room was plunged into darkness. Then she heard the distinct sound of footsteps. The swish of covers being pushed aside at the other end of the lodge drifted across her ears.

He had come back. He would ease his body into the other bed. He would stretch out and shut his eyes. And he would sleep.

Hannah wasn't certain she would ever sleep again.

"Grandfather the Sun has risen," Luke announced.

Hannah opened her gritty eyes to find him towering over her

bed, his great legs sheathed in buckskin leggings, his copper chest bare except for a strand of beads around his neck and a leather thong from which his shell gorget hung. Hands planted on his hips, he stared down at her with an expression of bemusement on his lips.

"Is it morning already?" She squinted in the direction of the door. A pale purple light filtered between the wall and the hide flap.

"The cook would ring, but he doesn't happen to have a bell," Luke informed her.

When she shot him a scowl, he was tempted to chuckle. Hannah certainly hadn't deceived him about her inability to wake at dawn. Grandfather had been spreading shafts of golden and pink light across the sky for half an hour, and Hannah hadn't budged. Now she was rubbing her eyes in an attempt to rouse herself.

She did look beautiful in the morning, Luke had to acknowledge. She was all tousled cinnamon hair, rumpled white underclothes, and pale silken skin. He fought the urge to sink onto the bed beside her and take her in his arms. She would smell of the musky buffalo robe on which she had slept. Her neck would be warm. Her breasts downy. Her legs soft and pliant.

"There's no bell," he said, cutting into his own unacceptable thoughts, "but I do have tea for you."

"Tea?" She sat up, and he watched her hair spill over one bare shoulder. "Actual tea? With milk and sugar, perhaps?"

"Actual columbine tea."

Her face fell. "I knew fine black oolong was too much to hope for. I suppose I'll have another strip of jerky."

"Try this." He held a cup of steaming, fragrant liquid under her nose. "It's powdered columbine seed dissolved in boiling water. There's nothing better first thing in the morning."

Leaning forward, she breathed in the sweet perfume of his offering. Her injured hand ached, and her stomach turned over in hunger. The brew did smell good—and at this ungodly hour of the morning, she knew she would try almost anything to stay awake.

She had hardly slept all night. Telling herself it was merely the unfamiliar surroundings, she had tried to rationalize her wakefulness. The framework of the lodge creaked as it swayed in the night breeze. The hides that formed the roof over her head rustled and sighed. The mattress beneath her crackled, while the buffalo-skin rug kept her so hot she could barely breathe.

But she had to admit these weren't the only reasons sleep eluded her. The primary culprit was standing over her at this moment, his wonderful hands cupped around a mug of tea and his deep brown eyes searching her face for secrets she didn't want to reveal.

"You can hear the crackle of the mulberry wood in the fire," he said in a low voice, "and you can smell the fruit of the milkweed and the stems of cattails I'm boiling for your breakfast. There's a persimmon cake, too, and a bowl of wild strawberries."

Though the foods sounded strange, Hannah swallowed against her raging appetite. She didn't want to slip into an easy truce with this man—not after what had passed between them the night before. In fact, during the sleepless night she had decided she would ride back to Bolivar this morning, and she would stay with Ruth and Martha whether they wanted her or not.

"There's a stream outside for bathing," Luke continued, still holding out the cup of columbine tea. "I have a parfleche filled with clean shirts you can wear. It's hanging on the twig over there."

He pointed at the decorated bag she had inspected. Realizing suddenly that she was half-naked, she placed one hand on the bare skin above her chemise. "No, really, I don't believe—"

"There's a roof over your head," Luke said, stopping her words. "There's food enough here for both of us. And, Hannah, there's a man who offers you his apology."

She glanced up, startled.

"I promised not to touch you," he continued, "but I broke that vow last night. You told me you wanted to return to Boston. You said you would never want to bear my child—"

"It was *you* who despised the thought of my carrying your child," Hannah countered, cutting him off before he could finish. "You want an Osage wife and lots of little Osage children. I'm not good enough for you, remember? I'm just a silly, helpless Heavy Eyebrows woman. Isn't that what you said?"

"No, I didn't mean—"

"You did mean it! And last night you took me to a place where I was so weak you could make a fool of me." Standing, she brushed aside his offering of the tea and walked to the fire, where the kettle bubbled. "You told me it was a game we could play without consequences. You lied, Luke! You left me feeling hot and . . . and aching . . . and so miserable I wanted to die. It was a cruel trick, and a hundred cups of tea could not make up for it. You were right when you told me never to trust you. You can't be trusted!"

Luke stared at her, his heart hammering against his ribs. "I made a mistake. I've never touched a woman the way I touched you last night, Hannah. I've never wanted a woman the way I wanted you. The way I want you now."

She turned away from him, unwilling to let him see the need mirrored in her own eyes. Was this just another game of his? Was he toying with her again—leading her down the primrose path to her own destruction?

"I'm returning to Bolivar this morning," she announced, squaring her shoulders as she faced him again. "I don't trust you, Luke Maples."

He watched her gather up her discarded skirts and bodice before she strode to the door. As she marched outside to dress, the sun caught fire in her hair—blazing orange and red. The sight shot through Luke's chest like a flaming spear.

Trust me, Hannah. For the first time in his life he coveted such a gift with a passion he could taste in his mouth. *Trust me now. Trust me forever.*

Chapter
Thirteen

❦

Hannah knelt beside the stream and splashed chilly water over her face and arms. This was exactly what she had needed, she thought. A brisk shock to start the day would help her wake up and see her life for what it was—a hopelessly tangled mess. Instead of solving her problems through this ill-conceived marriage to Luke Maples, she had made them worse.

With effort, however, she felt certain that what was done could be undone. She dunked her head in the water and rinsed the dust of the past days' travel from her hair. After she had dried and dressed, she would demand that Luke pay her whatever he had left of his savings, for her efforts to secure the land he wanted. She would ride into Bolivar, collect her manuscript from Martha Strickland's house, and take the first wagon to Rolla. Then she would go straight home to Boston, where she belonged.

Squeezing the water from her hair, Hannah shut her eyes and drank in the early morning scent of summer. As much as she had disliked this woodsy, backward state, she couldn't deny that Missouri had begun to intrigue her. It was mysterious and rich with life, a teeming Eden that alternately delighted and disgusted her.

Pretty, pretty, pretty. A crimson cardinal danced down the dogwood branch near her, its black eyes bright as it chirped out the call Hannah easily recognized now. *Pretty, pretty, pretty.*

"Why, thank you," she said, giving the bird a curtsy. "And you are pretty, too. Or rather, handsome. I'll put you in my book, shall I? You can sing your song to Elizabeth Heartshorn. *Though her heart ached for the loss of her one true love, our young Elizabeth could not but rejoice in the song of the cardinal outside her window. Her husband had been dead two months now, slain by the . . . brutal . . . savage . . . trickery . . . of the Indian warrior.*

Hannah paused a moment, then lifted her chin. *Elizabeth was wounded in spirit and tormented by sadness . . . confusion . . . the desire for human love—but she was not defeated. The cardinal's song reminded her that life must go on. There were those who needed her . . . her family. Work there was, and the work would do her heart good. Like the scarlet-plumed bird, she would lift her eyes to heaven and set her sights upon the future. She would go forward . . . and never look back.*

The bird studied Hannah for a moment before taking wing. As it vanished into the thick greenery, she dropped the hank of wet hair down her back. In spite of herself, she would miss this enchanting place. She had become intimate with the wildflowers, and as she walked back toward the lodge, she named the ones she saw—blazing stars, coneflowers, butterfly weeds, compass plants, broomweeds, partridge peas, trumpet flowers. She could recognize songbirds, too—woodpeckers, doves, bluejays, sparrows.

There was more to the forest, of course, hundreds of creatures and plants she didn't know at all. Strange mushrooms and odd lichens on rocks and in the crevices of rotting logs. Animals she couldn't name and nuts she'd never seen.

But she would be thankful to get back to civilized Boston, Hannah reminded herself as she stepped behind a vine-covered tree to slip on her dress. In Boston, a woman could visit a shop without first making a three-day wagon ride to the mercantile.

In Boston, a woman could cultivate friends and take callers. In Boston, a woman could refuse to see men who wanted to play games that made a fool of her.

Frowning at the recurrent memory of the night before, Hannah lifted her chemise to arrange it before lacing on her corset. Her eyes fell on three bright red spots on her stomach, and her breath hung in her throat. Right in the center of each dot was a small, perfectly round . . . insect! Attached to her!

"Luke!" she shouted. She touched one of the bugs. It was fat . . . and it had minute black legs . . . and . . . "Oh, Luke!"

He crashed through the brush. "Hannah?"

Catching her, he brandished his knife. "Who's there?" he growled. He drew her against his chest, one arm protectively around her shoulders as he turned in menacing circles.

Hannah made a futile attempt to push him away. "Let go of me, Luke! Don't touch—"

"I won't hurt you, Hannah!"

"No, it's not you. It's these . . . these appalling creatures!"

"Creatures?" He lowered his knife. "What creatures?"

"Oh my stomach." She lifted the hem of her chemise.

Luke studied the angry red spots for a moment, then he broke into a grin. "Ticks," he announced.

"Great ghosts!"

"Come back to the lodge, and I'll put some witch hazel lotion on the bites. The swelling will go down, and you'll feel better. Then I'll boil a kettle of yarrow tea. You can splash it over your skin before we got out into the forest to work this morning. It'll keep away all appalling creatures."

"Ticks . . ." She stared at her blemished stomach as Luke led her into the lodge. Her mission to return to Bolivar was quickly forgotten as he seated her on a stool near the fire and proceeded to load a plate with breakfast foods.

"Pull off the ticks," he commanded, "and then eat this."

When he saw the expression on Hannah's face, he knew he might as well have instructed her to fly. "All right, I'll do it for you," he said gently. "That is . . . if you don't mind my touching you again."

She shook her head. Lifting her chemise, she watched in fascination as he took a piece of burning kindling and carefully

held the heated end against each insect. Immediately the
parasites withdrew their hold on Hannah's flesh, and Luke
destroyed them. Then he swabbed some witch hazel on the
open sores. His fingers felt warm, comforting as they moved
over her skin. She shut her eyes, unable to keep from enjoying
the moment.

"How is your hand feeling this morning?" Luke asked.

"It throbs," she said. "Your bird is a demon."

He glanced at the falcon, who was eyeing them from its
perch. "True," he acknowledged. "But to a hungry man, a
demon like Gthe-don can be a valuable possession. Here, let
me clean that wound."

He unwrapped the bandage and poured a little witch hazel on
the injury. "Check the rest of your body for ticks," he said as
he tied a clean cloth around her hand. "They like to latch on
around necklines and other places where your clothes are
tight."

"Another reason you Osage wear so few garments?" Hannah
tossed out as she walked behind the hanging screen to disrobe.

"You might try it sometime." His voice carried through the
lodge. "There's a good reason for most of our savage customs."

Scalp-locks? Hannah wondered how he would explain away
that barbaric practice. But she lost her concentration the
moment she began to discover more of the tiny intruders. As
Luke had predicted, she found five ticks, two on her neck, two
more on her back, and one . . . oh, heavens, one on the
delicate patch of sensitive skin where her thigh joined her
abdomen!

"Luke," she managed to croak.

"Found some more?"

"Umm . . . yes."

"Need help?"

"If you wouldn't mind."

Luke walked around the edge of the hanging buffalo hide to
find Hannah curled on her bed, a bright pink flush staining her
cheeks. The ribbons on her chemise hung loose, and the button
that held her white cotton smallclothes together was open. She
looked up at him with eyes like morning glories.

"One of them is located in a private place," she whispered.

His heart began to thud heavily. She had said she didn't trust him. Now was his chance to prove she could. But would he be able to look at her body and feel nothing . . . do nothing?

"It's all right, Hannah," he said with more assurance than he felt. "Let's get it over with so we can have breakfast."

She regarded him for a moment. Then she turned around on the bed. "My neck and back first. Four, I think."

Luke sat beside her as she drew aside her damp hair to expose her neck. The scent of fresh water and summer air clung to her skin as he bent near. A stab of desire ran through his loins. Stifling it, he heated and removed the insects and wiped cooling witch hazel over the bites.

But when Hannah lifted the back of her chemise, he had to turn away for a moment to steady himself. *One caress,* his body demanded. *Just one caress of that smooth, satiny skin. Just one lingering kiss* . . .

No, he couldn't. He'd promised.

Quickly he cleaned and dabbed the red-spotted bumps, then he lowered her chemise. "That's four," he said.

She took a deep breath. "There's one more. I'll do it."

"All right."

He held out the hot ember, the witch hazel, and the cotton rag. She studied them for a moment. "Luke, I—"

"I gave you my word, Hannah," he cut in. "I won't step beyond the boundaries we set. I want to . . . to earn your trust."

Her eyes darted up. Did he mean those words? After all his declarations that he would never trust—and wanted no one else's trust? And how could he ask Hannah to believe in him when he knew he was holding back the identity of the man who might be her brother? But if he told, he would lose her. He couldn't do that. Not yet. He coveted these moments with her—talking, touching, teasing, eating, bathing, even picking off ticks—even though he knew he must live with his own deceit.

Swallowing, Hannah began to slip the gathered white fabric over her hips. As her smallclothes slid down her legs, she watched Luke's face. He was staring at the bowl of witch hazel in his lap, but she could see a flicker of tension in his jaw.

"It's right here," she said softly.

Gritting his teeth to keep his face from revealing any

reaction, Luke turned toward her naked body. She had spread her thighs, and one hand held a clump of fabric over the pale flesh. The smallclothes covered her pelvis, but he could see the edge of her downy nest . . . auburn curls . . . blue-white skin . . .

"Right there," she whispered, placing one finger near the minuscule red spot. "Can you see it?"

Luke nodded, unable to speak. Forcing himself to remain steady, he placed one hand against her bare thigh and removed the insect. As he dabbed on the witch hazel, he allowed himself the brief pleasure of absorbing this moment—the smell of her clean skin, the feel of her tender flesh, the sight of her spread before him as though she were welcoming his desire.

But she wasn't, he reminded himself firmly. She had told him she was going to Bolivar today. She was leaving the place he had prepared for them . . . leaving him.

He tossed the strip of cotton into the bowl of witch hazel and turned away. "From now on, don't forget to rub yourself all over with the yarrow tea," he said, standing and walking back toward the fire. "Don't even step outside without it."

"Ticks," Hannah said with a shudder. "Missouri."

She pulled up her smallclothes and tied the ribbons on her chemise. All the more reason to return to Boston at once. Not that Bostonians had never seen a tick—but one didn't encounter them in the city. Never. One didn't encounter anything as wild and unpredictable in Boston as the things one encountered here in Missouri.

Blood-sucking insects. Bushwhackers. Murderers. Indians.

She peered around the hanging buffalo hide at Luke. He was brewing yarrow tea from some blossoms he had stowed in another of his many bags. At least he had managed to restrain himself while assisting her, she thought. Of course, he didn't want to risk another scene like the one the night before. Neither did she.

"Would you mind holding my laces while I pull?" she called across the lodge.

He lifted his head. "While you pull what?"

"The laces. On my corset." She let out a sigh. "I usually tie them to my bedpost, but there isn't a post on this bed. In fact, there's nothing in this house strong enough to tie them to. One pull, and the whole batch of sticks would come tumbling down."

Luke gave his brew a stir. "I doubt you could sway a single pole of this lodge, Hannah. I buried them deeply into the earth. Anyway, why don't you just leave off that stiff corset? It'll make you hot and sticky while you work."

"I'm not going to work out here," she shot back. "I'm returning to Bolivar when you go in to work with the surveying crew this morning. I'll fetch my manuscript and hire a wagon to take me to Rolla."

"It's Saturday. I'm not going to work until Monday."

She blanched. "Then I'll take the horse by myself."

"What about your promise to me?"

"Pay me for my trouble in securing this land, and I'll consider it satisfactory conclusion to our arrangement."

"Except that I don't have money to give you. I spent almost everything I'd saved on land fees, equipment, and seed." He poured the steaming yarrow tea into a bowl. Flinching inwardly at his own deception, he tossed out a final caveat. "Anyway, you have to stay here to wait for word on your brother."

Hannah clamped her mouth shut. She felt trapped again. Cornered. But it wasn't so much her difficult situation that hemmed her in. It was Luke. She didn't want to be near him. She couldn't bear the thought of eating with him, living with him, sleeping so near to him. Not with all the tension between them.

"I don't want to stay here," she said.

He held out a plate and bowl filled with aromatic food. "Stay, Hannah. It'll be all right between us. We'll grow used to each other. We'll learn how to live side by side in peace."

She looked into his brown eyes. "First you instructed me not to trust you. Then you told me you wanted to earn my trust. You tell me we'll live side by side in peace, but last night you played me for a fool. How am I to know what to believe?"

"By staying. By seeing that I'll keep my distance. I'll fulfill my promise to protect you and provide for you while you wait to hear about your brother. What happened between us was a mistake, not a trick. Don't go, Hannah."

She eyed him for a long moment, then she walked across the

lodge and took the proffered plate. "It'll be one day at a time between us? And if I change my mind, I'm free to leave?"

"One day at a time. Nothing more."

Tucking her skirt beneath her, Hannah sat on a low stool near the fire. She still wore nothing but her chemise on top, but such an indiscretion hardly mattered. Luke had seen her body—her naked skin, her bare breasts.

It wouldn't matter if she decided to forgo her corset either—though the thought of such a social blunder still made her feel negligent. It wouldn't even matter if she wore one of Luke's embroidered shirts. If she stayed out here with Luke, no one would see anything she did. No one would know.

She dipped her spoon into the stew of boiled milkweed fruits and cattail stems. Shutting her eyes, she took a sip. The rich broth filtered down into her shriveled stomach, warming and relaxing her. She chewed on a bite of milkweed.

"It tastes like cabbage," she said.

Luke smiled. "If only we had some corned beef."

Hannah gave him a return grin. "And a cook with a bell."

"Try the persimmon cake. I brought it from the reservation."

She sank her teeth into the flattened round fruit. It was dry, sweet, and delicious. "You made this?"

"My mother." He chewed contentedly for a moment. "When I was a little boy still living in my mother's lodge, I watched everything she did. Persimmon time is in November, the month we call Bucks-Rattling-Antlers Moon. My friends and I always helped our mothers gather ripe persimmons. Then the women used hickory or post oak wood to craft a flat board with a handle. They spread buffalo tallow on the board, then they placed a layer of seeded persimmons on it. They spread on another layer of tallow followed by more persimmons. After they had built up four layers, one of the mothers would hold the board over the coals of a fire until the first layer was cooked."

"Only the first layer?"

"That's right. Then she would set the board aside to cool. After it cooled, the persimmon cakes would be put into a parfleche for storage. These cakes last all winter long."

"You Osage make everything? You don't buy what you need?"

"Sometimes we go to the trading post for flour, bullets,

whiskey, beads, blankets—that sort of thing. But most of our food we gather ourselves. Now, with the loss of our Missouri land, we rely on the buffalo too much."

He took a sip of columbine tea and pondered for a moment. "I've seen the herds thinning year by year, Hannah. Buffalo are harder to find each summer when we go out onto the plains to hunt. When we locate them, they are always fewer in number than the year before."

"Why?"

"Because many tribes have been pushed out of their old lands and forced onto the prairie. Most of these tribes come from the East, where they once hunted deer and gathered their food. But in Kansas, there are few forests, and deer aren't so common. We've all been forced to rely on the buffalo. With guns, it's easier to slaughter great numbers of them. They're dying not only for meat and hides to supply the Indians' needs. The white man is killing them as he clears the land for homesteaders and railroads. I fear one day the buffalo may completely vanish from the prairie."

Appalled by the picture of devastation he had painted, Hannah let out a breath. "Luke, I'm glad I was able to homestead this land for you. I hope you can make all your dreams come true."

"Thank you, Gthe-non'-zhin."

But as Hannah rose to place her empty dishes in the kettle of warming water, Luke wondered why the old dreams that once had burned so brightly in his heart now looked dim, faded, even empty.

The woman he had married wandered across their lodge toward the parfleche that held his Osage clothing. Her drying hair shone a vivid cinnamon as it ran like a river down her back. Her hips swayed beneath the long skirt. Her breasts pushed upward against the thin chemise. "I believe I shall wear one of your shirts after all," she said, turning to face him.

Her eyes sparkled like dew-laden chicory blossoms on a summer morning. Curving into a soft smile, her lips seemed to beckon him. She placed her bandaged hand down into his parfleche and pulled out an embroidered shirt. "Will this one be suitable?"

He couldn't make himself answer. Nodding, he watched her

lift her arms and slide them into the scented folds of his garment. When her head emerged through the neck-hole, she grasped her hair and drew it out. Then she looked down at herself and gave a light chuckle.

"I know I shall never be an Osage," she said, lifting those blue eyes. "But one day, if I stay here long enough, I might find that I'm not altogether a Bostonian either. Would that be all right with you?"

Luke's fingers tightened around his cup. Would it be all right for this woman to slip slowly out of her world and into his? Was it all right that he had found himself easing away from his own world and into hers? Could it be possible that one day they would find a comfortable meeting place somewhere in the middle? Somewhere they could rest . . . and find peace . . .

"It would be all right, Hannah," he said. "It would be very much all right."

After breakfast, Hannah went outside to look around his lodge. While he banked the fire, Luke's thoughts again turned to the Butterfield Stage representative, Ethan Brown. How much longer could he continue to live with Hannah and remain silent? Though he hadn't seen the man again or heard anything new about him, it was obvious the stranger matched Hannah's description of her brother.

It stood to reason an educated Boston man might find employment with Butterfield, Luke had to admit. Even though Ethan Brown was vocally prejudiced against Indians and black men, he was clearly considered a valuable stage line employee. How would such a person react to learning his sister intended to return him to his family in Boston? How would he react if he knew Hannah had married a "redskin"?

On the other hand, Luke thought, wasn't Ethan Brown too old to be Hannah's brother? And wouldn't a man in such a comfortable position have contacted his family following the war? Surely he would have wanted to learn about his father's welfare. No, the stranger couldn't be Hannah's brother.

Was he, then, Luke's enemy—the murderous Ethan he'd been seeking? Without seeing the man again and talking to him, there was no way of knowing the truth. Luke made up his mind to put off telling Hannah anything until Monday, when he would seek out Ethan Brown and find out who he really was.

"I'm going to finish clearing the trail down to the road," Luke announced when he joined Hannah outside the lodge.

Arms filled with wildflowers, she turned and gave him a smile that tightened his stomach. His shirt hung to her knees, over her full skirt. She had pinned up her hair and tied on a diminutive hat. Trimmed in ostrich plumes and a length of dotted veil that hung down in back, the hat perched on her head like a strange bird. Luke hoped it would soon go the way of the corset.

"I'll arrange these flowers in one of your kettles," Hannah told him. "Then, if you have a needle and some spare fabric, I shall begin on some fancywork. I should like to make a coverlet for my bed."

Fancywork? Coverlets? Luke tried to mask the scowl that tugged down the corners of his mouth. He hoped his irritation had nothing to do with his guilty decision to keep information from Hannah. He couldn't let his own secret offense affect his attitude toward her. All the same, she needed to be set straight.

"There's no time for stitching today, Hannah," he informed her. "You'll be harvesting squashes and wild potatoes this morning. This afternoon, you can collect wild plums and dig blazing star roots. Later, we'll ride down to the pond together and gather lotus fruits and roots."

Her mouth slid open. "But I'm planning to write my book this afternoon. And I thought I should like to pen a sketch of these wildflowers in the evening."

"There's no paper out here. No pens. No ink. But there's work to do. Women's work . . . and you're the woman."

She bristled. "What constitutes women's work is a matter of opinion. I wouldn't know a wild potato vine from a poison ivy vine. Miss Ruth sternly warned me to stay away from any growing thing I'm not certain of. 'Leaves of three, let them be.' That's what she taught me, and I would never go against her instruction."

"Do you want to eat, Hannah?" he asked. When she didn't answer, he went on. "If you want to eat here in Missouri, you'll learn to tell the difference between poison ivy and wild potato vines. You'll learn to put yarrow tea or crushed pennyroyal on your skin to keep away ticks and chiggers so you can go into the forest to gather and harvest. You'll learn that wildflowers don't grow so you can pick them and put them into a kettle where they'll wilt and die."

He took the bunch of flowers from her arms. "This is chicory," he said, pulling out a stem of delicate violet-colored blossoms. "We'll eat its leaves in a salad or blanch them for a vegetable. We'll use the root to make a coffee."

Lifting up a specimen with powdery yellow flowers that rose into a point at the top of the stem, he handed it to Hannah. "Goldenrod. The blossoms make a good tea."

"Tea from flowers instead of leaves?"

"Of course. All these white blooms you picked are ox-eye daisies. If we bruise the leaves and flowers, they'll reduce the swelling of an injury. They make a tea, too."

Intrigued in spite of herself, Hannah touched the tip of a tiny golden flower that nodded on a wispy stem. "What's this?"

"Prairie dock. We can use it in a tea to help with a tickling cough. Its leaves relieve the itch of poison ivy, and its roots help bad skin conditions. If you sprain your ankle, you can use dock tea to make a compress."

"But couldn't we purchase the things we need at one of the Bolivar mercantiles? In Boston our family druggist supplies medicines for sprained ankles and bad skin and such. You have a steady job with the surveying team, Luke. Why don't you earn the money you need and buy your provisions?"

He focused on the clump of flowers in his hand. "I have a choice, Hannah. You're right when you say I could live in town and earn wages as a surveyor. With those wages I could buy the things I need for basic survival. Or I can live out here on my own land, where I find peace and contentment. But if I do that, I have to work hard from the moment Grandfather the Sun peers over the horizon until Moon Woman begins to shine her face in the night sky. Every minute of my day must be spent clearing, planting, hunting, gathering, harvesting, storing, drying, cooking."

"And you've chosen the land."

"Without hesitation."

"That's why you need a good Osage wife, isn't it? A woman who knows the difference between poison ivy and potatoes. One who can butcher a buffalo and make jerky from the meat.

One who understands that wildflowers belong in ointments and tinctures and teas—not in vases on the dining table.''

Her blue eyes looked so sad, her expression was so deflated, it was all Luke could do to keep from catching her in his arms and holding her tight. "Hannah," he said, his voice gentle now, "if you want to live here with me, you can learn everything an Osage woman knows. I'll teach you. But if you want to go back to Bolivar, I won't try to stop you.''

"But you don't have money to give me. Without money, I can't purchase a ticket home to Boston.''

"I'll continue working for the surveyor until I've earned your money. I promised you I would, and it shouldn't take long. When you have the money, you can buy your train ticket and return to your family. Then I'll quit my job so I can work all day on my land in preparation for winter.''

Hannah studied the forests surrounding the lodge. Once, she would have viewed these woods as merely a huge thicket of indistinguishable trees. Once, she would have judged flowers merely by color and fragrance. Now she knew the secrets of this Missouri timberland—that mulberry wood could make a fire crackle and snap, that hickory limbs were strong enough to build a home, that chicory flowers made a nourishing tea, and that prairie dock could heal a sprained ankle.

"I'll stay," she said suddenly. "I'll stay here and help you gather the things you need for food and medicine. But I ask you to fulfill your part of our agreement, too, Luke. I want you to continue working for the surveyor until you've earned my money so that I can go home.''

He nodded. "Agreed.''

"And I want you to do everything in your power to help me find my brother.''

Luke glanced away. Everything? Taking a deep breath, he faced her. "In time," he said.

She rewarded him with a smile that brightened her eyes with a blue light. "Then let the lessons begin. Teach me everything I would need to know if I were your wife.''

Luke observed her for a moment. *You are my wife, Hannah,* he wanted to say. *You are my wife, and what I want to teach you is best learned on a soft buffalo robe beneath the silver light of the Moon Woman.*

But she had turned away, her skirts lifted high as she waded straight into a thick patch of poison ivy.

Hannah scratched all day. No amount of goldenseal paste, prairie dock leaves, or jewelweed sap seemed to provide much relief. In spite of her discomfort and her sore hand, she was determined not to allow this wilderness to get the better of her.

She tramped through brush in search of columbine seeds, which grew in tiny pods that made her think of tall, five-pointed crowns. Luke taught her to chew the seeds and blow them onto her clothing to make the garments smell fragrant and sweet. Most important to daily survival were the potatoes and beans that grew untamed in the forest. Hannah learned to spot these immediately, and she took pride in the heavily laden bags she was able to set inside the lodge for storage.

She harvested roots of a plant Luke called by its French name, *pomme blanche.* She collected the mature fruit of the milkweed and the leaves of the sheep sorrel. In the lodge Luke showed her how to boil the greens of wild lettuce, lamb's quarters, and pokeweed for their lunch.

Afterward she accompanied Luke and his falcon on a hunt. She practiced the beckoning whistle, and she tried carrying Gthe-don on her leather-gloved fist. When the falcon brought down two rabbits, Hannah fed him the choice bits of brain and liver, and the wariness between the two mellowed into a comfortable truce.

Later, under the watchful eyes of an Indian and a falcon, she undertook the job of skinning and dressing the rabbits. She cut away the rabbits' pelts and soaked them in a tanning solution created naturally by rainwater drawing out the tannic acid in a hollow oak tree trunk. Her pale hands had begun to stain a deep brown; her dress was splattered with blood; the bridge of her nose was sunburned—and she felt happier than she could ever remember.

On Saturday night Hannah fell across her bed, her muscles aching, skin mottled with poison ivy and mosquito bites, and hair tangled with bits of vine and burrs. She could barely lift her head to sip a mouthful of the wild onion and venison stew Luke brought her. Exhausted, she slipped into a deep sleep, unaware of the man who sat by her side and gazed at her until the hoot of an owl reminded him it was late and time for his own body to rest.

Sunday morning, when Hannah reminded Luke it was time for Mass, he took her to the top of the bluff that overlooked the river. They sat beside the mouth of the cave where the gnarled oak tree grew. "We'll go to church another Sunday," he said, "but we can worship God anywhere."

Then he began to pray aloud—a long, heartfelt communion between a man and his creator. Humbled by the power in his words, Hannah listened as Luke brought his needs and praises before God. This was no rote repetition of a memorized prayer, and she marveled at the depths she was discovering in the man she had wed.

The worshipful experience drew Luke and Hannah closer. They worked hard all day without a disagreement or misunderstanding. He cleared the forest of brush all the way from his lodge to the road—a path wide and smooth enough for a wagon to follow. Hannah filled basket after basket with her wild harvest.

Late Sunday afternoon when Grandfather had spread his orange mantle across the bluff, Luke decided it was time to take Hannah down to the swampy pond to harvest lotus fruits and cattail stems. Though he had wanted to go the day before, he had determined she should first chew yonkopin to prevent malaria.

"I want you to wear a pair of my leggings," he said as he entered the lodge, where Hannah sat pounding columbine seeds into powder to make tea. "They'll protect your legs from reeds in the water, and snakes can't bite through the leather."

"Snakes?" Hannah looked up from the elm-wood mortar and pestle. "What sort of snakes?"

"Cottonmouths. The local people call them water moccasins. They live near streams and river sloughs around here. You'll recognize them by the cotton-white lining inside the mouth. Also, we'll keep our eyes open for copperheads. They're gray-brown or pink-tan in color, with dark crossbands along their back."

Hannah swallowed at the image of herself getting close enough to any snake to see the lining of its mouth. "I'm not fond of reptiles," she said.

"Don't worry. Wear my leggings and you'll be fine." He walked toward the back of the lodge to collect a few baskets.

"But leggings aren't proper on a woman," Hannah whispered. As soon as she'd said the words, she realized how foolish they sounded. It had become clear to her that here in Missouri a woman didn't concern herself with propriety.

In the past two days, she had realized that her ostrich-plume bonnet with its dangling ribbons and lacy veil was more a hindrance than a help in the forest. She had abandoned it and had begun to wear her hair in a long braid down her back. One of Luke's wide-brimmed straw hats kept the sun from her eyes.

Grateful for the absence of her corset, she had learned to wear Luke's shirts hanging loose and cool over her skirt. When her delicate white gloves proved useless against the thorns she encountered while harvesting, she had taken to slipping her hands into a pair Luke fashioned for her from deer hide thick enough to allow her to fly Gthe-don from the fist if she chose. Her shoes with their raised heels and slick soles were no good on the sloping hillsides and rocky bluffs around the lodge. She had readily accepted a pair of soft buckskin moccasins which molded to her feet and protected her toes from sharp stones.

Again and again as she reached into a clump of brush to pluck dock leaves or milkweed stems, Hannah had thought of her sisters in Boston. What would they say if they could see her in her Indian shirt and moccasins? Would Sophie be appalled at the sight of Hannah's hair in a thick braid instead of pinned on her head in coy loops? Would Brigitte gasp that her sister had failed to use her curling iron for days? Would Elizabeth laugh at the sight of Luke's enormous shirt hanging to her big sister's knees?

And what would their mother think if she knew what her eldest daughter had done with her newfound independence?

Hannah had worked out her pent-up emotion as she dug for wild potatoes on the hillsides. A refrain of maternal admonitions played through her mind in a haunting chorus. *A lady wears her gloves at all times. A lady wears a bonnet to keep her skin white and pure. A lady uses her fork and knife with feminine deftness. A lady does her needlework to express her God-given talents. A lady is polite but never forward with a gentleman. Never allow a man to touch more than your hand*

*or elbow, Hannah. Never allow a man to see any portion of
your unclothed person save your pale cheeks and gentle brow.*

"You can wear your skirt over the leggings if you want,"
Luke was saying as Hannah contemplated her many infrac-
tions. "But in that pond, it won't be long before you're soaked
and muddy up to your hips. That getup you wear will drag you
down and slow your progress. All the same, if you want to look
proper—"

"Where are the leggings?" Hannah cut in. "I'll wear them."

Luke reached into a parfleche and found his thick winter
leggings. He tossed them to Hannah, who stepped behind the
hide to change. Returning to his task of sorting through empty
baskets, Luke pondered the hours that lay ahead.

If he and Hannah could harvest a mass of lotus fruits, he
thought, the night would end with a delicious, nourishing meal.
They had both worked so hard they hadn't taken time to tend
to basic needs like bathing, resting, and feeding their worn
bodies. His own muscles ached from swinging an axe against
forest that was always encroaching, and he knew Hannah must
be sore from the many loads she had carried from the woods.

As he packed the baskets one inside another, Luke reflected
with satisfaction on the past two days. He took pride in the fact
that he had managed to avoid Hannah most of the time—and
when they were together, he had treated her as he might a sister.
He had taught her things without touching her hands. He had
sat beside her at meals without looking into her eyes. He had
slept a few feet away without giving in to his desire to go to her
bed.

He looked forward to this evening. Maybe he would teach
her the moccasin gambling game his people loved so well. Or
perhaps he would cut and sew a leather apron with large
storage packets so she could wear it while gathering. While he
worked, she could continue her tale of Elizabeth Heartshorn
and her family, telling him aloud what she would write the
following evening after he had retrieved her manuscript from
the *Nika-sabe* women.

Contentment spread through his chest as he reflected on how
well the arrangement was working out. Hannah was his
companion, his associate in the business of survival. Nothing
more.

"All right," she announced, emerging from behind the buffalo hide. "Let's go."

Luke turned, and his tranquillity was snuffed out in an instant. Hannah, the tip of her long braid brushing across the rise of her hips, strolled across the room like a vision out of a dream.

She had tucked his shirt into the leggings, and her breasts strutted boldly forward. Around her narrow waist, she had tied one of his woven belts. From there the leggings molded down her long, slender legs, emphasizing the curve of her bottom and the turn of her thighs.

"Are you ready?" she asked, pausing and setting her hands on her hips.

Luke could hardly force out an answer. Yes, he was ready. Instantly, forcefully ready. As he stood to join her, he wondered if she could see the swell beneath his own leggings that would tell her just how ready he was.

Chapter
Fourteen

"*I need a bath,*" *Hannah sighed as she waded out of the small* swampy lake. She lugged the basket, heavy with green lotus fruits, up the shore and set it beneath a pin oak tree.

Still thigh-deep in water, Luke dug at a patch of roots with his toes. As the starchy, tuberous vegetation drifted to the surface, he swept it up in his arms and tossed it into the basket on his back. Muddy water swirled around his legs, mosquitoes danced in front of his eyes, and decaying leaves clung to his hands and arms. He needed a bath, too.

But the thought of being anywhere near an unclothed Hannah was almost more than he could take. All evening they had worked in the lake together, she plucking cone-shaped fruits from the leafy surface of the water, he digging roots with his feet. She had sung little songs for him as she harvested— nonsensical rhymes and children's ditties. When she talked, she spoke of her dreams of being a famous writer like Mrs. Henry Wood, whose work she respected greatly.

Unable even to look at her without thinking disturbing

thoughts, Luke had focused on his work. Filling basket after basket, Hannah's fingers flew across the water. He tried to ignore her, but she would have none of it. Her questions poured like rainwater down a tepee. *Why do you eat these lotus fruits? How do you cook them? Do they taste good? Can you eat the leaves? Can you store them? What are you planning to do with all those roots? Can they be dried?*

When she had inadvertently stepped into an underwater hole and sank to her neck, Luke had rushed to her rescue without thinking. In the process of righting her, he had wrapped his arms around her waist. Her wet bosom had brushed against his chest, and he could feel the tight chestnuts of her nipples.

"Luke," she was calling from the shore. "I'll start back now with these baskets. We'd better leave right away, if we're to have them all home by dark."

Home. Luke shut his eyes and took in a deep breath. She had called their lodge home. More and more in these past two days, he had grown to treasure Hannah's presence—her laughter, her songs, her chatter. What would the lodge be like after she returned to Boston? It wouldn't feel much like home; Luke was sure of that.

"We'll just take what we can carry and what we'll need for supper," he said as he waded out of the water with his basket of lotus roots. "I'll come here with the wagon at dawn tomorrow to haul the rest."

"I can tell I'll have my hands full tomorrow."

She set one leg to the side and surveyed the array of produce they had gathered. At the unconscious act, her hip jutted out in a provocative gesture that sent a ripple of sparks down Luke's thighs. Gloved in wet leather, her body steamed in the damp heat of evening. Perspiration had curled her hair into tiny cinnamon corkscrews that hung around her forehead and onto her neck.

"I'll remove all these seeds from the fruits first thing in the morning, as you said," she continued, oblivious to the man who observed her from a distance. "Then I'll hull the seeds to remove all those hard shells. When you come home from work tomorrow evening, we'll build a fire and roast them. If we continue coming back to the lake and gathering, we should be able to collect enough to last us through winter."

She paused and glanced around her shoulder at him. "*You,*" she corrected herself. "They should last *you* through winter."

Luke walked toward her. "Hannah—"

"You'll teach me how to grind the seeds, won't you?" she interrupted quickly. "I'll bake bread out of the flour."

She crossed her arms protectively as Luke approached. Only twice had she seen such an expression on his face. Once when he had kissed her in the wagon. Once when he had lain with her on the bed in the lodge. Wanting his touch so badly that she could taste the ache in her throat, she forced herself to continue speaking as though she felt nothing at his nearness.

"Of course, I don't know how to bake bread either," she told him, "so you'll have to teach me that, too. And I do want to learn. I want to know everything you know. Never in my life have I felt so awake . . . so interested . . ."

He paused a pace away. "You like the Osage ways."

"Yes, I do."

"I'm glad." He reached out and ran one finger down her arm. "You've worked hard these past two days, Hannah."

"I don't mind. Other than the poison ivy, these forests are wonderful. I couldn't have imagined such abundance."

She spread her arms, and he glanced down at the abundance of her bosom. Catching himself, he pulled his focus back to her face. "You've changed. Not long ago you told me you hated Missouri."

"It's certainly not Boston." She studied the depths of his brown eyes. "But then Boston doesn't have everything a woman needs."

"Hannah—" He stopped himself again, remembering the secret he kept, remembering he had plans that didn't include her. Clenching his jaw, he turned away. "It's late. Let's go."

He bent and lifted four full parfleches, two for each shoulder. Hannah picked up two baskets and rested their handles in the crooks of her elbows as they set off through the forest. The sun had dipped beneath the horizon, and Hannah knew it would be completely dark by the time they reached the lodge.

All the same, she no longer feared the woods. Understanding the secrets of the shrubs, trees, wildflowers, and animals, she had gained a comforting sense of power. She also felt reassured at the sight of Luke walking ahead of her on the narrow trail, and the knowledge that their lodge waited in the distance.

Luke would build a cooking fire while she prepared lotus roots and peeled potatoes. They would work together cleaning a mess of dock to boil and smoking the rabbits Gthe-don had taken down. The picture was relaxed and satisfying. In some ways, it was more serene than the image of her own home in Boston—four girls in front of the mirror primping over shabby bonnet ribbons or faded ruffles, and a mother made disconsolate by her losses.

The hours alone with Luke made the present more appealing, Hannah realized. She enjoyed laboring at his side for a common purpose. She appreciated the way he listened to her and responded with his own thoughts. Learning from him was a pleasure as he sat beside her and patiently explained the ways of his people.

The only disturbing times were those moments when she caught herself gazing at him and dwelling on the memory of the night he had held her so close. As they worked side by side, it seemed almost impossible for her to keep her eyes from his hands, his mouth, his bare chest, his muscled shoulders. Bemused, she discovered she particularly liked the sight of his firm buttocks as he bent over to gather lotus roots. Taut, rounded, and sheathed in wet leather, they drew her attention like a magnet. Chastising herself for such untoward preoccupations, Hannah tried her best to keep her thoughts on practical matters.

It would never do to go wishing for another passionate interlude, she reminded herself. Luke had no intention of ever truly caring for her. He saw no future for the two of them together. He wanted nothing from her but the agreement they had made. And, of course, she wanted nothing more from him.

"Set your baskets by the fireplace," Luke instructed as they walked into the lodge. "I'll gather kindling and heat a kettle of water for you to wash in. Then I'll go down to the stream."

Hannah dropped her burden and leaned against a hickory post. Wiping a hand across her damp brow, she let out a breath. "Is the water in that stream cool?"

"It originates from a spring under the ground. It's chilly."

"Would it be safe for me to go to the stream myself to bathe? I'm so hot that the notion of warm water seems unbearable."

Luke pondered the suggestion. "I've never seen a snake around the pool—maybe because I'm there so often, they prefer to stay away."

"What about other animals?"

"The moon is full tonight, so you should be able to see anything that moves. Water always draws living things, and in Missouri there are many creatures of the night. Don't worry about it, though. When you step outside the lodge, turn south. I cleared a trail, so you can follow it down to the stream."

Conjuring up all sorts of unfamiliar nocturnal beasties, Hannah brushed a hand behind her damp neck. "Would you come down with me and stand guard?"

Luke studied the empty fireplace. How could he say no? To leave a woman unguarded would be a breach of honor. But to stay near Hannah while she disrobed? To wait a short distance away as she poured cool water over her bare skin?

"You can take my gun," he said.

Her eyes darted to the weapon that hung in a rack over the door. "I wouldn't have a clue how to fire it. Never mind, Luke. I'll wash in the lodge."

Giving a grunt of acquiescence, he turned away and began hunting through his clothing parfleches for his breechcloth. He didn't want the temptation of this woman. He hadn't asked for it. He didn't have time for it. He couldn't manage it.

As he thought over the situation, he could almost hear his mother's voice. "Are you weak, my son? Can you not control yourself long enough to allow this woman the pleasure of cleansing her body?"

From the darkness, he eyed Hannah. She was kneeling at the fireplace, setting out lotus roots and placing the seed-filled fruits in a pile. Her muddy braid had swung over her shoulder, its end brushing the dirt floor. Moccasins tucked beneath her round bottom, she worked diligently, unaware of the consternation she was causing one Osage warrior.

"All right," he snapped. "Go down to the stream. I'll stand guard."

She turned, her eyes bright with warmth. "Thank you, Luke. I feel as if cool water would ease all these bites and stings."

He grabbed his breechcloth and gun and stalked out the door. After all, he reminded himself as he marched down the path to the stream, he had counted coup many times. He had taken enough scalps to make him a respected warrior in the reservation village. Boldness was in his nature. He had never had time or patience for the timid and weak in this world. Of course he could guard one Heavy Eyebrows woman for a few minutes without any trouble.

"I've been scattering columbine seeds in my trunk," Hannah commented as she followed Luke along the moonlit trail. "They smell heavenly. I think even Sophie would like the fragrance. She's so particular, you know. She believes French perfumes are the only sort that smell nice. In Boston I love to place stems of lavender under my pillow. Have you ever smelled lavender?"

"No." He wished she would stop speaking. Just the sound of her voice sent hot knives down his skin.

"Drifting off to sleep in the fragrance of fresh lavender is the most relaxing thing I can think of after a long day. In Boston, I have a large bed with four tall carved posts. I sleep on a feather bed, you know, and when one can air it in the sunshine, it smells nice enough. But on rainy days it gets so musty. There's simply nothing like lavender to erase the scent of damp bedding."

Did she *have* to talk about her bed? Luke scowled at the path. He could almost see her stretched out on the billowy white feather bed, her long legs bare and her flaming hair spread around her shoulders. Lavender . . . Hannah . . . bed . . .

"The mosquitoes don't seem so thick around here," she said as they pushed through the last of the brush and emerged on the bank of the stream. "I thought they liked water."

"Stagnant water. This stream runs fast and high, so there's no place for them to lay their eggs. The bathing pool is downstream about fifty paces. You won't find many mosquitoes there either."

She looked at him as he stood tall and motionless in the moonlight. "You know so many things, Luke."

"I know about my world. You know about yours." He hooked his thumbs into the waist of his leggings to keep from touching her. "I don't have any idea how to waltz or do fancywork."

She smiled. "As you well know, waltzing is not an essential skill in life."

"All the same." He shrugged. "I can't do it."

Fighting the urge to offer to teach him beneath the silver glow of the moon, Hannah listened to the rush of the stream. "It shouldn't take me long," she said.

Clutching her bundle of garments against her stomach, she made her way along the edge of the stream. A bullfrog croaked. Crickets grew silent at the sound of her footsteps. Silver coins glittered on the water's surface, cast there by the full moon. Moon Woman, she corrected herself.

It was odd how Luke's Osage expressions had become a part of her thoughts. She had caught herself referring to Grandfather the Sun that afternoon. Luke had given her a look she couldn't read.

He did that often. Many times she caught him watching her. But she never knew what he was thinking. A veil that masked every emotion hung over his deep-set brown eyes when he studied her. His falcon's hooded gaze could not have been more inscrutable.

What did Luke think of her? He had never again mentioned the night they lay together. It was almost as if it hadn't happened. He never touched her unless by accident. He looked at her only when he thought she didn't know. It was as though he were doing his best to separate them.

But if she meant so little to him, why was he making such a great effort to remain aloof? If they were nothing more than friends, couldn't they carry on an easy banter? Couldn't they labor together as a pair of casual companions?

Hannah hung her clothes on a denuded walnut branch that jutted out over the bank. Raising her arms, she tugged Luke's wet shirt over her head. Her sodden braid tumbled out of the neck-hole and fell against her bare back. Quickly she unwound the three thick strands that formed her plait. Then she tugged the clingy leather leggings over her hips and down her legs.

The truth was, she realized as she stepped into the cool water, she didn't want merely companionship and easy banter with Luke Maples. She coveted those brief instances when

she'd caught him watching her. She reveled in the accidental
brush of his hand over hers as they worked. She cherished the
memory of those moments when he had held her and kissed her
with such desire.

Wading to the depths of the pool that had been cut by water
rushing over a limestone lip, Hannah reflected on the man who
waited for her in the distance. She had never found the men of
Boston interesting, she thought as she sank to her shoulders in
the chilly water. But Luke Maples was interesting. Very. She
couldn't imagine ever growing tired of his voice as he told her
about the Osage or taught her how to harvest and prepare food.

She hadn't found other men particularly attractive, either.
Most of her gentlemen callers had worked in downtown
businesses, and they were stiff and proper. They wore crisp
white collars and natty checkered suits. Their hands were as
white as the papers she imagined they stacked in their offices,
and as soft as clumps of uncooked bread dough.

Oh, but Luke's hands . . . Hannah dipped her hair under
the water as she thought of the moment when she had felt his
fingers slide over her breasts. Would she ever know his touch
again? She brushed her palms over her bosom and lifted the
weight of her breasts. What wouldn't she do for one more
touch. One more kiss.

Curls of need slid down the backs of her legs as she ran her
hands over her body to wash away the residue of the day's
labors. If only everything weren't so impossible. If only Luke
weren't an Indian determined to live his life with an Osage
wife. If only she hadn't promised to find Ethan and return to
Boston. If only her mother and sisters didn't need her so
desperately. If only she could relinquish her dreams of becoming a successful novelist, or Luke could abandon his goal of
reestablishing his tribal heritage in Missouri.

As she emerged dripping from the pool, Hannah lifted her
eyes to Moon Woman. At this moment everything seemed
right . . . and nothing was right. She knew what she wanted,
yet she couldn't have it. Leaving a trail of water droplets on the
smooth, rounded stones, she reached to the branch for a linen
towel.

"Hannah?" Luke's voice was so low she almost didn't hear
it.

A shallow breath caught in her chest. Silhouetted in a dusting of pale moonlight, he stood beneath the overhanging limbs of a black willow tree. She could just make out the shape of his shoulders and head, but his features were shrouded in darkness.

"I didn't hear you," she whispered, drawing a corner of the towel to her neck so that the rest of it draped down her body.

"You've been in the water a long time. I thought I'd better check on you."

"Oh . . ." She swallowed as he moved out of the brush and onto the bank. "I forgot the time. I was . . . I was thinking about things, I suppose."

"What were you thinking, Hannah?"

Flickers of heat scattered up her neck. "I thought about today and how much I liked it. Learning. Working with you."

"I liked that, too."

"I was thinking about you."

He paused in front of her. "What were you thinking about me?"

"Of all the men I've ever met, you're the finest."

A deep chuckle rumbled in his chest. He placed his hands on her arms and turned her until her face was bathed in moonlight. "You flatter me, Hannah. I think you must have forgotten about the handsome men of Boston and the soldiers who came courting you and your four sisters."

"No, I haven't forgotten them at all. I remember them very well, in fact."

"Then perhaps you have forgotten I'm a savage."

"Don't!" She caught his hands. "You know I no longer see the color of your skin. You know your heritage fascinates me. I won't play your games, Luke. I can't pretend to myself that you're foreign and somehow beneath me. When I think of you, I think of a man who's bold and intelligent and gentle. You have great wisdom and maturity. You speak your mind, and you follow your dreams. Those are attributes I admire. And when I look at you, Luke, I see . . . I see . . ."

"What, Hannah? What do you see in me? An Indian with black hair and copper skin? A man who wears leggings and hunts with a falcon? A warrior who knows how to trail an enemy, how to cut his throat, how to take a scalp? I'm all of those, Hannah."

"When I look at you, I see the warmth in your eyes. I see the strength of your hands. I see a mouth that speaks considerate words and lips that . . . that . . ."

He trailed his finger down her cheek. *Oh, beautiful Hannah.* Waiting for her in the darkness had been almost unbearable. Minute after minute his thoughts had circled, forming images of her naked body as she swam in the pool.

"You see lips that have burned to kiss you," he said in a low voice. "You see eyes that drink in the sight of your fire-hair as a thirsty man drinks water on a summer day. You see hands that hunger to touch your skin and learn every soft curve and hollow of your body."

Shivering, she let her eyes drift shut as his fingers trickled down her bare neck. "Luke, I told you I won't play games. Don't torment me and then abandon me as you did before. You know who I am as well as I know who you are. I'm not an Osage woman. I'll never have black hair and copper skin. I'll never fully understand the ways of your people."

"Gthe-non'-zhin," he murmured. "Shall I tell you what I see when I look at you?"

She nodded, unable to answer aloud.

"I think you are a woman with a mind of mystery and magic. You find beauty where other women see only the labors of daily life. You're fascinated with the smallest things—wildflowers beside a stream, the weave of a basket, the twist of a hickory limb. Your thoughts constantly surprise and intrigue and amaze me. Your laughter shimmers like midnight stars in my heart. Every morning when Grandfather the Sun wakens me, the first thing I think of is you, Hannah. Not my plans, not my dreams. It's you . . . always you."

"Luke, don't say anything more."

"Why not?"

"Because I feel as I did the night you held me in the lodge. I want your words to go on and on. I long for you to touch me and hold me. I think if you don't kiss me, I shall . . . I shall be forced to kiss you."

Luke bit back a smile. "Would that be so wrong?"

"You told me what we did in the lodge was just a game. You

said it meant nothing. But it wasn't silly to me. It wasn't safe or frivolous. I felt as if something inside me came to life as I lay in your arms. That living thing is crying out, demanding satisfaction. But I won't be made the fool. I won't have you torment me and then discard me because you believe I'm nothing but an awkward Heavy Eyebrows woman who isn't fit to be your mate."

He stood a heartbeat away, his hand on her shoulder and his breath so close she could feel it brush across her cheek. Droplets from her wet hair fell onto her bottom and trickled down the backs of her legs as she waited for him to respond.

Had she said too much? Would her words drive him away again? She almost hoped they would. He was so close, and she wanted him so much . . . and it all seemed so very dangerous.

"Hannah," he whispered, "you are not a foolish, unworthy Heavy Eyebrows. I told you what I thought of your mind and your spirit. How do I see you? I'll tell you. This hair . . ." He ran his fingers over and through the rumpled strands. "It weaves a fiery spell around my thoughts. This white skin is like cream that I want to lap with my tongue. Like milky, velvet cream . . . so soft and fragrant . . . so sweet . . ."

Drawing her toward him, he brushed his lips across the rise of her shoulder. A ripple of tension slid down her arms. Did she truly want him as she had said? Would she become his mate, no matter the consequences? Or would one of them become the discarded pawn in this game they played?

"Luke, I don't care," she murmured. "I don't care about anything. Finding my brother . . . going back to Boston . . . none of those things matter when you hold me."

He swallowed with pleasure at the release of guilt her words brought him. She ran her hands over his back, and flames spread down his skin like a prairie fire on a windy night. He felt as though he were a wild mustang stallion, head held high and nostrils flaring. His heart drummed like galloping hooves across an open plain. Every sense hummed with his drive to have this woman—no matter the cost, no matter the dangers.

"Come into the pool with me, Hannah," he said against her ear.

Her eyes fastened to him, she waited on the bank while he

turned away and stripped off his leggings. Then he left her and stepped into the cool water. Would she come to him?

He made a shallow dive beneath the surface. The swirling water brought a healing to his fevered skin. It seeped through his hair and rinsed away the debris of the mucky lake. If it had been daytime, he would have been able to watch frogs darting for cover and minnows flashing like silver darts at the water's edge. Now, in the darkness, he could only think of one thing. Hannah. His woman . . .

And then from behind him a pair of hands slipped around his chest. A body drifted against his. He turned beneath the water. Hips like the sides of a smooth sun-baked clay pot. A waist so small his hands molded easily around it. And then . . . then . . . oh, the easy weight of breasts . . . soft, full, round breasts . . . bare breasts . . . nipples like small, hardened acorns beneath his palms . . .

He floated to the surface and studied Hannah's face in the moonlight. Her eyes were deep and hungry . . . confident, yet timid . . . Her hair drifted loose in the water.

"Gthe-non'-zhin," he whispered. "Returns-and-Stands. You came into the pool."

"You summoned me."

"I wanted you." He held her close against him, running his hands over her satiny body. "Oh, my woman, you have brought the greatest happiness I've ever known. And the greatest confusion."

"Yes," she agreed. "And fear. But never doubt." She placed her lips on his chest as she drifted in the touch of his fingers rippling up and down her wet skin. "When I'm near you, Luke, I can't think about what's right or wrong."

"This hunger between us is right. I don't know what *Wah'kon-tah* has planned for us, Hannah. Only tomorrow will tell. But I know that He brought us together, and I know that my desire for you is pure. It rises not only from my body, but from my spirit."

Their lips came together in a fiery meeting. Luke cupped Hannah's head in both his hands, supporting her as his mouth worked its magic. Her fingers kneaded his back. Her thighs brushed his. Her breasts crested against his chest.

"This is what I ache to do with you, Hannah," he murmured.

Then, as he had imagined during the long silences of the night, he touched the tip of her tongue. Deftly he probed her mouth with soft, sensual caresses, and then penetrated with hard thrusts.

"But not only with my tongue," he continued as his hands began to slide around her shoulders. "Can you feel how strongly I desire to come into your warmth, my woman?"

She nodded, lost in the tantalizing stroke of his fingertips across her bosom. "Luke, it's not safe for us to touch. You were wrong about the game."

"I've been wrong about many things where you're concerned. I thought I could stop . . . and I did. But the pleasure between us vanished. We became angry and resentful, as prickly as a pair of porcupines trying to live in the same burrow. Tonight, Hannah, let's play until we're satisfied."

"Yes," she whispered against his cheek. "Yes, please play with me, my mate."

He eased his arousal against the firm flesh of Hannah's stomach and then began to kiss the tips of her breasts. She drifted upward a little in the swirling water as she sought to encourage him.

She couldn't help but marvel at the wonder her own body had become. Silver light dusted her skin. Her nipples stood out like cherries atop a pair of rounded sugar cakes. Luke ran his tongue over first one and then the other, tasting and savoring her as if she were indeed a delectable dessert.

Shivers shot down her spine and into her thighs as his lips covered one jutting crest. He licked around and around in torturous circles, then he began to suckle. At the sweet tugging sensation in the pit of her stomach, Hannah gasped. The stars overhead in the indigo sky began to swirl and dip.

Taking Luke's swollen shaft in her hands, she cupped and toyed with him. In response, he pressed her closer and his mouth began to move hungrily from one breast to the other. Stroking him, she prayed her touch was as magical to him as his was to her.

As she drew him out, further and further toward the apex of release, Luke felt the thudding in his blood begin to hammer. He had to have her. He couldn't stop this time, no matter what.

Images of his boyhood fantasies drifted through his thoughts as he suckled her taut nipples. He remembered the spring morning when he had inadvertently came upon a group of maidens bathing in the river. Wonder of wonders, he had glimpsed the full majesty of their bronzed breasts and small brown nipples. He had stood behind a sycamore tree and watched in mesmerized fascination, unable to move, until one of the older women standing guard had caught sight of the clandestine observer and had driven him away.

In the night . . . oh, in the nights of his boyhood, he had dreamed of those young women's breasts. He had imagined their softness against his lips. He had ached for their taste on his tongue.

But not until he met Hannah had his fantasies been transformed into reality. It wasn't the Osage maidens he craved—Hannah was the woman he wanted. By day he had watched her, stealthily observing the jutting peaks of her firm nipples beneath his shirts. By night, he had conjured her, and in his visions he had stroked her lithe body until dreams merged with reality.

An unbidden memory of his boyhood returned. He recalled nights when he was aroused and in agony of need, and he had satisfied himself alone. Slipping out of the lodge, he knelt beneath the concealing shadows of a tree where no one would know, no one would see the thing he did to find relief.

Were those nights of torment gone forever? Luke wondered as he reveled in the beauty of the woman he held. Would this creature who had stepped out of his fantasies ease his throbbing hunger in days to come? Would she be the fulfillment of every dream? Would she be his hot-blooded mare, and he her stallion thundering across the plain . . . nostrils dilated to drink in her fragrance . . . muscles straining . . . ?

"Hannah," he whispered, "will you ride me?"

"Anything."

Cupping her bottom, he scooped her up in his arms. "Spread your thighs to me, my woman. Wrap your legs around my hips."

Obliging, she grasped his shoulders as he lifted her against him. The feel of him pushing toward her, then bumping and sliding gently against her sent Hannah's body into a cloud of ecstasy. His hands sizzled down her wet skin, feathered across her back, and massaged her buttocks. She felt as though she were aglow.

This was the secret of which no one ever spoke, she realized. This was what husbands and wives did together under the cover of night. And Hannah knew it was this man . . . only Luke . . . who could take her this far. She felt as though she were perched in a swing on the top of a great, high cliff. She swooped out over the canyon, then took a giddy drop toward earth, then swooped out again. Just when she was certain she had tasted the heights of pleasure, she felt Luke's hand move around her thigh . . . under and up . . .

"Oh!" she cried out.

"Do you like this, my spirit mate?"

"Oh, Luke . . . this is . . . Don't ever stop . . ."

He smiled as he played her. To see Hannah's head thrown back on her shoulders, her eyelids drifting shut, her nipples tight and hot, and to run his fingers through the creamy welcome she had prepared for him went far beyond his greatest dreams.

"Hannah, I wait outside the door to your lodge," he told her softly. "I want to come in. Will you invite me?"

For a moment she couldn't answer. Never, never had she dreamed of such a wondrous pleasure as the stroke of Luke's fingertips. All she could do was to push against him, spread her thighs farther, beg for more with the urgent thrust of her body.

"Come into me, Luke," she managed. "Please . . . please come inside me."

He tilted her chin and forced her to meet his eyes. "Have you heard that when a man opens a woman's door, he must bring her pain along with his gift of pleasure, Hannah?"

She pressed her swollen breasts against his chest. "My mother . . . that's all she told me. A wife's duty to her husband brought pain and unpleasantness."

"That's all your mother told you?"

He could hardly fathom such a thing. He had been taught from earliest memory that the loving between a man and his wife brought a union of souls. How could it be anything but beautiful?

"I don't care about the pain." Hannah's mouth moved against his ear. "Luke, take me."

At her words, his doubts vanished. Turning her around and around in the pool, he continued to caress her breasts and titillate the pebble of pleasure in her secret nest. When she gasped out loud, and when her fingers dug into his back, he knew she had climbed to the peak of her desire.

"Now," he said, "we fly."

Rigid with barely leashed control, he thrust into her. She stiffened for a moment, then sagged against him. He held her close, nuzzling her neck as his body reveled in the majesty of union. Unable to keep still, he slipped slowly in and out. Her tight, silken sheath caressed him. Her heels pressed into his buttocks.

"Luke, please take away the pain," she pleaded. "Take me high again."

"As high as we both can soar, my woman."

In the liquid embrace of the water, they drifted while Luke transported Hannah upward to the top of the cliff. As he stroked into her again, her senses began to tingle. His fingers plucked a tune on the crests of her swollen breasts. Images of him in past days drifted through her mind—broad shoulders bent over the fire, muscled arms swinging an axe, taut buttocks braced against a stone, hard thighs cocked in a waiting crouch as his falcon soared.

Fantasy mingled with reality as she reflected on the times she had hungered in silence for this man. The morning she had caught him boldly studying her breasts. The time she had peered through the scrub oak brush and focused for leisurely minutes on the fine bulge beneath his breechcloth. The night she had crept out of bed, gathered up his leggings, and held them to her cheek, lost in the musky scent of leather and male skin. She had ached to touch him, to drink him, to taste him. And now he was hers.

Instinctively she moved her hips, joining him in the dance of passion. Her body sang and waltzed as she swayed with her mate over the edge of the high cliff and then back again . . . over and back . . . over and back . . . over and—

She fell, plummeting through heaven on a shower of stars and moonbeams. Ecstasy shuddered through her. Wave upon wave. Shower upon shower.

Just when she knew the bottom had dropped out of her

world, she felt Luke's muscles [...]
gripped her thighs and tore into h[...]
exploded within her—a cataclysmic, p[...]
some in its intensity.

She clung to him as they swirled heedless[...]
pool. Then his mouth found hers again, and he [...]er
softly. His hands held her close, stroking her back and[...]s.

"Hannah, Hannah," he murmured. "You are my woman, my
wife, my mate. You're everything I've desired, more than I
could ever have dreamed. You're all I want and all I will ever
need."

"Oh, Luke." She swallowed against the tight knot in her
throat. "I'm so happy, so full. You've brought me the greatest
gift I could wish for. You've given me yourself."

Luke shut his eyes as they drifted together, drinking in the
silence. Yes, he had given himself to this woman—more than
just his body. He had given her his future, his trust, his heart.
And she had surrendered herself to him. How long could this
peace between them last? What would become of their union in
the days to come? He had no way of knowing.

Chapter
Fifteen

❦

Hannah awoke to the sight of a great expanse of bronzed male chest. A thin sheen of perspiration dampened the skin, as though the man's flesh had been brushed with a honey glaze. Sinew and muscle stretched across his rib cage and rose into a hardened plain to form his upper torso. Like a pair of copper coins, his flat nipples rose and fell with each deep, chest-expanding breath he took.

Luke, Hannah thought. *Luke Maples.*

My husband. My lover.

Stretching, she brushed her nose into the musky buffalo-hide blanket beneath her. The thick brown fur tickled her nostrils. Indolence and satisfaction rippled through her as memories of the hours she had spent in Luke's arms sifted slowly into her consciousness like sugar through a sieve.

A sense of wholeness permeated her heart for the first time in her life. Sometime during the night of lovemaking, she had stepped over the line from girlhood to womanhood. Her body

glowed with ripeness. Her mind filled in the gaps of understanding she had lived with for so long.

Now she knew the person she had been growing into all
these years. Now she felt certain of the woman she was at this
moment. Now she understood the magic her future could hold.

Nothing outward had changed so much. She could certainly
go on writing novels of romance and adventure, Hannah
realized. She could now say she'd experienced both in large
measure. If she chose, she could return to Boston and live the
rest of her days in a snug brick home with a rose garden in the
backyard. In fact, she felt at this moment that she could
accomplish anything.

No matter what became of her outwardly, she knew that
inside her heart she would never again be the same Hannah
Brownlow. It was Luke, of course, who had brought about the
changes. He had opened her door. He had taken her high into
the clouds, and she had touched ultimate bliss.

Rolling onto her elbow, Hannah studied his face relaxed in
sleep. Her throat constricted with a mixture of tenderness and
passion. In the space of a few short days, Luke Maples had
shown her more joy than she had ever known.

He had taught her the beauty of his world. He had filled her
thoughts with stories of a wonderful culture. And he had
explored her body in a way that unlocked the mysteries of life.

Could she leave him? Hannah ran her eyes down the profile
of his brow, his nose, his magnificent mouth. How could she
return to Boston and never again know this man's touch? Did
her books, her sisters, her mother, and her missing brother
really mean more to her than Luke Maples did?

No. She couldn't deny the truth. She would sacrifice
everything she had strived for to spend her life in his embrace.

But did Luke want her as much as she wanted him? What if
the night's pleasures had been merely an enjoyable interlude
for him? There was no question he desired her. But did desire
always bring commitment? Probably not. Especially for a man
with dreams as vivid as Luke's were to him.

What could she do to win from him the promise of a future?
Nothing could erase the fact that she was no Osage wife. She
was a Boston miss, through and through. In spite of the
changes she felt inside, she remained unschooled in the basics

of Missouri existence. She might make a willing lover for Luke, but in the middle of winter as they huddled cold and starving, he would find little use for a paramour when what he needed was a mate who could provide.

She still didn't know most of the things an Indian wife would know—how to make warm clothing, how to cook nourishing food, how to build a fire, how to construct a drying rack, how to plant corn . . . The list of things she couldn't do nearly overwhelmed her, until she reflected on one bright hope. There *was* someone who could teach her what a woman needed to know in this wilderness—someone who had all the answers.

With a chill of excitement, Hannah bent over and kissed Luke's shoulder. Her solution was perfect. By nightfall she would be well on her way to ensuring a lifetime of happiness with this warrior who had captured her heart.

Lifting a hand, she trailed her fingertips over his chest. Minuscule bumps rose on his skin. The centers of his copper nipples contracted into tiny seeds, and he let out a deep breath.

"Luke," she whispered. "Grandfather the Sun has already peeked over the ridge. Are you going to sleep all day?"

With an unintelligible murmur, he slipped his arm around her and pulled her close. "Hannah," he whispered. Nuzzling against her ear, he spoke a flow of words in his native tongue. Though she couldn't understand the endearments, their meaning was evident in the soft rhythm of tender accents.

"Mmm," she moaned as she kissed his warm neck. "You taste delicious in the morning."

"Are you really in my bed, Gthe-non'-zhin?"

"No . . . you're in my bed."

He smiled, and his eyes slid open in a drowsy gaze. "From now on, this lodge will hold only one bed, so there can be no confusion."

"I'm not confused about anything."

"No? Then tell me—what does the future hold for this man and his mate?"

"Happiness. Peace. Prosperity."

"Union?"

"As often as possible."

Laughing, he gathered her into his arms. "Yes, Hannah, my fire-haired woman. As often as possible."

"But right now, Grandfather is calling you to breakfast and then to work."

With a mock frown of disappointment, he ran his fingertip down her cheek. "How can I leave you?"

"You won't have to. I'm riding with you into Bolivar."

"I thought you'd planned to roast lotus seeds."

"First I must speak with Miss Ruth."

"The old *Nika-sabe?*" A curl of doubt flickered through Luke's stomach. "Why, Hannah?"

"Oh . . . women's matters."

He looked into her blue eyes. "Hannah, I've heard there are ways to keep a baby from growing inside a woman. Charms she can wear around her neck and things she can put into her body. And I know it's possible for a mother to drink a potion that will tear the growing child from her womb. Hannah, you told me you would disdain the thought of bearing a son from my loins, but please—I beg you—don't try to prevent our baby."

Shocked at his erroneous assumption, she could hardly bring herself to respond. "Oh, Luke, no . . . I would never . . . No, of course not."

His face relaxed. "Then?"

"I want Miss Ruth to teach me how to be your wife. A proper Missouri wife. I want to learn everything."

"Hannah . . ." He stroked her pale shoulder. "Last night you showed me everything you will ever need to know about being my wife."

"No, Luke, you don't understand. It's the cooking and sewing. It's storing and drying. Miss Ruth can teach me."

Overwhelmed by the expression of devotion in her eyes, Luke could do nothing but draw her against his chest and hold her tightly. Did she really mean to become his wife in every sense of the word? Did she want to live in his lodge forever? Did she hope to bear their children?

Swallowing, Luke contemplated a new future. Certainly it was not the one he had planned so carefully on the Kansas reservation. Could he release the dreams that had driven him so far for so many years to settle permanently with a woman of the race he had good reason to despise? Could he betray his determination to restore the heritage, the lineage, the lands of

his tribe? And what about the search for his father's killer?
What about Ethan Brown? This was the day he had sworn to
find out who the man really was. But did he really want to
know?

He shut his eyes, struggling with questions that surged
through him like a whirlpool. The vision he had begun to see
last night as he held Hannah was not the life he had planned.
But with this woman at his side, might it not be even better?

"One day a week I'll visit with Miss Ruth," Hannah
whispered. "The rest of the time, I'll stay out here on our land."

"Writing your book?"

"Yes. And harvesting what we'll need"—she paused and
took a deep breath—"what we'll need for the winter."

"Winter . . . with you." He studied the depths of her
morning-glory eyes. "Hannah, at this moment I can think of
nothing more beautiful than the sight of you lying on our
buffalo robe when the first snow is falling outside our cabin."

"Cabin?"

"Now that you speak of staying here with me during the cold
season, I want to begin construction of a log cabin. A lodge is
adequate shelter for an Osage family who live and hunt in the
hills in winter, then move to the plains in search of food in the
summer. A lodge can keep out winter winds, and a tepee is a
fine summer dwelling. But a cabin is essential to a family who
plan to stay in one place for the rest of their lives."

Shivering with happiness, Hannah wrapped her arms around
Luke's neck and rubbed herself against him. He smiled in
delight at her boldness. Cupping her silky bottom, he posi-
tioned her so he could feel the mound of her soft nest against
his pelvis.

"I think I might be late for work today," he surmised.

"It's permitted, you know." She wantonly draped one leg
over his hip. "A man never goes to work on his honeymoon."

Palming her breast, he rolled her nipple between his thumb
and finger. She wriggled with pleasure. His eyes traveled down
her from the rise of her full breasts to the flat, white satin of her
stomach to the slender circumference of her thighs.

"Honeymoon?" he murmured, unfamiliar with the term. "I'd
like to taste your honey, my mate."

As she lay in shimmering arousal, he rolled onto his knees

and parted her thighs. Gently he dipped his tongue into her damp silk. Instantly intoxicated, she tangled her fingers in the buffalo fur behind her head. Again he tasted her. And again.

Her hips swayed. Danced. Pounded into the bed.

She reached for him and ran her hands through his hair. As his mouth sent flames racing through her, her nipples distended into tight buds that ached with wanting. Like a pair of wild gourds ready for harvest, her breasts grew large, ripe, and heavy.

"Please," she said, the word no more than a shuddering breath.

Pausing on the apex of release, she sensed Luke hovering over her. His mouth had ceased its ministering, but the emptiness was quickly filled. Plunging into her, he immersed himself in dewy paradise. As he rose and fell, stoking her flames to a roaring bonfire, she clutched his shoulders.

Their mouths met again and again, seeking, savoring, drinking. Their bodies thrust into the soft bedding. Their skin went liquid and hot.

As his caresses broke the final dam that had held her back from the crest, Hannah cried out. Rolling waves surged through her body with blinding heat. Her release triggered Luke's eruption into the same blinding sea of rapture.

"My wife, my wife," he whispered again and again as he surged into her until his strength was spent.

Her body sagged with euphoric exhaustion. Feeling like a pool of melted butter, she drew him close. His chest met hers, then his stomach. Collapsing, he gathered her against the full length of his body and rolled onto his side, taking her with him.

"Hannah." His palm slipped comfortably over her bare breast as if it had always been there. "Hannah, the heavens are smiling."

She brushed her lips across his mouth. "Amen and hallelujah."

"I'll return for you at five this afternoon," Luke called while he walked across Lillian Street to the fencepost where his horse was hitched.

Standing outside the front door of Martha Strickland's cabin, Hannah waved in farewell. Beside her, Ruth Jefferson crossed her arms beneath her ample bosom and surveyed the situation, a skeptical frown drawing down the corners of her mouth. Luke gave his horse's reins a flick, and the two women turned away to walk across the yard.

But as reality filtered through the happy glow suffusing her thoughts, Hannah suddenly paused. She swung around, lifted her skirts, and trotted out onto the street. "Luke!" she cried.

He pulled on the reins and turned around. "Hannah?"

"I almost forgot. Please check at the post office for word of my brother!"

A heavy lead weight sank to the bottom of Luke's stomach. "All right, Hannah." He gazed at her for a moment, then reached down and ran his fingers through the soft hair at her forehead.

Shivers skittered down Hannah's arms as he nudged the horse into a trot. Before she felt ready to let him go, he had turned a corner at the end of the street and disappeared.

When Hannah let out a sigh, Ruth chuckled. "My, my, things do change in a hurry, don't they?"

Hannah tried without success to prevent the flush that spread across her cheeks. "Where's Miss Martha?"

"Out back with the washin'. I ought to warn you, she ain't gonna be happy to see you today."

"Why not? Am I interrupting something?"

"We got troubles, sure enough." She reflected a moment. "Besides, Monday is laundry day, girl. Don't you know that?"

"That's exactly why I've come!"

"Martha don't take white folks' washin' no more."

"No, I want to help her with the laundry. And with the cooking and cleaning and whatever else Miss Martha does today."

"Lord have mercy." Ruth took Hannah's hands and drew her into the sheltered side yard. "You didn't come here to write?"

"I've come to learn from you and Martha. I want you to teach me everything you know."

Ruth's soft brown eyes grew wide. "Don't you recollect what I told you? I ain't never been to school. There's not a thing in this world an old slave woman could teach a lady like you."

"You're not a slave any longer, Miss Ruth. And you're

wrong about not knowing anything. What's the name of that purple flower growing over there by the rain barrel?"

"That's a coneflower."

"There! You see what I mean?"

"A coneflower won't do you no good, honey. You can go on down to the mercantile and buy whatever you need."

"Not in my financial straits, I can't. So tell me, Miss Ruth—could I eat that coneflower raw if I were hungry? Or could I boil it, or brew it into a tea?"

"Why, a body don't eat purple coneflower for food. It's an ailment cure. Take care of most anything you can think of—snake bite, bee sting, poison ivy, headache. It's good for distemper in horses, too. If you put just a piece of it on your tooth when you've got a toothache, it'll make everything go numb. You can rub its juice onto a burn, and it'll ease the pain straight away."

"Aha!" Hannah said in triumph. "I didn't know a thing about coneflowers, but now I do. And it was you who taught me."

Ruth gave a skeptical snort as she walked behind the house. "Hey, Martha, look who's here."

Martha glanced up from a huge tub of steaming water. Her curly hair was hidden under a bright red scarf, and perspiration made her skin glow like polished ebony. Dressed in a walnut-dyed brown homespun dress, she had strapped her baby to her back with a sling made of soft fabric.

"Good Lord," she said under her breath as Hannah approached. "What next?"

"Morning, Miss Martha," Hannah said in greeting.

"You better not come around here no more, Miss Hannah." Martha gave the laundry a final stir and then made her way across the yard toward Hannah and Ruth. Chickens scattered as her barefoot stride took her through a pile of spilled grain. Her baby peered around his mother's shoulder from his perch in the sling. The two older children looked up from their play beneath the spreading branches of a pin oak tree.

When she got close enough, Martha lowered her voice to a whisper. "We been havin' trouble, Miss Hannah."

Hannah paused. "What kind of trouble?"

"Trouble over you. Folks seen you over here, and they been talkin'. I'm afraid Jim's gonna catch wind of it."

"Has anyone threatened you?"

"No, and I ain't afraid if they do. Not too much, anyhow—so long as they don't touch my babies. But you got to watch yourself, girl. It's you they been meanmouthin'."

Hannah breathed a sigh of relief. "I long ago stopped caring what people thought of me, Miss Martha. Besides, Luke won't let any harm come my way."

"The Indian? Lawsy, I'm surprised your scalp ain't hangin' off his britches by now."

"Not hardly a chance of that," Ruth interjected. "From the cozy looks of things, that man ain't been in his britches none too often these days. Nor has Miss Hannah been wearin' her skirts."

Martha cackled as Hannah turned a brilliant pink. "Happened faster than we thought, huh, Ruth?"

"You shoulda seen them moonin' over each other a minute ago. Grinnin' like skunks eatin' cabbage. And now Miss Hannah says she wants us to learn her everything about bein' a good wife."

"Lawsy mercy." Martha clucked as she wiped her hands on her apron. She surveyed Hannah up and down. "So that Indian has truly made you his wife, girl?"

Glancing toward the children, who had returned to playing with their corncob dolls, Hannah cleared her throat. What went on between her and Luke had nothing to do with Martha and Ruth. Nothing at all. "It's really not important—"

"You gonna feel kindly 'bout bearin' that man a baby?" Martha cut in. "Your mama gonna take a half-breed grandchild into the family? You gonna send that little one to the white man's school and let all the other children laugh at him and tease him?"

Hannah bristled, but Martha's words hit close to thoughts of her own. "I don't know what the future holds, Miss Martha," she said. "I only know I came to ask you and Miss Ruth how I can become a good wife."

"There's more to being a good wife than cookin' and cleanin'," Martha said. "More than rollin' around on a feather bed. There's money to be made and in-laws to be got along with. There's days when you can barely walk 'cause you're all swole up with an unbirthed baby—but you got to hoe the fields and wash the clothes and cook your man's supper over a hot fire anyway."

Ruth nodded sagely. "There's children to tend in the middle of the night when they's got the chills and is spittin' up all over you. There's babies to bury when they don't live through their first two years. And there's a man who comes in from the fields too tired to love you and too worn to listen to your heartaches. Oh, Miss Hannah, you might as well know what you're in for."

"But you're the ones who told me to find the pleasure in my marriage," Hannah protested. "Not a week ago, you both told me I shouldn't bother to be married without claiming the joys."

"If a woman's got to be married," Martha acknowledged, "the least she can do is get some good times out of it. Sure we told you to find the pleasure with that Indian. You'd already done married him. Besides, we knew he wasn't gonna waste no time liftin' them ruffled petticoats of yours. Might as well know the pleasure, 'cause there's sure enough gonna be pain."

"Don't be so hard on her, Martha." Ruth took Hannah's hand and clasped it between her own. "As long as you know what to expect, girl, you can make the best of it."

"And, believe me," Martha added, "a man can bring a woman some mighty fine times."

"You gonna get started on that again?" Ruth said with a reluctant chuckle. She leaned over toward Hannah's ear. "The minute Martha sees that big hunk of husband of hers a-walkin' up the street toward the house, she's got only one thing on her mind. She wants to boil him a mess of greens and fry him a pork chop, and then get them children of hers off to bed so's she and Jim can settle down to business."

Martha laughed. "How do you know what Jim and me do, Miss Smarty-britches?"

"You two make enough racket to wake the dead. There's me and Willie up in the loft just a-sleepin' like babies, and the next thing we know, the two of you is down there hootin' and hollerin' and whoopin' it up. I'll swear if the sounds of you folk havin' such fun don't half get me in the mood sometimes."

"Hoo, Lawsy! Willie wouldn't know what to do with you if you got all het up, Ruth."

The older woman covered her mouth as she snickered. "Now, what you know about old Willie? Let me tell you, that man can ring my bell. Amen! Light a fire under him, and he'll chase me around the bed in circles like an old rooster after a hen."

"Old Willie's the cock of the walk, is he?"

"Mercy sakes!" Ruth exclaimed.

She and Martha bent over in a gale of hearty guffaws. Hannah's mouth twitched, and then she burst into laughter. When the three women were wiping tears from their eyes, Martha gave Hannah a big hug.

"Listen, honey, if old Willie still has enough lovin' in him to chase Ruth around the bed, there must be somethin' pretty fine about a man and woman livin' a long life together. I reckon you seen the good in that Indian husband of yours, and no matter what comes your way, you and he can fix it for the better."

Hannah smiled. "I hope so, Miss Martha. Luke is a fine man. Even though things are stacked against us, I mean to do my best by him. Do you suppose you and Ruth could help me?"

The two women regarded each other, and Hannah knew they were weighing the risks. "White folk wouldn't like it," Ruth said finally. "Jim and Willie wouldn't like it if they ever found out. Ain't nobody would like it."

"I'd like it," Hannah said softly.

Martha looked at Ruth for a moment, then her mouth curved into a tentative smile. "I'd like it, too," she said. "Mr. Abraham Lincoln didn't set me free to live like a coward. You want to learn from us, Miss Hannah, we'll teach you all we know."

Ruth glanced nervously at the road. "Lord help us if folks find out."

"Aw, Ruth, it'll be fine. Listen, Miss Hannah, when that first bitty baby of yours gets ready to be borned, why, you send your young husband after Ruth lickety-split. We'll get Jim to hitch up the wagon and drive her out to help you."

"I am the best around at midwifin'," Ruth confirmed.

"It liked to kill me when she and Willie headed north, and then I found out I was gone with this little feller." She gave her baby a pat on the bottom and then adjusted the sling on her shoulder. The little boy's chunky legs dangled behind her as she set off toward the huge iron kettle. "Roll up your sleeves, Miss Hannah," she hollered over her shoulder. "I'm gonna set you to makin' starch."

* * *

"Where you been this mornin'?" Tom Cunnyngham called as Luke stepped into the courthouse office. "We nearly left without you."

Luke took off his hat and set his equipment bag on the floor. "I've been on my . . ." He searched for the word. "Honeymoon."

"Honeymoon!" Tom's face split wide in a grin that lit up the room. He took Luke's hand and pumped it up and down. "You been holdin' out on us, boy! We didn't know you was courtin'. Who's the lucky gal?"

"Her name is Hannah."

"An Indian, I hope?" The voice came from behind the open door of a cabinet. In a moment Ethan Brown's pale blue eyes peered across the dimly lit room. "She's Osage, I trust?"

Luke scowled. Instinct told him to turn and walk away, but he knew he had to face the man and find out the truth. "My wife is a white woman," he said. "Is that a problem for you?"

"That's a problem for me," Brown said. He stood and walked slowly toward Luke, his stocky body squared and threatening. Jim Jones, the county clerk, followed, tapping on the man's shoulder to try to draw his attention.

"You're from Boston," Luke said. "Why do you care how an Indian lives?"

"No redskin should look at a white woman, let alone touch her. It's an abomination."

"What do you have against the Osage, Mr. Brown? What have my people done to you?"

"You exist. That's enough."

At that, Tom clapped his hands together. "Well, boys, sun's up and time's awastin'," he said with forced cheer. "Let's head out."

"Mr. Brown, surely you have someone you care about no matter what people think," Luke said, ignoring Tom. "Don't you have a mother, a father . . . sisters?"

"I have sisters—and were you to lay a hand on any one of them, I would personally blow your brains out."

Luke clenched his jaw. The men in the crew were gathering by the door, and Tom was nervous, but Luke had to know more. Was this man his Ethan or Hannah's—or both?

"You would kill me over such a thing?" Luke said. "You must hate my people for some reason. Maybe you knew the Osage when you were in Kansas?"

Brown laughed, but his pale eyes were mirthless. "Know them? Yes . . . oh, yes. And I know you, too, Luke Maples. I've recorded your name in my little book here, and I mean to see you sent back to your reservation, where you belong."

Fists clenched, Luke started for the man. He would wipe that smirk off his face. He'd slit open his throat and drain every drop of blood from his pale body. As Luke lunged forward, Tom grabbed his arm. The others in the crew leapt to hold him back.

"Come on, Luke," Tom said. "Ain't no use talkin' to that ol' turkey buzzard. You got yourself a bride and a good-payin' job. You got too much at stake to stir up trouble with the likes of him. Let's go set up our survey flags and see if things don't look better out in God's country."

Breathing hard, Luke glared at the man. Brown gave him a cocky smile. "Watch yourself, Redskin," he sneered.

Luke bit back a threat and allowed Tom to maneuver him through the door and into the hall. As they walked out into the sunshine, Luke swallowed against the knot of anger in his throat. Ethan Brown—no matter who he was—deserved the devil's hell. Luke intended to see that he got it.

Hannah's dress was drenched with sweat by the time Luke tied his horse to the post on Lillian Street late that afternoon. Like a flaming halo, her hair stood out around her head in wispy curls. Her cheeks glowed bright pink from a combination of sunburn and working over a fire most of the day.

The hem of her skirt had been peppered with tiny sparks that had scorched holes right through the fabric to her petticoat. Blisters covered her palms, and every muscle in her back ached. But as Luke sauntered across the road, she gave him the happiest smile of her life.

"Luke! Oh, Luke!" she called.

He lifted a hand. "Had a good day, Hannah?"

Her morning-glory eyes shone with joy as she danced toward him, manuscript in one hand and fresh butter in a small basket that hung on her arm. "Luke, I've learned how to make starch and bluing," she sang out. "I've cooked a mess of hominy and churned cream into butter and fried a chicken."

"She wrung the critter's neck all by herself, too," Martha said, stepping out of the house. She dried her hands on her apron and stuck one out in greeting. "Martha Strickland's the name."

Luke gave the woman's hand a firm shake. "Luke Maples. I'm Hannah's husband."

"I had that figured right. So what kind of an Indian are you, anyhow?"

"Osage."

"You folk used to live around here?"

"All these hills were once our hunting grounds."

"From what Miss Hannah told us, sounds like you been havin' hard times."

Luke nodded. "Your times have not been so easy either, Mrs. Strickland."

"No, they ain't. But we's makin' it now that we got our freedom. You want to come around the house and set a spell?"

Ruth, who had been hanging back in the shadows, cleared her throat. "Willie and Jim be home soon," she warned Martha. "Bad enough we had a white woman here all day workin' with us side by side. What are folk gonna say to an Indian? We're gonna get ourselves lynched for puttin' our noses where they don't belong."

"It's all right," Luke said. "Hannah and I need to ride for home anyway."

"I'll be back next week," Hannah added. "If it suits you to teach me more lessons, I'll return on Monday."

"Better come another day of the week," Martha informed her. "That is, if you want to learn somethin' new. Monday's always wash day. I ain't gonna change that, not even for you, Miss Hannah. Come on Tuesday, why don't you? We'll be—"

"Ironing," Hannah finished. She looked proudly at Luke. "Washing on Monday, ironing on Tuesday, mending on Wednesday, hoeing on Thursday, cleaning house on Friday, and baking on Saturday. Sunday is church day. All the spare time on my hands I'll use to tend the garden, churn butter, can, pickle, black the stove, gather eggs, and milk the cow."

Luke's mouth tugged upward into a grin. "Which cow are you planning to milk, Hannah?"

"We must purchase a cow with the very next pay you earn. How can we survive without milk, butter, and cheese?"

"That's right, Master Luke," Martha confirmed. "And chickens, too. Now, you go out and buy a few hens and a good rooster first thing, hear? Cookin' ain't decent without eggs."

"Would you be willing to sell us a few of your chickens, Mrs. Strickland?"

Martha beamed. "Why, surely I would. Be proud to. We got ourselves more than enough here. Fat, healthy ones, too. You come on around next week, and I'll fix you up."

"Thank you, ma'am," Luke said. "I suppose we'll need a kitchen garden, too, if Hannah's planning to tend one."

"It's too late in the year to grow most things. But you could put in some beets and set out a mess of onions."

"We can dig wild onions in the forest."

"Maybe so, but they ain't as good as the planted ones. You sure can't get through the winter without turnips. You can eat the greens, of course, and come fall you can harvest yourself a fine root crop. Dig a big old hole and bury them turnips good and deep. Then you can dig some up every time you get hungry, and they'll last you right through the cold."

"I don't know much about turnips, but if you say we should plant some, we will."

"Clear you a big patch of ground right next to the house. Pull out all the stumps—every single one. Haul away all the big rocks, too. Then get your plow and turn over the ground as deep as you can. Keep turnin' and turnin' till the dirt's plumb soft. Then spread out some manure to help things grow. Plant your turnips, and I guarantee you'll have yourself a dandy crop."

"All right," Luke said.

"And don't forget to turn over your garden after the harvest. Come spring, your patch will be prime for plantin' again."

"Thank you, Mrs. Strickland." Smiling, Luke slipped an arm around Hannah's shoulder. "I'll get right to work on that."

"You do it."

"And make her a good churn," Ruth put in from her hiding

place in the shadows. "Our girl don't need to keep wearin' her hands to blisters like she done today."

"Yes, ma'am."

"And fetch her a fine big iron kettle, too. She'll need it for renderin' lard and washin' clothes and such. You buy the biggest and best you can find so's it'll last her a lifetime."

"Yes, ma'am," Luke said again. "Anything else?"

"Treat her good."

"Nothing but the best for my wife." Luke gave Hannah's shoulder a squeeze. "Now, if you ladies will excuse us, we'll head for home. Sounds like I've got my work cut out for me before the sun sets."

As he and Hannah walked toward the horse, Luke could hear the two women whispering behind him.

"He's plumb decent for an Indian," Martha said. "And a right handsome devil at that."

"Amen to that," Ruth confirmed. "Lawsy . . . what a man! You reckon he'll do her right?"

"Reckon so."

"Lord have mercy, here comes Jim and Willie!"

Luke spotted the two *Nika-sabe* men walking down the street toward the house. One was a fine-looking fellow in the prime of life—tall and brawny with muscles that bulged and a chest as wide as an old oak tree trunk. His dark skin glistened with sweat against the white of his homespun shirt.

The other man was much older, bent and worn. His hair was dusted with tiny white curls, and his eyes were buried in deeply etched lines. Luke recognized him immediately as the one who had taken his rabbit that evening on the road to Bolivar.

"What you doin' at my place?" the younger man barked.

Luke stiffened and tucked Hannah against him. "I was asking your wife about selling some chickens."

"What you want my chickens for? Ain't you an Indian? Go shoot a deer with your bow and arrows, why don't you?"

"Say, I know that feller," Willie said. "He was out in the woods a-huntin' rabbits with a doggone bird. And that's Miss Hannah Brownlow right there beside him. Ruth and me brung her all the way from Jefferson City in our wagon. I'll never forget them hoops in her skirt. Like to drove me plumb crazy."

"Hello, Mr. Jefferson," Hannah greeted him as she stepped

out of Luke's protective embrace. She clutched her manuscript in one hand and extended the other. After Willie finally shook it, she gave Jim a polite curtsy. "You must be Martha's husband."

"What you know about my wife? She don't do white folks' washin' no more. We're free now, hear? We ain't slaves to nobody. Martha don't got to work a lick if she don't want to."

"Oh, hush your mouth, Jim," Martha said. She ignored Ruth's pleas for silence as she swung her baby onto her hip and strode across the street. "This here's Miss Hannah. She's hitched to Master Luke, and they's settin' up housekeepin' out a ways in the woods. Ruth and me is teachin' her how to manage, seein' as she's come here from the East, where folks is backward."

"Backward?" Willie took off his battered hat and scratched his forehead. "You mean to tell me you're teachin' things to a white woman, Martha? Out here in front of God and everybody?"

"Cookin', washin', cleanin'. Them Easterners don't know nothin', Jim. They're plumb ignorant."

"Lawsy," he said. "I never would have figured such a thing."

Willie gave a snort that silenced the crickets along the road. "Ignorant is right. Wasn't too long ago Miss Hannah tried her derndest to shoot that there Indian. I saw it with my own two eyes. She grabbed the shotgun right out of my hands and pulled the trigger so fast the blast knocked her clean onto her fanny in the wagon bed. Now you mean to tell me she's up and married him?"

"That's right," Hannah said.

"What fer?"

"Because . . . because . . ." She fumbled. Could she blurt right out how she felt about Luke? That he had come to mean more to her than anything? That she loved the sound of his voice and the touch of his hands? That she found him fascinating, kind, brave, intelligent, handsome—

"What do you think they got hitched for, Willie?" Ruth asked as she joined the group. "Why do most folks hook up? First off, they reckoned they could help each other out. Pretty soon, they found out they was hot for each other's britches, too."

"That'll do it," Willie acknowledged. "Now I reckon they got themselves a full-blowed case of love. Ain't that right, Miss Hannah?"

Hannah gripped her manuscript and glanced up at Luke. He was staring at her, waiting for her answer.

"Well, Miss Hannah?" Willie repeated. "Ain't you in love?"

Chapter Sixteen

~~~~~~~~~~

"Dadburn it, Willie," Ruth *snapped.* *"If Miss Hannah loves her* man, that's her business, not yours. Now, you two get on over to the house and wash up. We got fried chicken for supper."

Willie turned without a backward glance, but Jim eyed Luke up and down. "I don't reckon you and your missus better come round here no more," he said. "Wouldn't want nobody thinkin' we was steppin' out of our place."

Hannah's blue eyes narrowed. "Mr. Strickland, not two minutes ago you informed me that you and Martha are free. And I'm a free woman. I don't believe other people need to have any say about what we choose to do or whom we choose to befriend."

"Maybe they don't need to say, but folk is gonna think what they want. And I know that when white folk decide black folk is settin' too high on the hog, they gonna knock 'em down a peg or two. Now, I got me three children, Miss Hannah. I don't want no harm to come to their daddy, you hear?"

"Quit your frettin', Jim," Martha said. "Nobody's gonna

bother about what we do. Far as I'm concerned, Miss Hannah can come over here anytime she wants. And she wants to come next Tuesday to learn how to iron. If one woman can't teach another how to iron, ain't none of us free."

"A black woman teaching a white one to wash and iron? Now, don't that beat all?" Turning on his heel, Jim stomped off toward the house.

"Don't pay him no heed," Martha told Hannah. "Till I get some food in that man, he always acts like an old bear. Besides, he don't understand that this war gave us a new hope. Folk who's been property all their lives can't hardly think past it. Sometimes I wake up in the night and lie there just a-tryin' to puzzle it out. Can it be that me and Jim actually got the freedom to get married? Can it be that our three children belongs to us and not to our master? Ain't nobody can take . . . can take my little babies away from me and . . . and sell 'em?"

Her great dark eyes clouded with tears. Ruth patted her on the back. "Now then, Martha, don't you fret."

"Ruth here done birthed fourteen children," Martha told Hannah through her sniffles. "Nine of 'em lived to grow up. But when they got to be four or five years old, her master sold off every one of 'em. Ruth don't even know what become of her babies. All she's got is old Willie now. Fourteen birthin's . . . nine children . . . and all she's got left is old Willie."

Dismayed, Hannah folded Martha into her arms. "Nobody will take your children from you, Martha," she whispered. "You don't have to worry anymore. Nobody can take them away."

"She done already lost two," Ruth said in a low voice. "Them that was growed enough, her master sold."

"Two little boys," Martha wept. "Zeke and Ab. I don't know where they is, Miss Hannah. I never will know. Not never till I see 'em in heaven."

"Oh, Miss Martha, I'm so sorry." Hannah held her tightly as she sobbed. "So very sorry."

"Now you know why Jim don't take kindly to you bein' over here at the house," Martha said softly. She lifted her head and wiped the back of her hand over her ebony cheeks. "He don't truly believe things is different. He don't trust white folk. He reckons he'll have to go back to slavin' one of these days. Tells me we should keep to ourselves and do our work best as we can. Don't go gettin' uppity nor expectin' life to be changed. And I try . . . I do try. But, Miss Hannah, ever since you come around, I been thinkin' about the way things might be for me."

"How do you mean, Miss Martha?"

"I think about how we's friends, good friends. I like that, Miss Hannah."

"So do I."

"I think about what you told me and Ruth—that we know things you don't know. That we's smart, and we can teach you. I think maybe the world *is* a-changin' a little. Maybe I will get to keep my babies till they's growed up. Maybe I'll get to live in this house till my dyin' day, and nobody'll take it away from me. Maybe my children will grow up thinkin' better of themselves. They might even go to school and get a fine job one day."

"Oh, Martha," Ruth said with a laugh. "You dreamin' now."

"Maybe so. But maybe not." She swung her baby from her hip to her stomach and looked him in the face. "You gonna live with your mama and papa till you're a big boy, ain't you? I'm gonna see that you learn to read and write and cipher. Maybe one day you'll take yourself off to St. Louis and open up a mercantile. You'll marry yourself a fine wife and have lots of babies and make a passel of money. And maybe when you're an old man with a head of white hair like old Willie, you'll walk down the street and look every white man you meet straight in the eye. 'Good mornin',' you'll say. 'Good mornin', Mr. Strickland,' they'll say. And they won't even notice you's black as midnight, and they won't even care that your daddy was a slave."

"Lawsy!" Ruth exclaimed. "Martha, you been out in the sun too long today. You's a mite tetched."

"No, she's not," Hannah countered. "I think she's right. At least . . . I hope she is."

"So do I," Luke said. He took Hannah's arm and drew her close. "I hope all your dreams come true, Mrs. Strickland. Although we come from separate worlds, when I listen to your

words I understand that one person is not so different from
another. We all want fairness, equality, freedom to dream. We
want hope."

"Well, I want my fried chicken supper," Ruth said. "You all
is talkin' too high and mighty for me. I been a slave all my life,
and I don't reckon things is never gonna change too much.
Sure, I lost all my fourteen babies, but I knew from the start I
would. I cried buckets of tears, but them children is gone and
not a thing I can do to change that. Maybe all I got left is old
Willie, but at least he's fit enough to earn a wage. Amen."

"And chase you round the bed like an ol' rooster after a hen."
Martha gave a weary chuckle. "Come on, girl. Our men is
gettin' impatient. Miss Hannah, we'll see you Tuesday, hear?
And don't forget about how to do the washin'—heat your
water, shave in a whole cake of lye soap, sort out your three
piles—"

"One pile of white clothes, one pile of colored clothes, one
pile of work britches and rags," Hannah finished. "Scrub
the white clothes on the board and then boil them good. Scrub
the colored clothes, but don't boil them. Make starch out of
flour and water. Rinse the clothes and starch them, but blue the
white ones first. Pour all the rinse water in the flower bed, and
scrub the porch with hot soapy water."

"Wait a minute," Luke cut in. "We don't have a flower bed
or a front porch."

"One of these days we will," Hannah stated before returning
to her recitation. "Turn the washtubs upside down, then go put
on a clean dress, brew a cup of tea, sit down, and rock a spell."

"And don't forget to count your blessin's." Martha gave
Hannah a farewell smile as she turned to walk away.

"I'd never forget my greatest blessing," Hannah said, lifting
her eyes to Luke. "Shall we ride for home?"

Grandfather the Sun was fading from bright gold to soft
orange as Luke and Hannah rode their horses past Bolivar's
square on the way out of town. Luke was certain he'd never felt
as full and happy in his life as he did at this moment.

There were many victories in the life of a bold young
warrior, and Luke's experience was no exception—the times
he had counted coup on his enemies, the raiders he had slain in

battle, the honor his clan had bestowed on him for his bravery.

Luke could count other, perhaps smaller victories, too—the day he had won an award at the mission school for having read the Bible through from front to back in Latin. The evening when Father Schoenmakers had told Luke he was the brightest hope for the future of the Osage—brighter even than Not-Afraid-of-Longhairs, whom Luke had always admired. The morning Luke had climbed to the top of a cliff and first laid a hand on the soft ball of feathers that would become his hunting partner and friend, Gthe-don the prairie falcon.

Mingled with these moments of triumph and pride were the ephemeral memories of happy hours—gathering lotus roots with his mother, sitting around the fire as his grandfather told stories of the Little People, playing the moccasin game with his friends, stalking a deer through a glade.

But none of those could half equal the feeling that swelled his heart as he slipped his arm around the slender waist of his fire-haired woman. Hannah. His mate. His wife.

He dipped his nose into the fragrant strands of hair that had escaped her bun to lie in soft curls against her neck. She smelled of soap and sunshine and fresh, clean air. He could hardly wait to lift her down from the horse and press her body tightly against his.

During the morning, he had pondered the incident with the Butterfield investigator. Every time he conjured the man's smirk, he felt murderous. But when images of Hannah began to encroach, Luke found himself wondering at the value of revenge. Could he give up his quest to find his enemy? Could they prevent the Ethan who had drawn them together from tearing them apart?

All afternoon, Luke's thoughts had been consumed with Hannah. He could almost see her firm breasts as they peeked out of the pool of water where he had bathed with her the night before. He could almost taste the sweetness of her skin and feel the small, ripe cherries of her nipples as they rolled against his tongue.

While holding the survey chain for Mr. Cunnyngham, he had suddenly pictured Hannah lying naked on the buffalo robe. Instantly he had hardened with desire at the image of her pale thighs spread open to him. A shout from the surveyor had brought him back to attention.

"I thought of you all day, Luke," Hannah said, breaking into his thoughts with her silky voice. "Miss Martha kept having to draw my eyes back to my tasks."

Luke smiled at the reflection of his own powerful feelings. "I could hardly wait to hold you again, Hannah. In my mind you were with me every minute."

"Were you out in the woods long?"

"All day. The crew left right after I arrived. When I told Tom I'd just gotten married . . ." Remembering something suddenly, he reined the horse. "I didn't have the chance to ask for your mail."

"You can bring it to me tomorrow if there's anything."

"I promised to check for you today, Hannah," he said. "I will never break a promise to you."

He slid from behind her and dropped to his feet. Seated on the horse's back, Hannah watched him walk into the large building where the postal clerk kept an office. Curls of anticipation slid into her stomach as she observed Luke's straight, broad shoulders, narrow waist, and long legs. Would he want her tonight? Would he stroke his fingers across her bosom and wet her skin with his kisses?

Oh, she didn't know how she would survive the duties of gathering kindling, building a fire, cooking, and serving dinner. All she could think about was the moment when she would drift into Luke's arms and feel the swell of his hunger for her. The thought of that firm pressure against her pelvis brought rivulets of heat sliding down to the tips of her breasts. Her heart began to thud against her ribs. If he didn't come out of the courthouse soon, she didn't know what she would do. She needed his touch so badly!

Perhaps, when they were safely out of town and on the trail, he would slide his hands over her breasts and strum her nipples. As they rode along, he might toy with her until that delicate ache began to throb in her back and that sweet melting warmth seeped between her thighs.

"Hannah!"

She lifted her head, her eyes drowsy with imagined passion. Luke took the steps two at time. In one hand he waved a pair of letters. "Mail!" he called. "From the Confederate office. There's something from your mother, too."

Thoughts of lovemaking scattered as Hannah watched Luke return to her. He thrust the letters into her hands. "Maybe they've found your brother." He swung up behind her onto the horse and tucked her against him.

With trembling fingers, Hannah tore open the letter from the military office. Scanning it quickly, she felt her mouth go as dry as a sun-bleached bone.

" 'To: Hannah Brownlow,' " she read. " 'From: The Army of the Confederate States of America, abolished. Records indicate that in June, 1862, an Ethan Brownlow from Forsyth, Missouri, volunteered for service in the cavalry division of the army of the CSA. Records show that Brownlow served under the command of General Jo Shelby. He saw action at the battle of Newtonia, Missouri, in July, 1862, and again in Newtonia in October, 1862. Brownlow served under General Shelby during the attack on Tipton, Missouri, in October, 1863. Brownlow also served under General Shelby's command during General Sterling Price's invasion of Missouri, August through November, 1864. Records indicate that Brownlow was last seen alive but wounded on the battlefield at Mine Creek, Missouri, in October, 1864.' "

"Wounded?" Luke peered over her shoulder.

"It doesn't say how badly." Worried, Hannah finished reading the letter. " 'The Army of the CSA holds no further records of Ethan Brownlow.' "

"That's all?" Luke asked. "Did they abandon a wounded man on the battlefield?"

"I suppose the Confederates were in retreat from the Federals. But to leave my brother all alone . . ."

"Do you believe these are your brother's records, Hannah?"

"I don't know what to think. A Confederate? It hardly seems possible. Ethan was brought up just as I was, a strict supporter of the Union. But here in Missouri . . . perhaps something happened to change his heart."

"Friends, maybe? Sometimes a man will join his companions, even if he's not certain they do the right thing."

"Oh, Luke, I have to find my brother. But this letter says he was wounded last October, almost ten months ago. Anything could have befallen him. Do you think he would have returned to Forsyth, where he enlisted? Can we go there? Tomorrow?"

Luke turned over the situation. It was time to tell Hannah about Ethan Brown. Forsyth was a dangerous place. It lay in Taney County, deep in the Ozark Mountains. The White River ran beside the town, which Luke knew had been a strategic Union outpost during the war. Hundreds of women, children, and refugees had thronged the soldiers' quarters begging for bread crusts, clothing, and shelter. The town's gristmill had been razed and its three-story courthouse burnt to the ground.

Taney County was well known as a center of bushwhacker activities. The last place a renegade Indian with a white, Federalist wife needed to set foot was Forsyth, Missouri.

"The town is dangerous, Hannah," he said gently. "Why don't you write a letter?"

"To whom?"

"The sheriff, the clerk." Luke let out a breath. "I don't know. Let's go home, Hannah. I need to talk to you there."

As the horse started down the street again, Hannah tucked the report from the Confederate Army down into the bodice of her dress. Then she broke the seal on her mother's letter. Riding through the forest, she read in silence.

Dearest Hannah,

How we all love and miss you! Your sweet face lingers in our thoughts as each bright morn we remember the joys with which you gladdened our lives. Darling Hannah, we entrust your welfare to God Almighty, yet the poignant absence of your laughter lingering in the parlor as we gather around the hearth has filled each of us with a deep, abiding sorrow. In the cool of the evenings, I find myself often drawn to tears at the haunting ache of my losses.

I think of dear, good, loving Ethan. What has become of the boy who lifted our hearts with his cheery presence? Can it be that I will never again see the one whose presence most clearly evokes my late adored husband?

With such anguish that I fear my heart may burst, I remember the blessings your beloved father bestowed upon my life. Tears of mourning fall to my bosom as I recall his blessed face. How dearly your father loved you, darling Hannah! You cannot plumb the depths of his devotion to you and your sisters. Had it not been for a call to the grand and glorious service of the Union, your noble father would be with us still. Could I but see his form emerging from the shadows of the long walk behind our house, how great would be my happiness and ecstasy!

Were your father still the champion of our home, then you, my precious eldest daughter, would never have been compelled to embark on the daring search for your brother who is now our only hope. Hannah, my darling girl, how do you fare in the wilderness of our frontier? I covet each letter I have received from your hand, and yet I live in dread of the day I may learn that some ill has befallen you.

Hannah, oh gentle daughter, never be swayed by the call of the world. Remain true always to your devoted mother and sisters. Keep yourself from all evil. Remain pure, unstained, holy. Be a light in the darkness of a world filled with heathens and savages. Most of all, my star, my pride, my joy—come home to me!

Gentle Sophie has taken employ as an instructor of singing and dance for young ladies. Without her pittance, I fear we should starve. Pearl, the dear child, has been courted most wholeheartedly by a fine young soldier. How we lift our prayers toward heaven that she may be joined to him in marriage so that he will provide her with home and sustenance! Brigitte, our quiet one, takes mending from the ladies along our street. If only you could see her laboring by night over the tiniest of stitches! And young Elizabeth, who longs to aid us in our delicate straits, bakes bread and cakes to sell. Yet, I haven't the heart to sell them when so many in this world are more needy than we. Thus, I have been compelled to send every loaf and every torte to the Soldier's Aid Society of Boston for distribution.

Most treasured Hannah, I implore you to find your brother and return to me with the greatest of haste! Let your waking days and sleeping nights be consumed with nothing but your search for your departed brother.

Return, oh my child, that my days may be long upon the land which the Lord my God has given me!

With warmth and love forever, your mother,
Lydia Brownlow

Hannah let out a shuddering breath.

"What's the matter?" Luke drew away from her and tried to look at her face. "Is something wrong in Boston?"

"My mother needs me desperately. Two of my sisters have taken employment to help the family fend off starvation."

"Starvation?" Luke's heart began to thud. He knew all too well the impact hunger could have. More than forty years earlier, his tribe had set out on their winter buffalo hunt when they were attacked by Cherokee. Although the Osage warriors defeated the That-Thing-On-Its-Head People, many of the Little People were killed, including twenty-nine women and children whose bodies the Cherokee had thrown to their hogs to be devoured. The winter hunt had been ruined, and the Little People faced starvation.

Without their primary food of buffalo meat, they were compelled to hunt for skunks and opossums to feed their children. They ate cattail roots, acorns, and lotus roots. The wild grapes had all been eaten by birds, so they hurried to gather hackberries, pecans, black walnuts, red haws, persimmons, and wild rose fruits. On this meager nourishment, the Little People had barely survived the winter of 1821–22, and Luke had heard many grim stories of what hunger had meant for his tribe.

"Has your mother laid in stores for the coming winter?" he asked Hannah.

She shook her head. "We don't store food as you do, Luke. Not in such great quantities anyway. Almost everything we eat is purchased daily at the market or weekly at a mercantile. But without money, my mother can buy nothing."

"Then we'll send her fifty cents of every dollar I earn."

Hannah's eyes misted at such a generous offer from a man who didn't even know her family. But she realized that what he earned would never be enough to allow five women to maintain a comfortable Boston lifestyle.

"Luke, without your money," she reminded him, "you won't be able to buy a wagon or any of the other supplies you need to ensure that *you* will survive the coming winter."

He considered this thought, but he couldn't rationalize the rightness of providing for his own survival when others for whom he felt responsible went hungry. "Will your sisters' employment bring in enough money for the family?"

"Sophie teaches music and dance. Brigitte is taking in mending. Genteel labors, to be sure, but certainly not lucrative. My mother is too proud to allow her daughters to labor at anything common or coarse. She won't even allow Elizabeth to sell the breads and cakes she's been baking."

Luke pondered this news. It didn't surprise him that Mrs. Brownlow was a proud and noble woman. Hannah must have learned confidence in herself from her own mother. Esteem for oneself and dignity were virtues to be admired in a woman. But to lead a family toward starvation by insisting on outward decorum? No, Luke couldn't understand how anyone could do that.

An Osage mother would not endanger the health of her children for any reason. And an Osage man would never allow his mother-in-law and his wife's sisters to starve to death. He would do all in his power to help them.

"I'll ask Tom to lend me enough money to send five train tickets to Boston," he told Hannah. "Your mother and sisters will come to Missouri and live with us in our lodge. I'll hunt deer with my rifle, and rabbits and quail with Gthe-don. Together you and I can harvest enough wild foods to fill all our storage parfleches. With the turnips we grow and the meat we smoke, we'll be able to feed everyone in your family, Hannah."

"Oh, Luke . . ." Turning, she slipped her arms around his chest and pressed her cheek on his shoulder. Deeply moved by the innate goodness of this man, she was also dismayed at realities he would never fully fathom. "Luke, you don't understand," she said softly. "My mother would never come to Missouri. She's . . . she's like I was in the beginning. The wilderness would frighten and appall her. She would despise the forests, the insects, the feral creatures, the sodden skies. Missouri would seem backward to her. Uncivilized. And, Luke, she would think of you as—"

"As a savage."

Hannah fell silent. That was exactly what Lydia Brownlow would think of him. She would be mortified to learn that not only had her eldest daughter entered into an arranged marriage with such a man, but she had actually been intimate with him.

The pages of her mother's letter rustled in Hannah's hand. *Oh, gentle daughter,* Mrs. Brownlow had written, *never be swayed by the call of the world. Remain true always to your devoted mother and sisters. Keep yourself from all evil. Remain pure, unstained, holy. Be a light in the darkness of a world filled with heathens and savages. Most of all, my star, my pride, my joy—come home to me!*

The words played tag around and around inside Hannah's mind as she contemplated the consequences of her actions. She had done exactly the opposite of her mother's instruction. For the burning touch of an intriguing stranger, she had betrayed her family. For a night of passion, she had abandoned her own purity.

Yet Hannah couldn't bring herself to repent anything she had done. She had wanted to love Luke Maples. She still did.

"My mother lives in a world where everything is either black or white," she explained. "For her, there is no gray. No compromise. She sees things as she has been taught to see them. Her scruples are unchangeable. In many ways, this is good. It has seen her through difficult times, through death and loss and indigence. But it also means she cannot open her heart to people she doesn't understand. Luke, it would take a miracle to alter my mother's perception of you."

The image of this unbending white mother-in-law disturbed Luke. No matter how strongly he cared for Hannah—and he cared enough to want to grow old with her—he would never be accepted by her family. Such a thought was almost beyond his grasp.

"To an Osage," he said, "family is everything. We hold our parents in the highest esteem. No Osage child would ever go against his parents' wishes. To venture out away from the tribal village is almost inconceivable. The only reason I felt comfortable with the idea of coming here to Missouri is that I spent so many years at Father Schoenmakers's Osage Mission School, and I learned to exist alone. But, Hannah—you're telling me your mother will never accept me, and that you went against her instructions when you married me."

"Our marriage was to be only a short-term arrangement," she reminded him. "We agreed that I would never even have to mention the marriage to anyone in my family. But now—"

"Now I have touched your soul . . . and you have touched mine."

She smiled and stroked her hand up his thigh. "Yes," she whispered, "but it was wrong for me to marry you, Luke. I was desperate, and your solution seemed so practical. It may have been a greater mistake to give myself to you as I did last night."

"No, Hannah," he said, gathering her closer. "I can't make myself believe what we did was wrong. Do you?"

"No," she admitted.

"But I won't allow your widowed mother and her daughters to starve to death. That would be dishonorable."

"There's only one solution, as there has always been only one. We have to find my brother. We must go to Forsyth."

Luke clenched his jaw as he struggled to force out the truth. If he told Hannah about Ethan Brown and the man proved to be her brother, she would go back to Boston. Luke had no doubt of it. But would she return to him in Missouri? No, Brown's hatred of the Osage would seal off that option. Hannah would never fly in the face of her own family. Luke couldn't allow himself even to wish for such a thing. She would go away with her brother, and once in Boston she would be seduced into her former life of comfort and luxury. Luke would lose her forever.

He guided the horse onto the trail that led from the road to their lodge. Whether Ethan Brown was Hannah's brother or not, Luke couldn't allow her to step into the path of peril.

"You should know," he told her, "that Forsyth is a dangerous town. Bushwhackers make their hideouts in caves near the White River. After they strike a farmhouse or a traveler, they rush back to their lairs. If Missouri authorities come sniffing them out, they ride across the state line—south to Arkansas or west to Kansas."

"Kansas? Did you see bushwhackers on your reservation?"

Thankful for the shift in topic, Luke lapsed into memory. "In the years before your war over the *Nika-sabe*, we witnessed the struggle between the Heavy Eyebrows for control over the land. Before Kansas became a state, the territory was known as Bloody Kansas because of the battles between those who wanted it to be a slave state and those who wanted it free. Those Heavy Eyebrows raiders . . . they . . ." Unable to continue, he fell silent.

"What, Luke?"

Summoning up words to express the bitterness in his heart, Luke gritted his jaw. "The Heavy Eyebrows man who murdered my father . . . perhaps he was a bushwhacker. Hannah, I must tell you about something that—"

"Why would bushwhackers do such a thing?" she cut in. "What did the Osage people have to do with the trouble over slavery?"

"Nothing, but there were Heavy Eyebrows men who tried to persuade us to take sides. John Mathews, who owned two trading posts on the reservation, persuaded the chief of the Big Hills people and the chief of the Buffalo-Face clan to favor pro-slavery partisans. The priest, Father Schoenmakers, whom we called Black Robe, led others among us to side with the abolitionists."

"And you think some Missouri bushwhackers may have attacked your village because you opposed slavery?"

"It's possible. The raid on our village happened a few years before the Heavy Eyebrows war. When my father was murdered, I was still a boy. I didn't have the skills of a warrior trained to defend or attack. My mother forced me to hide during the raid, so I only saw part of it . . . the worst part."

He gazed at the trail, so lost in memory that he saw nothing of the wildflowers and leafy brush that touched the horse's legs in passing. "I'm not sure whether the man who killed my father was a bushwhacker or not," he said finally. "The men all wore hoods. All I know is they hated my people. In the end, that's all that counts."

Hannah studied the first stars glittering against a misty purple sky. As her eyes focused, she realized that the mist was an illusion. "Luke!" she gasped, digging her fingers into his arm. "Look—the sky!"

His head snapped up. As he centered his attention on the treetops, he saw that a drifting gray haze hung above the crest of the hill. The evening breeze carried a faint, acrid pall. Luke's heart slammed into his throat.

"Smoke," he whispered, the word no louder than a breath.

"Luke, it's above the clearing where our lodge is."

"Gthe-don!" Luke shouted suddenly, goading the horse into a gallop. As the animal thundered to the top of the hill, Hannah heard her pulse echo every hoofbeat. The lodge . . . someone had burned it! Luke's falcon had been tethered inside. Everything destroyed . . . their storage parfleches . . . the buffalo robes that would see them through the winter . . . their beds . . .

"Oh, no!" She stared in horror as the horse broke into the clearing. Smoldering ashes formed an oval of charred earth. There was nothing else. The lodge was gone.

Burned to the ground.

Luke leapt from the horse and tore across the grass to the smoky remnant of his home. At first he said nothing. Then he lifted his head and emitted a heart-shattering wail. "Gthe-don!" he cried.

Hannah's spine crawled at the animal intensity in his wail of mourning. As she slid to the ground, she saw Luke raise his clenched fists skyward and throw back his head. Again the cry of desperation was wrenched from his throat. Gthe-don had been more than Luke's hunting partner. The falcon had been his companion in the long silences, his provider in desperate times, his only living link to his distant tribe and the prairies of Kansas.

Hugging her manuscript to her breast, Hannah stood in silence as the agony poured out of Luke's heart. His falcon had perished. His embroidered shirts had been burned to ashes. The trunks that had held her own clothing . . . gone. The carefully dried potatoes, mushrooms, lotus roots . . . gone. The sack of columbine seeds . . . gone. The hickory framework, the buffalo robes, the pots, pans, gourds . . . gone.

How had it happened? They packed their fireplace with dirt every morning to snuff any live coals. There had been no violent rainstorm. No lightning. How?

Luke's shoulders slumped as he stared at the desolation. But when he lifted his head again, he immediately strode toward a nearby oak tree. Hannah peered through the evening gloom to spot the hatchet that had been buried in the tree's trunk.

Lifting her skirts, she dashed across the clearing to Luke's side. He jerked the hatchet from the wood and took down the attached scrap of paper.

"A note!" she said. "Someone's been here. A human did this!"

Luke scanned the message, then thrust it into Hannah's hands. "Billings," he said.

She stared down at the paper. *Injun go hom,* it read. *Capt. J. Billings CSA.*

"Joshua Billings . . . the bushwhacker! The man who attacked us on the road to Springfield. Oh, Luke, he did this to us!"

"Travis, too, I'm sure. And others. This was not the work of one man."

"They burned everything."

"They stole everything," he corrected. "They burned the lodge."

"How can you be sure?"

"There would be more here—some trace of your trunk, the iron skillet and kettle. But there's nothing."

"Only ashes."

For a moment, neither spoke. Then Hannah turned to Luke and slipped her arms around his waist. His hands came around her shoulders as he drew her against him. Holding, touching, they clung together as though their embrace might barricade them against destruction.

"Gthe-don is dead," Luke muttered.

"I'm so sorry."

He stroked his hands through Hannah's hair, seeking comfort in the warm silk. Hatred swirled around him like flames— first Ethan Brown's, then the bushwhackers'. His urge to retaliate, to kill in revenge, was dampened only by his sorrow at his falcon's death.

What could one man do against such turmoil? How could a single person overcome hatred and prejudice? Should he tell Hannah everything he knew and then give her up, or should he keep secrets and learn to live with guilt? Should he strike back at his enemies or should he slink away from Missouri with his tail between his legs?

As Luke held Hannah close, her body worked an unexpected magic in his heart. Fingers of peace filtered into his chest. A relaxing balm curled through his stomach, easing the knots of pain. A misty solace drifted into his throat and dissolved the gritty lump of sorrow.

"You are like a cup of sage tea," he said in a low voice.

The first hint of a smile lifted one corner of Hannah's mouth. "Sage tea?"

"You lift my sadness, Hannah. You soothe away my gloom."

"But I feel so helpless. I can't do anything to bring back Gthe-don. I can't rebuild our lodge. I can't undo the hatred that made those men steal and burn."

"You are Gthe-non'-zhin. That's enough for me."

"Returns-and-Stands?"

"You've come back to our home, Hannah. Will you stand with me now against this trouble?"

Chapter
Seventeen

❧

"Of course I'll stand by your side," Hannah answered *without* hesitation.

Luke took her hand and squeezed it hard. "All right, I'll get the rifle from the saddle scabbard for our protection. We'll use the bushwhackers' hatchet to cut limbs and build a lean-to to sleep in tonight. Tomorrow evening, after we return from Bolivar, we'll start a new home. Maybe we'll begin our log cabin."

"Luke, I want to stay here tomorrow to work on our land. I'm longing to put into practice what I learned from Ruth and Martha. While you're away, I can gather more wild potatoes and lotus fruits. I'll chop kindling and—"

"No, Hannah. I can't leave you out here alone. If Billings and his men return and find you, who knows what they would do? You're not only a Federal, you're married to an Indian. We'll have to tell the *Nika-sabe* women about this, too. It's probably not safe for them to spend time with you any longer.

The bushwhackers could attack their home, and I couldn't guarantee anyone in town would help defend them.''

Hannah reflected on the strong, kind faces of her friends. How could she bear never seeing Martha and Ruth again, never sharing the pleasant moments she had come to relish, never having the opportunity to learn more from them? But she would not endanger the women or their children. They had suffered so much already.

"All right, I'll go to Bolivar with you, Luke," she said. "I want to tell the sheriff about this incident anyway. He can round up Joshua Billings and his despicable cohorts and bring them to justice. The signed note they left ought to seal their fates.''

Luke reflected on the scene Hannah might cause were she to storm into Bolivar demanding retaliation. And at the courthouse she would stand a good chance of running into Ethan Brown. "I ask you again to leave the authorities out of this," he told her. "Around here you can't be sure who's a bushwhacker sympathizer and who isn't. For all we know, the sheriff himself may be one of the men who torched our lodge." He stroked his fingertips down her cheek. "Come on, let's see what we can find to eat in the forest and then settle down for the night. We have a hard day ahead of us tomorrow.''

While Luke lopped off long hickory branches and wove them into a wall to construct a sheltering lean-to, Hannah dug wild potatoes from a patch near the clearing. Using her skirt as an apron, she gathered up the potatoes and added some blazing star roots. She found a few wild grapes, which weren't very sweet but would add variety to the meal.

When she returned to the glade where the lodge had stood, she saw Luke bending over the rounded stones that had been the inside fireplace. Sparks brightened the encroaching darkness, and in spite of the emptiness in her heart, Hannah found herself anticipating the comfortable, homey taste of baked potatoes.

They ate in virtual silence. Luke kept the rifle propped against his knees. Hannah's spine prickled at the slightest sound. He had spread a layer of soft moss on the grass beneath the slanted shelter of branches near the fire. Over the bedding, he laid his shirt. Hannah took off her petticoat to form another layer, and they lay down for the night.

Luke gathered Hannah in his arms, holding her so close she could feel his heartbeat against her ear. He didn't sleep. Though her own eyes slipped shut, she knew he was awake, staring up at the woven limbs, seeing beyond them to the scattered stars.

"The truth is . . . I have nothing to offer you, Hannah," he murmured just as she had begun to drift into sleep. "I have no wealth. Even this land is yours by right. The meager things I owned—pots and pans, a few clothes—all are gone now. I can't even promise you safety and peace for the future."

When she said nothing, he began to stroke her hair, running his fingers through the loose strands again and again. She nestled her cheek against his bare skin, welcoming the scent of his flesh and the firm tone of his muscled chest. Wanting to tell him that nothing mattered but this moment—his arms holding her and his presence surrounding her—she found that she was too tired even to speak.

The blisters on her hands stung where they had gripped the handle of the churn. Her arms ached from the repeated up-and-down motion of transforming cream into butter. But she knew she would do it again—and gladly—if it were her own butter she was churning. Butter for Luke, butter for their pantry, butter for their children . . .

"There's nothing for you here," he was murmuring, "and everything for you in Boston. A strong home, security, family. Nothing here but violence, thievery, poverty—"

His hands stiffened suddenly. He lifted his head, listening . . . alert. Gripping her arm so tightly she gasped, he reached for his rifle.

"Hannah!"

Instantly awake, she struggled to her elbows. "Luke?"

"Can you hear that? Someone's coming up the trail. Men— and horses, too."

"Bushwhackers, Luke! They've come back for us." Memories of Joshua Billings's first attack flooding through her, Hannah gathered the fabric of her skirt close around her legs as she fumbled in the darkness for her manuscript. She couldn't find it! She would have to leave it behind. "Let's go, Luke! We can hide near the stream in that cave—"

"Wait." He held up a silencing hand. "Women's voices."

"Women?" Hannah strained to hear. "What can they want? They've stolen everything. Luke, they must mean to kill us. Please, let's—"

The blast of a shotgun cut off her words. It was followed by another blast, and then a third. Beneath the roar of the guns sounded the trumpet of a fox horn. And then the loudest banging, ringing, and gonging Hannah had ever heard shattered what was left of the night. Cow bells, dinner bells, horns, washtubs—anything that would make a sound filled the air with a cacophony of noise.

"It's them!" she cried. "Bushwhackers!"

"Come, Hannah!" Luke grabbed her arm with one hand and clutched his rifle with the other. Hand in hand they dashed from the lean-to and started toward the shelter of forest. Running on the rough ground in her bare feet, Hannah winced in pain. It was so dark she could barely see Luke's form just ahead of her.

"There they be!" someone hollered. A swarm bearing torches, shotguns, washtubs, and bells burst into the clearing. Laughing, whooping, shouting, they headed straight toward Luke and Hannah.

"Run!" Luke called. "Hannah, stay with me!"

"Got any treats for us?" a man shouted.

"No, they don't got treats!"

"Get 'em then! Get 'em!"

Hauling Hannah behind him, Luke broke headfirst into the forest. He knew his single rifle and few bullets would never protect them against the bushwhackers. Their only hope was to cross the stream, climb the bluff, and find the old cave.

"After 'em, boys!" The sound of breaking brush followed them into the woods. "Cut 'em off. They's headin' for the crick!"

"Run, Hannah!" Luke whispered through clenched teeth. "Run, run, Gthe-non'-zhin!"

"Oh, God, dear God, help us!" Scrambling blindly through the forest, she struggled to breathe as her feet flew over sharp stones, brambles, and vines. The sound of the bells and gongs and shotguns only grew louder as the trees closed in around her. She could see nothing, smell nothing, feel nothing but the wrenching grip of Luke's hand on her wrist.

"Now!" he said as they burst out of the forest onto the stream bank.

Hannah turned in the direction of the bluff just as her feet went out from under her. Crushed beneath the weight of a massive man, she heard her breath explode from her lungs. A huge hand knocked her head to the ground, smashing her cheek against a round river stone.

"Got her!" her captor shouted. A moment later she heard someone else call, "We got him, too! Ride him on the rail, fellers!"

Gasping, Hannah was hauled to her feet and propped against the trunk of a dogwood tree. Two men whose features she couldn't distinguish pinned her arms to her sides while the other attackers swarmed around Luke. In moments they had felled a sapling and stripped it of branches. Hannah watched through tears of horror as they forced Luke to straddle the pole. While a group of men lifted the front and back ends of the rail, others steadied their swaying cargo.

"Luke!" Hannah cried.

He said nothing as the men hoisted him onto their shoulders and began to trot along the stream bank. Laughing, swigging long drafts from jugs of whiskey, banging a gong made from a circular wood-cutting saw, the bushwhackers carried Luke into the forest back toward the charred clearing.

Hannah searched the darkness in vain for his rifle, knowing even as she did that it must be in the hands of the mob. She had bitten the inside of her cheek, and the taste of blood mingled with her salty tears. Every time she struggled to free her wrists, the two men holding her clamped down harder.

"What's the matter?" one of them asked as she tried to wrestle out of his stranglehold. "What's troublin' you, woman?"

"I don't want you to kill Luke! He's a good man. He isn't hurting any of you."

"But he ain't got no treats for us," one of the men responded with a cackle. "Got to ride him on the rail."

"Leave her be now, boys," a woman said in the darkness.

Hannah swung toward the sound of the voice, hoping for sympathy. "Please! You're a woman—you know what it means to love someone. Surely there's a measure of tenderness in your heart. Don't let them hurt my husband! Please, I beg you, stop them!"

But even as she spoke, the men were tramping back onto the stream bank. Luke sat balanced high on the pole, barely keeping his grip. The deafening beat of horns and washtubs almost masked his voice as he called to her.

"Hannah!"

"I'm here!" she shouted. "I love you, Luke!"

Raucous laughter and rowdy comments followed her cry, but her ears went deaf as she watched the men begin to swing the rail back and forth over the pool where she and Luke had bathed.

"Into the water with him?" someone asked.

"You're the boss!"

"Dunk him!"

The men let go of the rail, and Luke flipped head over heels into the water. The splash showered everyone with droplets, which only seemed to add to the merriment.

"Break out the whiskey, boys!" someone called. "Gotta warm up the bridegroom."

"Jim already uncorked the jug."

"Well, pass it over here."

The man who seemed to be the ringleader stood at the edge of the pool and watched Luke bob to the surface. In silhouette, the assailant looked nothing like the bushwhacker Hannah remembered. Joshua Billings's stocky build, grease-matted beard, and filthy hat were a sight she would never forget. Tall and thin, the man thumped his suspenders against his chest as he studied his victim.

"Hey, Luke!" he said, cradling his shotgun. "Luke, old boy! How's the water? A little cold for ya?"

Hannah clenched her eyes shut, waiting for the blast of the shotgun. When nothing happened, she peered through slitted lids. Instead of making for the opposite bank, Luke was treading water in the pool. Then, to her horror, he began swimming toward his attacker.

"Say, you doin' all right, Luke?" the man on shore asked.

"Tom? Tom Cunnyngham?"

"Why, who'd you think it was? Ain't nobody but me and the crew knows where you live."

"I'll be damned, Tom." Luke waded out of the pool and raked a hand through his wet hair. "You scared the hell out of me, you old buzzard. Where's my wife?"

"Zeke's got her. What're you so riled up for? Ain't you never heard of a shivaree, boy?"

"Reckon not, him being an Indian," one of the men commented. The onlookers groaned and laughed. "Let's pass out the food and drink. Tom, you tell Luke what this is all about."

Zeke released Hannah as Luke crossed to her. Though he was dripping, he clasped the trembling woman tightly in his arms and held her close. Together they watched in bewilderment as the men and women in the group began uncovering wicker baskets. Where had the baskets come from? Hannah wondered. She hadn't noticed them before. Why had Zeke let her go? Who was Tom Cunnyngham, and why was Luke acting so friendly toward him?

Out of the baskets drifted the aroma of fried chicken, buttered corn on the cob, baked beans, and pies of every kind. Jugs of liquor traveled from hand to hand. The banging and clattering subsided to soft chatter and laughter as women spread tablecloths near the stream and began to set out food.

"A shivaree is what we do for folk out here in the Ozarks right after they's married," Tom Cunnyngham explained. "Sometimes the shivaree happens the night of the wedding, sometimes a few nights later. Everyone from town—all the bride and groom's friends, anyway—comes out to their house just a-whoopin' it up, shootin' off guns, and makin' as much of a ruckus as we can. We ask for a treat of cigars and candy, and if the groom don't pay up, why, we ride him on the rail and then dump him into the nearest mud hole or pond. It's a Missouri tradition."

At the explanation, Hannah's knotted fingers loosened, and her heartbeat began to slow. She realized she had seen the speaker before. Hadn't he been one of the men inside the courthouse her first day in Bolivar? Thomas Cunnyngham . . .

"You're the county surveyor!" she said suddenly.

"Sure," Tom acknowledged. "Luke works on my crew. When he showed up late for work and told us all he'd up and got married, why, there was nothing to do but put on a big shivaree to get you two started off the right way. Come here, Luke, and fill your plate. No one will start till you do."

Luke reluctantly moved away from Hannah. She let out a shaky breath, and a woman standing beside her smiled. "You ain't from around here?"

Hannah shook her head. "Boston."

"I'm Tom's wife, Lavinia Cunnyngham. I remember when they shivareed me and Tom, I cried the whole time—just sure they was gonna kill him or shoot our cabin full of holes. And I'd grown up with shivarees my whole life."

"I've never heard of such a . . . such a strange custom." Hannah barely held her tongue. She had a good mind to tell these people how barbaric their behavior looked in the eyes of a well-bred woman.

"Folk mean well at a shivaree. It's to welcome the bride and groom to married life and show 'em a little fun." The woman, hardly older than Hannah, peered at her in the moonlight. "Lord-a-mercy, you're white as a ghost, girl. You all right?"

"I can't seem to stop shaking. I was so sure Luke would die. I thought you were . . . someone else."

"Now, who else would we be?"

"Bushwhackers," Hannah said. "They burned down our house today and left a note warning Luke to leave Missouri."

Lavinia stared. "Bushwhackers burned down your house today," she repeated. "And you thought we was them come back to kill you? Good Lord."

"We saw the smoke as we rode up the hill after we'd been in Bolivar working all day. The bushwhackers stole everything we had and burned the rest. There's nothing left of our home but ashes."

Shaking her head, Lavinia laid a hand on Hannah's arm. "I'll be dadburned. Come here, now." She drew Hannah against her side to give her a warm hug. Then she lifted her fingers to her mouth and blew an ear-shattering whistle.

When the crowd fell silent, she held up a hand. "We got more on our hands than a shivaree tonight, folks," she said. "We got trouble."

"What's the matter, Lavinia?" Tom asked.

"Bushwhackers burned down Luke and Hannah's house today. Stole everything they owned."

"Damn!" Tom glanced at Luke.

"They left a note warning me to leave," he confirmed. "I've had trouble with them before. But I'm not leaving my land."

"That's for damn sure, you ain't. I never seen anybody work as hard as you to get what he was after." Tom looked over the group gathered around the spread tablecloths. "What do you say to a weekend house raisin', men? And ladies, how about a quiltin' bee?"

"I've already got two quilts put back for just such an emergency as this," Lavinia said. "I'll donate both of them and five jars of my blackberry jam, too."

"I've already pieced a wedding-ring quilt top," another woman added. "I'll bring the backing and batt, and we can quilt it while the men work. That'll give Luke and Hannah lots of bedding come winter."

"We have an extra kettle that come from my folks' place after they went north during the fightin'," someone said.

Before Hannah could respond, the crowd gathered closely around her. In darkness so deep the contributors were all but anonymous, offers of gifts continued to flow.

"I've got an old sow. She ain't good for breedin' no more, but they could get some bacon and ribs and such off her."

"They can have half my rhubarb crop. I got so much I don't know what to do with it."

"I just built my Lizzie a new kitchen table. We was gonna give the old one to the church, but it's good solid oak, and I reckon Luke and Hannah need it more."

In the cover of night, Luke slipped to his wife's side again and enfolded her in his arms. Neighbors patted them on the back and offered sympathies for their trouble.

"Bushwhackers killed our boy Robert," someone said. "We'll help you out all we can."

"We'll put you up a good strong cabin and a door with a bar."

"I'll bring you by some of my pickles."

"Our dog just had puppies. We'll let you have a pair of 'em.

Make fine watchdogs sure enough. No bushwhackers ever gonna get past our hounds.''

The night changed from a terrifying ordeal to a lighthearted picnic so swiftly that Hannah could hardly adjust. She and Luke were seated together and were fed chicken and beans until they could eat no more. They both turned down the whiskey, but Lavinia had brought a jug of apple cider to cool in the stream.

In the soft light of stars and lanterns, Tom strummed a tune on a dulcimer while another man accompanied with his zither. Everyone sang ballads and hymns that Hannah had never heard—"Nearer My God to Thee," "When I Survey the Wondrous Cross," "Come Christians Join to Sing." There was more laughter and joke-telling than Hannah had ever heard. And the pies were certainly the sweetest, flakiest she could have imagined.

By the time everyone started back to the wagons they had left at the bottom of the hill, Hannah was so sleepy she could hardly lift a hand to wave farewell. Though the terror of the night had faded, she could still clearly recall every moment. Her neighbors had meant well, but she didn't like shivarees. She and Luke walked back to the lean-to and settled in a second time.

"Do you think they really will help us?" she whispered as she ran her palms down his bare chest.

"Tom Cunnyngham is a good person." He paused for a moment before speaking words he never thought he would say about any man. "I trust him."

"In spite of their strange ways, I trust our Missouri neighbors, too. At least those who came tonight." She smiled at the promise of the weeks ahead. "A cabin of our own, quilts and chickens, a table, skillets, even a sow . . ."

Luke fingered a strand of her hair. "Hannah, tonight when you thought they meant to kill me, you said something to me . . . Did you mean those words?"

She shut her eyes and drifted in the pleasure of his touch. "Yes," she whispered finally. "I meant those words."

He drew her against him and kissed her lips. "I love you, too, my wife."

*   *   *

Hannah agreed to postpone her trip to Forsyth for a few days. Their Bolivar neighbors had offered to construct a cabin that weekend, and both knew that if they left on the long journey south, the new home might never be built. Harvest was drawing near, and the men in town would be working day and night in their fields through the rest of summer and into fall.

Believing Hannah's mother and sisters to be near starvation, Luke struggled to make himself tell Hannah about Ethan Brown. At the same time, he convinced himself he could find out all he needed to know about the man before bringing his wife into it.

As a precaution, Hannah accompanied Luke to town every day for the rest of the week. Though she told Martha and Ruth about the bushwhacker attack, they agreed she should continue coming to their home to work at their side. After all, Martha informed her husband when he protested, if Miss Hannah was to survive the coming winter, it was up to her friends to see that she learned how to cook and clean and tend her family.

"Friends," Jim Strickland had snorted. He maintained that he would never understand how a black woman and a white woman could call themselves friends. Such a thing wasn't natural, and no good could ever come of it.

But Martha's growing sense of security in her own independence had opened her heart to Hannah. As they shared laughter and secrets, and as their hands labored together, their friendship was sealed.

The elderly Ruth remained kind and generous, though at times distant, and Hannah knew her aloofness was a result of years of slavery. All the same, as she and the two other women made cheese together, put up wild plum preserves, darned socks, and planted turnips, Hannah often realized how much Ruth had assumed the role of mother to her. The older woman gave advice and support in these first days of marriage, just as Hannah had always expected her own mother would do. Remembering that Ruth's children had been torn from her arms, she knew how deeply blessed she was.

Full and content with each day, Hannah was surprised at the gift of yet another new companion. One morning as she was hurrying into a mercantile, Lavinia Cunnyngham waved to her.

They discussed the night of the shivaree and the bushwhacker attack, and Lavinia invited Hannah to her house for afternoon tea.

Within moments of settling on Lavinia's horsehair settee, Hannah discovered that she and her hostess were almost the same age, each had four sisters, and both liked to read good books. Beside herself with happiness to learn that Hannah was a published writer, Lavinia shyly produced a basketful of her own poems that she kept hidden under her bed.

Hannah found them delightful, and she urged Lavinia to try to place them with a publisher. Soon the two women had agreed to spend their afternoons together. While Lavinia composed poems and prepared to submit them, Hannah labored over her novel.

The story had progressed beyond the Indian massacre, and Hannah felt her portrayal of the scene was adequate. But could she make Elizabeth's plight as a widow realistic? Could she elicit the sympathy her character demanded?

Gentle reader, Hannah penned after much thought, *never assume for one moment that our young Elizabeth would abandon the precious memories of her beloved husband. His tragic death at the hands of angry, marauding Indians was an event that would tear at Elizabeth's heart for the remainder of her life.*

In spite of her pain, however, Elizabeth would not hold back her forgiveness. Both wise and good, she understood that the Indians had struck out in blind revenge for the loss of their tribal lands. Hunting, fishing, and gathering wild foods in the forests had sustained their people for generations. Faced with starvation, they had been led to commit an act more despicable. Though Elizabeth well perceived that her own children might go hungry, she could not refrain from pardoning the Indians for their heinous crime.

But if they believed their murder would send Elizabeth fleeing eastward, they mistook our brave and stalwart heroine. In fact, as you shall see, she grew all the more determined to face the approaching winter and to give her two small and innocent children a life of joy, contentment, and security.

Gathering them about the hearth one evening not many days hence the vile tragedy, she gently explained that their darling father would no longer grace their table at dinnertime, nor would he lift his prayers heavenward on their behalf.

"Lambs," she explained, "your father has no need to pray for us from his earthly domain. He has journeyed to heaven himself in order to better watch over us and to personally lift our needs to God Almighty. We must take great care to make him proud by the actions of our hands and the passions of our hearts."

"Yes, yes, Mama, but look!" cried her young son, who since his father's cruel death was aflutter at the slightest movement. "Who is that man at the gate?"

Before Elizabeth could summon herself to admonish her bright little Johnny for his straying attention, she heard a knock that sent a stab of breathless terror to her heart. Had the Indians returned? Would she again be called upon to face the wicked hand of death, as her little ones huddled around her in vain hope of protection?

"Who knocks?" called she, trepidation casting a tremble to her voice.

"It is only me, Caleb Williams," came the sure response.

"Mama, the farmer who lives over the hill has come to visit us!" shouted Johnny. "Perhaps he has brought Papa with him."

Lest tears brim her eyes again, Elizabeth settled her baby daughter on her hip, took Johnny by the hand, and approached the door. "Mr. Williams, how kind of you to pay us a call," said she, lifting the latch to welcome him. "Do come in."

"Mrs. Heartshorn," responded the gentleman, tipping his hat. "I have come with a wagon of provisions from my larder. My good servants have stored away more food than I can ever hope to consume this winter. Sacks of flour and sugar, strings of onions and garlic, even a slab of bacon and a side of beef await you."

"Shall we have candies, too?" burst out little Johnny in an exclamation of joy.

Before his blushing mother could correct her son, Caleb Williams had produced from the pocket of his frock coat a handful of sugary sweets to delight and amuse both children. While her kind neighbor undertook to settle the youngsters by the fire with their treats, Elizabeth could not restrain her eyes from the form of the tall, black-haired—

"Wait a minute now—I thought Caleb had blond hair," Lavinia commented late on Friday afternoon. "Yes, I'm sure he did in the beginning of the book."

"Blond?" Hannah recollected for a moment. "On the other hand . . . perhaps I did change him, now that I think of it."

"I don't reckon you ought to change the color of a man's hair plumb in the middle of a story, Hannah. What were you thinkin'?"

"Hmm." Tapping her chin, Hannah recalled the moment Caleb Williams had been transformed. How was it possible so much had happened to her since that first night in the Springfield hotel! Bill Hickok had shot his gambling companion dead; she had married Luke Maples on an impulse; she had filed a claim for one hundred sixty acres of Missouri land; and . . . of course . . . she had learned the pleasures of the marriage bed.

"What I was thinking of," she told Lavinia, "was a man whom I had just met—but one who had already touched my heart."

"Luke?"

Hannah smiled. "Do you suppose . . . even then . . . that I knew he would come to mean more to me than anyone? Could I have suspected that I would be willing to leave my family, my friends, the security of my home, to live in this wilderness with him?"

"I don't know," Lavinia said. "But I hope you're plannin' to stay around. All the talk in town is about you and Luke. There were some who weren't sure about you in the beginning—you being friends with the coloreds. There were a good many uncomfortable about Luke—him being an Indian. You were both uncommon—you from the East and him a native. But now most of us hope you can forget that bushwhacker attack and build yourself a fine life right here in Polk County!"

"I believe we shall, Lavinia," Hannah mused. "I am trusting in it."

Dipping her pen in the ink bottle, she leaned over the page and began to shape Caleb Williams into the man of Elizabeth's dreams.

Chapter Eighteen

꧁ꕤ꧂

By Saturday morning, Hannah was certain her heart could hold not a moment more of happiness. As the long, burning days and stifling nights had stretched on, she had grown more and more certain that she desired a permanent future with Luke Maples.

Desire was hardly the right word to describe what she felt for the man who lay beside her in the purple light of early dawn. She thirsted for him. She craved him.

If the hint of his memory crossed her mind during the day, a crackle of lightning shot into the pit of her stomach and made her weak in the knees. If, while weeding in her garden or roasting lotus seeds, she imagined she heard his voice, her whole body tingled with goose bumps. She could hardly wait for him to call for her at the end of the day. And the nights . . . oh, those summer nights!

As she lay drifting in thought beside him, Hannah recalled one scorching afternoon with particular clarity. Martha had treated her to a cup of river-chilled dandelion wine. The taste of the cool liquor against Hannah's lips had trickled through her like thick honey. Within minutes her carefully assembled reason had scattered like seeds blown to the wind. She had felt suddenly hot and wild and languorous—and so ravenous for Luke that she had hardly been able to wait for him to arrive on his horse.

Even now, at the image of his mouth brushing across her nipple, Hannah felt that warm honey begin to throb in the sweet nest where it always pooled these days, waiting to be stroked and caressed. Hours in the sun, aching muscles, blistered fingers—nothing could blot the pervasive, delicious pulse of her damp desire.

How could she have lived so many years in ignorance of the magic that had lain dormant inside her body? Now that her sensuality had come to life beneath Luke's expert hands, she couldn't suppress it—and didn't want to.

"Are you awake, Gthe-non'-zhin?" he murmured against her neck. Stirring sleepily, he ran his palm over her flat belly in gently provocative circles. "I can hear your mind turning with thoughts."

Smiling, she traced a finger down his bronzed back. "Oh? And what am I thinking, my Mystery-hawk?"

"Mmm . . . You're thinking about sinking your teeth into a big slab of fried ham and a couple of fluffy biscuits."

"Wrong."

"You're thinking about quilting with your women friends this morning while we men build the log cabin."

"Wrong."

"You're thinking about our young Elizabeth Heartshorn and her intriguing neighbor."

Hannah laughed. "Wrong again."

"I'm sure I heard you thinking."

With a sly grin she snuggled up against him and slipped his hand between her warm thighs. "I was thinking about you," she whispered, her voice husky with longing.

Luke shut his eyes and gave a groan of ecstatic disbelief. To wake in the morning and find his woman already soft, damp, and eager for his touch went far beyond his greatest imaginings. In the past week, Hannah's passionate loving had severed the bonds with which he had suppressed and restrained his youthful cravings for so many years. He felt like a man set free from prison.

Turning her body to his, he marveled at the magic of the sunlight as it kissed her skin. Like a marble urn, her curved flesh seemed to glow from the inside. He formed his hands around her breasts, memorizing their weight, fullness, silky velvet.

"Luke, sometimes I can't remember my life before you," she whispered, slipping her fingers around him and urging his arousal to its apex. "What gave it meaning?"

Struggling to concentrate on her question, he clenched his jaw. "Hannah," he managed, "before we came together, you had a good life. Better in many ways."

As his thumbs tipped her nipples into aching peaks, she shook her head in denial. It was impossible to imagine that writing books in a garret in Boston had ever held any significant appeal.

"But I didn't know about this," she said with a sigh. "If I was happy before you, it was only because I didn't know what I was missing."

"Come to me, my love." He cupped her hips and settled her against his pelvis. As his fingers dipped into the warmth of her sweet nectar, he stroked delicious circles around and around the focus of her yearning.

"Let me remind you," he said, "of what you didn't know you were missing."

As he played with her, he watched her face drift from bliss to urgency . . . her breasts tighten from gentle, rosy peaks to hard, throbbing buds . . . her hips move from an easy waltz to a pounding drumbeat . . . her hands clutch at his shoulders . . . her mouth burn across his skin . . . her thighs part and push toward him . . .

He taught her, once again, why she desired him. And in the frenzied storm of their dance, he prayed that his love would be strong enough to keep her . . . to hold her near . . . for the rest of their lives.

"Forsyth?" Lavinia Cunnyngham asked as she worked her best quilting needle through eight tiny stitches. "What in heaven's name do you want to go down there for, Hannah? Forsyth's plumb at the back end of nowhere."

Hannah twisted her thimble around and around on the end of her finger. Should she confide in this group of women—young and old—who sat around the quilting frame? Theirs were the faces of Missouri . . . worn with exhaustion, hardened from the trials of survival, weathered by the sun . . . and as beautiful as wildflowers in a field. These were her neighbors— kind, generous, patient. And trustworthy.

"My brother," she related, "may be living in Forsyth. Just before the war erupted, Ethan left Boston to seek his fortune as a merchant in Missouri. Our last letter from him had been posted in the southwestern part of the state. He'd had no luck establishing a mercantile, he wrote, and he was seeking other employment."

"Did he become a soldier boy?" Granny Ledbetter, one of the townspeople, asked.

"Perhaps."

"Then I reckon he'd have been stationed at that Union outpost in Forsyth. I heard tell it was a busy place. Folks just a-comin' and a-goin' like bees in a hive."

Hannah wove her needle through the layers of fabric. "I don't think he was at the outpost, Granny. The Federals had no records of an Ethan Brownlow among their ranks. But the Confederates did."

"Your brother was a Rebel?" Granny adjusted her spectacles and peered at Hannah. "And him a Boston man?"

"It does seem hard to believe. But the only Ethan Brownlow I've been able to find in all these months was enlisted in the Confederate Army. He was wounded during General Price's raid—"

"Oh, that! Now, there's a pretty picture—the glorious Sterling Price as fat as five barrels of lard. They say he rode in his mule-drawn ambulance up the east side of the state and told everyone how he aimed to restore Missouri to its southern roots. Missouri would take its rightful place as one of the Confederate States of America, Price said. He'd bring back slavery, and he'd put Jackson back into the governor's chair in Jefferson City. Ha! How anybody thought a man like Sterling Price was a-goin' to defeat the Federals I'll never know."

"General Price had a respectable reputation as a fightin' man, Granny Ledbetter," Lavinia countered. "His troops called him Old Pap. He was real polished and courtly—a true Southern gentleman. When he was organizing his raid, why, he rounded up nearly twelve thousand troops. I hear tell fellers left their farms and families and came out of the woods to volunteer."

"Bushwhackers," Granny announced with a snort. "Maybe Hannah's brother done the same thing—got caught up in the glory of the speeches. And then, like so many other of them poor young'uns, maybe he got himself wounded. Or killed."

"Anyway," Hannah said quickly, "this Confederate Ethan Brownlow may have gone back to Forsyth after the war. I have no choice but to find out whether or not that man is my brother. So Forsyth is where Luke and I are planning to search for him."

"You better arm yourselves good," Granny warned. "You already seen what them bushwhackers will do to folk they don't like. Burn houses to the ground. Rob everything that ain't nailed down. Kill innocent boys. Lord-a-mercy!"

"On the other hand, they can be plumb civil to women," Lavinia contended. "Downright chivalrous."

Several of the women around the quilt frame nodded. "They know we's unarmed and defenseless," someone said. "I don't think they never harmed a woman."

"Maybe they never took a woman down," Grace Odum said. Then she dropped her voice to a whisper. "But I know of a woman who was threatened and molested by them bushwhackers. After they shot her husband and two boys, they . . . they felt of her person."

"No!" the others gasped.

"Yes, indeed. And they used such shameful language she couldn't repeat it to me."

"I have a friend whose cabin they burned," Pearl Williams said. "First they robbed every scrap of food in the house, then they torched the place. After that they run her teams into the field and robbed all the family's corn and fodder."

Charity Gillespie nodded. "A friend of mine from down south in Taney County told me all her menfolk was shot to death by them bushwhackers. Then they made her play the piano while they danced around the bodies. You know what they done next?"

A chorus of "What?" circled around the quilt.

"They exposed themselves to her."

"Lawsy!" Granny Ledbetter exploded. "That's just what them Confederates would do, ain't it? They got no respect for decent women. None at all."

"Alf Bolin, Bloody Bill Anderson, Charley Quantrill, Ol' Sheppard over Clinton County way, Jim Green—them's all bad men. Meaner'n bitin' boars."

"The Union boys wasn't so wonderful at times neither." Mary Hough jabbed her needle into the air as she spoke. "Ain't you ladies heard of the Sand Creek Massacre last November? What the Federals did to them Indians was plumb terrible."

"What happened?" Hannah asked. Luke had never mentioned a word about a massacre.

"The First Colorado Cavalry slaughtered five hundred Cheyenne Indians—most of 'em women and children. Scalped all of 'em. They even mutilated some."

"No!" the women gasped in unison.

Mary leaned toward the center of the quilt and dropped her voice. "My brother told me the soldiers would cut out a woman's private parts and hang 'em on a stick or stretch 'em across their saddle bows. Some of the men even wore those poor dead women's privates over their hats while they was ridin' in the ranks."

Hannah could hardly breathe. "Union troops did that? And they killed children, too?"

"Colonel Chivington said, 'Nits make lice.' That's why he killed them little ones."

Moved to silence by the story, each woman bent over her section of the quilt. Hannah's fingers trembled as she worked her needle through the soft cotton fabric. Bushwhackers shooting men and boys in cold blood? Union troops slaughtering children and mutilating women?

The rosy glow that had surrounded her that morning in bed with Luke evaporated in a flash. The pleasant chatter, lush forests, and bubbling streams she had come to idealize were replaced by the harsh realities of life in a land where terror might be lurking just over the next hill.

Biting her lower lip, Hannah surveyed the sunlit glade. All morning the men had sung and laughed as they cleared the dense brush and felled more than eighty shortleaf pine trees. The notched logs—each a foot or more in diameter—lay in neat stacks as the men peeled them with drawknives and spuds.

In the distance, Luke was supervising the construction of a stone foundation for the cabin. Though the other men seemed to think a foundation was a waste of time and energy, Luke had told Hannah it would help their house to last a lifetime. With a smile on his face, he whistled and told stories with the rest of the men while they worked. Hannah didn't know when she had ever seen him looking so peaceful—so much like he belonged.

"I don't understand it," she said softly. "Why do decent, hardworking people like all of you go on living in the same place where others commit such depredations?"

Granny Ledbetter paused in the middle of humming a hymn. She pushed her spectacles up on her nose and regarded Hannah solemnly.

"That's the way things is in this world, honey," she said. "There's good folk and there's evil ones. Sometimes the line betwixt them ain't too clear. Good folk will do bad things when they's driven to it. And wicked folk might do good things now and then in spite of themselves."

"But to kill children, mutilate women, murder men and boys . . . it's monstrous."

"I suspect most of them bushwhacker boys was reared in decent families—but troubles drove 'em to the bush. I reckon if you'd get one of 'em alone and set him down for a cup of sassafras tea, why, he'd be just as harmless as a bee in the butter."

Hannah regarded the men working on her cabin. They all looked so amiable, so ordinary. "How can you know whom to trust, Granny?" she asked. "How can you distinguish which person is good and which one is evil?"

"Only time's gonna tell you that. Get to know folk day in and day out. Hard times and easy. Happy times and sad." The elderly woman smoothed her wrinkled hands across the top of the quilt. "Most of us has got a good streak a mile wide. But you can't judge someone just because they go to church or dress fancy or got schoolin'. Can't judge 'em if they bring you pickles or piece you a quilt top. Them outward things don't show what's in a person's heart. Why, you can't even judge a feller by the color of his skin. Look how you up and married that Indian. You must've decided he was a good man."

Hannah nodded. "I do trust Luke."

Mary Hough cleared her throat. "I bet you don't know all the things that husband of yours done before he met you, Hannah. He might have scalped somebody just for lookin' at him wrong."

"Now, Mary!" Granny chided. "What you talkin' like that to a new bride for? Don't you know better than that?"

Hannah lifted her eyes beyond the circle of women to the clearing. Focusing on the man who stood head and shoulders over the others, she pondered the things she had chosen to overlook in Luke since their hasty wedding—his heritage of disdain for the "Heavy Eyebrows" who had stolen his people's home . . . his determination to rebuild his tribe's strength through marriage and land acquisition . . . his status as the Osage warrior Mystery-hawk . . . his scalp-lock leggings . . .

"I'm just tryin' to be helpful, Granny Ledbetter," Mary protested. "How can Hannah be sure that man won't turn on her one of these days? Maybe he'll take a notion and cut off her scalp. He's an Indian, ain't he? Them folk has been our enemies for nigh onto a hundred years. I think it's only fittin' for Hannah's white friends and neighbors to look out for her. If she needs a word of caution now and then, why I'll be the first to give it to her."

"You would," Granny said under her breath.

"I hear tell she's been fraternizin' with Martha Strickland. Martha and Jim been slaves all their life up till now, and I don't know where they got the idea they's good enough to talk friendly with anybody—let alone a fine Boston lady like Hannah."

"They's gettin' plumb uppity if you ask me," Charity put in. "Even that ol' Ruth looked me straight in the eye the other day at the mercantile. Straight in the eye! Said, 'How-do, Miss Charity. Say, what you think of them pickled pig's feet in the barrel over yonder?' as if I wasn't no better than her!"

"What makes you any better than Ruth Jefferson?" Hannah

said softly, turning on Charity. "Granny Ledbetter just now instructed us to look beneath the color of a person's skin in order to judge her true worth and value in this world."

"Can't see nothin' under skin as black as the ace of spades. Next thing you know they'll be thinkin' they can walk right in the front door of the mercantile just like us white folk. They'll be thinkin' they can send their children to our schools. They'll be thinkin' they can worship at our churches."

Hannah's cheeks flamed. "Why shouldn't they worship at our churches?"

"I guess you never heard of the Bolivar slave rebellion. Six years ago—just before the war—a Polk County slave owner gave an order to one of the mercantiles to let a slave of his have as much whiskey as he wanted from Christmas to the new year. Well, the grocer decided the slave was abusin' his privileges and cut him off. So that slave entered into a plot with his friends to cut the grocer's throat and burn down his store. Two slaves was thrown in jail, and one of 'em was given twenty lashes. After the insurrection—"

"What insurrection?" Hannah blurted. "Did the slaves actually hurt anyone?"

"No, but they planned to sure enough. *The Courier* said so."

"Libelous pro-slavery newspaper," Granny Ledbetter muttered.

"Rumors was just a-flyin' around town," Charity went on. "In defense, a group of concerned citizens formed the Bolivar Mounted Riflemen. The adjutant general of the Missouri Militia heard about it and told them they'd be called the Polk County Rangers instead. They was subject to state military regulations. I heard Jim Strickland was one of them murderin' slaves—"

"Murdering! You just told me the slaves never did anything. You said the plot against the grocer was nothing but rumors."

"Listen here, Miss Federalist Fancy-Pants—"

"Now, you two quit that argyin'." Granny poked her needle into the quilt and crossed her arms. "Charity, your tongue wags at both ends. Mary, you ain't hardly better. And Hannah, you'd better get used to folks' ways around here if you want to get along in this town. Swaller some of that spitfire and get on with good deeds in silence. We don't want to start up the war again right here around our quiltin' frame, now, do we, ladies?"

Hannah eyed the two women across from her. "Forgive me for speaking hastily. I do cherish your friendship . . . Charity, Mary, Lavinia, Granny . . . all of you have been so kind to me. I also love my Indian husband and my two dark-skinned companions, Ruth and Martha. You will excuse me, I trust, when I come to their defense—just as I would rise to champion you were someone to call your character into question."

A smile softened Granny's face. "Well, ladies, now we know why she writes books—talks so highfalutin you can't hardly follow her meanin'. But, Hannah, we appreciate you and your friendship, too. We mean to make you and Luke a welcome part of our town. If you do some things a little different from the rest of us, why, we'll learn to get along with the notion. We'll let some time go by, and pretty soon we'll know whether you're the kind of woman we want to keep for a friend. And you'll know the same about us."

She cleaned her spectacles with the hem of her apron, then set them back on her nose. "Now, what do you womenfolk say to unpackin' the lunch baskets? We've got some hungry men to feed."

Hannah glanced up to see a man approaching the clearing on horseback. Dressed in a fine morning coat and shiny boots, he had thin hair that hung to his shoulders. Without veering his horse toward the working men, he stopped at the quilt frame and nodded politely. "Good morning, ladies," he greeted them.

"Yessir?" Granny Ledbetter stepped toward him. "How can we help you?"

"I'm looking for a man named James Jones."

"The county clerk? Yes, he's here. Now, let's see." Granny turned toward the cabin and pushed her spectacles up her nose.

As she searched the men gathered around the watermelon bucket, Luke broke away from the group. Axe still in his hand, he ran toward the women. "Brown," he barked as he came to a stop at Hannah's side. "You're on my land. What do you want?"

The man on the horse regarded Luke coolly. "It's Butterfield business."

"Then take care of it in town."

"Luke!" Hannah set her hands on her hips in surprise. "Perhaps we could offer the man a drink. Would you care to join us, Mr. . . . ?"

Luke held his breath as Ethan Brown took off the hat that had shaded his eyes. This was the moment he had dreaded, put off, avoided—until now it was too late. He glanced at Hannah, then back at Brown. The man was smiling.

"My name is Brown," he said. "Ethan Brown. Boston."

Hannah gasped. "Boston! Why, I'm from Boston, too. Do you know the Brownlow Print Shop?"

"I do indeed. It's near the Courthouse, I believe. My family used its services often. My father is Samuel Brown, proprietor of fine dining."

"Brown's Hotel?" Hannah laughed in delight. "I've eaten there many a time. The best baked clams in Boston."

Luke watched in disbelief as Ethan Brown transformed before his eyes. The spiteful, sneering demeanor was veiled by charm and gallantry. The man actually beamed as he chatted with Hannah. And he *wasn't* her brother! Luke could have kissed his cheeks.

"And what brings you to Missouri?" the horseman asked.

"I'm in search of my brother, Ethan Brownlow. Perhaps you knew him."

"A fine man. Rather remote as I recall. Kept to himself. Missing, is he? Have you spoken with the county clerk, Miss—?"

"Mrs. Maples," Hannah corrected. "I'm Luke Maples's wife."

The effervescence vanished as Brown cast a disdainful eye on Luke. "Her?" he demanded. "You defiled a Boston woman?"

Luke hefted the axe in his hand. Ethan Brown wasn't Hannah's brother, but he might be his father's killer. "Get off my land," he snarled. "And if I see you here again, I'll kill you."

"Luke!" Hannah cried.

Brown regarded Luke with malice for a moment, then he turned to Hannah. "You will never know happiness in that man's arms," he said. Spurring his horse, he rode away into the forest.

Hannah felt her cheeks flush as she scanned the curious faces of the gathered women. Then she looked at Luke. He turned to her, but the veil that shrouded his eyes was so heavy she could read nothing in them.

"Never speak to him again," he instructed her. She watched the axe in his hand swing back and forth as he returned to the cabin.

That night Hannah and Luke slept within the security and comfort of their own log cabin. The oak-shake roof blocked the starlight, and the lack of windows made the darkness seem even more intense, but Luke assured Hannah he would saw openings for windows the following day. He planned to chink the walls, too. Until he did, the fireplace opening and the spaces between the logs let in the night breezes.

Luke's muscles ached from endless hours of chopping trees, peeling bark, scribing and cutting notches, and hoisting two-hundred-pound logs with a slanted skid and ropes. Though he was sore and tired, he felt more than content with the work he and the men had completed. The ridgepole and purlins formed a roof strong enough to keep out the heaviest winter snow. The foundation would keep the cabin warm and dry.

Within the next few weeks, Luke planned to hew joists for the floor. With wide oak planks that he would split and nail to the joists, the floor would be easy to sweep and mop. He liked the idea that his children would one day crawl safely across a raised floor that would keep insects and snakes at bay.

At the thought of children, Luke laid his hand on Hannah's stomach. She sighed in her sleep and nuzzled her nose against his shoulder. For the first time since their wedding, they had chosen not to seek comfort in each other's bodies. Tired, sunburned, and a little out of sorts in their new environment, they had eaten a quick supper and crawled onto the pallet on their dirt floor. Neither had mentioned the incident with Ethan Brown, and Luke was thankful. He didn't mind, either, that they had not made love.

In fact, he realized as he lay with Hannah in his arms, this moment felt as good as any other with her. Maybe on this night their passion had calmed like a slow river in the heat of summer. But the deep pleasure of contemplating many years inside this home . . . with this woman . . . with their children . . . was just as satisfying to Luke as the magic of joining their flesh.

He stroked his palm in circles on her stomach and listened to the logs settling, creaking, sighing. Maybe he could abandon his quest to pin down his father's killer. Somehow revenge no longer seemed essential. Together he and Hannah would attend church in Bolivar the following morning. Later he would cut windows in their cabin. After hauling stone from the Pomme de Terre riverbed, he would begin to construct a wide, shallow firebox, a stone hearth, and a chimney.

Hannah had told him she was anxious to continue gathering and storing food for the winter. All but their buried stores had burned in the fire, and finding enough to eat each day had become a challenge. She had spoken of other things she wanted, too, things that had lifted Luke's heart—gingham curtains, pots and pans, a rendering kettle, a flour bin, a quilt frame. She wanted to purchase hens and a rooster from the *Nika-sabe* women, and she was eager to buy a cow. Would she be cataloging such necessities if she didn't plan to stay?

With the building of their cabin that day, Luke had begun to feel better about what he could give to this fire-haired Hannah of his. Maybe he could provide for her after all. Maybe he could keep her safe from harm. Maybe they would have friends and neighbors to support them, a school that would accept their children, a church to lend comfort and spiritual strength.

In the past few days, Hannah had rarely mentioned Boston, though Luke knew that finding her brother was always on her mind. Tomorrow evening they would pack their borrowed wagon with the few supplies they had been able to gather. Tom Cunnyngham had allowed Luke a week off from work to search for Hannah's brother.

In two days, or maybe three, they would arrive in Forsyth. Luke closed his eyes and let out a deep breath. Forsyth . . . Ethan Brownlow . . . Ethan Brown . . . Ethan . . .

"I've been so hot these days," Hannah commented late the following evening, "but I feel I really should wear my corset, hoop, and crinoline on the journey. It wouldn't seem proper to appear in Forsyth in one of these shapeless old dresses."

Luke looked up from the bowl of mortar he was mixing beside the fireplace and grinned. "Hannah, in that dress you're hardly shapeless."

"But my waist . . ." She ran her hands over her breasts and down the sides of her torso to her hips. "I think it has expanded a good two inches since I stopped wearing my corset regularly. Sophie would be mortified if she could see me."

"I'm bewitched by you."

She smiled at the endearment and picked up her hoop. "I shall have to wear it anyway. All of it. I want Ethan to be pleased when we meet again. If he truly did join the Confederates, he might feel reluctant to return to Boston. I'll have to be at my very best to remind him of the gentility and culture he's been missing all these years."

Luke's grin faded as he returned to mixing the mortar. Gentility and culture. Hoops. Corsets. Crinolines. Sophie. Did Hannah feel she'd been missing out on the best life had to offer? He recalled the sparkle in her eyes as she reminisced about Boston with Ethan Brown. Again the niggling uncertainty formed a knot in his gut. How long before Hannah would tire of the rough Missouri frontier and her savage husband?

"If there's a piano at that outpost in Forsyth," she was saying, "do you know what I'm going to do?"

"No."

"I'm going to play every lighthearted tune I know. None of these morbid Missouri hymns for me. Last Sunday it was 'Alas and Did My Savior Bleed?' and 'There Is a Fountain Filled with Blood Drawn from Immanuel's Veins.' Did you notice? Goodness, one would think the crucifixion was all there was to religion."

"It is pretty important to Christianity, as I recall from Father Schoenmakers's sermons."

Hannah flicked him on the shoulder with a towel. "Of course it is, silly. I know that. But there ought to be joy in worship, too. There's so much to be thankful for. Friends, flowers, music, dancing. I do miss the dances we used to attend in Boston. I have the most glorious pink dress you have ever seen, Luke. Seventeen yards of pale watered silk. White velvet ribbon trimmings. A pointed décolletage edged with a pleated frill of net. Puffed sleeves—"

"White gloves?"

"Of course!"

"But you don't wear your gloves anymore."

"They're hardly useful in this wildnerness. I would shred them to tatters in half an hour." She extended her palms. "Just look at these calluses. And the stains! If I continue picking up black walnuts, Luke, my hands will be as brown as mud. Did you notice how that Mr. Brown looked at me yesterday in my plain green dress? He could hardly believe I was from Boston."

With his trowel Luke buttered the edge of a flat slab of limestone. So Hannah did miss her pampered life in the East after all. The prospect of continued hard labor could not be appealing compared to her gay Boston life of waltzing, calling on friends, and singing songs around a piano. There was no way he could promise Hannah anything but a life of walnut-stained hands and making do. There would be no fine-tuned musical instruments in their log cabin, no pink silk dresses with velvet trimmings, no sumptuous dances to attend.

He studied her covertly as she folded her few garments that hadn't burned and placed them in a cotton feed sack. Lost in thought, she was humming one of those lighthearted songs she had spoken of. Would it be this failure to find a meeting place that parted them in the end? Not their differences in heritage. Not the prejudices of others. Not their marital expectations. Not even the threat of violence. They could overcome all of those if they worked hard enough.

But could Hannah ever fully let go of the comfortable life in which she had been reared? Could she ever learn to love the land and relish the hard labor as he did? Would Missouri ever be home to Hannah?

"In Boston," she said, "we had plates so shiny you could see your reflection in them. Do you like china plates, Luke?"

He buttered another limestone slab. "I don't know. I've never eaten on one."

"They're very delicate." Hannah watched his biceps contract as he lifted the heavy stone and set it in place. At moments like these—when she and Luke were going about the daily tasks of life—she felt at ease about him. But since her conversation with the women the preceding morning, Hannah had caught herself wondering and worrying. He had behaved abominably to that gentleman from Boston. Lavinia had assured her later that it was pure jealousy—a husband protecting his wife from admiring eyes.

Hannah wasn't so sure. Was Luke truly one of the good, the trustworthy—as she had avowed? Could she rely on him to be loving and loyal to her for the rest of their lives? Or might he suddenly turn savage and cruel as the women had hinted?

"When I think of our china plates," she said carefully, "I always remember my father. He was a kind man, you know. He never lifted a finger against anyone. Was your father like that, Luke?"

"My father was an Osage warrior."

"Of course." Hannah smoothed the gathers of her white morning cap before setting it in her bag. "Perhaps you never knew the quiet pleasures of home and hearth as I did, Luke. A mother seated at the piano . . . her daughters enraptured by her songs . . . a home filled with music and gracious peace and noblesse—"

"Hannah, listen to me." Luke cut her off. "I can't give you those things. This isn't Boston, and I'm not an aristocratic gentleman like your father."

Dismayed, she watched him pace back and forth, his trowel dripping wet mortar on the dirt floor. "This cabin will never be as genteel as your family's brick house in Boston," he said. "I won't smoke a pipe with my friends at the club. I won't read the newspaper in the evening and sip a glass of sherry. There probably won't be a piano in our home or glass panes in our windows or china on our table."

"But, Luke—"

"Missouri is a rough land with hard people." He crossed the room and took her arm. "My roots are Osage, Hannah. Nothing can change that. The ball of fire that rises in the sky every morning will always be Grandfather the Sun to me. The moon will always be Moon Woman. Christ is my Savior, but to me the name of God the Father will always be *Wah'kon-tah,* not Jehovah. I'll wear my mussel-shell gorget and my breechcloth. I'll hunt with my bow—"

"And will you one day grow tired of me because I'm a

foolish Heavy Eyebrows woman and not the dark-haired Osage wife you had planned to marry?"

"What?" Luke stared at her.

He reached out to her just as the front door burst open on its leather hinges. A dozen white-hooded men rushed into the cabin, their boots pounding the dirt floor, their shouts filling the room. Hannah screamed. Luke whirled and froze.

"There he is!" a torch-carrying figure shouted.

"Get him!"

"Don't let him escape!"

Hannah cried out again as Luke pushed her behind the pile of limestone slabs near the fireplace. Brandishing his knife, he momentarily halted the hooded invaders. "What do you want?" he snarled.

One man stepped to the front of the crowd. From behind the stone pile, Hannah observed the rough white fabric of his hood, the mud on his boots, the worn knees of his breeches.

"We want to know why you didn't leave for Kansas when we told you to, bastard," the man spat. "You've had two warnin's now. I reckon that ought to be enough, even for a dumb Indian."

"I have no quarrel with you, Billings," Luke returned. "Why don't you go back where you came from—you and your bushwhacker friends?"

Fear prickled down Hannah's spine as she recognized the voice of the man who had attacked their wagon on the road to Springfield. The man who had burned down their lodge. Joshua Billings! She searched the bare cabin for a weapon, aware that even with a loaded shotgun there was little she could do against this armed and angry mob.

"We ain't gonna leave till we teach you a lesson, Redskin," Billings growled. "A lesson you won't forget. We aim to slicker-whip you and then string you from the nearest tree."

Luke shuddered at the memory of his father's death by those methods. "Why?" he demanded. "What have I done to you?"

"Your cabin's settin' right here on white man's land. I call that a crime, and we's here to enforce the law."

Luke knew he could tell them the land really belonged to Hannah. But if the men realized he had married a woman of their own race, she could be in grave danger. "If you're the law around here, Billings," he hissed, "why don't you and your men show your faces? Only cowards hide beneath hoods."

"Cowards!" Billings jerked off his hood, and the other men followed suit. "Get him, boys!"

"Stop!" Hannah shouted, leaping to her feet. "Stop this madness at once. My husband has done nothing wrong. This homestead is mine—claimed and filed at the land office in Springfield. You're trespassing on the property of a United States citizen, and I demand that you leave immediately!"

"Your land?" Billings roared. "You married this renegade? Why, you ain't no better than—"

"Wait a minute, Billings." A stocky man with close-cropped dark hair pushed to the front of the crowd, his pale blue eyes pinned to Hannah's face. "You? *You're* the woman who married this Indian?"

She held her breath. "Ethan," she whispered.

Chapter Nineteen

~~~~~~~~~~

"Hannah?" Ethan Brownlow's eyes narrowed as he stared at his sister. "What in God's name are you doing here?"

She lifted her chin. "I came from Boston to find you."

"What for? I'm not going back there."

Hannah glanced at Luke. "Ethan," she said softly, "Father has died."

A momentary softness crossed his face. "Died? How?"

"He was killed in battle just before the war ended. Mother needs you desperately. I've come here to ask you to return to Boston and open the print shop."

"Print shop!" Josh Billings guffawed. "Brownlow, you never told us you was in business."

"No," Ethan snarled. "I don't owe a thing to that woman. She's not my mother."

"But Sophie, Pearl, Brigitte, and Elizabeth are your sisters," Hannah cried. "And so am I."

"Half sisters."

"If you loved your father at all, Ethan, you owe it to him to look after his daughters. They're falling into poverty, and their prospects are abysmal. Sophie and Brigitte have taken employment. I've been laboring as a literary domestic for several years. Even Lizzie has tried to do her part by baking bread to sell. Father's pension has proved inadequate. You simply must return to Boston."

"Your little story's just breaking my heart," he sneered. "Sounds to me like you're doing fine."

Hannah stared into her brother's empty blue eyes. This man was nothing like the gregarious youth who had taken his sisters to the circus and the park. Had his broken heart taken such a toll? Once Hannah would not have believed the loss of love could crush a person and transform him into an empty shell. Having loved someone herself, now she knew differently.

"What has happened to you, Ethan?" Hannah's voice was low, her words measured. "Why are you with these men? Bushwhackers go about the countryside wreaking havoc—robbing, burning, murdering. Why do you wear that white hood on your head? Why have you burst in on us and threatened to kill a man who has done nothing wrong?"

From behind her Luke watched as Hannah confronted her brother. He had never seen her so intense, so angry. Shoulders squared, she had planted her feet in a stance that dared the man to contradict her. Her fiery hair tumbled down her back.

"What lies have these men told you, Ethan?" she demanded, her fists knotted at her sides. "Don't you know the War Between the States is over? Don't you know it's time for peace and rebuilding? Justice has been served, and harmony should reign."

Ethan's mouth curled. "Harmony? Justice? What do you know about justice, little sister? Is it justice when a boy's mother dies, like mine did? Is it justice when a woman casts away her lover as my fiancée did when she spurned me for another man?"

"Ethan, that happened years ago. Anabel Adams betrayed you, it's true. But it does no good to—"

"Is it justice," he cut in, "when a man's stepmother and sisters ignore him . . ."

"That's not so! We loved you, Ethan."

"Did you know where I'd gone when I disappeared for years

at a time? Did you care? Did you even bother to ask? I was here—on the frontier, living with men who took me into their circle and made me a friend and a leader. We took care of ourselves, Hannah. We went on raids to get the food and clothes we needed. We burned out those who opposed us."

"Those are criminal deeds, Ethan. That's not the way you were brought up."

"We look after our own, don't we, boys?" he asked, glancing at his companions.

"Yeah," Billings agreed. His dark eyes flicked to Luke. "And we get rid of Indians and niggers and other vermin."

"Why would you kill Indians?" Hannah demanded. "The tribes are all in the Kansas Indian Territory—their people trapped on tiny reservations. What quarrel do you have with them?"

Ethan, too, transferred his focus to Luke. "They weren't *all* on their reservations where they belong. Just like they're not *all* there now. Back before the war, Indians made regular raids over the state line into southern Missouri. This had been their land, and they wanted it back. The Osage were the worst— retaliating, stealing, burning, killing. So we decided to teach them a lesson."

Billings snickered. "One time we swung down on a village and rounded up all the men—them brave warriors. Tied 'em to trees and whipped 'em with stripped hickory branches. If you ever felt the whack of a hickory switch with its bark peeled off so it's good and slippery, you'd know it don't feel too good to be slicker-whipped."

Ethan laughed. "The worst she's ever suffered is having a scuff on her shoe." He lifted his eyes to Luke. "After we'd whipped those Indians, we strung them up and left them dangling till they were good and dead."

Hannah caught her breath and looked at Luke. His face had gone as hard as stone. The knife in his fist glinted.

"Ethan," he said in a voice so low she could hardly hear it. Suddenly it had all come clear to him. Though he could track a deer down a streambed, in this most important hunt of his life he had taken the wrong trail. Ethan Brown was nothing more than a Butterfield Stage inspector. *This* guerrilla was his enemy. "Ethan," he hissed, "the murderer in the white hood."

"That's right," he confirmed. "I led the group of men that took out as many of you lice as we could. But did that stop you? Of course not. You can't teach an Indian."

"Ethan, you didn't kill anyone!" Hannah cried. "You were in Boston, remember? You took Sophie and Brigitte—all of us—to the park, to the circus. You carried Lizzie on your shoulders. You weren't a murderer. Please, Ethan—"

"That all happened before I began my travels, little sister," he cut in. "Before I was spurned by Anabel, the only woman I've ever loved, I was the man you remember. Before I realized that nothing I could do would truly win the love of my half sisters and their mother. You were never my family. When I wandered away from Boston and found myself in Missouri, I discovered I did matter to someone. Oh, I tried making a life again in Boston, but it didn't work out. I was a failure even in my own father's eyes. So I came back to Missouri a second time and joined up with my friends after the victory at Wilson's Creek. We volunteered to fight."

"For the Confederacy?" Hannah asked.

"That's where my friends were." He turned to Luke again. "I was with the twenty-one Confederate soldiers who traveled across the reservation border one night to try to rally the Plains Indians against the Union."

"We discovered you, of course," Luke cut in, recalling the incident with sparkling clarity. "You Heavy Eyebrows fools never were any good at secrecy. It took only ten of us to capture all you brave soldiers. We decided to transport you to the Union post at Fort Humboldt and let them handle the matter. But you tried to escape, didn't you? And in the attempt you shot one of our warriors."

"That's right," Ethan handed his torch to Billings and leveled his shotgun at Luke's chest. "Then you bastards went and rounded up two hundred warriors. You followed us and trapped us on a sandbar in the Verdigris River. When we ran out of ammunition, we fought you hand to hand."

Luke smiled slowly. "As I recall, we scalped and beheaded eighteen of you."

"Luke!" Hannah gasped.

"Three men got away," Ethan finished. "One of them was me."

"Too bad," Luke countered.

One of the bushwhackers stepped forward and held up what Hannah immediately recognized as Luke's deerskin leggings. Obviously the men had taken them from the lodge before setting it ablaze. Ethan snatched the leggings and shook them in the Indian's face.

"These scalp-locks," he shouted, "were cut from the heads of my friends!"

Luke raised his knife. "You murdered my father, Ethan Brownlow."

"Dear God!" Hannah cried. "Luke, did you agree to take me to Springfield that first time because you thought my brother might be the man you were searching for?"

Luke's eyes never left his enemy. "That's right. The name Ethan was all I knew about the man. But I didn't—"

"He obviously married you to get at me, too," Ethan told Hannah. "And you were stupid enough to fall for his scheme. Why did you marry him in the first place?"

"He wanted . . . this land," she whispered. "And he said he would help me find you."

Ethan laughed. "Sure he did. I'm certain he found lots of Ethans for you to look over."

"No, he . . ." Hannah suddenly saw the man on horseback—Ethan Brown. Had Luke thought he was her brother? It was obvious they had met before, so why hadn't he told her earlier?

"You're the loser all the way around, aren't you, Hannah?" her brother taunted. "It must have been simple for our redskin friend—take an ignorant white woman and talk her into filing for land he couldn't legally own. Convince her he wanted to help find her long-lost brother, when really that was the man he intended to kill. Maybe this snake is smarter than I gave him credit for. I bet he lifted your petticoats, too, didn't he, sister?"

Biting her lip, Hannah couldn't see beyond her tears.

"Was that part of your deal?" Ethan demanded. "That he'd have you breeding his filthy nits for him?"

"That's a lie!" Luke spat.

"It's too late, bastard. She knows you played her for the fool. But you're a fool, too. While you're over here enjoying your little game with my sister, your own people are on the verge of being wiped out."

"What do you mean?" Luke shot back.

"Oh, you haven't heard? Your Osage chiefs have just signed a treaty with the United States Government at Canville's Trading Post. They were forced to sell off the eastern thirty miles of their reservation, as well as a twenty-mile-wide tract running the entire distance of the northern boundary."

"You're lying," Luke said, though the look of triumph on the man's face told him he spoke the truth.

"It won't be long," Ethan jeered, "before your people are forced to sell off their entire reservation. You know the buffalo herds are almost gone, and you can't come running back to the Missouri hills to raid anymore. With no buffalo, no crops, and no land, the Osage are bound to die out. You have no future, Indian. As far as I'm concerned, that's a damn good way to get rid of vermin."

Rage, frustration, rancor flooded through Luke's veins. This was the man who had killed his father. These were the people who had stolen his lands—men who would destroy the Osage people.

Luke looked at Ethan and desire for blood-vengeance burned a bitter gall in his throat. Then he glanced at Hannah. Her blue eyes shone with tears as she stared, white-faced, at him. Paralyzed—torn between hatred for the man and love for his sister—Luke gripped his knife.

"Take him outside, boys," Ethan ordered, pulling Hannah to his side. "String him up from the nearest tree."

The bushwhackers surrounded Luke, wrested the knife from his hand, immobilized him. As they streamed out into the night with their captive, Hannah pushed away from her brother.

Luke could never defend himself against these men! In minutes he would be dead. Part of her said death was the fate he deserved. He had admitted to deceiving her about his motives . . . He had kept back news that might have helped her . . . He had admitted to slaughtering the soldiers . . . The scalp-locks on his leggings bore evidence of his savage nature. Moments before the bushwhackers had burst into the cabin, he had been telling her he would never change—he would always be Osage first and foremost.

If she kept her silence, Luke would die, and she would be done with the ugly mess she had made of her life. She could go back to Boston, write her books, forget everything that had happened. Forget the betrayal, the deceit, the arguments, the hard labor, the long nights, the shared laughter, the tender caresses, the soft kisses . . .

She rounded on her brother.

"Ethan!" she snapped as he shoved her out of the cabin into the night. "I demand you set Luke free. Let him go! He'll never come back to Missouri. He knows you would kill him if he did."

"We gave him two warnings already, and he didn't leave," Ethan said. "Fetch the rope, men!"

"Stop it!" Hannah shouted. "Ethan Brownlow, turn Luke free this instant! He'll leave. I know he will. His family in Kansas means more to him than anything. If they've lost most of their land, he'll have no choice but to stay there and protect them. All he has left is his mother—and I know he won't desert her in a time of need. You must let him go! He'll never come back, I swear it!"

Ethan hesitated a moment. His pale eyes fastened on Luke, who was pinned to a tree between two vigilantes. "All right," he said finally. "Turn him loose, men."

"You sure, Ethan?" Billings asked.

"Let him go."

Hannah stared across the torch-lit clearing as the bush-whackers released Luke. Before she could call out to him, her brother jerked her around in the opposite direction. "Let's get out of here," he said.

Half lifting her off her feet, he dragged her toward the trail that Luke had cut in the trees. Tears stung in her eyes. How could she leave the man who had become her husband? She loved him! She had been so sure he loved her.

Tearing loose from Ethan's grip, she swung around. In the distance, Luke had paused at the edge of the clearing. His dark eyes locked with hers one last time.

"Luke!" she choked out.

But as she stretched out her hand toward him, she saw the barrel of Ethan's shotgun take aim. Before she could knock it aside, the gunfire roared, and Luke fell to his knees.

"No!" Hannah screamed and ran toward him. She could hear Ethan behind her, branches cracking beneath his pounding feet. Just as they got to the fallen man, he staggered upward. Lunging at Ethan, Luke swung his fist. Ethan's head snapped back; he stumbled and fell.

Luke sprang, flattening his enemy to the ground. A knife glinted in the moonlight. Hannah screamed again. She could hear the other bushwhackers plunging through the forest, tearing across the clearing. In the moonlight she saw a line of blood spatter across Luke's chest.

"Ethan!" she cried. "Luke!"

The men rolled across the deep grass. Another arc of blood shot out to dampen Hannah's skirt. Leaping around them, she searched in vain for a stone or a stick—anything to separate the enemies.

"Now!" Luke growled suddenly. Springing onto Ethan's chest, he caught the man by his dark hair. The knife flashed in Luke's fist. Yanking Ethan's head backward, he exposed the throbbing jugular vein in his enemy's thick neck.

Arms pinned to the ground by his opponent's knees, Ethan couldn't move. Luke slowly lowered the knife and angled it against his throat. "You killed him," he ground out. "You murdered my father. I swore I would destroy you or die."

Rage almost blinding him, Luke pressed the blade into the murderer's skin. He couldn't think. Couldn't reason. Couldn't smell or taste or feel anything. The only sound he heard was his own heart, like a drumbeat calling for war. His own heart . . . and the sound of soft weeping. A woman's tears . . . Hannah.

Hannah.

Forcing himself to draw the knife away, Luke rose from the terrified man. "Hannah . . . ," he called, starting toward her.

At that moment Ethan rolled onto his knees. Drawing a small pistol from his belt, he came to his feet and aimed the weapon at Luke's back. In the torchlight of the approaching marauders, Hannah caught the glint of silver.

"Luke!"

The Indian whirled. As the pistol fired, Luke swung his knife. A flash of steel sliced across Ethan's throat, and he slumped to the ground. A pool of blood spread quickly where he fell.

"What's goin' on here?" Billings shouted.

Before Hannah could react, Luke had slipped away into the deep forest.

"Hey, what's become of Ethan?" Billings demanded. He fell to his knees beside the prone body. "Damn . . . he's dead, boys. Ethan's dead."

Hannah stared at the line of silhouetted trees. The piercing cry of a falcon echoed through the darkness.

Chapter
Twenty

~~~~~~~~~~

"Let's get out of here," Joshua Billings cried. "Grab the woman!"

"No!" Hannah tore across the clearing, skirts tangling around her ankles as she ran. Barely eluding her pursuers, she untethered the skittish horse and hauled herself onto the creature's broad back. Within moments the horse was thundering down the trail toward Bolivar as Hannah clung desperately to its mane.

In the moonlight every shadow was a hooded demon rearing to lunge at her. Every firefly was a vigilante's distant torch. Every owl's hoot gave a foreboding warning. Squeezing her eyes shut, she laid her head against the horse's neck as it galloped over hills and through hollows.

Luke! Luke! The hoofbeats pounded out his name. Was he wounded? Dead? Had the bushwhackers followed him into the forest? Or were they pursuing her? And Ethan! Her brother was gone forever. Killed by Luke—by her husband.

Hannah pulled the horse to a halt just outside Jim and

Martha Strickland's small log cabin. She slid to the ground and hammered on the door with her fist.

"What you want?" A harsh voice followed the sound of the door opening just a crack. The cold steel of a shotgun barrel pressed into her bosom. "Talk fast or I'll shoot."

"Jim," she gasped. "It's me—Hannah. Luke's wife. Oh, Jim, you must let me come inside! They're after me!"

As the big man grabbed Hannah's arm and half jerked her into the house, a lantern came to life in the back corner of the room. "What's the matter, woman?" Jim demanded, slamming the door behind him. "Who's chasin' you? Speak your piece in a hurry, and then fetch yourself back outta my house."

"Jim?" Holding a lantern high, Martha emerged from the shadows. "Why, Miss Hannah! What's goin' on?"

"The bushwhackers—they attacked us again. And my brother was among them! Years ago he killed Luke's father. Tonight the two of them fought, and Ethan tried to shoot Luke. But Luke cut Ethan's throat instead. Now Luke has vanished into the forest," she concluded breathlessly. "I'm sure he'll never come back!"

"Of course he'll come back," Martha said. "He's your husband, ain't he?"

"But he killed Ethan, and I'm sure he fears what the sheriff would do to him. He once told me that because he's an Indian he'll never get justice from white men."

"Can't deny that," Jim said. Ruth and Willie Jefferson had crept down from the loft and were crossing the room. Jim turned to the older man. "Willie here can tell you—no person whose skin ain't lily-white is ever gonna be treated fair and square."

"That ain't true," Martha countered. "You and Willie both been treated real good by them fellows you mix mortar for. They pay you decent, and they respect you for your work. Round the house, we been fine, too. Nobody's bothered us much since we been livin' here. Matter of fact, folks has been plumb friendly. And Luke didn't fare no worse—except with them bushwhackers. People in town take to him real good, Miss Hannah. I reckon he'll come back for you."

She shook her head. "Before the attack, Luke and I . . . we had words. We disagreed about our future. I expressed my fears that he would always long for his Osage ways . . . and he couldn't deny it. He'll always be an Indian first, Miss Martha. He's been driven away by the Heavy Eyebrows. Why would he come back here only to face more persecution?''

"Because he loves you."

Hannah let out a breath. "You don't understand. Luke cares for me—but he has stronger ties than our love. His own people are being driven from their land. The government is carving up their reservation piece by piece. He won't stand by and watch that happen. He'll go back to Kansas, Miss Martha. He'll care for his mother, and while he's there he'll remember how much his old ways meant to him."

"You reckon?"

"Of course. I'm nothing but a reminder of everything bad that white people have done to him—stealing land, killing children, mutilating women. My race burned down his lodge, destroyed his falcon, threatened to whip and hang him, shot at him . . . and murdered his own father."

"Lawsy mercy." Martha stared at her feet. Her small son slipped to her side and wrapped his arms around her leg. She absently fondled his soft hair.

"I reckon you're right, honey," she said finally, lifting her eyes to Hannah. "You done seen the last of that man. You're on your own now, and you might as well make the best of it. I don't suspect you never was much for this place anyhow. You belong back in your nice house with your mama and sisters. They're gonna need you, what with them losin' both men of the family. You better go on back to Boston, don't you reckon?"

"I reckon so," Ruth put in. "Miss Hannah, you never was gonna make a Missouri woman. You ain't got tough meat on your bones. You got tender ways, tender thoughts. Your dreams . . . well, they's beyond us common folk round here. Why don't you get on home to your Boston mama and let that Indian boy go on home to his? You got things to take care of, and so does he. It's best you part ways, I reckon."

"I reckon so," Jim added. "Ain't no sense in stayin' round these parts, Miss Hannah. Without a man to look after you, ain't no way you can stay out at that cabin all winter. Tell you what—I'll run fetch the sheriff, and you can tell him your story. Then, him and me, we'll ride up to the farm and check things out. We'll see if Luke's done come back. And we'll bring down your brother for the buryin'. That'll tell you what's what, don't you reckon?"

Hannah nodded. "I reckon."

Luke hadn't returned, and Ethan's body was nowhere to be found. The following morning, the sheriff informed Hannah that the bushwhackers had probably taken their slain companion and would bury him. Before she had time to sort through her thoughts, he had secured her a seat on a supply wagon bound for Rolla. Ethan Brown, as it turned out, would accompany her there, then ride with her by train to St. Louis, where he could continue his investigation of the Bolivar incident.

"Miss Hannah, you take this money, now," the sheriff said, placing a small coin purse in her hand as she sat dazed in the loaded wagon. "It's enough to get you back to Boston on the train. I'll sell your horse, the seed, and the other goods at your cabin, and we'll call it even."

"Here's some fried chicken, honey." Ruth Jefferson set a small calico-wrapped bundle in Hannah's lap. "There's cornbread and a couple of apples, too. Eat good, hear? Keep your strength up so's you can get on home. I reckon your mama be missin' you somethin' awful."

"Thank you, Miss Ruth," Hannah whispered.

Tears glistening on her ebony cheeks, Martha hitched her baby onto her hip and approached the wagon. "You're a good woman, Miss Hannah," she said in a low voice. "Think about us now and then, will you?"

Hannah could only nod. Leaning forward, she wrapped her arms around Martha's shoulders and kissed her damp cheek. "I love you, my dear friend," she murmured.

Then the team of mules tugged at the harness, and the wagon rolled forward. Hannah shut her eyes as she started back to Boston.

The journey east took Hannah farther and farther from the rolling green Ozarks . . . away from thickets of oak, hickory, and dogwood . . . away from log cabins and split-rail fences . . . away from homespun butternut-dyed dresses, bare feet, toothless grins . . . away from ticks, chiggers, poison ivy, mosquitoes, water moccasins . . . away from mountain air, delicate mists, golden sunshine, dancing wild-flowers . . . away from Missouri.

Mr. Brown was polite, if distant, company. His wife, Hannah learned, had been murdered by raiding Indians. The man had never recovered from his shock and grief. The mention of Indians sent him into fits of anger and such vituperation that Hannah quickly decided never to mention Luke. And so she fell silent. She bade Mr. Brown farewell in St. Louis, and there was no one to talk to after that anyway.

Hannah knew she should have been happy. Finally she could walk into well-stocked mercantiles and eat something other than venison and hominy. Rustic sheds gave way to small towns and then to sprawling cities. Deer were replaced by cattle and then by factories. Barefoot strollers became horse-back riders, who became carriage drivers. The pace of life picked up from a lazy amble to a hurried scamper to a frantic rush.

And then she was back in Boston. Orange, red, and yellow leaves barely clung to the trees. A chilly wind cut through her thin cotton mantle and crept around her mosquito-bitten ankles as she stepped down from the train. Riding a carriage along cobblestone streets past large brick homes, she studied her gloveless hands.

Why wasn't she happier?

The carriage drew up to the front of a two-story house with green shutters and an ivied wall. Hannah gazed at it a moment, thinking how solid and proper it was compared with a buffalo-skin lodge or a creaking log cabin. Solid, proper, and boring.

With a sigh she descended the carriage and climbed the steps. She let the heavy brass knocker fall against the door, then waited for the familiar sound of Molly, the housekeeper, coming down the hall. Instead the patter of scampering shoes and the sound of muffled laughter greeted her ears. Then the door flew wide.

"It's Hannah!" Elizabeth shrieked as she caught sight of her sister's face. After slamming the door she had just opened, the little girl fled through the house.

Hannah waited outside, a smile softening her lips. And then the door was flung open a second time. A bevy of females billowed onto the steps, clustered around her, enveloped her in warm arms, soft kisses, sighs, tears, the brush of silk, the scent of heliotrope and lavender water.

"Oh, Hannah! Hannah!" Her mother wept on her daughter's shoulder. "You've come home to us. I feared I would never see you again! Oh, my darling Hannah."

And suddenly the flood of anguish inside Hannah's heart spilled over. She clutched her mother's narrow, fragile body and squeezed her eyes shut against wracking waves of sorrow. It wasn't the loss of Missouri or her friendship with Ruth, Martha, and Lavinia. It wasn't the aching tiredness in her bones. It wasn't the burden of her experiences on the frontier— fear, pain, hunger, shock. It wasn't even the death of her brother that filled her with anguish. It was Luke . . . Luke . . .

"Hannah, do come inside out of the chill," her mother murmured. "Goodness, you're as thin as a sparrow, darling. Your cheeks are so pinched and pale. And look at these hands!"

"Where are your gloves?" Lizzie asked as they led their sister to a settee beside the fireplace. "You've been outside without your gloves. And just look at your bonnet, Hannah! What's become of the frill?"

Hannah smiled and touched her sister's soft cheek. "Elizabeth, you've grown two inches since I've been away." Then she glanced around her at the cluster of bright faces. "Tell me everything. Make me feel . . . at home again."

They did their best. Sophie elaborated on her activities as a music and dancing instructor—giving special note to the handsome widower whose daughter she was teaching to play the piano. Oh, but he was divine, Sophie insisted. Hannah simply must meet him!

Pearl displayed the delicate ring on her finger, a symbol of the betrothal that would see her wedded at Christmastime. "To think that I would be the first among us to marry!" she exclaimed. "Hannah, I can't wait for you to get to know Benjamin. Why, he's so kind and wonderful that you might even change your mind about never marrying!"

Brigitte had a clientele list miles long, she assured Hannah.

Her hats were the talk of Boston. Even the mayor's wife owned one. "I'm going to be just like you, Hannah," she told her sister. "I'm going to make my own way in this world. And I don't want a man at my side to drag me under."

Elizabeth brought out her fancywork and paintings to show Hannah. She sang the latest tunes and did a few turns on the parlor floor to demonstrate a new dance step. "Hannah, we've been so busy we hardly knew you were gone!" she announced.

A collective gasp went around the room. "That's not true!" Brigitte admonished her sister. "We've missed Hannah dreadfully. We've prayed for her safety day and night."

"Of course you have," Hannah said, gathering Lizzie onto her lap. "And I've missed all of you. Now, before I go upstairs to my room, I must tell you my own news."

Mrs. Brownlow sank onto a chair and her daughters gathered around her. "You haven't found Ethan, have you?" she asked.

Hannah wrapped her arms around her little sister. During the long miles across the country she had pondered how to break the news. She knew she must protect the delicate sensibilities of these women who knew little more of life's harshness than a forgotten glove or a stained parasol. Though war had touched them, they had never witnessed men battling for their lives with guns and knives, as she had. Death had trod heavily across their path, but it had altered their lives without revealing its hideous face. They had never experienced bloodshed, murder, or revenge, as she had. And she hoped she could spare them from it forever. After turning the situation one way and another, she had finally decided to use discretion.

"Ethan passed away," she told her family softly. "He has been buried in Taney County, in the southern part of Missouri."

"Oh my!" Mrs. Brownlow drew her handkerchief from her sleeve and covered her mouth.

"How did he die?" Lizzie asked.

Hannah stroked her sister's red hair. "Well . . . someone killed him, I'm afraid."

"When!"

"Not long ago." She paused for a moment. "You must understand. Missouri is . . . a different sort of place than Massachusetts."

"Wild and savage?"

"At times. But it's also mysterious and beautiful." She let out a breath. "At any rate, we must accept the fact that Ethan will never return to us. He has joined his father and ours in death, and we must permit his memory to rest in peace."

"Then we shall have to get on with our lives the best we can," Sophie said. "I think we should sell the print shop."

"Sell it!" Mrs. Brownlow's face crumpled. "That print shop was your father's pride and joy. Never shall I sell it!"

"Then I'll open it," Hannah announced. "Don't look shocked, Mother. What choice do we have? If we won't sell it, and Ethan will never manage it, then one of us will have to. I watched Father working there, and I know I can operate the press. If no one patronizes the shop, we shall be no worse off than before."

Mrs. Brownlow regarded her daughter evenly. Finally she shook her head. "Absolutely not. No child of mine will ever stoop so low."

Hannah let out a breath of exasperation. "Mother, we can't sit around in this house and wish our lives would change! We may be women, but we're not helpless. We must swallow our pride, roll up our silk sleeves, and set to work. I'm not afraid to get ink on my fingers, and I don't care what people say about me. I can manage the print shop as well as Father ever did."

Mrs. Brownlow gaped. "Hannah!"

"It's true!" She set Lizzie to one side and stood to face her family. "If Brigitte is so talented at making hats and dresses, why shouldn't she open her own shop? Brownlow Millinery and Tailoring. She could have twice the clientele and make enough money to support herself and you as well. Instead of hourly private lessons in the parlor, why shouldn't Sophie open a school for young ladies? She could charge a monthly fee for whole groups of girls and teach her pupils everything she knows—reading, writing, ciphering, fancywork, dancing, singing, piano. I'll open the print shop during the day and continue writing my novels in the evenings. If Pearl is married, and if Sophie, Brigitte, and I are working, we should have more than enough to get by."

"I want to be a doctor when I grow up," Lizzie announced.

"Hush, Elizabeth!" Mrs. Brownlow scolded. "Hannah,

you're rambling. You must be exhausted from your journey. Do go upstairs now and have a bit of a rest."

Hannah stared at the women seated around the fire. Suddenly they seemed like strangers. Turning away, she walked toward the kitchen.

"I'll heat some water," she said. "Before I do anything else, I want to take a long bath and wash my hair."

Behind her, she heard a gasp. "A bath!" Sophie exclaimed.

"Wash her hair?"

"In the winter?"

"She'll catch her death!"

It took less than a day for Hannah to realize how much she had changed. She found the morning needlework hour deadly dull, the luncheon rest time exasperating, and the afternoon callers boring beyond relief. When she caught herself dozing off during the evening piano and dance recital, Hannah knew something had permanently altered her.

It took less than a week for her to realize that the lifestyle she had once found interesting and comfortable now felt like a prison sentence. With her mother's refusal to alter the daily pattern of the family's existence, Hannah had no choice but to delay and possibly even surrender her notion of reopening the print shop. But how could she ever be content with nothing more stimulating to do than stitch an alphabet sampler? Or stand in front of a mirror? Or cut roses? She wanted to churn butter! Milk a cow! Gather lotus roots in a swampy lake! Oh, what she wouldn't give for a mess of wild greens and onions to boil over a fire and eat for supper.

It took less than a month for her to realize that not only were her desires, interests, and needs different—so was her body. Sophie noticed it first. "Why, Hannah, your bosom is twice the size it was! Whatever have you done to yourself?" And then Pearl chimed in. "Hannah, you're at least twenty inches around the waist this morning. I simply can't pull these corset laces any tighter. What have you been eating?" But it was Elizabeth whose innocent comment gave Hannah the truth.

"You're no fun at all," she pouted one afternoon. "You're tired and snappish every day. All you do is cry, morning, noon, and night. You eat like ten horses, and you sleep in that chair by the fire just like lazy old mama puss. But she's going to have kittens. Are you going to have kittens, Hannah?"

Hannah's face went white. "Kittens?" she whispered. "Why, how silly, Lizzy. Of course not. I'm a woman. Women don't have kittens. They have . . . babies."

She should have recognized the signs much sooner. But the train trip had been exhausting, and so she convinced herself that her constant tiredness was a result. The upset of her monthly cycle was due to all the travel and distress, she told herself. The food at home tasted so good, and she was simply eating to make up for all the days when she had gone hungry. Her tears and irritability and sadness—well, she missed Luke.

That much of it was true. How long the nights seemed without him. The days were all but unbearable. She could hardly stand to think that she would never again hear his voice, his deep laugh, his murmur of passion. Just the memory of his strong brown hands rolled through her like a wave that slammed into the pit of her stomach. His touch, his scent, his words, his kisses . . . how could she live the rest of her life without them? He had awakened her—not only to the ecstasy of loving, but to life itself. She had learned to embrace each day and to hunger for night.

Nothing she tried would erase the ache.

Now, as she stood staring down at her little sister, Hannah laid a hand on her own stomach. Luke's child . . . their baby . . . was alive inside her body! Utter happiness mingled with choking despair as she sank into a chair. How soon would she become a mother? Would her own mother ever accept a fatherless baby in the home? How could Hannah explain to her child what had become of Luke?

Pregnant without a husband! A half-Indian child without a father! Hannah gripped the arms of the chair and sat forward. The baby would be disgraced—called illegitimate, a bastard! Luke's child!

"Oh, dear God . . . ," she whispered.

"Whatever is the matter, Hannah?" Lizzie asked. "Shall I call Mama?"

"No!" Hannah exclaimed. How would she ever explain this to her mother? She wouldn't. Couldn't.

"I don't like you anymore," Lizzie announced. "And I know

why. I know what's wrong with you, Hannah. Even though you think it's a secret, it's not. We all know about it—Mama, Sophie, Pearl, Brigitte . . . and me, too. We talk about it at breakfast after you've gone to lie down. We talk about it at dinner when you're weeping in your room. We know what's wrong with you, Hannah."

"You do?" she mouthed, barely able to make the words have sound.

"Of course! We're not blind, you know. We see what's different about you."

"What?"

"You've stopped writing books, that's what!"

"Oh!" Hannah gave a slightly hysterical laugh. "Oh, that!"

"Yes. Mama says if you'd start writing again, you'd feel better at once."

"I . . . I left my novel in Missouri. I had to go away quickly, and there wasn't time to look for it. Besides, that book grew in a different way than I'd planned. Perhaps I meant to leave it behind, Lizzy. Perhaps I could never have finished it."

"Then write another one. Don't tell me you have only one idea for a story, Hannah. I know you better than that." The little girl marched across the room and picked up Hannah's wooden lap desk. "Here you are. Now start writing. And when you're done, see if I don't like you again."

With a forced smile, Hannah took the desk and set it on her knees. Lifting the lid, she stared down at her pens, ink bottles, paper. Yes, it was time to write.

Hannah's new book went to the publisher on the first day of January, 1866. Her new effort was nothing like the fictitious novel of love and adventure she had written in Missouri. This was the tale of her own travels—not only the places she had been, but the people she had come to know and the things she had learned. When she had sent her editor the first half of the book, he had purchased the project at once. "A breakthrough!" he had scrawled across the bottom of the last page. "A triumph! Hannah, you will be famous!"

But the day after the book went into the post, she began packing a trunk.

"Whatever are you doing?" Mrs. Brownlow asked as she

walked past the bedroom with a tray of tea cups. Pausing in the doorway, she stared at her daughter. "Hannah, honestly. You've done nothing but write for weeks now. You've completely ignored the family—other than beating us over the head with your strange ideas at mealtimes. Now Sophie and Brigitte have gone and turned the upstairs of the print shop into a school for young ladies and the downstairs into a milliner's shop—"

"And they're so happy, aren't they?" Lighter at heart than she had been for months, Hannah picked up a soft yellow skirt and hugged it against her expanding waistline. "I think this will be wonderfully cool in the summertime, don't you?"

"Summer? Hannah, dear, it's the dead of winter. Why are you packing a trunk? Where do you think you're going?"

"To Missouri."

"Missouri!" Mrs. Brownlow swept into the bedroom and set the tea tray on a table. "My darling girl, you'll do nothing of the sort! You will stay right here at home where you're safe and secure. Oh, you've been acting so strangely since you returned from that ill-advised adventure. I'm going to send for Dr. Harris immediately. A strong dose of laudanum should settle you."

"No, Mama. There's nothing wrong with me. Nothing that Ruth and Martha can't fix, anyway."

"Ruth and Martha? Who are they?"

"My best friends. They used to be slaves, and they know—"

"Slaves! Listen to me, young lady. You do nothing but write, eat, and sleep. That, and mourn. You've completely let yourself go. Just look at you!" Taking her daughter's shoulders, she propelled her in front of the pier mirror. "You're plump!"

Hannah laughed. "Yes! Isn't it wonderful!"

"Who do you suppose will want to marry a butterball?"

"It's only my waist, Mama. The rest of me is exactly the same size. And I don't plan to ever marry again."

"I know what you always say—" Mrs. Brownlow caught her breath. "*Again?*"

Hannah stepped away from the mirror. She lowered the lid of her trunk and sat down on it. "I'm a married woman, Mama," she said softly. "I wed a man in Missouri, and I'm bearing his child. Before you swoon—"

It was too late. With a shriek that would wake the dead, her mother dropped to the floor like a pile of limp laundry. The four sisters came rushing into the room, a bevy of colorful butterflies flittering around the fallen matron. Hannah observed the scene from a distance. Detached, for the first time. More estranged than she'd ever been. She was tired . . . so tired of all this.

Rising, she picked up a purse that contained part of the publisher's advance for her novel. Then she knelt beside her mother and took her hands. The graying lashes fluttered open.

"Mother," Hannah whispered, "I've sent for a carriage, and I'm going to the train station now. A man will come up in a few moments to fetch my trunk. I shall write to you all from Missouri. Good-bye now."

She bent and gave her mother's cheek a kiss, then she stood to go. Lizzie stared up at her sister, eyes clouding with tears. "You're leaving us again, Hannah? Oh, nothing will be the same without you. Who will read me stories?"

"You'll read them to yourself. And when you grow bigger, Lizzie, you'll go to school and study medicine. You mustn't wait for happiness to find you. You must pray, and be good, and work hard."

"Then I shall live happily ever after?"

"I think so, darling," Hannah whispered. "I hope so."

Turning away from her family, she walked out into the hall and set her heart toward Missouri.

Chapter
Twenty-one

The cabin stood in the clearing, its shake roof capped with a foot of crusty white snow. Hannah lifted her skirt and waded from the wagon toward the door. She almost expected to see Luke step around the corner, a parfleche over one shoulder and his falcon on his fist. But there was no smoke drifting from the half-finished fireplace. The door hung ajar on its leather hinges. The cabin was deserted.

"Now, you know you can't stay out here, Miss Hannah," Jim Strickland called from the wagon. "Don't get no ideas about that."

Ignoring him, Hannah pushed open the door and stepped inside. Time had frozen. The pallet of summer moss lay against one wall—shriveled and dried. The pail of mortar sat by the hearth, its contents as hard as a rock. The trowel Luke had been using had tumbled to the earthen floor, where it still rested, untouched since the night the bushwhackers had burst in.

"Miss Hannah," Martha whispered, following her inside. "Come on back out to the wagon now, and let's get on down to

Bolivar again. It's too cold out here for a woman in your condition. You're liable to take sick."

Hannah laid her palm on the fireplace. Luke's hand had been the last to touch these stones. His body had warmed this room. His dreams had filled its corners.

"I'm going to stay here," she whispered. "This is where my baby will be born."

"Law, no! What you talkin' about now? Are you crazy, girl? You can't live out here all by yourself. There ain't nothin' to eat, nothin' to keep you warm, nobody to protect you. You'll freeze yourself to death, and that baby, too. Come on, Miss Hannah. Don't say such things."

"Willie and Jim can finish the fireplace and chink the logs. They know how to mix mortar, and they've watched the bricklayers in town. I've brought enough money to pay them both. I'll buy the other supplies I need from the mercantile." She swung around, her face flushed with excitement. "This is where I belong, Miss Martha! Don't you see? I'm not a Boston girl anymore. Missouri is my home. My child must be born here on my own land. Mine and Luke's."

Martha shook her head. "You always was a passel of trouble, you know that?" Then her face softened, and she held out her arms. "Come here and let me give you a welcome-home hug. I reckon we can fix you up out here if this is what you really want. Ain't that what friends is for?"

Hannah laid her head on Martha's shoulder and shut her eyes. "I've missed you so. Yes . . . this is what friends are for."

They walked together back to the wagon, and when Jim had finished cussing and bemoaning his fate, he reluctantly agreed to help Hannah with her cabin. Work was slow to nonexistent in the winter, he admitted, so he and Willie would have plenty of time.

While Hannah was confined with Lavinia Cunnyngham and her family for the next two weeks, the two men labored from dawn until dusk, cutting limestone, mortaring it in place, and chinking the gaps between the logs. Ruth and Martha took Hannah's purse to the store and purchased a large supply of flour, sugar, and salt. They borrowed a bed and mattress from the Baptist preacher, a chair from the Methodist church, and a lamp from the Catholics.

The women in town donated the quilts they had promised, along with crocks of pickles, jam, and honey. The sheriff supplied Hannah with a side of smoked bacon, and the local butcher sent over a ham. A table appeared one morning on the Stricklands' front porch, and so did a cradle.

Finally, on a warm morning in early March, a team of mules pulled two loaded wagons up the muddy trail to the cabin. Bolivar townspeople—both dark-skinned and light—carried everything inside. They swept and dusted, built a roaring fire, set up the table, chair, and bed, and built shelves to hold the stores. A group of men chopped more wood than Hannah thought she could burn in a year and stacked it beside the front door.

Then old Willie handed her a shotgun. "You keep this close, now, Miss Hannah. Critters is hungry this time of year—and I don't mean just the four-legged kind."

Hannah smiled at the expression of kindness. "Thank you, Mr. Jefferson. I'll keep it near the bed."

"And if you feel any pains," Ruth whispered, "any at all, you climb on that mule Tom Cunnyngham let you borrow and get yourself down the hill. I'll help you with the baby, so everything will work out good."

"Thank you, Miss Ruth. I'm counting on you."

While Hannah stood outside the cabin, everyone climbed back onto the wagons, waved cheery good-byes, and set the mules toward town. "Good-bye!" she called.

"We'll check on you in a day or two!" Martha hollered. "Keep that bar across the door, you hear?"

"Don't worry, I'll be fine."

Stepping back inside the cabin, she shut the door and dropped the wooden bolt in place. She looked around at the bed, table, quilts, pickles. Why did it all seem so empty? So quiet? So still? And why did she feel so very much alone?

She spent the following day setting her house in order. The baby wasn't due until summer, but she had grown so unwieldy already that she found it difficult to work in comfort. The cabin was cold and the silence almost deafening.

But Hannah felt happier than she had since the night she had fled the bushwhackers. This was her home and none other. She dusted away old cobwebs and cooked herself a meal of bacon and eggs. But as she sat alone at the table, the scent of her dinner all around her, she suddenly realized tears had filled her eyes.

Luke had taught her to cook eggs. Luke had built the foundation of this cabin. Luke had laid the hearthstone and nailed the shingles in place. This was his home, too!

Laying her head on her arms, Hannah finally permitted herself to dwell on thoughts she had pushed away for months. Where was Luke now? No doubt he had returned to the reservation. She tried to picture him there, and couldn't. Did he live in a lodge? Was he alone . . . or had he taken an Osage wife?

Sniffling, she swallowed against the lump in her throat. Another woman in Luke's arms . . . his strong hands caressing someone else's breasts . . . his lips brushing her cheek . . .

Hannah felt a flutter of movement inside her womb as the baby turned. Laying her hand on her stomach, she prayed for the child's health in the conversational manner Luke had taught her. But how happy could a baby be without a father? And how could she herself ever make it through the years to come?

Oh, she would exist. Her own strength and inner power would see her through the hard times. She possessed an unwavering faith in God, loyal friends, intelligence, and wit. These were stores more valuable than flour, sugar, and salt.

But she knew her heart would always be frayed around the edges. Her arms—no matter how full—would always feel empty. There would be no laughter that could cheer her as his laughter had. There would be no touch but his that could set her ablaze. It was Luke . . . Luke . . . Luke . . .

Her eyes, swollen by tears, drifted shut. She let out a deep breath and relaxed in the heat of the room. As sleep made winding inroads, she thought she caught a glimpse of Luke walking toward her through the trees. He was pointing out patches of poison ivy, just as he often had.

"Be careful, Hannah," he whispered. His eyes glowed like the coals of her dying fire. "Be careful!"

He approached, and she could hear his footsteps on the bare ground. In one hand he held up a clump of poison oak, in the other a writhing copperhead snake. His lips formed words she couldn't hear. *Be careful, Hannah,* he mouthed. *Be careful!*

His footsteps grew louder as he approached. Not footsteps after all . . . the sound was his heartbeat. He dropped the snake and the ivy and held out a hand. One finger pointed in the direction of the sun. "Be careful! Be careful!"

It wasn't his heartbeat—it was hooves! A horse's hooves. They were thundering up the hillside toward the cabin. Bushwhackers! Billings was coming for her in revenge! She tried to scream. Luke! He reached toward her. The pounding grew louder, louder.

"Luke!" she cried out, but the word was only a muffled croak. Her head shot up from the table, and she stared blankly. The fire had burned down to a few glowing coals, casting the cabin in darkness. Though she could see nothing, she heard her own front door shuddering on its hinges as someone hammered against the wooden bar.

Bushwhackers! Hannah pushed away from the table, knocking over her chair in her scramble for the shotgun. It was by the bed, but where? And how to load it? And how to aim in this darkness? Wood cracked, splintered. The bar! She dropped to her knees and crawled across the floor in search of the weapon.

As her hand closed around cold steel, the door burst open. A mammoth figure stood outlined in moonlight. Thick brown fur from head to toe . . . a bear! A grizzly! Covering her mouth with her hand to keep from crying out, Hannah tried to wedge her ponderous body under the bed. The creature had come after her honey . . . or the bacon . . .

The bear moved across the floor on its hind legs. It lumbered to the table, then to the fire. Hannah clutched the shotgun against her breast and fumbled for the stock. Maybe she could beat the animal over the head and run out of the cabin. But where would she go? How long could she survive in the deep snow?

Breathing hard, she held her hand over her stomach as she watched the bear knock over the carefully stacked wood by her fireplace. It grabbed a bundle of kindling and shoved it into the coals. Instantly they sparked and caught flame.

Hannah squeezed her eyes shut as the animal turned around.
"Is anyone here?" The voice was deep, warm. Human.

Hannah gasped out loud. The torch swung toward her.
Bearskin robes fell to the floor. A man emerged. And it was
Luke.

"Luke!"

"Hannah?" Recognizing her voice, he hurled the kindling
torch into the fireplace and lunged for her. "Hannah!"

Gathering her out from under the bed, he swept her up from
the floor and cradled her in his arms. His lips found her cheek,
her forehead, her mouth. She slid her arms around his neck.

"Oh, my love," he murmured against her shoulder. "You
came back."

"Luke, you're here! I . . . I can't believe it."

"I rode from Kansas through the snow. I had to come. This
was the only place I felt—"

"At home," she finished. Cupping his face in her hands, she
searched his deep brown eyes. This was her Luke. Her
husband.

How many times had she tried to conjure him and found her
memories inadequate? But he was here now, alive and warm
and real. She stroked her fingertips along his firm jaw and up
his cheeks. Her gaze played across his forehead, the familiar
bridge of his nose, the sensual curve of his lips.

Slowly she arched upward against him. Their mouths met,
gently exploring. He smelled of winter air and leather, and she
ached to drink him. His fingers wove through her hair. His lips
caressed her mouth. Their tongues touched, a tentative meeting
that sent ripples of sensation down her skin. Deepening the
intimacy, he claimed her, and they drifted in the pleasure of
union, of memory, of promise.

Overwhelmed, Luke finally broke away. "Hannah," he
whispered, his voice husky. "My beautiful Hannah." His hands
gripped her shoulders, drawing her closer, tighter, harder as his
desire flowered. His embrace crushed the breath from her
chest.

Hungry for him, she clutched his back, pressed her fingers
into his firm muscle, laid her cheek on his shoulder. The feel of
his body reverberated through her like a familiar song. This
was her man.

"Luke," she whispered, "oh, Luke!"

He gazed at her. "I never expected to find you here."

"I was so sure I had lost you forever. What became of you after the bushwhackers attacked us?"

"I hid out in the forest. They returned that night and took away your brother's body. Then I saw the young *Nika-sabe* come with the sheriff. I didn't trust them, so I stayed in the woods hoping you would return. I had prepared a peace gift for you, Hannah."

"A peace gift?"

"Among my people, when a loved one is killed, a peace gift is given. If the wronged party accepts it, then all is forgiven. I wanted to beg your forgiveness for your brother's death, Hannah."

"Oh, Luke, I never blamed you. Ethan intended to kill you. You were only defending yourself."

He held her close as he spoke. "I had made up my mind to abandon my quest for vengeance. But when I saw your brother, I couldn't deny—in my heart—that I wanted to kill him. He had murdered my father, and I'd sworn revenge. Hannah, can you forgive me?"

"Of course." She ran her hands across his shoulders and down his arms. Then she took his hands. "Ethan was not the person I once knew. Disappointment and rejection had caused a root of bitterness to grow inside his heart, and it choked out everything else. His family had become the bushwhackers. They accepted him better than we ever had, and the fault for that lies with us. But all of that is over now. It's best put behind us, Luke."

"Your mother and sisters?"

"They're well—much better than they think, actually. In spite of their laments, they are succeeding well with their independence. I have no worries about them. They'll be fine."

"And what about you, Hannah? Were you all right after the attack?"

"I went back to Boston for a few months, but I knew almost at once that I didn't belong there. This is my home—Missouri, this land, this cabin. You are my family." She studied his face in the flickering light. "Oh, Luke, are you here to stay?"

"Forever." He sealed the promise with a kiss. "Now come, Hannah. Sit beside me while I build you a fire."

His presence was more than enough to warm her heart and heat her flesh. But she allowed him to lead her to a low stool by the hearth.

As he began stacking kindling and logs on the grate, he spoke. "I won't return to the reservation. My family is as well as can be expected. The Osage lands are shrinking, as your brother said, but no one can stop that. Not-Afraid-of-Longhairs tries. So do some of the Little Old Men. Yet I can see the truth in my mother's eyes. It won't be long before the Osage people are forced to move west again."

"I'm so sorry, Luke."

"At first I thought I should stay. I thought there might be something for me there—some way I could help or make a difference. There wasn't. I tried to fit back into the tribe. I went on the buffalo hunt. I raided a Cherokee village with my friends. But when I read your book—"

"My book? But I left it here. I assumed it had been destroyed by the elements or burned as fuel in someone's fireplace."

"I took your manuscript from the cabin before I left. That and my leggings." He stirred the fire to flame. "When I read your book . . . how the neighboring farmer's hair changed from blond to black . . . how his body was shaped like mine . . . how his words were ones I had spoken . . . and how deeply he was loved by the woman in the story, Hannah, I knew I had only one home. And that was with you."

Her eyes misted as she gazed at him. "So you came."

"I decided I would sell whatever I could from the cabin and buy a train ticket to Boston. No matter what it took, I intended to convince you to return to Missouri with me. But when I finally got here tonight and saw the footprints in the snow around the door, I was angry. I thought strangers were living in our cabin."

"But it was me."

"Yes, you, my love."

She studied his face in the firelight. "You look the same . . . and different to me somehow. I think your hair is shorter."

"When I went back to Kansas, I shaved my head in the way

of warriors. I wore a beaver-skin headdress along the center of my scalp. But when I knew I was returning, I let my hair grow."

"Luke, I don't mind if you shave your head," she declared, determined to resolve the conflict that had torn at their love. "You can wear your scalp-lock leggings and your gorget. You can call God *Wah'kon-tah.* It doesn't matter to me that you're an Indian. I like your Osage ways —"

He covered her hands to calm her. "It's all right, Hannah. I'm comfortable with both white and Indian ways. I've found my peace." Observing her, he let his focus trail down her fire-hair and over her soft, fair skin. To find her here . . . to see her again . . . to hold her . . .

Rising, he took her in his arms and held her against him. "Hannah, you're beautiful. My Gthe-non'-zhin, Returns-and-Stands, you have returned. You stand waiting and ready. So strong."

She smiled, suddenly shy with him. He touched her cheek with his fingertips. "You've changed, too, Hannah," he said. "The food at your house in Boston has made you healthy."

Wanting to chuckle, she lifted her eyes to his face. But when he placed his hand on her stomach, she held her breath. Would he know? Would he feel that growing life . . . the seed of their love?

His dark eyes searched hers. His expression shifted from pleasure, to concern, to disbelief. "Hannah?" he whispered. His palm molded around the firm, solid curve beneath her skirt. "Hannah!"

She laughed. "Yes, Luke!"

"You're . . . you're . . ."

"In the summer you'll have to fetch Miss Ruth to tend me. Miss Martha says she's the best around at birthin' babies."

Overcome, he buried his face in her hair and held her so tightly she could hardly take a breath. A baby . . . born of their love! A gift so precious he could hardly imagine it.

"This is our hope," he said. "This child—neither pure Osage nor pure white—may bring peace to those who cannot exist in harmony. My people will live on in the bloodlines of this baby, here in the ancient homeland of the People of the Middle Waters."

"My people will live through our child's blood, too," Hannah murmured. "A new breed—strong and hardy—who will build a nation from this wilderness."

"Hannah, you've taught me to dream in new ways," Luke said. "We'll dream great things for all our children. But now, more important than dreams, is love. Our love."

Bathed in the warmth of the fire, they held each other. Their lips met, their hands caressed. Clothing slipped aside. Bodies drifted in ultimate union, ultimate peace.

Overhead, Moon Woman cast her silver light on the snow. Stars glittered like ice. Perched on the topmost branches of a bare oak tree, a falcon surveyed the tiny cabin and the wisp of white smoke that sifted upward from the chimney. Bright brown eyes reflected the image of a man—strong and bronze of skin—a master to be obeyed. A woman, too, lingered in memory. Fragile but fierce. Soft but determined.

The falcon ruffled its feathers. Nights of terror, like the inferno barely escaped, might come again. But so would the trickle of melting snow, the flowering of white dogwood, the scent of damp earth.

Lifting from the branch, the falcon soared across the clearing, over the cabin, and away toward the resting place of Grandfather the Sun.

Afterword

A book is more than just words on paper. It arises not only
from the writer's heart but also from her experiences. Those
who helped bring *Falcon Moon* to life deserve my deepest
appreciation.

First, I thank my readers. You write to me, meet me at
conferences, and continue to believe in my stories. Your faith
in me and your enthusiasm for my books are what keep me
writing.

My editor, Judith Stern, has the uncanny ability to share my
vision for characters and plot. Her support, wisdom, insight,
and encouragement make the writing process a pleasure. Her
friendship is a rare treasure.

My husband, Tim Palmer, reads every word of everything I
write. The love and skill with which his purple pen touches my
manuscript give me the confidence to keep putting thoughts to
paper.

My agent, Patricia Teal, is always available with kind words

and optimism. Without her to champion me, I would still be
holding my manuscripts in the basement!

George Hooper, Polk County, Missouri, historian, provided
me with his library of newspaper clippings, from which I drew
many of the factual elements in *Falcon Moon*. He met with me
for interviews and supplied answers to my many questions.

Catherine Wilson of the Osage Tribal Museum in Pawhuska,
Oklahoma, gave me insight on Native American legal rights.

Leona Belle Buchanan taught me to recognize poke, dock,
lamb's quarter, and wild lettuce. She told me how much a
"mess" of greens was, described pawpaws, explained how to
heat a curling iron in an oil lamp's chimney, and detailed the
rigging, harness, and seat on a wagon.

The Missouri Department of Conservation provided me with
pamphlets and posters on native flora and fauna. Tim Smith
and Ann Wakeman took the time to teach me about the lotus
plant and the wild columbine.

The Thomas Jefferson Public Library in Jefferson City,
Missouri, opened their Missouri collection to my perusal. This
fine library not only supplied me with books, but its librarians
searched long and hard for answers to my questions.

For further information about subjects contained in *Falcon
Moon*, I suggest the following titles:

Back to Basics. Pleasantville, NY: The Reader's Digest Asso-
ciation, Inc., 1981.

Buchman, Dian Dincin. *Herbal Medicine*. New York:
Gramercy Publishing Company, 1979.

Evans, Humphrey Ap. *Falconry for You*. London: John Giffin,
Ltd., 1960.

Fellman, Michael. *Inside War: The Guerrilla Conflict in
Missouri During the American Civil War*. Oxford, 1989.

Gilmore, Melvin R. *Uses of Plants by the Indians of the
Missouri River Region*. Lincoln, NE: University of Nebraska
Press, 1977.

Hams, Betty. *Missouri's Early Home Remedies*. Sioux City,
IA: Quixote Press, 1992.

Hartman, Mary and Elmo Ingenthron. *Bald Knobbers: Vigilantes on the Ozarks Frontier*. Gretna, LA: Pelican Publishing Company, 1992.

La Flesche, Francis. *A Dictionary of the Osage Language.* Washington, DC: Smithsonian Institution Press, Bureau of Ethnology, 1932.

Massey, Ellen Gray, ed. *Bittersweet Country.* Norman, OK: University of Oklahoma Press, 1986.

Mathews, John Joseph. *The Osages: Children of the Middle Waters.* Norman, OK: University of Oklahoma Press, 1961.

Polk County Historama I-V. Bolivar, MO: Historical Society of Polk County.

The Resume: Newsletter of the Historical Society of Polk County. Bolivar, MO: Historical Society of Polk County.

Thomas, Robert. *How to Talk Midwestern.* Sioux City, IA: Quixote Press, 1990.

Wood, Mrs. Henry. *East Lynne.* New Brunswick, NJ: Rutgers University Press, 1984.